W9-DBG-281

GRAIL

OF THE

SUMMER

STARS

Books by Freda Warrington

* A Tor Book

Freda Warrington

GRAIL
OF THE
SUMMER
STARS

TOR®

A Tom Doherty Associates Book
New York

GRAIL OF THE SUMMER STARS

Copyright © 2013 by Freda Warrington

All rights reserved.

Edited by James Frenkel

A Tor Book
Published by Tom Doherty Associates, LLC
175 Fifth Avenue
New York, NY 10010

www.tor-forge.com

Tor® is a registered trademark of Tom Doherty Associates, LLC.

The Library of Congress Cataloging-in-Publication Data

Warrington, Freda, 1956–
    Grail of the summer stars / Freda Warrington.—First edition.
        p. cm. — (Aetherial tales ; 3)
    "A Tom Doherty Associates book."
    ISBN 978-0-7653-1871-8 (hardcover)
    ISBN 978-1-4299-8651-9 (e-book)
    1. Painting—Fiction. 2. Magic—Fiction. I. Title.
 PR6073.A75G73 2013
 823'.914—dc23

                                    2012042626

Tor books may be purchased for educational, business, or promotional use. For information on bulk purchases, please contact Macmillan Corporate and Premium Sales Department at 1-800-221-7945 extension 5442 or write specialmarkets@macmillan.com.

First Edition: April 2013

Printed in the United States of America

0 9 8 7 6 5 4 3 2 1

For all my friends, old and new.
Especially for my mum, Ida Warrington.
And as always, for my guardian angel, Mike Llewellyn.
With all my love.

Acknowledgments

There are almost too many people to thank for their support, both with the Aetherial Tales series in particular and with my writing in general over the years. In no order of favor, Jenny Gordon, Justina Robson, Storm Constantine, Stephanie Burgis, Keren Gilfoyle, Anne Gay, Stan Nicholls, Tanith Lee, Mark Robson, Anne Sudworth. Thanks also to the stalwarts of the Birmingham SF and F Writers' Group, and to my fellow members of The Write Fantastic: Kari Sperring, Juliet McKenna, Chaz Brenchley, Liz Williams, Ian Whates, Deborah J. Miller and Sarah Ash. Together as TWF we are doing our best to widen the appeal of fantasy fiction in the United Kingdom, drawing in new readers and raising the profile of the genre.

Special thanks are also due to my agents, John R. Parker and John Berlyne of Zeno Agency, to my editor at Tor, Jim Frenkel, and to the wonderful artist Kinuko Y. Craft for creating such stunning cover art.

As with *Elfland* and *Midsummer Night*, the settings for *Grail of the Summer Stars* are loosely inspired by real places, but entirely fictionalized for the purposes of the story. The museum where we find Stevie working at the start of the book, along with its staffing arrangements, administration and so on, is a confection of my imagination and not intended as a portrayal of any actual establishment.

However, I must note that the Jewellery Quarter of Hockley, Birmingham, United Kingdom, is a real and wonderful heritage area. The Birmingham Jewellery Museum, not *entirely* dissimilar to Stevie's place of work, is well worth a visit.

GRAIL

OF THE

SUMMER

STARS

Reprise

I see a city of gleaming black stone that shines with jewel-colors: crimson, royal purple and blue. I see labyrinthine passages and rooms where you can lose yourself for days, months.

Lofty pillars. Balconies onto a crystal-clear night full of stars, great sparkling white galaxies like flowers. Statues of winged men looking down with timeless eyes. I want to stand on those balconies and taste the breeze and hear the stars sing and be washed in the light of the moon. There will be ringed planets, and below, the tops of feathery trees blowing gently: an undiscovered land full of streams, with willow trees in spring green, and oak and hazel—with their elemental guardians, slender birch-white ladies with soft brown hair—and mossy banks folding into water.

And through this citadel walk graceful men and women with lovely elongated faces and calm, knowing eyes. They have seen too much. They might wear robes of medieval tapestry or jeans and a shirt but you would never mistake them for human. It's so much more than beauty. Look at them once and you can't look away. These are Aetherials in their oldest city, Tyrynaia.

They have been building the citadel for thousands of years and it will never be finished. Upward it spreads, and outward, and down into the rock below. It is their seat of power: their home.

They take the names of gods, on occasion.

Sometimes they are heroic and help the world.

And sometimes they are malicious and turn it upside down.

In the deepest depths of the citadel, a ceiling of rock hangs over an underground lake. Here is Persephone's chamber. She welcomes and cares for those who come, soul-sick with despair, to seek solace, rest and sleep. Here they need not speak, only sit on a black marble lip and contemplate the mysterious, glowing lake beneath. If you lie down in despair, Persephone will lie down with you.

—from the diary of Faith Fox

Prelude

Daniel's hands shook as he checked his watch. Five to six. Dusk had fallen two hours ago and he'd turned off the lights, relying on an orange wash of streetlight that spilled through the windows. The studio was an empty industrial space around him, darkness massing above the high steel beams. Easels and store cupboards stood stripped, the wide shallow drawers of plan cabinets yawning open. He hardly noticed the mess he'd left: scraps of paper, curled-up paint tubes, a layer of charcoal and gold-leaf dust coating everything. There was no time.

He worked fast, fumbling as he covered the surface of the last panel with protective paper, folded the outer wooden leaves into the center, then bound the triptych in layers of bubble wrap. Better too much wrapping than too little. Nothing cooperated: clouds of plastic billowed around him and he kept losing the damned scissors. The sticky tape clung to his fingers, to everything except the edges he was trying to seal. In frustration he tore the tape with his teeth. He could barely squeeze the last, overwrapped artwork into its packing case.

The tiny luminous bars of his watch hands moved on. Ten past six. Rain dashed the windows.

In his rush to fasten the lid of the last case, Daniel gouged himself with the screwdriver. He barely felt the pain.

Where the hell was the courier?

He heard the elevator rising one floor from ground level, its doors opening onto the landing. Footsteps rang out and wheels rumbled along the metal walkway that jutted above the art center's large public foyer. Hurriedly Daniel completed the delivery label. As an afterthought, he scrawled a note—too late to place it inside, so he folded the paper and stapled it to the crate. The noise grew louder as it bypassed other studio units, stopping abruptly at his door.

There was a loud knock. His heart jumped into a wilder rhythm. A figure waited outside the glass-paneled door, dark against the fluorescent lights of the landing.

Daniel held himself together long enough to exchange pleasantries with the courier as he double-checked the forms and handed over payment. Then the courier hefted all four packing cases onto a trolley, grunted a word of thanks, and went.

Softly, Daniel closed the door behind him. It was done.

For a moment, he thought of running after the courier, shouting at him to wait, he'd written the wrong address . . . Too late. Automatic doors hissed shut and he heard the elevator trundling downwards. No, his decision couldn't be unmade. He knew he'd done the right thing.

Oliver, though, would not see it that way.

Daniel walked to the middle of his studio and looked up at a steel beam above his head. He reached out to a low cabinet nearby and picked up the tangle of rope he'd left on top. The rope was a thin blue nylon twist, designed for lashing together heavy goods . . . strong enough to bear the weight of a lean human body. He positioned a high stool. Standing on the seat should give him enough height to lash the noose to the beam.

The letter he'd written to his mother lay inside the top drawer of the cabinet. There was nothing else to say.

He looked up, testing the strength of the rope between his hands. He felt no fear, only a whooshing sensation that shook his whole body. It was a trance-like feeling, a flood carrying away all clear thought. His visions would end and there would be peace . . .

"Daniel."

He heard the voice, glimpsed the flash of glass as the door swung open. Turning, he confronted a silhouette with light spinning a white-gold halo through the edges of its hair.

"Are you ready?" said the shadow. "It's time to go."

1

The Triptych

Even when the machines were silent, Stevie could still hear them. Ghosts thronged the empty factory: women in long dark skirts and men in overalls, busy in the dusty gloom. Their work clothes had no pockets or cuffs to trap even a speck of gold dust. The workers mouthed soundlessly at each other, lip-reading over the whir of lathes and the steady thump of presses . . . she wondered at the long hours, the sweaty heat, their overcrowded backstreet homes with shared toilets in outhouses, and no running water . . .

Stevie shook her head, pushing the ghosts away. Overactive imagination. She "saw things" so readily that doctors had diagnosed visual migraine, or even some odd form of epilepsy. She wasn't the only member of staff to sense *presences*, but her visions often went to extremes.

A pounding noise broke her trance.

"Stevie, are you there? Someone can't read the 'Closed' sign."

"Okay, Fin, I'll get it."

The old jewelry firm, Soames & Salter, was a museum now. Over thirty years ago, the owners had retired. Unable to sell the unmodernized business, they'd simply locked the doors and walked away, leaving a time capsule of work methods that had barely changed from 1880 to 1980. Tools had been left strewn on benches, dirty teacups abandoned . . . this sense of sudden desertion was so carefully preserved by the curators that it made visitors shiver.

Stevie made a last check that all lights and machinery were switched off, then closed the door on the old factory and hurried through the museum gift shop.

The person banging on the entrance door was not a late visitor, but a wet and fed-up-looking delivery driver, his van parked crookedly against rush-hour traffic.

He presented a large packing crate, addressed to *Stevie Silverwood, Museum of Metalwork, Hockley, Birmingham.* As she helped him drag the case inside, he muttered apologies for the delay, blaming "problems at the depot" over the weekend, and that they'd tried to deliver the previous day only to find the museum closed.

"Yes, we're shut on Mondays," said Stevie. "It doesn't matter, I wasn't expecting a parcel in the first place."

She signed his electronic notepad, said her thanks—receiving a curt "Orright, pet" in return—and relocked the door behind him. A note stapled to the crate was close to falling off. Stevie detached the scrap and frowned at it.

The world needs to see this, stated the scribbled handwriting.

"Oh, really?" she said aloud. "Is the world ready for it, whatever it is?"

Outside, streetlamps splashed the rainy grey dusk. Stevie watched the van pulling away into the sluggish traffic along Vyse Street. Although she'd turned off the main lights before he arrived, a parade of car headlights flashed over display cases full of jewelry, glinting on shelves stacked with local history books and souvenirs. Enough light to read by.

Please exhibit for me. Sorry can't explain. D.

"Who was that?" Fin, her assistant, called from a back room that served as an office-cum-kitchen. Stevie could hear the soft rattle of computer keys.

"Grumpy courier with a parcel," she called back.

"Didn't know we were expecting a delivery."

"Nor me."

The crate stood waist-high, heavy but manageable. She laid it flat, grabbed a screwdriver from a drawer behind the counter and set to work. Removing the screws and prizing off the wooden lid took only a minute. Inside she found a thick sandwich of bubble wrap, apparently protecting a canvas of some kind. She sat back on her heels, puzzled.

"Surely I didn't arrange an exhibition and simply forget about it?" Raising her voice, she called, "Fin, is there anything in the diary?"

"About what?"

"Someone's sent us artwork, I think."

The sender had sealed the package in overzealous haste, as if to make unwrapping it as frustrating as possible. Stevie took scissors to the job. A sea of bubble wrap mounted around her as she pulled off layer after layer.

"Who's the artist?" said Fin, emerging from the office.

In her heart, Stevie knew, but she needed to be certain. "See if you can find the documentation."

Fin inspected the crate and freed a label from a see-through sleeve. "Sent five days ago from a place called 'the Jellybean Factory.' North London postcode . . . Does that ring a bell?"

Stevie frowned. "Oh, yes, it's familiar. So's the handwriting."

"If someone's sent them on spec, that's naughty. It is normal etiquette to ask first."

"Unless I agreed to something that's slipped my mind. Am I going nuts?"

"I reserve my right not to answer that," said Fin, pushing her reading glasses into her curly brown hair.

Stevie pulled a face at her. She liked Fin, who was energetic, blunt and good-hearted. They made a good team. "Seriously. We didn't, did we?"

The annex housing the gift shop, café and further galleries had been refurbished in sleek modern style, in contrast to the factory. A large open arch led into a second room that they used as exhibition space. A clockmaker's bench occupied one corner. Fin glanced in and said, "There's not much spare wall area, and we've got the needlework guild next month . . . Any clues?"

"There's a note."

Fin took the scrap, dropping her glasses back onto her nose. "'*The world needs to see this*'?" She raised an eyebrow. "Modest. What was the artist thinking? 'Hmm, shall I submit my masterpiece to a famous institution in London or New York? No, I've a better idea—I'll send it to an obscure gallery in the outskirts of Birmingham.' Mysterious."

"Hey, not so obscure! We didn't win a 'best small museum' award for nothing, you know. We're world-famous."

"Okay, but still . . . Who's D?"

Stevie didn't answer. As the last pieces of wrapping and protective paper floated away, she rose to her feet with the object between her hands. The weight was unexpected. It was not canvas after all, but a wooden panel shaped like a Gothic arch, covered by two hinged flaps.

A triptych.

Stevie carried the panel to the counter and spread the side leaves at angles so that the structure stood up on its own. She felt a thrill of magic in opening the panel to reveal the artwork inside, like a child with an Advent calendar window.

She saw a vibrant wash of orange and red, lots of bright gold leaf reminiscent of a Byzantine icon, a pair of fiery female eyes staring at her . . . In the gloom, the effect was luminous.

"Wow," said Fin behind her. "This is your brain on drugs!"

The central image showed a goddess-like figure in a mountainous red desert. In the foreground lay a tumble of stonework: a fallen temple? The female, stepping from behind the stump of a column, had auburn hair swirling around a pale golden face with glaring eyes. A face or a mask? Her complexion had the sheen of fur, and strong-boned features more feline than human. A regal, feral cat deity. One hand was holding a crystal sphere up to the heavens, the other pointing at a molten yellow fissure in the earth.

The brushstrokes were so precise and detailed that everything seemed to be in motion, vibrating and rushing around the central figure. There was so much light and energy, it hurt the eyes.

The side panels showed equally enigmatic visions. On the left sat statues of a king and queen, side by side like pharaohs in a ruined palace. On the right, a silver globe emitted a beam of light towards the stars. In the background stood a priest-like figure with a severe expression.

Stevie was silent, wondering.

"The artist's gone a bit crazy with the gold and silver leaf, hasn't he?" said Fin. "I need sunglasses. The way he's caught the light is amazing, but it looks like everything's vibrating. I wouldn't want it on my wall, would you? Imagine confronting that, with a hangover." She bent closer. "I can't read the signature."

"I can. I know the artist." Stevie gave a soft laugh. "I went to college with him. Danifold." A strange shiver went through her. "Well, bloody hell."

"Who?"

"Daniel Manifold," said Stevie. "We used to call him 'Danifold.' I'd know his work anywhere. He was obsessed by Byzantine religious icons and that was his thing, adapting those methods to his own ideas. He was always arguing with his lecturers, who frowned on his non-modern style, but he stuck to his guns. This is amazing."

"What's it supposed to be, though? It's all sort of . . . wrong. It doesn't look like any religious subject I've ever seen."

"No," said Stevie. "He took the style and played with it. Dreams, folklore, myths . . . whatever came into his head, I suppose."

"He sounds very creative."

"You could say that. Passionate. Driven."

"So, have you been in touch with him lately?"

"No, hardly at all since we left college." She smiled wistfully. "Since he's working in London, why would he send stuff to me? It doesn't make sense."

Fin began to pick up discarded wrapping, only to stop with a panicked glance at the clock. "Damn, look at the time! I have to collect the kids from the minder. I've counted the cash, locked it in the safe and put the figures on your desk. Everything's done."

"Yes, it's fine, you go," said Stevie, startled out of a semi-trance. "I made the mess, so I'll clear it up."

"Okay, let me shut down the computer," Fin continued as she went behind the counter into the office. "How long since college?"

"Oh . . . seven years. We drifted apart."

Fin reappeared in a black overcoat and scarf, settling her bag on her shoulder. "Was he an old flame?" she said, her lips quirking.

"Not really. Well, sort of." Stevie deflected Fin's cheerful nosiness with a flick of her hand. "It was a very long time ago. I'm more than happy to exhibit his work, but an email or phone call would have been nice. This is odd, even for Daniel."

"Is there some way you can contact him?"

"Not sure." She stood with arms clasped, trying to outstare the fiery goddess. "Probably. I'll have a think."

Fin plucked car keys from her bag. Hesitating, she added, "Look, why don't you come to ours for supper tonight?"

Stevie didn't mean to be unsociable, even though she felt like the anti-Fin: slightly built, willowy and untidily bohemian in appearance, her hair a long shaggy mess of amber shades—an oddball, in so many ways. Fin was a tall sporty type, dark, chic but . . . "ordinary" wasn't a fair description. Fin was simply of the mainstream; down-to-earth, bright and breezy, normal. That didn't stop them being friends, but . . .

Stevie thought about Fin's house. The rooms would be ablaze with light and warmth, cooking smells, two children arguing in front of the television, Fin's jokey, talkative husband, a couple of large dogs bounding around . . . The mere thought of all that heat, food and chatter was enough to wake a thin headache behind her eyes.

"I'd love to, but maybe another time? It's been a long day. I need an early night."

Fin nodded in resignation. "It can't be great for you, living alone in that grotty apartment. You're welcome any time, you know."

"Thank you." Stevie mustered a smile. "It really isn't *that* grotty. Anyway, I need groceries, and I have paperwork to finish. We'll deal with Daniel tomorrow."

"I can't wait," said Fin. "Hey, you want a lift to the supermarket? It's foul out there."

"No. I'll walk. I don't mind the rain, and I do need the exercise."

And space to think, Stevie added to herself.

With Fin gone, Stevie tidied the sea of bubble wrap, stowed the triptych and packing crate safely in the office, finished her final checks. All was clean and neat in the café, mini-spotlights in the display cases turned off. In the exhibition room, distorted shadows of the wording engraved on the windows—*Soames & Salter, Metalsmiths*, and in smaller letters beneath, *Birmingham Museum of Metalwork. Preserving the industrial heritage of the Jewellery Quarter*—slid repeatedly across the polished oak floorboards. She pulled down the blinds, set the alarm and let herself out of the rear exit.

Outside, the wind stung her face. Stevie lived in a small apartment above the museum gift shop, just a few steps across a yard to a fire escape that wound two stories up to her front door. She'd thought of taking Daniel's triptych upstairs, but decided not to risk rain damage. Besides, she wasn't sure she wanted those disturbing images staring at her all night.

Rain fell hard as Stevie walked the length of Vyse Street. The street was dark and shiny, awash with traffic on a typically British December evening: wet and piercingly cold. She hadn't thought to bring an umbrella, so she wrapped her long Indian cotton scarf several times around her neck, pushing her chin down into the folds. She passed the multistory parking garage and a long row of stores selling gems and watches.

The Jewellery Quarter wasn't pretty, yet it possessed a unique character. The streets had an industrial feel. Buildings of Victorian grandeur were interspersed with rows of old red-brick houses—mainly occupied by jewelry stores, with design studios and repair workshops on the upper floors—and marred by occasional blocky constructions from the 1960s. There were tiny shops stuffed with antiques, glamorous high-end boutiques, contemporary designers, discount gold merchants, clockmakers and more, all nestled side by side along every street in the vicinity.

Stevie loved the place. She'd fallen in love the moment she stepped off the new light railway at Hockley station, looked up and saw the station sign: a modern sculpture of cogs, like a giant skeleton clock. An air of dilapidation persisted in places, but historical conservation projects were restoring the area into a prime heritage site. Stevie was proud to be playing a part, however modest.

She wasn't her own boss as such. She'd been deputy curator/manager for five years, officially supervised by tiers of city council administrators. Fortunately, they left the day-to-day running to her. The pay wasn't great, but Stevie was happy. The job came with an apartment, and the museum was her life. There was nothing more she needed.

On the opposite side of the road, a cemetery lay dark and peaceful, untouched by the bustle around it. Reaching the Jewellery Quarter clock—a handsome green and gold tower—she crossed the road to a small supermarket on the far side.

The store's harsh lighting made her blink as she bought basics: milk, bread, a ready meal and a bottle of wine. Soon she was on her way back, with rain blowing into her eyes, half her shopping list forgotten. All she could think about was Daniel.

Tall and skinny, with spiky brown hair, bright blue eyes shining through his crooked glasses, a permanent grin . . . the memories were vivid and fond. She still missed him. He'd been her first lover, the first person she'd ever allowed close to her.

Art college had been a great time in her life. Although her talent for fine art proved minimal, the college let her transfer to a jewelry-making course of study that suited her better. The curriculum covered all kinds of metalwork, allowing her fascination with clocks and other mechanisms to blossom alongside her love of gold and gems.

When college ended and her fellow students went their separate ways, she felt bereft. For those four years, she'd been part of a large, flamboyant family. With Daniel at the center, like a flame.

Fin had guessed right: she and Daniel had been an item at college, although it hadn't exactly been a grand passion. The initial excitement of sexual discovery faded within a year or so. Affection remained, but sheer physical chemistry seemed to be lacking between them. He'd always been eccentric, verging on unstable, and Stevie had her own interests, so they poured their ardor into work rather than each other. Yet there had been a sweetness in their mostly platonic love that still made Stevie smile. By the end, they were more like brother and sister.

Then the search for work took them in different directions. Daniel's mother hadn't helped, of course; she disapproved of his career choice and disliked his friends, Stevie in particular. Really, it had been easier to let him go than fight his mother or cope with his driven self-absorption.

Still, Daniel was special. She would always love him. Sending artwork with an urgent, cryptic note attached . . . even for him, that was damned weird.

Something was wrong.

As she passed the cemetery, she felt an ominous prodrome, a fizzing in the top of her head . . . *No, not now*, she told herself, but couldn't push the feeling away.

The world changed around her in a horrible, indefinable way. Reality tilted. Traffic faded to silence. A cobalt glow replaced the darkness and sparks danced in the corners of her vision. Static tingled on her skin. She was dizzy, holding her breath with an overwhelming sense of a presence behind her . . . watching her . . . something dark and slithery, so close she could feel its breath on her neck.

And in front was a white shape, kitten-sized, like an animal specter. It kept glancing back, drawing her onward.

Stevie kept walking, willing herself not to run or otherwise behave crazily in the street. This feeling could last for half an hour or more. And every time, it was no less terrifying.

Migraine. Epilepsy. Some kind of neurosis. We'll try you on this drug, or that . . . She no longer spoke to doctors about these episodes. Their drugs had only made her worse. It couldn't be the world that changed, revealing weird hidden dimensions. Therefore it must be her own malfunctioning brain.

A horn sounded, headlights flashed. Shock jolted her back to herself. She'd stepped into the road without looking, straight into the path of a car. The handles of her grocery bags bit into her palms. The driver swerved around her, gesticulating angrily, and the street was normal again. The spooky cobalt glow and malevolent stalkers vanished. Stevie let out a shaky breath and strode on.

A security man in a dark suit, standing in the doorway of a large diamond merchant, greeted her with a friendly "Evening, Stevie," as if nothing had happened.

Nothing happened, nothing. Where was I? Daniel . . .

She quickened her pace along the slight downhill curve of the street until she reached the museum, a handsome nineteenth-century building fronted by a row of imposing arched windows. The sight of the place she loved steadied her, gave her a surge of pride, every time.

At the far end of the building, Stevie let herself through a steel gate to an alley that brought her into the rear yard. She climbed the fire escape and let herself into her apartment. Luxurious it wasn't; she always felt a frisson of dismay at the brown linoleum and a tiny kitchen cramped under sloping ceilings. To the right, the small sitting room resembled student digs, with a threadbare carpet and sagging sofa. The colors were mostly faded browns and greens set against dingy white walls. However much she cleaned, a musty scent of damp hung around, reminding her of an attic.

Stevie had made no effort with the place, because it came with the job, and was not truly hers. Since she'd never had a proper home, she wasn't sure how one should feel . . . With a brief shudder, she blocked out her murky memories of foster homes. The past was over, firmly rejected as if it had happened to someone else. The museum was her anchor now; the rooms above were merely somewhere to sleep.

She flicked lights on, turned on the television for background noise, discarded her wet outdoor clothing and wrapped herself in a thick cardigan. While her lasagna heated in the microwave, she sat on the sofa with a glass of white wine and booted up her laptop.

Danny might have a website. He might even have sent her a message.

She waited impatiently for the laptop to pick up a Wi-Fi signal from the museum office. Soon she was balancing a plate full of lasagna on her knees, eating with a fork in her right hand while manipulating the keyboard with her left.

She scanned a long list of spam, searching for the rare gem of a personal message. From Daniel, nothing.

There was only one address she recognized. From Dr. Tom Gregory, the message was headed, "Our meetings."

A thin breath escaped between Stevie's teeth as she clicked Read.

Dear Miss Silverwood, I'm dropping you a line to see how you are. I'm sorry that you couldn't make our six-monthly follow-up—glancing at my calendar, I see that it's nearly a year since we last spoke. Please do drop me a line or phone the office to make an appointment so I can fit you in before Christmas. You've made wonderful progress but I must emphasize the importance of continuity. It's all too easy for clients to slip back into difficulties, so this is just a friendly reminder that I'm always here for you, a phone call away. I appreciate you are busy, but it is so important that we keep up our regular chats. I look forward to seeing you soon.

Yours,

Dr. Gregory

Stevie paused, feeling a small flame of annoyance in her stomach. She closed the message and pressed Delete.

The lasagna was a disappointing mush. She mentally kicked herself for forgetting to buy chocolate cookies. There might be a can of peaches in the cupboard. Perhaps she could mix the juice with her wine to create a sort of cut-price peach Bellini. Grimacing, she washed away the fatty cheese taste with more wine, undiluted.

She paused to watch the television news. There were floods devastating a Caribbean island, an earthquake near Pakistan's mountainous border. Film was shown of people wandering about covered in dust, weeping, devastated. She changed the channel. Her throat tightened and she felt guilty for turning away, but there was so much devastation every day that her emotional reservoir was dry.

She opened her web browser and tapped Daniel's name into the search engine.

There weren't many results, but the most useful appeared at the top: a website for the Jellybean Factory, an arts and media cooperative in North London with studios, offices and function space to rent. It was so long since she'd heard from Daniel, over a year, she'd forgotten he worked there until the parcel came. She clicked the link, clicked again on "Daniel Manifold" in the list of artists in residence.

There was only one example of his work: a thumbnail of the triptych he'd sent her. The auburn-haired sorceress stood in all her mystical glory, one hand raising a crystal globe to the heavens, the other pointing to a boiling-yellow crack in the earth.

The title was *Aurata's Promise*.

The accompanying text was minimal. "Daniel Manifold is a twenty-eight-year-old from the Midlands who works with a mixture of materials to create 'Icons for the New Age.'" A few more words described his background, and noted that he'd been at the studio for two years. He was just a name in a long list of artists, designers, filmmakers. The only contact number was for the Jellybean Factory itself.

Stevie put her dirty plate in the sink, picked up the telephone. She dialed, but got an answering machine; of course, they were probably closed by now.

Was it his own decision, to offer so little information? That was hardly great publicity. If he wanted the world to see his work, surely there were better ways. Websites, exhibitions . . . She took the folded note from a pocket and reread it. *Sorry can't explain. D.*

Just not right. Crawling anxiety threw the world off-kilter. The ceilings seemed to press down, and she glimpsed the pale shape again, like a tiny leopard lying, tail swishing, along the arm of the sofa.

It had to be a visual anomaly, seen from the corner of her eye. She'd even joked to Fin about her "ghost cat," but the apparition always unsettled her. Not knowing what it *meant*, that was the worst. She half-wished she'd gone to Fin's after all, rather than stay home alone with her neurological disorder and endless footage of natural disasters afflicting the world.

She took the phone and a second glass of wine into the bedroom, found her old address book in a bedside drawer. Sitting on the edge of the bed, she found the page and stared at Daniel's home number in apprehension.

Shoving her nerves aside, she dialed. Five rings . . .

"Yes?" snapped a female voice at the other end.

It was Daniel's mother. The familiarity of her voice brought back sharp memories. By reflex Stevie became her polite, deferential student-self again.

"Is—I'm really sorry to disturb you, but I don't suppose Daniel is there, is he, please?"

"What? *What?*" the voice lashed back. "Who is this?"

Stevie was taken aback, unsure how to respond. "Am I speaking to Professor Manifold?"

"Yes, this is she. And you are—?"

"Stevie Silverwood. I went to college with Daniel. I'm sorry if I've called at an awkward time, but is he there?"

There was a protracted silence at the other end, a dry intake of breath. "No, I'm afraid he isn't. I thought you would have . . . but I couldn't expect everyone to be aware . . . No, he's not here."

"Do you remember me?"

Again the clipped tone. "Yes, I remember you, Stephanie."

"Do you know how I can get in touch with him? He's sent me a painting without any explanation. I can't find an email address for him, only the number for his London studio, but there's no one there."

"He sent you a painting?" The voice crackled with disbelief. "When? Did you see him?"

"No, a courier delivered it tonight, about five. It was sent last Thursday, I think. There was just a brief note asking me to exhibit the work. It's odd, because we hadn't discussed an exhibition. We've been in touch maybe once a year since college, if that. His work arrived out of the blue."

"I see." There was a pause and a couple of faint gulping noises. Stevie realized in consternation that Daniel's mother was wrestling with tears. Stevie remembered her as a no-nonsense type; brisk, arid and intimidating. Not the sort to break down easily.

Stevie asked softly, "What's wrong? Has something happened to him?"

She heard a faint crackle at the other end: a dry tongue trying to moisten drier lips. Eventually the professor spoke, her voice shaky but controlled. "Stephanie, could you possibly come and see me?"

The request was startling. The Frances Manifold she remembered had no time for her. She would never have issued an invitation to visit, not socially, and certainly not as a cry for help.

"Yes, of course, but can you tell me anything?"

"It won't do over the phone," came the brittle answer. "We need to talk face-to-face. I'm sitting here with a letter from him in my hand." Another pause. "My son's gone missing. I'm . . . I'm terribly afraid this might be a suicide note."

2

Sea Birth

Mistangamesh stood on the shore, reborn.

His reflection hung suspended in the wet sand. The sea from which he'd emerged lay as sleek as jade under the setting sun. Salt water rolled from his sodden black hair, plastering to his body what was left of his shirt and trousers. Seaweed trailed from him.

He looked up and saw gulls wheeling in the air currents, the only sign of life above the empty beach. His memories flickered, like a silent film projected onto fog—lives lived by someone else—yet he remembered everything.

In a previous existence, he'd thought himself to be a man called Adam who'd endured a hundred years of suffering, ended by a cliff fall. Yet he hadn't found death, exactly, but a sea change. So he wasn't human after all. He was Aetherial, a creature of the Aelyr race.

Only a few hours ago, he'd been rolling on the ocean bed at the tide's mercy. His sense of being dead, yet aware and all-seeing, had seemed natural. It was said that the resting soul-essence of each Aelyr spread throughout space and time, and he believed it. He'd found peace.

And then came the wrench. All the scattered parts of him rushed together and he surged back to life, fighting the cold weight of the ocean, exploding upwards through the foam into a world of violent sensation.

Reborn in his true Aetherial form. Washed clean by the sea.

A long swim from the ocean depths had drained him and his legs felt too heavy to bear him up. His eyes dazzled and stung. His heart labored, the raw air hurt his lungs . . . and yet it felt so good to be alive. He relished every sensation, even the wet cling of his clothes and the sea breeze drying salt on his skin. Mistangamesh stood poised on the threshold between land and sea, between surface world and Spiral, life and death.

And there was no sign of Rufus.

This was the first time he'd ever felt free of his eternal tormentor, his brother, Rufus Dionys Ephenaestus. For thousands of years they'd feuded, beginning in the lost glory of their Aetherial past and continuing through human history. Now, at last, he had the choice to walk away, vanish, never to see his brother's beautiful, cruel face again. For a second or two, his heart soared.

Mist pushed back dripping hair from his face and groaned.

"Not free," he said to the sky. "As long as Rufus is out in the world, it's still my duty to find him and stop him."

The thought of his brother was vivid and hard-edged. Their eternal feud: sharp images of betrayal, blood and grief: obsession, tangled in coils of love and loathing . . . so much business unfinished. Every time Mist thought the game was over, it began again.

Perhaps, he thought, *this time on my terms.*

He turned and began to walk along the shore.

Reality bit as he found a steep path to take him up the cliffs. Aetheric energy and the altered reality of the Dusklands had cocooned him when he first rose from the tide. Now clouds obliterated the sunset and he felt winter in the bitter, salty wind.

The climb brought him to a bleak landscape of hills coated with heather and stunted shrubs. All was grey. The ocean roared softly behind him. Ahead lay distant, dark lines of conifers.

His awakening Aelyr senses suggested that he was still in Scotland, albeit many miles from where he had fallen and drowned. He had no urge to return to Cairndonan House, where, in mortal form, he had lived for a time. Cairndonan was in the past.

He was different now. Someone new, yet ancient. And because Mist knew himself to be Aetherial, not human, he didn't pause to worry that he was wet and frozen and looked like a shipwreck survivor, or that he had no money and no means of transport except his bare feet. He was above such concerns. He had strength enough simply to walk until he caught the skeins of Rufus's aura.

And where was Rufus? Was he still doggedly searching, or had he given up at last? The harsh truth was that he was bound to find Mist eventually. He always did.

For that reason alone, Mist needed to find Rufus first. It wasn't a question of revenge. His duty was a promise made thousands of years ago, a vow to halt Rufus's endless rampage of destruction. If Mist did not try, no one would.

Where to start? In the vast, darkening landscape he was lost, but if he kept the coastline on his right and kept walking, he would be traveling south, towards England and the big cities that Rufus had always loved.

His brother could be anywhere by now. Paris, Vienna, Moscow—who knew? London was the obvious place to begin.

Once he found Rufus, then he would know what to do next.

Mist walked in a trance, suffering the shock of rebirth and not considering that a walk of five hundred miles or more was unrealistic, even for an Aetherial. How long had passed since they'd been together? It might have been days or months. Did Rufus actually believe him to be dead this time?

Aetherials called themselves semi-mortal, since they couldn't fathom the strange paths of their lives. If they were physically killed, the flesh might heal and return to life, but more often the soul-essence would flee the corpse and rest in elemental form for years or centuries. Some would gradually take on solid form again, while others would be literally reborn. One might even be born into a human family and not know any different, never awaken to his deeper self. Or he might morph into animal shape, or fade into the Otherworld. Nothing was predictable.

Mist had experienced nearly all of those incarnations.

Not many went on and on unchanged, as Rufus had.

Let him believe I'm gone, thought Mist. *I spent centuries trying to escape him. Was the effort all for nothing? Can I watch him like a spy, without him ever knowing I'm there? And if he's still causing mischief . . . somehow I must avenge our father and mother, and all the countless others he has destroyed.*

Helena.

When Mist's way was blocked by a sea loch, he turned and walked inland until the waterway was narrow enough to swim across. Soaked again, he went onwards over rocks and heath. He had no need of food, rest or physical comfort. He was Aelyr, indestructible.

Mountains rose on either side, their rounded snowy peaks vanishing into thick cloud. Presently he reached a narrow road that felt like iron beneath his feet. Freezing air blasted into his face and he was utterly alone amid the desolation. *Keep moving. Nothing else matters.*

The long bitter night passed. When flat grey daylight returned he was still walking, like a machine. The asphalt was brutal but grass was worse, the blades so tough it was like stepping on tiny knives.

Now and then a car roared past, startling him. As Mistangamesh, he'd lived in a time long before motor vehicles, but he also retained Adam's more recent memories. So, although the world was strange, it wasn't wholly unfamiliar.

It didn't occur to him to hitch a ride, but as a second evening fell, a huge truck rumbled to a halt beside him. A bearded driver in a red flannel shirt leaned towards the open window and called out amiably, "Hey, d'ye need a lift, pal? Where are you headed?"

Mist's face was so solid with cold that he could barely speak. The driver began to frown. At last he forced out the words, "Anywhere. South. London."

"London?" The driver gave a gruff laugh. "Ye'll be lucky. I can take ye tae Carlisle."

As Mist climbed in, the driver stared in shock and asked what the devil had happened to him. He struggled to find an answer. Somehow his cool, Aelyr self found the words. "It's a long story. I got lost, and caught in the sleet."

The driver put the truck into gear and it moved off with a deep, shuddering growl. "Your car broken down? Anyone needing help back there?"

"No, only me."

"You English tourists!" the driver exclaimed, as if this explained everything. "Ye wouldnae believe the idiots who go mountain-walking in the middle of bloody winter! Ye sure you're okay?"

Mist affirmed that he was and the man shrugged, accepting his word. The cab was stifling hot, the air rank with diesel, sweat and stale food. Mist sat staring out through the windshield, watching sheets of rain being swept away into a clear semicircle by the wiper blades, again and again.

The driver—a big man, blunt and easygoing—showed no sign of being offended by his silence. When Mist offered no reason for walking barefoot in the middle of nowhere, the driver constructed his own explanation—that he'd fought with his wife or girlfriend, and she'd thrown him out of the car on a highland pass to make his own way back to civilization. "Either that, or you got lost up a mountain and you're too embarrassed tae admit it!"

Mist said nothing to contradict him. Amused by his own tale, the driver produced a lunch box and offered him half an egg-and-bacon sandwich. Mist ate without appetite, accepted a drink from a bottle of fizzy orange liquid. The taste was chemically sweet and revolting, yet he felt better after a few sips. He'd needed food after all.

He fell asleep for a time, but memories kept jolting him awake, like electric shocks.

The driver tuned the radio to a talk station. Several commentators hotly debated restoring the death penalty for murder. After a while, Mist found himself asking softly, "Do you believe in the death penalty?"

"Oh, aye," said the driver. "Hang the bastards! Cut down on the prison population. Me, I'd have 'em taken out the courtroom and shot."

"How many crimes, though? How many last chances do you give them?"

"What? One's enough. One strike and you're out, eh?"

"But when it's been going on so long, you've lost count . . . and you're dealing with someone who can't die . . . What's the worst crime? Wiping out a whole civilization? Or a single, cruel killing, for the hell of it?"

"Och, I don't know. That's what war crimes tribunals are for. However many murders he's committed, you can only hang the bastard once."

"Rufus didn't mean me to die. I don't think he meant Helena to die, either, but he didn't *care*." As Mist's thoughts unspooled, he barely realized he was saying them out loud. "Yes, he drove himself mad with guilt for centuries, trying to bring me back to life again. But I didn't want to come back. It's because he didn't care about *her* that I can't forgive him. She was human, truly dead forever. And Rufus never got it."

The driver turned up the radio, an unsubtle hint that Mist's rambling was interfering with his concentration.

Mist murmured on, "I meant to stay in elemental form, so that Rufus could never touch me again. But I came back as a human—I don't know how, strange things happen to us that we can't control—and for years I thought I was a man called Adam Montague. Adam had two sisters who loved him. He wanted to be a priest, but instead he got sent to the trenches and witnessed all his friends killed in the mud around him . . . and he was never well again. Then Rufus came, and saw Adam, and kidnapped him. He inflicted ninety years of torture, as he tried to wake up poor Adam and turn him back into *me*."

Mist sighed, rubbed his forehead. "He couldn't do it. Only the sea could do it. What Adam's disappearance did to his family—that's another story. But Rufus *enjoyed* their pain. How can you reason with someone like that?"

Mist was half-aware that the driver was giving him alarmed sideways looks. "Hey, why don't you take a wee doze? Long road yet, and you're nae making a lotta sense. Tired and cold will do that."

"What would you do," he asked, undeterred, "if this monster, this war criminal and murderer, was your brother?"

"Ma brother?"

"Would you give him up to the police? Would you still want him taken out and shot?"

"Man, that's deep. Family's different."

"Is it? So would you protect him? You know he's a lost cause, but part of you still loves him . . . but if he's hurt people you love?"

"Well, that'd be different. Say if he'd hurt ma wife or bairns, I'd kill him with ma bare hands."

"So if you knew he was guilty, but the courts let him go free and he vanished—would you let him go, or hunt him down?"

"This conversation's doing my head in, pal. Reach behind your seat; there's an old jacket and boots. They're a wee bit skanky, but you take 'em. Better than walking around in rags."

Mist found the items; the jacket, once green, was grey and oil-stained, the boots stiff with age, yet to him they were a priceless gift. "Thank you."

"All the thanks I want is for you to shut up, because I've zero patience with hitchhikers' weird life stories. Okay?"

Mist stared out into the sleet. The road grew broader, traffic increasing. In the distance, city lights sparkled like a lake of stars cupped within bleak sur-rounding hills. *Weird?* No, the driver misunderstood because he didn't know Mist was Aetherial, didn't know what he'd been through.

"Sometimes I'm so angry with Rufus that I could strangle him, but that's emotion, not justice. To be honest, he still frightens me. But that's Adam's fear, not mine. All I ask is the wisdom to deal fairly with him when I find him. I don't know how humans experience death, but for me it was a sudden striking out of existence, like a curtain falling midscene in a play. Then wak-ing up somewhere dim, peaceful and strange . . . peaceful until the memories come back, because you know it's too late to change anything. I can't leap back in time to prevent the horrors happening. It's like being severed. First from my true self, three, four hundred years ago? And severed again from being Adam. But you wake up again and the journey goes on."

"No fer much longer," the driver muttered.

Mist paused, remembering Adam's beloved sisters, who'd devoted their lives and sanity to searching for him after he'd been abducted by Rufus. They were long dead. And he thought of those who'd helped him when he'd escaped after decades of captivity. Juliana Flagg, the artist who'd inherited Cairndonan House, her niece Gill and their scarlet-haired friend Peta . . . Mist smiled sadly at the memories. He couldn't go back, because Cairndonan was in the past and he was someone different now. Had they grieved for Adam at all?

Had Rufus left them alive?

Mist's breathing quickened. The cab's heat was suffocating and he began wrenching at a handle, trying to crack the window. Instead, the door came open.

The driver braked, bringing the truck to a violent halt at the side of the road. "All right, pal, that's it. I cannae take ye any further. Get out."

"What?"

"You're too weird, even for me! We're nearly in Glasgow. Last stop before I hit the motorway. Ye can get help here, and man, do you need it. Guid luck, pal."

Shaken, Mist thanked him, obediently climbed down from the cab and resumed his walk under the vast grey sky. His feet throbbed inside the ill-fitting boots. The jacket stank, giving bare protection from the wind. Dimly he was aware of gnawing hunger, but he didn't fight his bodily discomfort, any more than he'd questioned how mad his rambling must have sounded to the driver. It wasn't his fault he didn't understand.

All around him were concrete roads roaring with vehicles. The cityscape was festooned with long ropes of metal, and ugly buildings poured smoke or steam into the sky. Wild hills were still visible in the far distance as he walked into the heart of the city. Mist ignored the exhaustion that was beginning to overwhelm him. His thoughts dissolved into a waking dream, in which roads became murky canals. At some point, he fell.

A huge deafening sound awoke him. It was like an earthquake above, filled with the rattle and squeal of metal. He found himself lying on cold damp concrete beneath the arch of a railway bridge. Weak street lighting spilled into the darkness.

"Are ye awright, mate?"

A grizzled face peered into his, sour alcohol fumes wafting from a snaggle-toothed mouth. The accent, slurred, was almost impenetrable.

Mist's first thought was that the old man was after money. Laughing weakly, he tried to pull out the linings of his pockets to show he had nothing. The vagrant stayed his hand, making gravel-voiced protests. "Nae, what, ye think Ah'm going tae rob ye? Wait. Wait. You stay there. Ah'm going tae call the ambulance."

This was unreal. Mist's voice emerged as a faint rasp. "No. There's nothing wrong with me. I'm looking for . . ."

"You're no druggie or alky, that's plain as day," the man whispered. Mist realized that his rescuer wasn't old after all; no more than forty. "There's a light around ye. Ah know the hidden folk when I see one. God strike me down dead if I don't get ye some help."

Mist dreamed that he stood on the edge of the world. Islands rose like grey walls from the ocean; beyond, there lay no land between him and the coast of North America, only thousands of miles of sea and sky.

Next he was walking. Endlessly walking.

Rows of town houses loomed on either side of a canal. Venice? Trees lined the banks and there were cobbles beneath his feet . . . No, not Venice. Amsterdam. He was going to meet someone and it was urgent. *Helena.* He would take flowers to her, tulips like soft bright cups of paint, red and peach and bright yellow.

Mist saw multiple images. First he watched the human thread of Adam's memories, like images flickering on a spool of film: two beloved sisters who were long gone; mud and blood and shell-fire all around him, a bullet entering his gut . . . then a long nightmare of abduction into the Otherworld by Rufus and his heartless, beautiful friends, held prisoner while Rufus tried every technique of pleasure or pain he could devise to make Adam admit he was really Mistangamesh Poectis Ephenaestus. After he escaped, he enjoyed a short time of safety until Rufus came after him once more . . . and then the bullet completed its journey. It tore through his body and sent him plummeting into the waves.

The memory of Rufus's face—passionate, obsessive, devoid of empathy—sent shivers through him. So close . . . yet they couldn't reach each other.

Time meant little in the Otherworld, but it meant everything on Earth. In seventeenth-century Amsterdam, Mistangamesh was hurrying along the canalside towards Helena's house. He was panicking in pure terror as if the world was collapsing.

His memories wound back in time. He recalled a nightmare, in which his sister was trapped in a strange house and calling his name, but he could never find her . . . What came before that? A gulf of darkness. He was staring down a tunnel of whispering phantoms. A point of golden light shone at the far end but he dared not look too hard. *Seeing* would be like diving into the sun.

A voice murmured deep in his brain, *It is always like this.*

"Is it?" Mist said softly to himself. "We carry this chaos inside us?"

His subconscious self was wiser. It commanded him to be quiet and watchful, to pay careful attention and to learn fast.

He became aware of someone beside him: a woman who was silver from head to foot, with a halo of pale hair, a glint of white gold and pearls, a long thick coat of figured velvet trimmed with white fur: Juliana Flagg, an angel in a dream.

He opened his eyes and she was really there.

Consciousness came as a violent shock. His last memory was of lying on concrete beneath a bridge, engine noise growling above, a fog of foul smells enveloping him. Now he was on a bed, walled in by blue curtains. Bright lights dazzled him and he heard a buzz of activity in the background. Juliana leaned towards him, her aged yet beautiful face alight with amazement. He caught the warm, powdery fragrance of her velvet coat.

"Adam?" she said softly. "Oh my god, is it really you? I can't believe this."

"Juliana."

His voice was a rasp. Her eyes widened as he spoke. "You recognize me?" Her fingertips pressed his cheekbone, as if touch was more certain than sight. "I've been sitting here for an hour, so I've had a very thorough look at your face, but I still can't comprehend . . . Adam, what happened? We saw you die."

He glanced around. This was a much brighter, stranger place than the grim wards that human Adam remembered, nearly a century earlier. "Is this a hospital?"

"Yes, you're in the Acute Admissions Unit. Next step up from Accident and Emergency." She looked at him with grave, concerned eyes. "Oh, my dear boy, what a state you're in. Whatever happened?"

Everything and nothing, he thought. This was all wrong. He should not be in hospital because he was Aelyr, indestructible. Juliana was in the past, so she shouldn't be here, either. All wrong.

"Well, let me tell you what I know," she said when he didn't speak.

"Yesterday I received a phone call from this hospital. A young man had been found unconscious in the middle of Glasgow. This city sadly has its share of homeless people, and one of them called an ambulance for you; I wish I could have thanked him, but he was long gone. You had no identification on you. You were wet through, dressed in rags and a stinking old jacket. At first the doctors thought you'd been attacked, but they found no injuries, no drugs or alcohol in your blood. They concluded you'd collapsed with hypothermia. You were a mystery. However, while you were half-conscious, you kept saying my name and mentioning Cairndonan House. So the hospital staff found my number and telephoned me. It took me half the night to get here, but here I am."

"You should not have come," he whispered.

"Why not? Who else would have come to look after you?"

"I don't need looking after."

She gave a short laugh. "You were brought in half-dead! And I've spent all this time thinking you were *genuinely* dead! How could I not come?"

He shifted in the bed, trying to prop himself upright. They'd dressed him in a hospital gown and there was a silvery blanket over him. Juliana plumped up the pillows to help him. He had a flashback to Cairndonan House, of Adam lying in bed because—confused—he'd tried to hurl himself through a window. Mist looked down at his palms, which had been badly cut. There were no scars now. The skin had healed smooth.

"You look as if you need food," she said. There was an awkward pause. "This is beyond strange—but then, so many strange things happened at Cairndonan, I shouldn't be surprised. You do remember me, and what happened there?"

"As if through a veil, yes."

"Good. That's a relief. So, the tide washed you up and you walked away . . . ?"

"Something like that." The understatement made him smile.

"How long have you been sleeping rough?'

He was puzzled. "I wasn't sleeping rough. I was walking. I don't remember collapsing."

"Well, I'm extremely curious to know how you're even still alive. Oh, my dear boy. You were shot through the chest by a raving madman who was actually aiming at Rufus. For good measure, you fell a hundred feet onto rocks and were swept away into a stormy sea. And yet you survived?"

It was time to tell her.

"No. Adam died. I am Mistangamesh." The last word was a whisper. "Mist."

"Ah." She released a long, quiet sigh. "That was the name of Rufus's long-lost brother."

"Yes. That's who I am."

Juliana looked keenly at him, her head tilted, as if trying to work out if he was telling the truth or plain mad. "Are you saying that Rufus was right about you?"

"He didn't understand that Adam had to die before Mist could wake up. Or realize that he had to let me go before I could return. I was deep in the ocean but I swam back to shore. Then I climbed up the cliffs and began to walk southwards."

"How long were you walking?'

"I'm not sure. Two or three days."

"Without stopping to rest or eat?"

"A truck driver gave me a lift and shared his food. When he dropped me at the edge of the city, I began to walk again."

"Where were you going?"

"Towards London."

She was staring at him, aghast. "Do you realize how far— You set out to walk several hundred miles from the wilds of Scotland with no help, no money, nothing? What were you thinking? Oh, dear god, Adam. Mist, I mean. Has rebirth made you insane?"

"I am Aelyr. I thought I'd left behind all human needs."

"Obviously not. Are Aetherials, excuse the pun, superhuman? Are you a god of some sort, who never gets tired or hungry, never needs to sleep?"

Her questions threw him. He considered his answer. "I never claimed we were gods. We change between different states . . . but when we're in physical form, yes, we need food and rest eventually."

"Yet you somehow forgot this, did you?"

"It seems so."

"Well, you're an idiot!"

Mist laughed. She was right. Finally it dawned on him that he had been out of his mind. "I thought I was indestructible. I'm ashamed to discover, after all, that I'm as weak as any human."

"Don't knock humans," she replied tartly. "You'd be surprised what we can endure."

Her words reminded him that he'd no idea what harm Rufus might have done after Adam's demise. Alarmed, he touched her forearm. "Where's Rufus now?"

"Oh, he's long gone. Don't worry, he's not with me!" Juliana shrugged. The gesture was slight, but soaked with contempt. "He ran away, vanished over the horizon."

"He didn't hurt anyone?"

"Oh, no, my dear, not at all." She covered his hand with hers, reassuring him. "After you, or rather after *Adam* died, Rufus went to pieces. He was insane with grief and no threat to anyone, so I let him stay for a few days. Then he perked up. Grief turned into anger, perhaps. He stole a car and off he went in a spray of gravel and exhaust fumes, sticking up a finger at the rest of us. Haven't seen him since, don't want to."

Mist sighed. He was trying to clear his mind, to engage with the new reality he'd entered. "So he's been gone for . . . a few days? Perhaps a week, at most?"

Juliana gave him a measured stare. "My dear, those events didn't happen last week. They happened over two years ago."

Some hours later, they were sitting in a coffee shop in the center of Glasgow, as crowds of shoppers passed the windows. Already the sky was growing dark again, but the streets were bright with Christmas lights, strings of sparkling red and gold stars.

Juliana had gone out and bought Mist some new clothes: underwear, black trousers and T-shirts, a dark grey sweater and a warm, waterproof jacket, sturdy black boots. The doctors had wanted to keep him for a day or two. He'd discharged himself against their advice. They wouldn't understand that, despite everything, his Aelyr flesh would heal fast.

Once he'd consumed soup, toasted sandwiches, a large chocolate muffin and half of Juliana's too, he felt . . . well, "human again" wasn't quite the phrase, but substantially better. They sat facing each other, cradling fresh mugs of coffee.

"Two years?" he said.

"Nearly two and a half."

"It seemed only days . . . It was like a dream, though. Time can't be relied on when you're part-elemental and in the Dusklands."

"You must be in shock," said Juliana. "Nearly as much as I am, finding you alive."

"Gill and Peta . . . they were such dear friends to me. Are they still with you?"

She waved a hand. "Goodness, no. They buggered off backpacking together. But you were missed. Gill said something very telling: that she couldn't stay at Cairndonan because, if she did, she'd always be watching the sea."

Mist felt a pang of human regret, so intense it stole his breath. "I'm so sorry. I wouldn't have wished that on her . . . She and Adam . . ." He had to stop until the pain abated. Softly he went on, "But I'm not *him* anymore. So please don't tell her, or anyone, that you've seen me."

"I understand."

"It could be worse. I might have lost twenty years. I wonder what Rufus is doing?" Pushing aside any tender thoughts of Gill, Mist focused on his brother. "I need to know where he is."

"Well, I didn't report the car stolen because we were so glad to see the back of him. He could be anywhere." She touched his hand. Her fingers felt hot on his skin. "My dear, I'm sure you're safe. He thinks you're dead. He has no reason to return to Scotland."

"He'd head to the capital." Mist smiled sourly. "He always liked crowds, places of power. Extremes of poverty and wealth. They were his playgrounds."

"London has a population of roughly ten million people. Plenty to play with. Or he could have even more fun in New York, Tokyo . . ."

"I know, but London is somewhere to start looking." A shudder of fear went through him. So it began again, his never-ending duel with his brother.

"Are you sure you *want* to find him?" Juliana was a graceful figure, a goddess carved from silver-grey marble. Human, yet something more. "I'm confused. All the time you, and/or Adam, were with him, Mist was dormant. As if you were so hell-bent on not letting Rufus win, you'd rather stay 'dead' than let him think he'd found you. You said yourself that you reawakened *only* when he was safely out of the way. Yet now you want to go looking for him?"

"I don't want to. I have to."

"Why?"

His fingertips padded softly on the tabletop. "Wherever he goes, there is trouble and pain and death. I need to stop him."

She swallowed. "I must admit, things were somewhat interesting while he was on the scene. Do you remember the trial?"

Mist nodded. Certain Aetherials had tried to convict Rufus for crimes against both his own race and mortals. They'd failed. Her words woke images of a vast black chamber, a jury of near-invisible figures. Lord Albin of Sibeyla, owl-white in the darkness, was the keenest prosecutor . . . but Albin had been thwarted. "It was a joke. Even the Spiral Court couldn't pin him down. Rufus escaped Aelyr justice and now he can't be touched. He must think he's invincible."

"A frightening thought, but . . . you should know that all the fight went out of him when he lost Adam. Taking the car was bravado. I think what I'm trying to say is this." She chopped at the table with the edges of both hands. "You had your brother *there*, right in front of you, for years on end. He held you, or rather, a person he *thought* was you, prisoner. Now that you've managed to break free, why on earth would you seek him out again?"

Mist sank back in his chair. "Because the game isn't over yet. Yes, he imprisoned me, but I wasn't truly *me* at the time. Adam was powerless. Things are different now. Rufus has a mountain of debts to pay. Let him feel guilty about my death! He's done far worse than kill me."

Juliana raised her eyebrows. "I've heard of sibling rivalry, but this is ridiculous. So what is it now, your turn to kill him?"

"Oh, I wish I could turn away and forget him, but I can't. I want the upper hand this time. I'll be watching him from the shadows, but he'll never know I'm there."

"But how on earth do you ever expect to find him?"

"In the past, wherever we were, we always found each other in the end."

Juliana gave a slight shiver. "How?"

"I don't know. We were always both drawn to places where history was being made, or the world changing. We knew each other too well, or perhaps we were simply very predictable."

"I'd hardly call either of you predictable." She gazed at passersby in the street for a few moments, then turned to him again. "Look, here's a radical thought. How would it be if you let this go? Travel, or settle somewhere, or return to the Otherworld, whatever makes you happy—but forget your brother. Live your own life."

Mist laughed. "That sounds tempting. Don't think I haven't thought of it."

"Is it impossible?"

"Wherever I go, he'll find me. That's why I have to find him first. To end it."

Juliana gave him a long, wistful look. "At least stay a few days, first. You're like a newborn seal. You've barely dried off."

"I can't. And you shouldn't have had to come and rescue me. Some Aetherial I've proved to be, unable to survive without human aid. I feel ashamed."

"Nonsense. There's no shame in needing a little help. You can thank me by staying until you're fully well. Couple of days' rest in a decent hotel?"

He shook his head. In his mind he saw mountains stretching away, roads stringing together villages, towns, cities . . . the idea of hunting Rufus through the world made him despair. No use resisting, though. The idea also held a strange thrill. "Sorry, Juliana, but I have to go."

Now she was exasperated. "And how far d'you think you'll get with no money, no identification? You'll need documents. Not being of criminal inclination, I don't know how one goes about creating a false identity, but it can't be that hard. You'll need more clothes. Money. Look, I'll lend you a credit card until we can get one in your name. And I'll pay the balance each month, at least until you're established."

Mist had learned what a credit card was when she'd used one to pay for their food. He shook his head. "I can't take money from you!"

She waved a hand. "Oh, pay me back when you can. Listen to me: You'll get nowhere without cards and cash."

He groaned, knowing she was right. "Thank you. I wish I didn't need such help, but I'm grateful. And I will pay you back."

"Damn right you will. So it's settled. We need to get your paperwork sorted out, finances, a cell phone—"

"A phone?"

"Yes, so I can make contact in order to forward stuff to you, wherever you happen to be. You want to find Rufus, so I'm oiling the wheels. Hop on a train, and you can be in London in a few hours. After that, you're on your own."

"I'm so grateful, Juliana." An awkward silence fell for a moment. Then he looked up at her and said, "I feel foolish. The truth is, I don't really know where or how to start searching."

"Well, there's always the Internet," Juliana said wryly.

"The what?"

"Come on, Mist. Even I have a creaky old computer. As Adam, you must have noticed. The side room with a collection of yellowing plastic boxes?"

"No. That I don't remember." He smiled. "Still, I am a fast learner."

"I'm sure you are." She reached into her bag and placed a shiny oblong device on the table. "Start learning."

"What's this?"

"This is me, entering the twenty-first century. It's one of those tablet computer gadgets. You touch the screen and it tells you what you want to know. Magic."

Mist stared at her in disbelief. Then a smile pulled at his mouth. Perhaps there would be sparks of wonder in the journey after all.

"Honestly, it's easy, even for someone of my great age. Look."

She powered up the device, and had to show him only once how to use the search engine. Mist was entranced by the small, glowing screen that could call up any part of the world, any piece of information, at the touch of a few keys.

Hardly knowing how to start, he typed in his brother's name; Rufus Dionys Ephenaestus. The result came at once.

Your search did not match any documents.

Entering his most recent assumed name, Rufus Hart, yielded 774,000 results.

Mist sat back in his chair and laughed, causing people at the next table to look at him. Ignoring them, he tapped on some of the links, but found none that bore any relevance to his brother.

"He wouldn't use that name again, would he?" Juliana put in. She'd shifted her chair around to look over his shoulder.

"Not Hart. But he nearly always used Rufus, as if he was winking at the world, saying, 'I'm pretending to be someone else, but we all know who I really am.'"

"I noticed that about him. He was proud of being infamous, didn't even try to disguise himself. The way he brazened it out before the Spiral Court was quite breathtaking. You should have seen it! Oh . . . you did."

"Well, Adam was there, and I have all his memories."

"Of course. Try being more specific. Aelyr, or Aetherial?"

He tried. Links to foreign language sites appeared for "Aelyr," while "Aetherial" had over 30,000 results. Apparently it was too generic a word to be of much help. All it meant—according to an online dictionary he consulted— was *"of the aether," "pertaining to the higher regions beyond the Earth,"* and *"from the Greek verb, to blaze."*

Mist sighed to himself. He continued entering every word or combination of terms he could think of. Azantios. Poectilictis. Theliome. Aurata. Places and people he had not seen for countless thousands of years.

For "Aurata," images of beetles, fish and caracal lynxes appeared. The name meant nothing more specific than "golden." How had they spelled it, in the ancient days? That alphabet no longer existed. The language of Aelyr and Vaethyr alike had evolved along with the Earth and the humans who'd taken it over.

On the fifth page of results, a title caught his eye. "Aurata's Promise. Central panel of triptych, tempera and gold leaf on wood panel. Artist: Daniel Manifold."

He tapped on the link and found a website for an art gallery, a working studio whimsically called the Jellybean Factory. He scrolled a list of names with a thumbnail image beside each one. Mist pressed on the stamp-sized picture beside Daniel Manifold's name and up came a bright image like a religious icon. He sat back, stunned.

There was a red desert landscape and a city of towers, gold and pale yellow and white, so glassy and weightless they seemed to float. But their perfect shells were crumbling, open to the sky. Smoke rose. A woman with flowing auburn hair and the face of a feline goddess stared straight at him, enigmatic, one finger pointing at a volcanic crack in the ground, the other hand holding up an orb to the fiery sky.

He recognized the place. Even with her stylized, cat-like features, he knew the woman, too.

"What is it?" said Juliana, leaning forward.

"Aurata," Mist said softly. "My sister."

3

Ghosts and Shadows

Stevie dreamed she was drowning. She was on her back, fully immersed in cold green water, enveloped in cushiony moss. The surface rippled above her face. No air bubbles rose from her mouth. Her struggles had faded to calm acceptance. She was now like an amphibian, part of this watery, mossy realm. She had always been here, a forgotten sunken treasure, watching the hypnotic play of sunlight and shadows far above . . .

A steel cord snared her, dragging her violently up to the surface. She gasped in the dry world like a hooked fish.

The "steel cord" was actually the shrill of her alarm clock. Stevie slammed her hand on the button to silence it. Seven-thirty. Waking brought a rush of adrenaline, her usual reaction to such disturbing, recurring dreams.

The boiler that supposedly heated the water and radiators clunked into life, jolting her back to reality. She stared at the sloping, off-white ceiling as she recalled the previous day's events.

She didn't believe Daniel was dead. He'd always been wrapped in artistic visions, but had he been making a decent living? Didn't a London studio equal success? Yet she knew too well that anyone could put on a confident front while quietly falling apart inside. Inner turmoil, provoking him to some crazy action . . . well, that was possible. But suicide? Surely not.

Stevie hoped with all her heart that his mother was wrong.

Daniel had been her savior. The first time she met him, she was seventeen-ish and working in a café, without family or hope. One lunchtime, there he was at a table, sketching. He looked up, caught her staring in fascination, and grinned. Warily sliding into the seat beside him, she saw that he was drawing her. They began to talk. He was so excited to be starting at art college that she decided, in a spontaneous rush of optimism, that she would apply too.

She had nothing to lose.

He'd helped her compile a rushed portfolio of artwork, told her what to say at the interview, and by a miracle, she scraped in. Horribly out of her depth at first, she abandoned fine art and found her vocation in working with metals.

Daniel had been her first true friend, her first lover. Until then, her only brush with boys had been fighting off the unwanted advances of older foster-brothers, who'd all learned the hard way to keep their distance. Daniel was different: gentle, nervous and equally inexperienced. They discovered pleasure together, until their bond faded naturally back into friendship again.

Did he have other girlfriends? Surely no one special; no one she could remember. Since leaving college, Stevie had had occasional brief affairs, all of which she'd ended because she never felt at ease. She'd concluded she must be too unconventional or damaged to connect with "normal" people. Perhaps both she and Danny were simply too weird to sustain a proper relationship.

Stevie made to get out of bed, but paused, recalling something else. His painting style had changed radically after he'd met her, or so he claimed. "I drew anything and everything," he'd told her, "but I had no real direction. Once I met you, though . . . I can't explain. It's like you give off an aura and my head's suddenly full of images that are really important, even though no one understands them, least of all me."

Thanks, she thought, *since you weren't painting pretty portraits of me. No, it was grotesque stuff like saints with snake heads, angels with lion paws and beaks—images that made your lecturers shake their heads in despair.*

Some muse I was. No, Dan, you had no business trying to shift the credit for your bizarre visions onto me. Credit or blame, whichever—it wasn't my doing.

She decided that when she found him she was going to tell him exactly that.

"So what's going on, Danifold?" she murmured. Reluctantly she pushed back the bedcovers and felt the chill of the air. "What's happened to you?"

The watery world of the dream haunted her as she took a barely warm shower and dried off. How frustrating, that she rarely dreamed of anything more pleasant than drowning. "Aquaphobia" was the official term for her fear of water, a doctor had once told her, although his simplistic diagnosis didn't begin to cover what she felt.

She chose a calf-length patchwork dress in blue-green shades, adding a thick jade-colored cardigan. Once dressed and sipping a mug of tea, Stevie finally stopped shivering. She smudged kohl on her eyelids and worked at her knotty hair until it was more a flow of russet-amber ripples, and less of a fright wig. Perhaps she should trim it to jaw-length, like Fin's, if only to save five minutes of pain and swearing in the morning.

But her hair was part of her, a kind of veil that gave her both identity and camouflage.

She hung strands of rough-tumbled beads around her neck: orange carnelian and turquoise. The color clash pleased her. She added silver gem-set rings that she'd made herself, and bracelets with dangling charms. Her spectral cat, like a tiny leopard, lay watching her from the bed with its claws digging into the duvet.

The water dream had been unusually intense. The triptych, the sudden reminders of Daniel and the past, awoke feelings she was always trying to bury.

By eight-thirty, Stevie was down in the museum shop, counting money into the till, firing up the computer, ensuring all was neat and ready for opening time. She checked the upstairs gallery, where examples of metalcraft stood on display behind glass: jugs, trophies, world globes, even a model battleship hammered from silver and gold. Her favorites were five skeleton clocks, each one unique, with their inner workings of cogs and spindles revealed like elegant kinetic sculptures.

She unlocked the doors to the factory, poked her head in and said, "Good morning," to the ghosts. No apparitions were visible, but she greeted them anyway, out of courtesy and a mild dash of superstition.

Back in the gift shop, she entered the exhibition space, put out fresh piles of leaflets and tacked up a poster advertising a jazz concert. The clockmaker's bench in one corner was her addition. However, one of the staff, Alec, was a lifelong clock-obsessive and often requisitioned her workspace. To her annoyance, he was untidy and failed to keep her tools in pristine condition. His latest repair lay in pieces strewn all over the bench. Yet Stevie indulged him, because visitors loved to stand and watch a craftsman at work.

Such a novelty, these days, to see anything made by hand.

By nine, her part-timers were arriving: Ron the retired engineer and Margaret, a cheerful, matronly type who'd worked in the factory in her younger days. Stevie had a dozen casual staff to call on, retired folk who worked for sheer love of the museum's history. This gave the place a happy atmosphere, and made it easy for her to be a popular boss.

"Morning, Ron," she called as he passed, leaving a trail of wet bootprints. "Still raining, I see?"

"And ruddy freezing," he replied, turning and noticing the mess he'd made. "Oh, look at that. I wiped my feet, honest. Sorry, I'll grab the mop."

"Don't worry, Alec can do it," said Stevie. "Get the coffee machine on!"

Stevie never went behind the café counter if she could help it. Preparing food was not her favorite activity. When Alec arrived, he headed straight for the workbench. Mildly irritated, she called out, "Hold on, Alec, would you mind cleaning the floor first?"

He stopped, giving her an ironically grumpy look over his spectacles. "Who's doing the tours today?"

"It's on the duty roster. You've got the two o'clock."

"Yes, ma'am." He went to collect a mop, adding wet footprints of his own.

Stevie sighed and went behind the counter. Alec was the only staff member who acted up; he was old-school and resented women telling him what to do. At least his sense of humor redeemed him.

In the back room, she unfolded Daniel's panel on her desk. The flame-haired goddess resembled an angel, offering a choice between heaven and hell . . . but no, that interpretation wasn't right. She frowned. Daniel's work appeared as puzzling as ever.

"Sorry I'm late!"

Fin breezed in, throwing her coat over a chair and complaining about the slow and rainy school run, and how if it weren't for her kids, she would be on a plane halfway to Florida by now. Without waiting for a response, she hurried into the café, reappearing minutes later with two large cappuccinos.

"Thanks," said Stevie, accepting the mug. "The coffee bribe always works."

"Third time this week, and you're not going to tell me off?"

Stevie took a breath. "No. I'm going to ask you an enormous favor."

"Oh-oh." Fin took a sip of her cappuccino, which left foam on her upper lip. "What dreaded task have you lined up for me?"

"Nothing awful. Mustache," Stevie added, grinning.

"Always happens." Fin wiped her lip with a tissue. "How come you drink yours so daintily? I end up with a Santa Claus beard if I'm not careful. This favor . . . ?"

"Right, okay, about the mystery delivery . . ."

Stevie explained about her phone call to Daniel's mother. Fin froze, staring.

"Oh my god. You don't really think he's done away with himself, do you? That's terrible."

Stevie's throat tightened. She gave a vehement shake of her head. "No. I can't let myself believe that. But his mother's in real distress, and she's not one to ask for help unless she's desperate. I promised I'd go and see her. Today. Now. Can you manage without me?"

"Absolutely. No problem. I mean," Fin corrected herself, "absolutely *not*, but we'll struggle through somehow. You want me to do anything with the triptych?"

"Leave it in the office for now. I'll make a decision after I've seen Daniel's mother."

"No problem. Yes, go, Stevie. After all, when do you ever take a day off?"

Only on Mondays, and only because we're closed, she thought. Days off, she never knew quite what to do with herself. Sometimes she'd go shopping, or to the library or cinema in the center of Birmingham, but often she'd find herself back in the museum, dusting, restocking or rearranging displays.

Stevie had to admit that her life was, frankly, a bit sad.

"Thank you. That wasn't the big favor, though." She gave an apologetic grin. "Please can I borrow your car?"

"What?" Fin sounded more startled than horrified.

"His mother lives in the wilds of Derbyshire. I could go by train and taxi, but that would take forever."

"Fine, but, er, do you actually possess a driving license?"

"Yes, of course. Look." She took her purse from under the counter and produced the document. "I live over the shop, and I can walk into town or take the tram, so there's no point in me owning a car."

"I know." Fin rolled her eyes. "And since my car's an old banger, only fit to run my kids around in—"

"Hey, I never suggested that."

"I'm stating a fact. Don't expect leather luxury. Yes, fine, when do I refuse you anything? We'll hold the fort." Fin passed her the keys. "Ignore the chocolate wrappers and dog hairs. My insurance should cover you . . . I *think* . . . just don't put any dents in it, okay? Any *more* dents."

"You're my fairy godmother," said Stevie. "Make sure Alec pulls his weight. Don't let him sit playing with his clock all day . . . er, you know what I mean."

"Sure, and please be back in time for me collect the children—five at the latest—if you don't want to be turned into a pumpkin," Fin retorted cheerfully.

Frances Manifold lived in a small village called Nethervale, deep in the countryside on the Leicestershire-Derbyshire border. The drive took Stevie only an hour. It was years since she'd passed along these narrow, hedge-lined roads, but as soon as she reached the village boundary, every detail was familiar, as if she'd never left.

She turned off the main street into a side lane that curved between a mixture of farmland, cottages, and barns converted into smart modern dwellings. A stream ran along the left-hand side. The wide, grassy bank was lined with trees. Crows cawed, high above in their leafless crowns. Presently she reached a row of old houses, each one set back in its own grounds.

Stevie pulled in at the side of the lane. Fog hung in the air and moisture dripped from the trees, soaking the grass and asphalt beneath. The lane was deserted, the air saturated with the wintry farm smells of wet grass and manure.

The Manifold residence was a small Georgian-style manor, poised on an incline in a walled, wooded garden. As Stevie walked up the curve of the gravel driveway, the house, with its greyish white walls and unpretentious shabbiness, woke vivid memories of Daniel.

His father had died when Daniel was nine. Lung cancer. That was all Stevie knew. She could only guess how hard his death had hit his wife and son, because they'd rarely talked about him. Frances Manifold was not one to show emotion.

Which was harder, Stevie wondered, losing a parent or having no family in the first place? The ache of chronic absence versus the acute pain of loss— could they even be compared?

Her feeling of dread rose as she approached the front door. She recalled Frances Manifold as a tallish, thin, acerbic woman, with copper hair cut in a short bob. Angular and tough, she was a paleontologist and looked the part in trousers and shirt of pale khaki. Her outdoorsy clothes and air of suppressed energy had made her seem always ready for action. She was a professor at a Midlands university, but Stevie suspected she was restless in lecture halls and yearned to be out digging up fossils in the wilds.

At their first meeting, Frances had shaken her hand, her grip powerful and bony, her eyes like those of an eagle locked on to prey.

Stevie had felt instant admiration for this strong, educated woman, and a desire for approval. Frances, unfortunately, had not reciprocated. The moment they met, Stevie felt she had been judged and found wanting.

Perhaps she subjected all Daniel's friends to the same caustic probing, challenging them to earn her respect. She made no secret of the fact that she'd wanted Daniel to go into science, like his parents. Art was not a proper career. And she seemed to consider Stevie a dreamy, shady reprobate who'd come to steal her little boy.

Stevie, shy and awkward in her presence, had never known how to break the ice.

Now she raised her chin and reminded herself that she was a grown-up, a professional in her own right, equal to anyone.

The door opened before she reached it. Frances Manifold stood waiting on the threshold. Superficially she looked the same, but Stevie saw signs of aging and stress. A few more lines around her eyes, her expression tight with worry. Grey roots striped the coppery hair. Always bony, Frances had lost weight, which made her appear more brittle than tough.

"Hello, Stephanie." No smile, but her tone was civil. "It's so good of you to come."

She held the door open and Stevie went in, breathing a miasma of floor polish, damp dog and stale cooking. The house hadn't changed. The large entrance hall was grand yet gloomy: defiantly unmodernized. The same black-and-white engravings of Victorian explorers still hung on the greying ivory walls. A grandfather clock ticked portentously. Two glass cabinets full of fossils stood opposite the door, as she remembered.

A golden cocker spaniel came lolloping out of a doorway, skidding on the buffed floor tiles. This was new. He snuffed at Stevie's knees, tail wagging wildly.

"Settle down, Humphrey," said the professor, as Stevie bent to stroke the silky head. "He's two, but still acts like a puppy. I seem to recall you're not a dog person?" The tilt of her eyebrows seemed to imply an accusation. "I can remove him, if he bothers you."

"Oh, no, he's fine, he's really sweet." Stevie was determined to defuse the tension that Daniel's mother created without trying.

"Well, I never thought I'd see you again, after you and Daniel parted company."

Yes, the edge was still there in her voice. Stevie sighed inwardly. "We never quarreled. No hearts were broken. We drifted apart, but we stayed friends."

"Hmm. Oh, let me take your coat and scarf. Chilly, isn't it? This sort of damp cold gets right into the bones."

Frances continued, as she hung the garments on a peg, "So-called friends these days don't see each other from one year to the next. It's all email and social networking. Perhaps if you and Daniel had stayed in closer touch—oh, I don't know what I'm saying. Come through and I'll make tea."

"Thank you, Professor Manifold."

"Call me Frances."

"Are you sure? And I'm Stevie, not Stephanie."

"I'm not calling you by a boy's name. That would be like you calling me Frank. Ridiculous."

Was there a hint of humor in the remark? Trying not to fall over Humphrey as he swerved in front of her, she followed Frances into a large reception room overlooking the back garden.

She looked around to see the same mismatched furniture, so antiquated it was almost in fashion again. Authentic "shabby chic." Stevie breathed in the musty scents and listened to the heavy tick of the grandfather clock. Nothing had changed here either. At the rear of the room, glass doors stood open to a conservatory, if that was the right word for the dilapidated glass house attached to the back of the building. The space was so full of potted plants that she could hardly tell where the garden began.

Daniel used to paint in there.

"Sorry about the cold. I leave the doors open for the dog, you see. I'm used to it. Make yourself at home while I put the kettle on," said Frances. She hurried through another door, Humphrey bounding after her. Chances were the kitchen hadn't changed either; Stevie recalled green-painted cupboards, a vast black oven range and an oblong sink flanked by wooden draining boards.

Stevie wandered into the conservatory, where the pungent scent of hibernating potted plants enveloped her. Condensation streamed down the glass. Rubbing a clear patch, she looked out at the garden. The lawn edges vanished under masses of shrubbery and dark conifers. The high walls surrounding the garden were thickly cloaked with ivy. A stone goddess tilted a shell towards a round, mossy basin, but no water ran.

She recalled long afternoons spent in here with Daniel, talking as he worked. His battered easel still stood in a corner. She shivered with an eerie sense of nostalgia.

Daniel had been gentle and quiet by nature—but once he got going, he would talk endlessly about *his* ideas, *his* visions. He rarely asked about her course; hammering and soldering fiddly bits of metal must have seemed a dull business to a fine artist.

Stevie hadn't minded. She'd never cared to talk about herself. There was no egotism in Daniel's character. Rather, he'd possessed a sort of wild yet innocent enthusiasm that he couldn't suppress.

A spasm of loss went through her. Daniel should be here but he wasn't. Where was he, what had happened to him?

Humphrey came scampering in. Frances was in the doorway with a tray. "Do come and sit down. Close these doors, and I'll try to get the fire going. We'll soon warm up."

Stevie obeyed, realizing that the house was almost colder inside than out. She sat on a sagging couch in front of the fireplace and poured tea into flowery cups while Professor Manifold added logs to the sulking fire. Sparks spiraled up the chimney.

With a faint huff the professor sat down at the far end of the couch, her knees making bony angles in her trousers. Stevie, seeing how underweight she was, how tired, felt her concern deepen. Frances sat straight-backed but brokenhearted, diminished by anxiety.

"So, you say he sent you some artwork?"

"Yes." Stevie handed Daniel's scribbled note to her. "This is all he said. That's why I'm trying to contact him."

Frances's hand tightened on the paper, making creases. "Damn. I so hoped you might be able to tell *me* something. Did you even realize that he hasn't been well?"

"I didn't know." Stevie felt irrationally guilty. She wished she hadn't let their friendship drift, but at times Daniel had simply been too intense for comfort. That was partly why she'd let him go in the first place. "He had a studio in London, so I thought he was doing okay. What happened?"

"He was overstretching himself in every aspect of his life. That was my opinion." The comment was waspish. "He wouldn't listen to me."

"But weren't you proud of him? You must have visited his studio, seen his latest work?"

A pause. Damp logs popped and whined on the fire. "No."

"Why not?"

"The rare times he phoned or came home, all we did was argue. He invited me, but I made a point of not going. And now I feel dreadful about it, of course, but I couldn't give my approval . . ."

She trailed off. Stevie said, "When you say he wasn't well, how do you mean?"

"Oh, you know how he was." Frances flapped a hand as if to push it all away.

"Well, not really." Stevie was trying to be sensitive. "At college, he was a bit eccentric, and he was a workaholic, but lots of creative people are like that."

Frances gave an empty laugh. "And you encouraged him, Stephanie; taking him food and strong coffee so he could work all night. I wouldn't indulge him like that."

She ignored the dig. "But none of that means he was ill, does it?"

"I suppose it depends on your perspective." Frances caressed Humphrey's head, not looking at her. "It's a shade of grey along a scale, isn't it? Many might regard me as eccentric, digging up old bones for a living. I don't think it's unreasonable to work for twelve hours preparing lectures, or cataloguing finds. However, I draw the line at moving from coffee to amphetamines to LSD or other dangerous substances. I do not suffer delusions that my fossils are talking to me."

Stevie felt dread trickling through her. "Was Daniel that bad?"

"Oh, Stephanie, he was out of control. Every time I saw him he looked worse; exhausted, manic, talking nonsense. I was extremely concerned about his lifestyle, the company he was keeping. He brushed me off, told me to stop interfering."

"What company? A girlfriend?"

"No, I mean the assorted low-lives who encouraged him because they think it's clever and radical to be constantly stoned. He needed protecting from himself! I wanted him to see a doctor, but just the mention of it made him furious, and I couldn't force him."

"That's terrible." The understatement was all she could manage.

"The warning signs were always there. You know that."

"But we didn't take drugs at college. An occasional joint at a party, maybe, but neither of us was into it." Stevie had to challenge Frances's view of her son. "Are you certain he was ill? Or is it more that you didn't approve of him?"

Frances sipped her tea and put down the cup. She looked haggard. "My disapproval is irrelevant. Things had gone far beyond that. He'd talk about the visions he was painting as if they were marvelous, when anyone could hear he was raving. He even tried to win me round by bringing home one of his supposedly wonderful new friends." Her mouth turned down in distaste. "Wonderful! This 'friend' was like some unwashed druggie off the streets. Each time I tried to reason with him, we'd descend into a dreadful argument and he'd walk out, or slam down the phone."

Stevie was quiet. The spaniel put his head on her knee, giving her a chance to think as she petted him. There were two possible interpretations. Perhaps Danny was excited about his work and simply wanted his mother to *understand*. Her indifference crushed him, yet he never gave up trying. Or maybe Frances was right. Daniel was mentally ill and in desperate need of help.

She began softly, "Professor—Frances, I know you didn't approve of him choosing art, but is it right still to be giving him such a hard time about it, ten years on?"

She tilted her head, meeting Stevie's gaze. "I don't know what went wrong. I so hoped he'd take after his father. His logical career path would have been the sciences, medicine, even law. It's a parent's worst nightmare to watch their child going off the rails into a fanciful occupation that's never going to bring any money or status."

"But he was so talented."

"Lots of people are talented, and still end up penniless."

"It hurt Daniel that you didn't like his college friends." Stevie took a sip of tea from the bone-china cup. "Couldn't you have accepted him the way he was?"

"Oh, that's the trendy thing to do now, isn't it? No. I was too disappointed, too worried by the bad influences on him, both then and now. I kept hoping he'd see sense."

"Bad influences like me?" The younger, nervous Stevie wouldn't have dared say such a thing, but she was more confident now, a match for the acid-tongued professor.

"Nothing personal. I wanted to protect him. He's always been drawn to types with an aura of anarchy and laziness about them. I hated my son being part of that."

"I don't recognize that description of our old friends. I'm not in the gutter on drugs. I manage a museum."

"Well, good for you. The funny thing, though, is that he's never stopped talking about you. He still claims that *you* were the one who made him paint so furiously."

Stevie felt a wave of shock and denial as she recalled having similar thoughts this morning. "After all this time? Are you suggesting this is somehow my fault?"

Frances shook her head, coppery hair bouncing on her thin cheeks. "No, no, of course not. But it's all so— Stephanie, I didn't mean to be accusatory. I'm not handling this well. But I don't know who else to turn to."

"Can I see the note? The one that made you think he'd . . ."

With a faint groan, Frances took a folded letter from her pocket. "They found it in his studio after he'd disappeared."

Stevie took the letter, recognizing the wild, cramped handwriting.

Dear Mother, this is hard. You know how it's been—or no, that's the point, you don't know. That's okay. I disappointed you and I'm sorry. But why be *disappointed* in me, any more than you'd be disappointed in the postman, or some random person you passed on the street? For the sole reason that I'm your son. That gives you the right to judge another human being, does it? Genes. But that's fine, you're entitled to your opinions of me—I'm very used to them, after all—but I want you to know that your expectations and disappointments *have got nothing to do with this.*

No. It's something else. Can't explain and you wouldn't understand. I'm trying to say it's not your fault. It's me. Me. I'm tired of arguing, of trying to prove myself, of hoping you'll understand, because I accept now that you can't. But I'm so tired. I need to make a clean break. Permanent. For your sake, as much as mine.

My brain is exploding with dreams. It's like trying to contain whole worlds in my head and I can't anymore. No sooner do I paint one vision than another rushes in to fill the gap and I don't know if anyone will ever see or understand any of it—so I have to make it STOP.

Give my love to my friends. Especially Stevie Silverwood, don't forget her. Tell them I'm sorry. Sorry to you too, Mum. Don't be lonely. Love you.

Bye, Daniel.

"So tell me," said Frances, "does it sound like a suicide note?"

Stevie waited for the ache in her throat to subside. How on earth to answer? "It could be. He sounds . . . angry. All he wanted was for you to accept him."

"It's the ultimate way to get back at me, of course. To show how much I hurt him. Very adolescent. But then I never thought he'd properly grown up."

Stevie decided to change tack, and not react to Frances's bitter remarks. "Did you call the police?"

"Yes, of course! They found the note, but the studio was virtually stripped bare, so they told me. I couldn't face going there."

"Are they still looking for him?"

"Yes, they're going through their missing persons procedure. They classed him as 'medium risk,' because of his precarious mental state, which means they're making serious efforts to trace him . . . but with no luck so far. Really, they were very helpful, but you can't help feeling he's just one of hundreds. I'm sure they think, privately, that this is a mere case of a son falling out with his mother. He's an adult, after all, and there's no sign he's come to any actual harm."

Stevie scanned the letter again, handed it back. "This is so ambiguous. Perhaps it's his way of cutting you out of his life and vanishing."

"So you're suggesting he'd rather I thought he was dead than ever see me again?"

"Er . . . I didn't mean that. It could be that he's exhausted and needs to get away. He might feel differently in a few weeks' time. Maybe you should give him the benefit of the doubt and . . . let him go."

Frances snorted. "That's what the police counselors hinted. Patronizing little devils, the pair of them looked barely fifteen! What do they know?"

One thing was clear: Frances and Daniel were equally difficult people. Stevie felt like walking away, but couldn't, because his mother's anger was so obviously a mask. Fear and misery shone from her like light through a cracked shell.

"What can I do to help?"

"Oh, Stephanie, I don't know. Daniel's right, I *don't* understand. This isn't about trying to control him. I'd take back every word, just to see him again. What does any of it matter? I need to know if he's dead, or ill, or run off to a new life. I won't even try to speak to him, if he doesn't want to. I simply need to *know*. He's my son. That's only thing that matters. Do you see that?"

"Yes, of course," Stevie said firmly. "And I'll try to find out for you. For his sake and mine, as well as yours. I'm no detective, but I'll do my best."

A gleam of hope lit the tired eyes. "Would you?"

"Yes, anything it takes. About his artwork—do you want me to display it, or send it to you?"

"Oh lord. I really don't care. He sent the damned thing to you, so there's your answer."

Again, her vehement rejection of Daniel's work was automatic, almost an expression of revulsion. Perhaps Frances didn't see it as rejection of Daniel himself, but he must have read it that way. How else to take it? If she hated his work, the most important part of him . . .

Yet Frances wasn't a hateful person. Only stubborn, too rigid in her views.

Stevie excused herself to visit the loo. Frances sent her to the upstairs bathroom, explaining that it was warmer than the one downstairs. From a window on the landing, Stevie looked out and saw the professor in the garden, scattering scraps for the birds. Several blackbirds, semi-tame, fluttered hun-grily towards her.

Is there is something she's not telling me? The suspicion lodged uneasily in Stevie's mind. The house had a desolate, haunted feeling. Dark shapes flick-ered in the edges of her vision, like the start of one of her hallucinatory epi-sodes. A cold draft moved across the back of her neck as if some creature was snuffling at her . . .

She whipped around to find herself looking at Daniel's bedroom door. She pictured the bed where they'd often sat talking—occasionally making love—and his bookshelves and glass display case . . . but the thought of peeping inside filled her with irrational terror, as if she might find his corpse in there. Ghosts of the past sighed all around her.

"I ought to be going," she said, reaching the bottom of the stairs as the professor came into the hall. Humphrey trotted after her, chewing on a ball. "Will you be all right on your own?"

Frances gave a dry laugh. "I'm not on my own. I've a lively dog and scores of garden birds to keep me occupied. But it's good of you to ask, Stephanie. I didn't expect such thoughtfulness."

"Why not? Did I seem rude in the past?" Stevie asked warily. "I was scared of you, that's all. I'm sorry."

"No, don't apologize. You were never rude. Only . . . Never mind."

She let the remark pass. "If I find out anything, I'll let you know."

She moved towards the coat pegs in the hall, but Frances said, "Stephanie . . . there's something else. During one of our arguments, Daniel told me he'd found a buyer for most of his work. I didn't believe him."

"Why?"

"Because he was implying that his work was too important and dangerous for the world at large to see. He sounded utterly delusional. That's why I wanted him to consult a doctor." Deep lines creased her forehead and she col-ored slightly. "I suppose he told you that I took him to a psychologist years ago?"

"Yes." Stevie swallowed a surge of complex emotions. "He thought you were making a fuss over nothing."

"Well, he would say that. But he was always . . . sensitive. His father's death hit him hard. And then his obsessive sketching—his insistence on go-ing to art college was bound to make things worse. I'm *not* blaming you. I've simply spent years trying to shield him from anything that fed his delusions. And I've failed."

"Perhaps you tried too hard." Stevie's head ached. These raw glimpses into his state of mind were too painful to bear. "You couldn't stop him being him-self."

Frances sighed. "Clearly."

"As I said, I'll do all I can to find him. Maybe I can dig deeper than the police."

Frances gave a tired grin. "What if he doesn't want his rotten old mother to know you've seen him, and swears you to secrecy?"

"Then I won't tell you," Stevie answered with a smile. "I'll contact you with a passphrase. I'll phone up and say . . . 'Humphrey has landed.'"

She laughed. "Then my dog's name would be the sweetest sound I've ever heard."

As she showed Stevie to the door, the mood between them was subdued, laced with pain. Frances said, "So you will let me know if there's any news?"

"Yes, of course. I'll come back anyway, to make sure you're all right."

Frances took Stevie's forearm in a bony grip. "Thank you." She held on for a moment. "Trust, Stephanie. I only deal in facts; I don't know what to do with 'maybe's. Promise you'll be straight with me from now on."

Stevie's breath stilled. "I'm not sure what you mean."

"You weren't always in the past."

"We barely knew each other."

Frances's lips thinned. "Just promise. I must be able to trust you."

"You can. I promise."

The museum was quiet when Stevie arrived. Two visitors were leaving with gift bags full of souvenirs or jewelry. Ron, sweeping the floors, raised a hand to greet her. There was no one manning the counter, but Stevie found the door to the back office open.

"Fin, I'm back! No dents in your car! I've had a very strange day. How was yours?"

Fin didn't answer. Stevie entered the office, saw her assistant's dark head bent towards the computer screen.

"Nutcases!" Fin exclaimed, making her start.

She leaned over Fin's shoulder and saw a busy website with news stories down the center, ad banners flashing at the sides.

"That doesn't look like a spreadsheet," said Stevie.

"I've finished the figures," said Fin. "Checked our email, got distracted by the news headlines."

"Who are the nutcases?"

Fin waved a contemptuous hand at the screen. "It's a summary of all this year's natural disasters. Hurricanes, earthquakes, tsunamis and so on. And they've included a statement by some idiot claiming that it's divine punishment on the human race!"

"For what?"

"Oh, the usual. For being gay, following the wrong religion, listening to the wrong music or daring to have some harmless fun." Fin gave an exasperated huff. "You'd think that ten minutes of scientific education would teach these crazies that it's nature, weather systems, the Earth's crust shifting around. But no." She threw her hands in the air. "Earthquakes are caused by human sin!"

Stevie grimaced. "Maybe they're being ironic."

"Nah. It's only irony if it's funny."

"Can I draw your attention to about a hundred comments underneath agreeing with you?" Stevie smiled, glad to be distracted by Fin's righteous indignation.

"Yes, thank goodness. I was going to add one, but I don't think all the effing and blinding would have got past the moderator." Fin closed the site. "You need the computer?"

"No, you can shut it down," said Stevie. "While we're quiet, I want to put Daniel's artwork on display. By the way, where's Alec?"

"Ah." Fin pulled a face. "He went home early in a huff. Don't know how to tell you this, but he's managed to burn out the motor on your bench lathe."

"Oh, great. Never mind, I'll sort it."

"The thing is, though, he tried to blame it on you."

Stevie's mouth fell open. "How is it my fault?"

"He was grumbling a load of rubbish about women damaging delicate equipment because they don't know what they're doing."

"*What?* Alec's the one who punishes the tools, *my* tools, and I haven't even touched the lathe in three months, because he's always on it. The nerve!"

"I know," said Fin. "So I gave him both barrels, and he went home in a huge grump. Sorry, I'm not diplomatic like you."

"Fantastic." Stevie pulled off her scarf, shook out her damp hair. "Never mind. If Alec doesn't come back, we'll cope—but he will. He always does. As I was saying, we can put the triptych on a table, because it's freestanding. People will see it as they enter the exhibition room."

"So is Daniel's mother okay about that? How did it go?"

"Awful," said Stevie, leaning on the counter. "Sad. Weird. Heartbreaking." Fin's expression turned sober. "And did you find out if he . . ."

"That's the worst thing. We don't know. He vanished, leaving a mysterious letter. The police haven't traced him so far. His mother's devastated. She puts on a brave front, but I'm really worried about her."

As they carried the triptych into the larger room and positioned it on a narrow side table, Stevie gave a brief account of the visit.

"Part of the reason Daniel and I split up was that his mother never liked me. She thinks I led her darling son astray. But I always *did* like her, in the perverse way that some people like sour lemons. I wanted her to trust me, and now she's obliged to."

"You need a drink," Fin said firmly, putting a hand on Stevie's shoulder. "Honestly, you look drained."

"Thanks." Stevie pressed her forefingers under her eyes, as if to press away the shadows.

She studied the trio of images, seeing a mass of detail she hadn't noticed before.

First the central panel, the auburn-haired goddess against a blazing white-gold background, one hand holding up a glass orb to the stars, the other pointing at a fiery fissure in the ground. What she'd taken for mountains in the background now appeared to be an evanescent city of transparent, crumbling, smoking towers. She picked out the words inscribed on the frame, AURATA'S PROMISE.

The left-hand panel showed a lofty hall of pillars, dominated by a pair of gigantic statues on twin thrones. A god and goddess, enthroned. Their faces were black and feline, possibly masked. The heights of the hall vanished into vague darkness that created a sense of desertion. Every pillar was covered in elaborate carving: decoration, or language? Some were broken stumps. Shafts of light fell through holes in the roof.

She looked more closely and saw what appeared to be number of dead bodies around the base of the thrones, half-buried by rubble.

In the right-hand panel, behind an exquisitely detailed armillary sphere, there was a rush of indistinct silvery creatures on all fours like hunting cheetahs. Not entirely cat-like, they possessed some disturbingly human qualities: a wild eye here, a human foot there. The sense of movement was intense, a race of life or death so ferocious that Stevie could almost feel the creatures' hot breath, smell their sweat.

The only still points of the image were the sphere itself, and the priest-like figure standing to one side.

Ron could be heard whistling as he swept the floor in the café. Fin spoke thoughtfully. "They're good. Do you think they're good? You're the art expert, not me."

"Hardly an expert. Striking, but very odd. That was Danny, though. A crazy genius."

"What's it meant to mean?"

"I wish I knew. Apparently these scenes were inspired by *me*," said Stevie. Her throat felt raw from too much talking, and the wintry air. "Don't ask me how that works."

Fin said, "Whatever your 'Danifold' has done, it's not down to you. I know you'll do everything possible to find him, and I'll help if I can."

Stevie grinned, grateful for her practicality. "Yes, what more can we do?"

"The very fact that his work is here might mean that Daniel turns up to reclaim it."

"It's possible." Stevie hesitated. "His mother thinks he's on drugs, delusional and even paranoid. He claimed some mystery buyer wanted all his work, because it's too dangerous for the world to see."

"Ah," said Fin. "That does sound a bit . . . loopy."

"But what if it's true? He might have made an enemy of someone for any number of reasons, and vanished because he's scared."

Fin mulled this over for a minute. "You're right, you can't rule out anything. Are you worried this putative enemy might turn up here?"

"It's a risk." Stevie folded her arms, recalling the unease she'd felt in the Manifold house, the impression of dark shadows circling her. A nebulous yet powerful fear squeezed her throat. She couldn't put her foreboding into words. "We might attract the very person Danny was frightened of."

"Then this is bait," said Fin, her eyes suddenly shining.

"And that's a good thing?"

"Aren't you curious to see if anyone turns up and shows an interest? Someone who might know what actually happened to Daniel?"

4

Light Through the Dust

Rufus woke, deep in the night, startled by a rumbling sound that began far away and rolled closer like a giant train. He tried to get up. The ground dropped beneath him, then bucked, throwing him against the wall of his tent.

"What the hell—?"

Earth tremor. Great. Rufus Dionys Ephenaestus looked up at a roof of sagging brown canvas a couple of feet above his nose. Through his thin sleeping bag, he felt the hard dusty earth and several hundred sharp stones digging into his back. What now? Go back to sleep as if nothing had happened? No point in panicking. There was nothing outside but the mountains of a dreary brown no-man's-land near the borders of Pakistan. Pulling open the tent flap, he looked up at the stars. No light pollution dimmed their magnificence. But he'd had thousands of years to gaze up at those stars and wasn't impressed.

It was also bloody freezing.

Warlords might come upon him, armed with the guns he'd sold them earlier, to steal back their money and leave him for dead. Surely someone would take his Jeep, leaving him in an even worse mess. Any sensible trader would be long gone, whisked back to civilization by a private plane or helicopter. Not Rufus. He couldn't find the energy to care.

He worked alone. He made himself an open target, took mad risks, sold consignments of rifles, machine guns and rocket launchers, yet didn't keep even a handgun to defend himself. Everyone he met thought he was insane, yet he survived. He knew why.

They were afraid of him.

That was useful, but the novelty had worn off. In the quiet of the night—whether he was in an African war zone, a Middle Eastern desert or the barren immensity of the Hindu Kush—he thought about his lost brother, Mistangamesh.

Another tremor came, disturbing, but not enough to push away his thoughts.

Beautiful, infuriating Mist, who'd accidentally "died" several hundred years ago. Ever since—echoing the legend of Estel the Eternal, who searched tirelessly for the scattered parts of her lover—Rufus had tried to find him, to restore him to life.

They were Aetherials, undying Aelyr. Mist had to be out there somewhere . . .

The tremor began again and the ground reared beneath him. This time the quake meant business, rumbling like a fleet of tanks towards his tent. Rufus tried to grab something solid for support. There was nothing. The Earth itself was rising and falling like the sea.

Somehow he clawed his way out of the tent, like a drunk negotiating the moving floors of a funhouse. It took forever. The struggle struck him as so ludicrous that he started to laugh hysterically. He couldn't even shift into the Dusklands, where the world might have been calmer. The earthquake was shuddering through every dimension.

He emerged on all fours into the open, in time to see his Jeep tumbling into a chasm that had opened in the ground. The vehicle slid from view with a crunch of breaking glass and buckling metal. Rocks and ground lurched violently, torn apart. The sound was overwhelming, deafening. Rufus flung himself to the convulsing earth and lay with his hands over his ears. He was afraid. How thrilling it felt to be afraid for once!

Presently it stopped.

He rose to his feet and stared around him, dumbstruck. The air was full of dust. The landscape, already bleak, looked as if it had been kicked around by a bored god.

In a daze, he started walking.

His mind was numb, so the inevitable thoughts of Mistangamesh trickled into the void. Rufus let them flow. *Where was I?*

At one point, Rufus was sure he'd found him in the form of a young man, shell-shocked and damaged by the Great War: the very image of his brother. Same flawless yet haunted face, thick dark hair shading his moody eyes. A tormented war poet; that was how he appeared. So Rufus had kidnapped him and spent ninety years trying to convince him that he was not Adam Montague, the scion of a wealthy British dynasty, but actually an immortal Aelyr, son of the ruling house Ephenaestus of the Felynx.

Rufus had failed.

Adam refused to "wake up." All the sultry beauty of the Otherworld, the sensual temptations of Rufus's followers, a good spell of sensory deprivation, even renaming him Leith to help sever his human ties—none of it had brought Mist back.

In the end, Adam had stupidly died, as he'd stupidly lived—a dumb human.

Rufus had lost his mind for a few days. Then he'd pulled his tattered self together, stolen the flashiest sports car he'd ever seen and roared towards the future. Free of Mist, free of false hope.

He'd headed for London and almost made it, crashing the Lamborghini with the police in full pursuit after he'd refueled and driven off without paying. The memory made him smile. Scrambling though fields and woods, a police helicopter hovering overhead unable to locate him because he moved through the Dusklands—the first layer of the Aetheric realms—thus foxing their infrared cameras.

It was a shame about the car, though.

Arriving in London, Rufus tried to lose himself in pleasure. He hung out in trendy nightclubs, befriended ugly politicians and overpaid footballers, sleek socialites, models and actors and all their hangers-on. He wasn't fussy. At their expense, he got drunk, imbibed an array of drugs, charmed every half-decent-looking human he met. In the morning he would be gone with their money, credit cards and jewelry before they woke up.

It was so easy, because he had an angel's beauty and knew how to work it.

The lifestyle was fun for a while, but . . . he'd done it all before, and for centuries. He was bored.

The truth was that nothing filled the void in his soul where his brother Mistangamesh should have been. Nothing ever would. He'd never doubted that Adam's eyes, clouded by animal fear, would light up with recognition and love. Probably with hate and rage, too, but he could have handled that.

It had never happened.

Finally Rufus was forced to admit that Adam was, after all, only a vessel of flesh. The physical resemblance to Mist, so poignant, had duped him. Now he resigned himself to being alone.

After all, he was used to it. For long centuries he'd been regarded as a pariah among Aetherials, a traitor on an epic scale. A long list of kidnappings, troublemaking and even murder, both on Earth and in the Otherworld, was the least of it. First and greatest was his alleged destruction of the legendary Aetherial city Azantios.

The Spiral Court—the pompous idiots—had tried to place him on trial, only to produce not one scrap of evidence against him. Rufus had been scared out of his wits for a while, but now the memory amused him. The ordeal had almost been worth it, to see the white face of his prosecutor, the puritanical Lord Albin of Sibeyla, set in frustrated rage.

One day Rufus realized why a life of hedonism and petty theft was so unsatisfying.

Don't be evil was the slogan of a huge Internet company. And Rufus had responded to himself, *Why the hell not?*

If his enemies wanted crime, he'd give them crime. He would plunge into the nastiest, shadiest, most dangerous career on the planet, so wicked it was a caricature, a veritable parody of evil.

One contact led to another and he found himself at glamorous charity balls, surrounded by world leaders and celebrity fund-raisers for good causes of every kind. Champagne flowed, light glittered on diamonds, pledges to end world poverty were made.

Soon he found himself on a darkened balcony at such an event, with a self-styled philanthropist—a short, unassuming man who resembled a schoolteacher—whispering into his ear. Offering an assignment.

Rufus wasn't naive, but this was confirmation that a few of these generous folk had perhaps not earned their millions through honest hard work. Illegal arms trading was shockingly lucrative. Also dangerous, grueling, raw and seedy, cynical, brutal, fatal. No one worked the raw edge of the actual hand-over unless they were crazy.

Rufus loved it.

He adored the hypocrisy, the corruption, the faux glamour of arms fairs, the shady deals laced with drugs and blood diamonds. He loved traveling to godforsaken regions of the world and selling weapons to desperate brutes, then venturing a little farther and selling more to their enemies.

At first, he was part of a team, dealing within the relative safety of an armed escort. That didn't last long. He was indiscreet and reckless, putting his colleagues' lives at risk. It was a miracle no one murdered him, not for want of trying.

Instead, he went freelance.

That worked for him. With each new deal, his arrival was greeted with consternation, awe and superstitious fear. How could someone as outrageously handsome as Rufus—with long burnished-brown ripples of hair, looking no older than his late twenties, as willowy as an angel walking the earth—how could such a man avoid kidnap, murder or worse? In fact he was as wily and tough as the most hardened bandit, untouchable and fearless, if not actually insane.

In the course of his travels, he worked his way through a series of lovers, male and female. Upsetting his customers by seducing their wives, daughters or sisters was not the safest way of life among the lawless yet brutally strict tribal zones he frequented, but Rufus was past caring. More than once, bullets ripped through his body and he simply stood there laughing. That tended to earn the healthy respect of warlords.

If he *were* to die, he assumed that his soul-essence would find its way into the Otherworld and along the Causeway of Souls to the Mirror Pool at the heart of Asru. Or perhaps it would, like a dryad, attach itself to some thorny tree. Whatever the case, he knew that in time he would be reborn. Perhaps, in his next incarnation, he would remember none of this. Then he might find peace at last.

But in thirty thousand years, no one had yet succeeded in killing him.

Dawn was breaking as he reached the edge of a town. Even Rufus felt a frisson of shock. The main road was torn in half by a long ragged chasm. Baked-mud houses had collapsed into the abyss, and the whole area resembled a scrapyard of torn concrete, corrugated metal and rubble. Wailing filled the air. The sun shone through a pall of dust, softening the scene with an ocher haze. Survivors wandered through the haze; he saw men in long pale garments, and women in saris that were incongruously bright against the ruins, lemon and blue and scarlet.

With no particular plan, Rufus wandered along the edge of the town, detached from the suffering around him. What was he supposed to do? Although he could see that this raw human anguish was horrible, heartbreaking, he felt nothing but bemused shock.

He spotted a vehicle with a red cross on the side. There were others, too, of military green. He saw dark-skinned soldiers, and Westerners in khaki fatigues. Rescue teams were here already, the ruined streets frantic with activity. A few individuals stood holding up cell phones to film the scene. There was even a television crew.

Rufus halted. Sweat was dripping from him. He simply stood and watched the carnage, not knowing what to do or feel. *Oh dear, not another earthquake. Mother Earth shudders and casts down another civilization into the dirt: great or small, she doesn't care.*

Through veils of dust, he singled out a moving figure: a female, very slender in beige shirt and shorts, her reddish hair coiled messily under a bush hat. Sunlight through the dust surrounded her with a golden aura. Like him, she seemed separate from the activity around her. Behind her, the rescue teams, the mothers and fathers wailing amid the ruins, their dark skins caked with dust—all seemed to move with the swarming speed of an anthill. By contrast, the woman moved in slow motion, taking photographs and scribbling in a small notepad.

Occasionally someone would stop her, as if pleading for help; and she would go and assist with the same slow, methodical grace.

Rufus couldn't take his eyes off her. A journalist, he thought. He watched for half an hour as she climbed over tumbles of rock or stared down into ruptured fissures.

No. Observation revealed that she was more interested in the geological destruction around them, the tear in the Earth's crust and the material it had thrown up. The victims around her were minor interruptions to her study.

A photographer, then, or a scientist? A geologist, perhaps, who happened to be in the right place at the right time?

The wrong place, he corrected himself.

Presently she looked up and saw him. She stopped; the world itself stopped. Closer she came until they were no more than four feet apart, their eyes locked upon each other. Around them, carnage and misery retreated behind yellowish gauze, and all activity froze as if a pause button had been pressed.

Her face was striking: heart-shaped with wide-set slanting eyes, golden-ivory skin caked with dust, and dark firm eyebrows. Her irises were liquid gold, ringed by dark brown. Red strands of hair escaped from beneath her bush hat.

Impossible. Yet, if it wasn't her, why had she come straight to him, and why was she staring with that so-familiar, knowing gaze?

Familiar, and yet he wasn't sure . . . or rather, he *was* sure, but daren't admit it yet. There was a game to be played first. He needed to be certain . . . and so did she.

"Hello," she said. "I'm Orla Connelly."

"Miss Connelly," said Rufus. Neither smiled; it didn't seem appropriate.

"Dr. Connelly," she corrected. "Or just Orla."

"Well, I'm pleased to meet you, Orla. I'm Rufus Hart."

"Rufus," she echoed. "And what brings you here?"

"Isn't it terrible? I'm in shock. I don't know where to begin."

"I know," she said. "I've experienced earthquakes before. It never grows any less appalling. Who are you with?"

He shook his head, not comprehending the question. "With?"

"Which aid agency?" she said patiently.

"Oh. Oh, I see. No one. I'm traveling alone."

Her eyebrows rose sharply. "Alone, in this region? You must have a death wish, Rufus."

"I just happened to be in the area when . . ."

"Just happened?" She stared into him with her unblinking golden gaze.

Lying came easily to him. Often he said the first thing that came into his head and didn't care if he was believed or not. With Dr. Orla Connelly, however, there was nothing for it but the truth.

"I was up in the mountains, selling guns to some belligerent types," he said levelly. "The earthquake ate my Jeep, and there's not much left of my tent, either. So I started walking."

"Poor you, Rufus." She gave a sympathetic frown. "We have food, water, medical supplies. You ought to be checked over."

"Did you hear what I said? I'm an arms dealer. Why do you want to help me?"

"Because I assume that's not all you are. You're not actually pointing a gun at me. What you are to me is an extra pair of hands. But you ought to be examined first."

"Can't you examine me, Dr. Connelly?"

"No," she said firmly.

"In that case, I'm fine." He paused. "Who's 'we'?"

"My team."

"Medical team?"

"No. We're seismologists. We were studying tectonic activity in the area when this happened."

"So it's your lucky day!"

She blinked at last. "In the eyes of a complete sociopath, perhaps. Unfortunately, it's difficult to gather data while people need our help."

"I saw you taking photographs, Orla."

"The geological damage needs to be recorded." She held out her hands and he saw that the palms were scraped and bloody. "I've also been helping to dig victims out of fallen buildings. And now I'm on my way to help in the first aid tents. Come with me?"

He took her left hand to examine the injuries more closely. Her skin felt hot and rough in his fingers. "Are you asking me to help?"

"Are you offering?"

"Well, considering that I sold a consignment of weapons that might be used against these very people in a few days' time, wouldn't that be hypocritical? As you suggest, I am a complete sociopath. Why would you think I'd want to help?"

"Because no one's beyond redemption, Rufus." She shrugged. "Even an arms dealer must find a humanitarian streak in a crisis like this."

"Perhaps."

"And because I'm asking?"

"Only because *you* ask. *You*," he whispered. They held each other's gaze, both basking in a secret that couldn't yet be spoken aloud. "This is unbelievable."

"Isn't it?" Orla said softly. Stepping forward, she kissed him on the mouth, parting her lips so he could taste her warmth.

He knew her mouth. He knew *her*. But he had to be sure.

Stevie sat cross-legged on the carpet in Fin's front room, watching four children under seven rampaging amid a sea of wrapping paper. Two were Fin's and the other two belonged to Fin's sister, Bernie. The room was bright and too hot, a good third of the space taken up by a huge, overdecorated Christmas tree. The television was on full blast, showing a corny seasonal musical that was on every year. Fin's father, in a green party hat, was circulating to top up drinks, while her husband, Andy, was on his knees trying to keep a pair of overexcited Labradors from knocking the children flying.

Fin, Bernie and their mother could be heard arguing and laughing at the tops of their voices in the kitchen. Andy's father—a sweet, widowed black man in his sixties—was sitting near Stevie explaining that he'd had to emigrate from the West Indies to England because he simply couldn't stand the heat in his home country. His humorous storytelling kept Stevie entertained.

Fin had a brother, too. Patrick was a quiet, good-looking young man with a shaven head and soft dark eyes. Skinny in dark trousers and a bright red sweater, he sat on the edge of an armchair, sipping red wine and watching his nephews and nieces at play. He looked as out of place as Stevie felt.

Part of her longed for the peace of her apartment, but she had to challenge her unsociable instincts. So here she was in the midst of a classic family Christmas. The same scene was being reenacted in millions of households all over the country, all over the world.

So too the scene of people drinking alone, like Daniel's mother, with no news of her son . . . Stevie had offered to spend the holiday with her, only to be turned down flat. She was relieved. She could only imagine how grim the day would have been for them both.

Now Stevie was embarrassed to realize how little she knew about Fin. She hadn't known her family was originally from Ireland, nor that she had a brother and sister. Patrick, Fin and Bernie sounded English, but their parents, the Feehans, retained their rich Irish accents. Although it was hard to miss the fact that Andy was black—also skinny and handsome, with the same irrepressible sense of humor as his father—she hadn't known his folks were from Trinidad.

I'm hopeless, Stevie thought. *Memo to self, start taking an interest!* She didn't mean to be self-centered. It was fear that kept her at arm's length from the everyday world.

Over Christmas dinner, Fin's mother grew pink-faced and garrulous, a party hat askew on her dark-dyed hair. She began asking Stevie cheerful yet probing questions that she didn't want to answer.

"So, you're not with your family on this special day?"

"Er, not this year, no," Stevie answered with a polite half-smile.

"What do they think of that, then?" Mrs. Feehan exclaimed.

"Well . . ."

"Mum, don't interrogate her," Fin said quickly. "More potatoes, anyone?"

"I think it's a shame. Patrick works over in California, but he still makes the effort to come back and visit."

"Oh, what do you do?" Stevie asked quickly, to change the subject.

"I write music for computer games," said Patrick.

"He's a partner in the company!" Mrs. Feehan puffed up with pride. "You wouldn't believe how much money they make! But you're doing really well too, Stevie, aren't you? You run the museum, you and Fin between you."

"She's my boss," said Fin. Her mother ignored the remark.

"Your parents must be so proud, Stevie. Where are you from?"

"Er, quite local, really."

"Well, so there's time for you to see them later."

"Mum!" growled Fin.

"What? I'm only making conversation. It's lovely that you're here. Isn't it, Patrick?"

"Absolutely," he agreed. Sensing his embarrassment, Stevie didn't look at him.

"So, any brothers or sisters, Stevie?"

"No, I'm the only one," she answered, lightly, willing the questions to stop. "As far as I know."

Wrong thing to say. Mrs. Feehan's eyes almost popped from her head. "Oh? Oh my goodness, I hope I'm not putting my foot in my mouth."

"I'm surprised you can get any turkey in there, Mum!" Fin cried.

Even the children were listening now. Stevie grimaced. This was why she hated social gatherings: having to explain herself to nosy strangers.

Fin's small son joined in. "Is your dad is a serial killer? That's why Stevie can't tell us anything. You can't spend Christmas with serial killers, because they're in prison."

"Where's her mum, then?" said the daughter. "Did her dad murder her mum with a big knife?"

"What?" Fin shrieked.

"It happens on the television," the daughter said defensively. Stevie started to laugh, couldn't help it.

"Right, no more TV for either of you. Ever."

Fin's sister Bernie caught Stevie's amusement. "I bet it's worse. She might be one of those child murderers living under a secret identity." Bernie raised her hands like monster claws at the children, making them giggle with pretend fear.

"Bernie!" Fin exclaimed. "All of you, stop interrogating her!"

"Yeah, give her a break," Patrick added.

"Honestly, it's okay," said Stevie, taking a sip of wine before she choked. "There's no big secret. I was brought up in foster care, that's all."

A murmur of sympathy rose around the table, while the children soon distracted each other by listing school friends who lived with foster families. Stevie cringed inwardly.

"And she hates talking about it," Fin added.

"Well, you could have told us, Fin." Her mother turned bright red. "Stevie, I'm so sorry."

She patted her hand. Stevie flinched. "There's no need. It's no big deal."

"I'm so sorry," Mrs. Feehan repeated, beginning to gabble. "Me and my big mouth! You're so right, it's no deal at all. Thousands of children are brought up in care. You're none the worse for it. Is she, Patrick? Such a lovely looking girl, you are, and look how successful!"

"She's not on the streets, shoplifting," said Patrick. "I call that a result."

He and Stevie exchanged a grin.

"Mum, stop!" Fin said with a meaningful glare.

Some time ago, Stevie had had a similar, awkward conversation with Fin. Since then, Fin tried to protect her from people's benign nosiness. Unfortunately, this was a double layer of embarrassment; Stevie twigged that Fin's mother was checking her out as potential girlfriend material for Patrick in a none-too-subtle manner.

Stevie quelled an urge to laugh. Families. A hothouse of tension, mixed with forced joviality. She felt like a biologist observing a colony of meerkats. They were fascinating to watch, but she'd never be part of their community.

Later, Stevie and Fin retreated to the kitchen, declining offers of help with the washing-up and closing the door behind them. Fin looked hot, flustered and slightly drunk. "Stevie, I am so, so sorry about my family. They're a nightmare!"

"It's all right. Quite funny, really."

"Are you sure? You looked . . . uncomfortable, to say the least."

"No, I'm fine. My real problem was thinking about Daniel's mother. Has Frances spent the day alone in that cold old house? I offered to go, but she said no. We'd both have felt miserable and awkward all day."

"More awkward than my mother?"

"Well . . ." Stevie gave a brief, sad laugh. "They've got something in common: the torment of fretting to death over their beloved sons."

The kitchen door opened and Patrick slipped in, offering to dry the pots and pans. Fin handed him a tea towel and said, "Good timing. Take over. I need to chill upstairs for ten minutes before I murder someone."

"Christmas, eh," Patrick said ruefully, as Fin closed the door. He spoke softly, standing close as Stevie handed him wet crockery.

"Sometimes I think I'm better off without a family," Stevie said with a grin.

"No kidding. Please accept my groveling apology. My mother does it constantly: any time there's a halfway eligible female in the room, she tries to pair us off. Why d'you think I moved to America?"

"Halfway eligible? That makes me feel special."

"No, I didn't mean— I think you're absolutely gorgeous, Stevie."

"You're quite cute yourself."

"No, really, you're stunning. Mum actually chose well for once."

Stevie turned, holding a large glass dish that dripped soapy water onto their shoes. "So, don't you think it's about time you told her you're gay, Patrick?"

He went white. "Fucking hell, is it that obvious?"

She smiled. "To everyone except your mum, and maybe your dad, too. Andy's father couldn't keep a straight face."

"Don't say anything. Please don't say anything!"

"Hey, calm down. Not a word. How old are you?"

"Twenty-seven."

"Got someone special?"

Red blotches spread into his pale cheeks. "Yeah. My business partner in California."

"So pretty soon you have to tell her the truth. It's for the best. Put a stop to the excruciating matchmaking attempts."

He groaned. "Yes, I know. I think she knows, secretly. But we're Catholics; denial is her default setting. If I sit down and tell her, all her illusions come crashing down."

"I'm sure she'll survive," Stevie said crisply.

"Hey, you know, it's really nice meeting you," Patrick said, sounding more relaxed. "Any time you're in the States, you have to call me and we'll meet up. I'll write down my phone number. Promise?"

"It's a deal," she said, knowing she'd never go. No time, no confidence. Also, no passport.

The day rolled into evening, full of games and chocolates and cakes and more drinks, overexcited children, too much television. By nine o'clock, Stevie was exhausted. She made her excuses.

"Andy will drive you home," said Fin.

"You're kidding. He's more drunk than you are. And it's only ten minutes' walk."

"Fifteen. He and Patrick can walk with you then."

"There's no need. Please. I promise not to get murdered."

"How're you fixed for tomorrow?" The question was too polite. Stevie knew the score. Fin knew she was alone, and found it a pleasure to invite her on one special day. But for the entire holiday season? That was different. There was a line where genuine sociability edged into obligation, a time to say enough and good night.

Stevie didn't want to be treated as a charity case. They both knew, and acknowledged it with awkward, ironic smiles. "Tomorrow," Stevie said, "I'm going to an old folks' home."

"I know how you feel." Fin laughed. "My family has that effect on me, too."

"They're not that bad." Stevie shared her amusement. "No, I go a few times a year. I help to serve party lunches, blow up balloons, all that festive stuff."

"You kept that quiet."

It was on the tip of Stevie's tongue to add that there was a reason. In the foster home where she'd stayed the longest, the only person who'd shown her any understanding was the grandmother, Nanny Peg as they'd called her. Now Peg was small and frail and in a care home, but Stevie visited her even though Peg often did not remember who she was. Tomorrow she would sit and hold Nanny Peg's hand and stroke her white hair. Not for the first time, Stevie felt guilty that she didn't visit more often.

She didn't say this to Fin, because that might have led to explaining an episode of her life she was always trying to forget.

"Anyway, I must get home to the ghost cat. Even though she's departed the earthly plane, she still gets mad if I leave her alone for too long."

"You and your ghostly cat!" said Fin, rolling her eyes. "Honestly, I don't know whether to laugh or call a psychiatrist!"

"Stevie's cat is a ghost?" exclaimed Fin's daughter from the hall doorway.

"It's a joke," Fin replied. "Don't start pestering her. Night, Stevie. Happy Christmas, take care."

"See you in the New Year."

They hugged. Stevie closed the door on the treasure box of light, tinsel and merriment, and stepped out into the quiet, dark night.

Night fell. Rufus and Orla lay close together without touching, still fully clothed, gazing into each other's eyes. Her tent was considerably better-appointed than his had been, with an air-filled mattress to cushion them. Her sleeping bag lay loosely over their bodies as an extra layer against the growing chill of the night.

For hours they'd labored to help the victims of the earthquake, but the human world no longer seemed real. All the time, their eyes had been on each other, waiting for this. How incredible, Rufus thought, that their intimacy had once been so easy and natural: even more so, for bordering on the illicit. Now they daren't touch each other. Their last encounter had been such a long, long time ago . . . He'd never dared dream they would meet again.

Among modern human societies, their relationship would have been considered beyond sinful: an absolute taboo. Even in their own ancient, Aetherial civilization of the Felynx, where morality had been very much more relaxed, there had been raised eyebrows—not to mention Mist's quiet disapproval—that only inflamed their passion.

Orla touched a tongue to her lips. Her eyes glittered with fire—exactly as he remembered. Their auras mingled, heating the space between them until the ache of anticipation became unbearable. Yet neither of them made a move. Was Orla really *her*, or a perfect simulacrum, like Adam, sent to torture him? If she was real . . . he could barely believe this was happening . . . was it possible to recapture what they'd once shared? Perhaps they shouldn't even try . . . yet her warm, alluring expression suggested otherwise.

The ground began to tremble with a prolonged aftershock.

"Now one of us should make a joke about the earth moving," said Rufus.

"The earthquake is due to faulting within the lithosphere of the subducted Arabian Plate as it grinds beneath the convergent plate boundaries," she murmured.

"I'm not sure that's funny, but the way you say it sounds incredibly sexy."

"Oh, it is." She smiled, more with her eyes than her mouth.

They lay in silence, waiting for the movement to subside. Orla stared upward, as if absorbing every nuance. He still couldn't believe that she'd become a scientist, a doctor, part of a team. That was true human camouflage. He'd never troubled to learn anything in particular, still less to attend a university or give any credence to human qualifications. She'd evolved, and he felt oddly inadequate. But, after all this time, who wouldn't change? Even the ancient, timeless Felynx. The question was not whether they'd changed, but how much the changes actually mattered?

Now they were engaged in a strange dance around each other, both secretly knowing the truth but daring the other one to speak first.

"One of us should begin," said Orla. "What are you thinking?"

Finally Rufus said, "I used to dream about you. You were calling to me from some kind of limbo with grey walls. Nine-tenths of me was sure you perished in Azantios, but the last tenth insisted that you must still exist . . . somewhere."

He heard her release a small breath of exasperation. "Who do you think I am? Rufus, we both know, so why can't we say it aloud?"

"It might break the magic," he said softly.

Her eyes narrowed, irresistibly seductive. "Magic? Rufus, please. Is it gunselling that's turned you so romantic?"

"All right." He paused. "It's gentlemanly to go first, but I hesitate because I've made grave mistakes in the past. I was convinced I recognized someone, so convinced that I couldn't accept I was monstrously wrong. Now I have the same feeling about you, but I don't trust it."

"This time, you probably should trust yourself, Rufus. I *have* been calling you. Gods, it took you long enough to hear me!"

"Calling . . . ?" He stared into the deep fire of her eyes. "Tell me your real name. I've already told you mine."

"No. You must say it; then I'll tell you if you're right."

"This is turning into a game."

"No game." She trailed a finger from his shoulder to his elbow. Her voice was honey. "This is more important than you can imagine."

Grinning, he leaned off the mattress and picked up her notebook and pen lying nearby. "All right, I'm going to write your true name on a piece of paper. Then you say it out loud, and we'll see if it matches what I've written."

Theatrically, she laughed and closed her eyes. "Fold it up and let me hold it, then. I don't trust you not to scribble the name down as I speak, then swap bits of paper around. You're an illusionist."

"You're not wrong," he said. "You remember me, after all." Turning his back to her, Rufus wrote her name, tore out the page and folded it three times to make sure she couldn't feel an imprint. Then he slotted the paper between her thumb and forefinger. "There. Now say it."

As she spoke, she opened her eyes and swiftly unfolded the note. "Aurata." Together they looked at the name written in slanting letters, *Aurata*.

Rufus could barely breathe. "Sister," he gasped. "Sweet sister."

5

A Winter's Trail

The arts center, jauntily named the Jellybean Factory, was a renovated 1930s printing works in North London. Stevie looked up at an expanse of red brick set with huge metal-framed windows. Fire escapes wound down from the upper floors into a courtyard landscaped with gravel areas and quirky sculptures. The look was industrial art-deco, ugly yet trendily urban at the same time.

A week into the New Year, this was the first day the center had been open after the Christmas break. Three hours of travel by train and taxi had left her cold, tired and hungry. Even the fake fur of her thrift-shop winter coat couldn't keep out the chill. Drizzle was eroding a light coating of snow as she hurried across the courtyard to the glass double doors of the entrance.

How frustrating, that she'd never visited Daniel here while she had the chance. If only they'd talked, maybe she could have helped him. *Maybe.*

Heat smothered her as she entered. She slid out of her coat and looked around at a vast, brightly lit gallery, with signs that pointed to a concert hall, function rooms, a filmmakers' suite, art studios. She was reminded of the museum gift shop, albeit on grand scale. This place had the same minimal look of pale wood and bright track lighting.

Twenty or so visitors were studying the contents of display cases, admiring colorful canvases on the walls and freestanding sculptures. Racks of leaflets advertised cultural events. In one corner was an information desk. Stevie slipped straight past.

At the rear of the gallery she found signs pointing to a café, restrooms . . . and artists' workshops. The arrow by Daniel's name sent her up a flight of metal stairs to the next floor, where she followed a long walkway with balcony rails on her left overlooking the foyer below. On her right lay a row of individual studios, their interiors visible through glass panels.

Stevie passed a ceramics workshop, then a jewelry studio where a spiky-haired girl sat at a bench, directing a fierce blue flame onto some tiny item. She resisted the temptation to watch.

The third unit was the one she sought. She felt a pang of loss and anxiety on reading the name beside the door: DANIEL MANIFOLD. ICONS FOR THE NEW AGE.

Stevie peered through the glass-paneled door. The only light was wintry gloom falling through wide factory windows. She saw a good-size space with high ceilings, walls of bare brick, cupboards, easels, stools, a drawing board. To the left, an inner door to a small utility room stood ajar.

The studio looked abandoned. Her spirits fell. She'd known all along this might be a wasted, and very expensive, journey.

She tried the door and was startled to find it unlocked.

"Danny?" she called softly, on the slim chance he'd returned. No answer. She draped her coat over a stool. Surfaces were scattered with dried-up tubes of paint. Cupboards stood with their doors open. A tangle of nylon rope lay on top of a low, wide cabinet amid rolls of sticky tape. A layer of fairy dust glinted, gold and silver, on every surface, betraying his fondness for metal leaf. In the side room she glimpsed empty shelving and a big white sink.

The sense of desertion was unbearably sad. Had Danny been in debt, or in danger?

Stevie felt like a thief as she walked around. The only clue found, as far as she knew, was his "goodbye" letter to Frances.

The softest noise . . . Her head jerked up. A rush of alarm overwhelmed her.

"Daniel?" she called out. "Who's there?"

She felt an unseen presence in the side room. Her insides solidified to ice. Yes, she had a tendency to see specters—and the last thing she wanted to see was Danny's ghost—but this was different. Real.

There was a heart-stopping pause. Then a figure moved into the doorway, as if taking shape out of air and dust. He'd been lurking behind the storeroom door all the time.

Not Daniel. This man was taller, with abundant inky-black hair brushing the shoulders of a dark overcoat. Wintry half-light illuminated a strong-boned face with a complexion as pale as the thin snowfall outside. Bright grey eyes, framed by thick eyebrows and long dark lashes, fixed her with an intense stare. Stevie felt faint with a head rush of terror and lust-at-first-sight combined. He was stunning, so damned attractive that even Fin's brother Patrick seemed a troll in comparison.

Her lips parted in an involuntary O. There should be a law against a total stranger conveying such warm, velvety, almost supernatural allure. It wasn't as if she'd never met a decent-looking male before, but this was different, a lightning strike. Never had she seen a stranger about whom she felt it would be perfectly reasonable to walk up to him, wrap her arms around his waist and introduce herself with a deep, hot kiss.

Not reasonable. She mentally doused herself in cold water. His unblinking gaze disturbed her enough to cancel his outrageous masculine beauty. *Lights on, but who is home?*

Stevie was long-practiced at presenting a cool front: her survival strategy. And the outer walkway overlooking the public foyer was only a few steps away, with a score of people below to hear a yell for help.

"Ahh." She put a hand to her chest, making light of her shock. "I'd no idea anyone was here! I nearly went through the ceiling."

"I apologize." His voice was deep and gentle. He lowered his gaze. "I didn't mean to startle you. I shouldn't be here, so I made a futile attempt at hiding. Stupid. I'm sorry."

"So, er . . . why are you here?" She tried to sound casual, subtly backing away until her hip collided with a corner of the low cabinet. She winced, suppressing eye-watering pain.

"I was looking for Daniel Manifold."

"Me too," she said. "Do you know him?"

The stranger's expression relaxed into a slight smile that made him appear more human. "No. I was hoping to meet him."

"A fan of his work?" she asked warily.

"An admirer." Evasive. That was not good. "Do you know where he is?" he asked. "Are you a member of staff?"

"No to both. But I am a friend of his," she said, uneasy. She owed this man no explanation of her presence, and was annoyed that she now couldn't explore freely. "Did someone let you in? Has anyone told you why he left, or if he's expected back?"

The man stepped towards her, his hands in his overcoat pockets. "No. I suppose I should have asked, but I found the door unlocked."

"That's strange." Stevie felt protective of Daniel, certain she'd more right to be here than the shadowy intruder. "So, you didn't contact him first? You just turned up?"

The stranger drew back at her assertive tone. "I'm afraid so. I saw his work on the Internet. I wanted to see it in reality."

His deferential, quiet manner steadied her nerves. "I'm Stevie Silverwood."

He hesitated. "Adam Leith. I'm pleased to meet you, Miss Silverwood."

He held out a hand to shake hers, and she reciprocated. The old-world courtesy of the gesture took her aback. He gave out such an unsettling mixture of signals, she didn't know what to make of him.

"Well, it looks as if he's taken everything and gone." She folded her arms. "Since you don't know him, this isn't your problem. Sorry you've had a wasted journey."

"I wouldn't say that." Adam Leith tilted his head and his smile grew friendlier. He managed this gesture without seeming remotely suggestive or, threatening. Stevie felt another heat-rush, but checked herself sharply. She never flirted; it wasn't in her nature. Friend or stranger, it was safest to trust no one.

"Have you been a fan of his for long?" she asked, crisp and business-like.

"Not long. I saw an image called *Aurata's Promise*. I was intrigued."

A small shiver went through her. She was not going to admit that she had the triptych.

"Well, I'm here on behalf of Daniel's mother. She's ill with worry. The police have found nothing yet, so I'm sleuthing instead."

He frowned. For an awful moment, she thought he was going to reveal that he *was* a police officer. He only said, "I could help you.'

"But why would you want to?" Adam Leith was so evasive that she bristled with impatience, an antidote to risky feelings of attraction. "You've obviously been poking around."

"Guilty," he said softly. "I had no right."

"And have you found anything?"

"Miss Silverwood . . ."

"Stevie."

He gave a brief, dry laugh. "Everyone is so quick to use first names these days. I still can't get used to it."

"These days?" Again she was ambushed, in a pleasant way, by his unassuming good manners. "'Miss Silverwood' sounds like an ancient schoolteacher, so please . . ."

"As you wish." He gave a gracious nod, with a touch of self-effacing humor.

"Adam, it's obvious you know something. Tell me."

"When I saw his work, I thought I recognized . . ."

He was struggling. She frowned, still suspicious. "What?"

"It's complicated. And unbelievable. But . . . Stevie?" His friendly gaze turned serious. "D'you know if Daniel knew someone called Rufus Hart?"

"I've no idea," she said. "Who's Rufus Hart?"

He didn't answer, but drew his left hand from his pocket to reveal a small sketchbook. "I found this. It had fallen behind the shelving in the side room."

"You've really had a thorough look round, haven't you?" she said acerbically. Accepting the book, she found it was an old one with yellowing pages. There were sketches of trees and animals, one of Frances and several of their house. And then—Stevie gasped to see it—the sketch he'd made of her, the very day they'd first met in the café.

Flipping pages, she found that the drawings grew stranger. Humans morphed into bizarre animals. There were detailed sketches of a thick stone disk, covered with Aztec-style carving. Next, leopard-like creatures raced on all fours through an unearthly stone landscape. Then came a monk tied to a stake, his head thrown back in anguish as flames engulfed him. Then a tall, thin mountain in a snowscape. The pencil lines were vague but trembling with energy. There were also dozens of thumbnail sketches for icons.

"I can't believe he was still using the same old pad," she murmured.

Looking over her shoulder, Adam flicked back to a page with a drawing of the stone tablet. "What is that?" he asked.

"I don't know."

"I recognize it. But that's impossible. I need to know why Daniel drew these things . . . it can't be coincidence, but . . . it makes no sense."

His words were cut short by the clunk of boot heels approaching. The door creaked open and a light flicked on, dazzling them both.

"Hello? Are you meant to be in here?"

It was the spiky-haired jeweler from the unit next door. She was tall and skinny, dressed all in black with a studded leather belt, her face and ears bristling with piercings. Stevie recalled the nameplate on her studio: Jan Lindeman.

"We're looking for Daniel," said Stevie. "You haven't . . ."

"Well, you can see he's not here," the woman said sharply, folding her arms. "Unless you've got permission from management, you're trespassing."

"The door wasn't locked," said Stevie.

"It should have been. If you need to speak to someone official, I'll take you downstairs; otherwise, you can't be in here."

Stevie confronted her, disregarding her stern attitude. She sensed Adam close beside her. "Do you have any idea why he left?"

"Friends of his, are you?" The jeweler's blue eyes narrowed at Stevie. "You do look familiar. No, everyone here's as much in the dark as you."

"Didn't he leave a forwarding address, or email?"

Jan shook her head, imperious. She angled herself toward the door, her message as plain as an Exit sign. Adam persisted, "Did he know someone called Rufus? Youngish-looking man with long brown hair?" He touched one hand to his hip. "Very long, reddish brown, slightly curly. He's my height. Slim. Flamboyant. He'd wear bright clothing, colorful waistcoats . . ."

Jan's mouth thinned. "No. Daniel had his share of visitors, but someone like that, I would have noticed. Look, the word is that he left because he couldn't keep up the rent. Wouldn't be the first time someone's done a flit. These units aren't cheap."

"I'm sure he wouldn't do that," said Stevie.

"Whatever. If *you* locate him . . ." Jan Lindeman broke off. She wagged a finger at Stevie and said, "Wait, I know where I've seen you. You run that museum in Birmingham Jewellery Quarter, don't you? The place with the old factory, Soames & Salter?"

Great, thought Stevie, *now Adam-the-weird-stranger knows where to find me.* "Erm, not single-handedly, but yes."

Jan's demeanor changed. Her piercings glinted as her face opened up in delight. "I *knew* I'd seen you before! Amazing place, I've been there twice. We never spoke, but I noticed you behind the counter."

"That explains why you look familiar, too." Stevie gave the warmest smile she could muster. "You know, if you'd like to display your work in our gift shop, just say the word."

"I might take you up on that. Thanks."

Stevie gathered her coat, tucking the sketchbook inside. She guessed she wouldn't get much further, but she made one a last try. "You must have spoken to Daniel most days?"

"Only in passing. Everyone's busy. Artists who stand around chatting don't get anything made or sold. Daniel rarely came in. He was a sweet guy, but preoccupied."

"Did you see his work?" Adam put in.

"Oh, yeah. Some of it was stunning. Like those old Eastern Orthodox icons, but when you look closely, it's something else. The figures were like pagan gods, with animal heads and all sorts of weird things. Played with your mind. Very cool."

Stevie persisted, "Did he seem depressed, or worried? Not his usual self?"

Jan laughed. "His usual self was crazy enough. We're all workaholics here, but he took it to another level. Or should that be paintaholic? You probably know that the police were here. All they found was a letter for his mother."

"I know," said Stevie. "I tried to reassure her, but she's worried it's a suicide note."

"God, I hope not," Jan said softly. "Honestly, I'm not being obstructive. All I can say for sure is that he fell out with management because his opening hours were so erratic. I mean, he'd be here working, but he'd lock himself in and not let the public browse around. If you refuse to open, you don't sell any work, right? And you can't pay your way. The answer is usually the most obvious one."

"All right, well . . ." Stevie looked firmly at Adam, giving him a clear cue to leave. Once they were on the walkway, Jan flicked off the light and shut the door. Stevie gave her a business card for the museum. "If you hear anything, please, will you let me know?"

"Absolutely I will. It's been great meeting you, Stevie. Circumstances aside."

A few minutes later, Stevie stood outside with her strange new friend, Adam, not knowing what to say to him, or how to shake him off. The wind blew sideways around the factory, stinging her face with darts of ice. She still didn't know who he was, but thanks to Jan Lindeman, he now knew her address.

His face was half-lit by streetlights, and specks of snow gleamed on his hair. On a very base level, she would have been more than happy to take him home . . . The impulse felt downright disturbing, so she quashed it. Again.

"I'll report back to his mother," she said. "No news is good news, I suppose. And I'll give her the sketchbook, since it's rightfully hers until he comes back."

"I do apologize for trying to take it," he sighed.

"Thanks for being honest, anyway," she said coolly.

She began to turn away, but he said, "Stevie, if you do find Daniel, will you let me know?"

Again she silently wondered what business it was of his. "How? Have you got email?"

His mouth twitched. She wondered why he found this funny. "No."

"Phone number?"

Looking sheepish, he shook his head. "I really should get around to buying a phone."

"Well, if you can't be contacted, how can I? I won't in any case, because I don't know you. It's a private family matter."

"I understand," he said. Before she could ask anything else, Adam was gone, melting away into the darkness through a swirl of fine, wet snow.

Stevie's last stop was Daniel's address, a couple of streets away. The tall, dilapidated Victorian town house appeared to be a shabby lodging house for students. There was a Room to Let sign in front. Having pictured him in a nice apartment, she felt shocked and sad to think that he'd been living in a single rented room. How lonely. She saw a scruffy-looking man, aged around seventy, dragging two full black garbage bags down a short flight of stone steps from the front door to the street. A dirty grey sweater strained over his beer gut.

"Excuse me," she began. "Does Daniel Manifold live here?"

The man gave her a look of sneering disgust. "He owes me three weeks' rent. Haven't seen him for days."

"He's gone missing."

"You're telling me."

"I'd like to take a look around his room."

"Fergeddit," growled the landlord. "After the police finished nosing around, I changed the lock. Everything he left behind is in these bags."

"Can I take them?"

His bushy white brows jumped halfway up his forehead. "Yeah, do what you like, darlin'. It's only rubbish. Believe me, if he'd left anything valuable, I'd have taken it. Not a sausage."

"Any personal papers?" Stevie shivered in the snowy air.

"I dunno. It's all in there, the crap he left behind."

Impulsively she took a twenty-pound note from her purse and pushed it into his hand, realizing too late it was all she had left to pay for a taxi back to Euston Station. "Did he say where he was going? Did he have any visitors?"

He looked at the note and emitted a grunt. "He owed me a lot more than twenty quid."

"I'm not paying his rent for him," Stevie retorted. "I was hoping you'd tell me something. Did he have a girlfriend?"

"Never saw one. There was some bloke he used to kick around with."

"What did he look like? A slim man with long brown hair?"

The landlord sniffed. "Nah. White hair up in spikes and an overcoat, like some old punk rocker. Called him Ollie, Oliver? That's all I know."

"Can't you think of anything else?"

"Sorry, darlin'." He pocketed the money and went stiff-legged up the steps to his front door. "Nothin' else to tell."

Rufus and Aurata spent two days amid the ruins, helping rescue teams haul survivors and corpses from fallen buildings, assisting in the medical tent, comforting children when the ground shuddered with aftershocks.

Rufus was not helping out of compassion. He was doing so entirely to be with his sister: to watch her, to learn what she'd become by imitating her. He felt like a phony, but this didn't disturb him. He'd always been an illusionist.

More television crews arrived. Helicopters buzzed in and out, dropping supplies. Troops arrived to protect the aid workers—probably, he thought, from the tribesmen in the hills, whom Rufus had so lavishly equipped with weapons a few days earlier.

During her rest breaks, Aurata was out with her camera, recording the rifts that split the landscape. Or she'd rejoin her team of seismologists to examine data. Rufus kept out of that, since he had no interest in squiggles on graph paper.

How strange to find Aurata had become a scientist. She seemed so human and yet—when they were alone in her tent at night—she was still the beautiful creature he'd lost so many thousands of years ago. Her languid body language invited a resumption of their deliciously sordid, incestuous union . . . yet, although it half-killed him to hold back, he still dared not touch her.

An incredible stretch of time had passed; thirty thousand years, at the most conservative estimate. And he'd committed the vast and terrible crime of turning against his own family and civilization, and leading an army to crush their city, Azantios.

Had she lost her memory? Surely not; she was too sharp. So why didn't she raise the subject? Was she leading him on while secretly planning to slit his throat in his sleep? What was she playing at?

Finally, on the second night, he broke the silence. "There's a rock song that could have been written for me, Aurata. 'Bad to the Bone'—that's me. I caused the downfall of Azantios."

"I know," she said evenly. She lay close, her head propped on one hand, her auburn hair flowing over her burnished shoulders.

"So what are you doing with me? Stringing me along until you can deliver me to the ghastly punishment I deserve?"

"Is that what you think? No, Rufus." She laughed, softly and without smiling. "That would be a waste. I have other plans."

"What plans?"

"Wait and see."

"But why aren't you blazing with fury? Why didn't you spit in my face, the moment you recognized me? You're acting as if nothing ever happened, but you can't have forgiven me. No one ever could."

She lowered her feline gaze. "True. What happened was far beyond forgiveness. But we have to set it aside, because . . . the truth is that the destruction of Azantios was as much my doing as yours."

Her words threw him. "I heard tales . . . afterwards. That the Felynx finished the job themselves rather than let my mob of proto-human savages defile the city. But that's not in the same league as my treachery."

"Isn't it? Can we please let this rest, and talk of it another time?" She touched his cheekbone. "All I ask is that you trust me."

"This will be a leap into the unknown." He grinned. "I've *never* trusted you, my fiery sister. But you know I'm yours, body and soul."

On the third day, Aurata announced that it was time for the two of them to leave. With her belongings in a small rucksack, she led Rufus to a waiting helicopter. Soon the devastated brown landscape was dwindling beneath them. They landed at a dusty airstrip and transferred to a small plane that took them to Lahore airport. Amid seething crowds and sweltering heat, Aurata used her credit card to buy both of them plane tickets and new clothes.

"I don't understand," said Rufus. "Can you just walk away like that?"

"I can do whatever I like."

"But you were working before the earthquake struck. What about your human colleagues?"

"My work with them was only ever a means to an end. It was our destiny to meet again, Rufus. The fact that you're finally here is my sacred sign to move onward."

"Sacred?" He laughed. "What if I don't stick around, Dr. Connelly?"

Aurata gave him a look. "Oh, you will."

She was right. The moment he'd seen her, everything else ceased to matter. She'd become his sole reason to live again. "Where are we going?"

"I'd love to keep it secret until we arrive," she replied. "However, unless you consent to wear a blindfold and earplugs for a day, you are going to know as soon as our flight is announced."

Venice.

He'd visited before—there were few places on Earth he hadn't seen—but a fresh enchantment lay over the city as they arrived. Pale mist hung over the lagoon, backlit by sunlight. Everywhere was white and gold, the Doges' Palace standing proud like a gigantic Rococo wedding cake. Aurata led Rufus away from the main thoroughfares, over bridges, down ever-narrower streets, crossing canals where water lapped between buildings in dank, fetid chasms.

VIALE DEI BELLI SEGRETI. He saw the sign bearing the name of the alley and translated it to himself. Avenue of Beautiful Secrets.

"What are the beautiful secrets?" asked Rufus.

"Now if I told you, they wouldn't be secrets, would they?"

He felt a subtle shift of atmosphere, colors becoming more intense. "Ah. A Dusklands place. So only Aetherials know of its existence, only Aetherials live here?"

"Others, by invitation only," she answered with a smile.

Her house had a facade of flaking grandeur. The creamy walls were decorated with gold and lapis lazuli, the tall windows framed by ornate carving. She opened the front door to reveal a grand, oval hall with a double staircase sweeping up the curved walls. Soft blue-green light filled the space. The floor was tiled with black and white marble in a familiar pattern; a single giant spiral, the most potent symbol of the Otherworld.

Rufus could imagine ghostly Aetherial guests at a masquerade, could almost hear the whisper of their skirt hems across the tiles. Or something more serious: a ritual for the warping of reality? He tasted subtle energies in the air, like ozone.

Aurata led him upstairs to a salon lined with gilt-framed mirrors. Crossing to the window, Rufus looked out at a row of houses facing him across the canal. Their pastel walls were stained with age, by algae and waterweed where the water sucked at their foundations. Water taxis plowed the turbid surface. The scene had a foggy look, as if a fine muslin scrim were stretched tight in front of it. Could the boat passengers see him at the window? Or was it some other house they saw as they glanced upwards, an Earth-bound construction occupying the same space as Aurata's hidden Dusklands mansion?

"Do you live here alone?"

"For the time being. My people are elsewhere."

"You have 'people'?" He laughed.

"Friends."

"No, you mean worshippers. Naturally. So did I."

"Of course you did, Rufus."

"We always were so alike."

"Were we?" She blinked. "On the surface, perhaps." Her words stung a little. For a few seconds, she seemed aloof: a scientist with mysterious plans, while he was just the same irresponsible reprobate he'd always been.

Aurata excused herself, and returned with a tray bearing food and a bottle of ice-cold white wine. If she had servants, he wasn't interested; such mundane matters would have spoiled the dream feeling. They sat in the salon in gilded chairs and refreshed themselves with olives, *ciabatta* bread and soft cheese.

Haphazard fragments of their stories came out. They spoke of living disguised within human civilizations; some of Rufus's tales were real and some fabricated. He avoided mentioning Mist, which left large gaps in his narrative. He told her he'd been a stage illusionist in the 1920s and 1930s: that was true. He claimed to have flown as a fighter pilot in the Second World War, a complete lie. And his latest, incredible claim, to have forced the British government to call a general election, also happened to be the truth. Aurata listened with a look of serene amusement.

"I've done everything and nothing," said Rufus. "Mainly, I've amused myself with humans. Seduced them, poisoned them against each other. Withheld knowledge, or let slip a little too much. I like to think I've changed the course of history, in some small way."

Aurata gave an ostentatious sigh. "And it never occurred to you to do something more constructive?"

He raised his eyebrows. "What for? I had Mist for that. He was the good guy, so I had to play the baddie. That was the role in which our father cast me. I had a reputation to live up to."

"Wait," she said sharply. "Mistangamesh was with you?"

He kicked himself for the slip; he'd meant to tell her in his own time. "Not all the time. Some of it, yes."

"So he survived Azantios?" She rose and paced about restlessly. "I *knew* you were hiding something! I was wondering when you'd admit it."

"And I can't hide anything from you, can I?" He grimaced. "When I behaved particularly badly, Mist felt the need to rein me in."

"But where is he now?" Her whisper echoed in the big, bare room. "What happened to him?"

Rufus swallowed hard. "He did what humans do," he said brusquely. "He died."

Later, they lay naked and entwined on a huge bed, curtains wafting gently at the windows, a breeze bringing in the sulfur smell of the canal and the noise of water traffic. Night drew in. Candles glowed, spinning a golden web around them. Aurata was no longer "Dr. Connelly," but the gilded feline angel he remembered. Despite his wariness, rekindling their passion had proved as natural and divinely sweet as if they'd never been apart. He'd given a ragged outline of the Adam story, and even of the Mist and Helena disaster, and afterwards she had soothed him until the pain faded.

"We thought you were dead, too," said Rufus.

"Did you grieve?"

"That's a feeble word for what I felt. There isn't much I care about, but I'll admit to one weakness. You and Mistangamesh, and our beloved mother, are the only three people I've ever truly loved. My grievance was against Poectilictis, never against you."

"And yet you were angry enough with Father to forget who else you were harming?" When he didn't answer, she added, "Would you go back and change the past?"

"That's a redundant question. Give me a time machine powered by hindsight, and I'll give you an answer! We can't change what happened. But this . . ." He cupped her face between his palms. "This matters, doesn't it? Not the past. The present."

"And the future, my sweet, unrepentant brother. Yes, we've lost Mist, but we've found each other."

"We could have been great, you and I," Rufus sighed. He kissed her neck. "Ah, the alchemy of siblings."

"We still could." Aurata was quiet for a time. Then she said softly, "So, you know what happened after your army invaded and began to cut down hundreds of defenseless Felynx in the streets?"

"Yes. Mist told me." Darkness stirred inside Rufus: an uneasy remnant of conscience. From afar, he'd watched his primitive warrior horde flood the city—ants swarming a pale honeycomb—eager for the riches he'd promised them. When flames caught the delicate spires of Azantios, he'd only sneered. This was his perfect revenge against their ruler, his own father.

But then the land began to shake. The scarlet mountain reared and shook the golden-white palaces of Azantios off its spine. The city crumbled and burned, swallowing the proto-humans in its own death throes. Soon it was as if Azantios had never been.

"You remember Veropardus, the Custodian of the Felixatus?" said Aurata.

"That pompous misery," said Rufus. "What did you ever see in him?"

"Useful secrets." She half-smiled. "There was always a plan in place, in the unlikely event of an attack, but it went wrong."

"Wrong, how? You did a perfectly good job of self-destruction, as far as I could see." Rufus's voice sounded hoarse. "Mist told me, days later when he crawled out of the ruins. He said you were dead, that everyone was dead. Suicide before surrender."

"Yes, that was the *official* plan. However, Veropardus and I had other ideas: we hoped to use the power of the Felixatus to shift Azantios right through the barriers and into the Otherworld. But we failed, and the Felixatus was destroyed."

Astonished, Rufus struggled for a response. Eventually he said, "I thought we were close, you and I, yet you never told me a word of these schemes!"

"Because I didn't trust you," she said bluntly.

Rufus felt strange. He'd intended to be blasé and detached. Instead the conversation was distressing him beyond words. "I deserved that. But . . . how did you not die?"

"Rufus, I'm Aetherial. I *was* lifeless for an immeasurably long time. I became an elemental, haunting the ruins, with no more awareness than the wind. However, eventually I woke again. I was alone, and quite deranged."

"I wonder what became of . . . our parents?"

"I believe that their last sacrifice was the end for them," Aurata said gravely. "I hope their soul-essences found peace."

"I wish peace for Theliome, at least. How strange it is to think of them . . . and the three of us in our glory days. You and me and Mistangamesh."

"Always at each other's throats." Aurata spoke idly, but her eyes gleamed.

"Foolish rivalry. Still, it was fun at the time."

"Until it grew a little too serious."

Rufus fell silent for a while. "I still can't claim I'm sorry," he said. "Father accused me of a crime I didn't commit, and that was the least of it. He always despised me. There was no love lost—"

"Hush," Aurata cut him off, her tone mild. "Haven't you changed at all? You were always such a child."

"A *spoiled* child," he amended. "So? Change is what humans do. Isn't the point of being immortal that we don't have to bother changing?"

"I think you're mixing us up with angels."

"That makes me Lucifer, then." He propped himself on one elbow and toyed with her hair.

"None of us is blameless," she said. "Perhaps it was time for the Felynx empire to end. Now it's vanished behind a veil of time, I'm simply ecstatic to have found you, Rufus. And no one's beyond redemption."

"What's wrong with you? Have you caught a human religion? I find you with a doctorate and doing humanitarian work . . . who are you, and what have you done with Aurata Theliet Ephenaestus?"

She bit him gently on the shoulder. "Aren't Aelyr allowed to evolve? I can be anything I want. So can you."

"Yeah," he said. "I'll become a fucking saint, if it pleases you, my lady."

"No need for that." Her breath warmed his cheek. "Are you composed enough yet to tell me more about Mistangamesh?"

Rufus pressed into her flank. "I can't talk about him. Not now. Let me make love to you again, while you whisper in my ear about rifts overflowing with molten lava."

"Ah, you like that, do you?"

"I like the way your eyes get moist when you tell me about tectonic plates and magma chambers and spurting geysers . . ."

"Well, all right," she murmured, her sleek body moving against his. "But there will be questions later."

"Oh, *you* have questions? I like a mystery, sweet sister, but at some point you might like to tell me why we're here."

Aurata slid off the bed and crossed the room to an ornate cupboard. Rufus sat up, indignant. "Hey, where are you going?"

She returned with a large, heavy book that looked and smelled a thousand years old. It landed on his thighs like a stone block, narrowly missing injury to a sensitive place.

"Careful! I may be more than human but I still have nerve endings, Aurata. What the hell is this?"

"It's the reason we're here. You did ask."

The volume was a bound medieval manuscript, filled with elaborate calligraphy in a language he knew: the ancient tongue of the Felynx. There were illustrations, some colored in lapis, red and gold, others unfinished. Rufus realized he was looking at a history of Azantios.

"Turn to the page with the bookmark. The diagram. What do you see?"

The sketch appeared to be a world globe. Instead of continents, strange animals sprawled over the curved surface. Complex struts supported the sphere, which appeared transparent, with a smaller sphere nested in the center and a separate lens poised above the north pole.

"The Felixatus!" he said, entirely forgetting sex, at least for the moment. "But who the hell created this book? It's not from Azantios."

Aurata gave a radiant smile. "Veropardus wrote it, in the twelfth century. He had his own renaissance. Now this is our best record of what the Felixatus looked like. We retrieved a few pieces from the original, which I have here, but parts are still missing."

"And?"

"The Felixatus was special to the Felynx, our holy grail. We thought it was lost, but now I see it's not consigned to the past after all. It's our future! And we must put it back together again." She bounced onto the edge of the bed, kneeling with parted thighs. "This house—haven't you worked out what it is? It's a museum, a safe place that I created to bring together all that remains of the Felynx. It's taken hundreds of years, but at last things are happening. I wove Aetheric webs and sent out calls until Veropardus and a few others finally heard me. And now you're here too, at long last."

Rufus frowned, bemused by her excitement. "What has this to do with earthquakes and volcanoes? Forgive me for being dense. Did *you* create this whole street to hide in? Are these the 'Beautiful Secrets'—an old book and some scraps of a crushed artifact?"

She glared at him in exasperation. "Rufus, please. Too many questions. It will all make sense eventually, I promise. But for now, am *I* not one of the beautiful secrets?"

Rufus leaned back on the pillows, grinning. "Oh, most certainly, the ultimate. I don't pretend to know what you're up to, Aurata, but you always were a treasure trove of mysteries. If you want to reconstruct the Felixatus, I have a surprise for you. Close your eyes and hold out your hands."

"What?"

Putting the book aside, he leaned off the bed and rummaged in the pockets of his old jacket until he found an object. He loosened its silk wrapping and placed it into her cupped hands. "Now you may look."

Aurata stared, breathing fast. "How did you get this?"

Her delight pleased Rufus. The lens was the size of her palm, convex, smooth and as heavy as a paperweight. Glassy and diamond-clear, it was fashioned from a rare Otherworld mineral that some called Elfstone.

"Mist found it, before we fled the ruins of Azantios," said Rufus. "The lens ended up in my keeping, somehow."

"And you took care of it, all this time?" She leaned forward to kiss him. "I never thought it was in your nature to treasure anything, Rufus."

"You misjudge me. I don't care for much, it's true. But that which I value, I never let go. You're pleased?"

She pressed a fingertip to the ink drawing of the Felixatus, her nail indicating the lens suspended over the globe's north pole.

"So thrilled, I can't speak."

"Is that a tear I see in your scientific eye, Dr. Connelly?"

"This is destiny. All the scattered pieces are coming together." Aurata rewrapped the lens in its black silk covering, and placed it on a table by the bed. She twined Rufus's hair around her wrists, pulling him to her. "And on the subject of coming together . . ."

Deep in the night, Rufus woke to hear Aurata's voice, and wondered if he'd fallen asleep in mid-conversation. "No, hide them all," she was saying. "I need to know how this happened . . . Human eyes are profane. Of course it's wrong. No, I can't leave, the doors are all iced shut. There are glaciers blocking all the ways out . . . I'm so cold . . . Qesoth grant me the power of fire to melt Sibeyla's ice . . ."

"What?" Rufus said softly. "Aurata, what did you say?"

When she didn't answer, but went on murmuring to herself and shifting restlessly, he realized she was talking in her sleep. Or in a nightmare.

6

The Thief

Stevie was showing the two-o'clock tour group around the factory when Adam Leith reappeared.

It was three days since she'd met him. The museum was busy, and she was shepherding a mix of retired couples and jewelry students from a nearby art college. Adam wasn't there at the start; she would most definitely have noticed. First she showed the group a wall-mounted life-size photograph of the founders, Messrs. Soames and Salter with their loyal workers, then drew them onward through the offices as she told the firm's history, pointing out typewriters and antiquated filing systems, old catalogues of bangles, brooches and buttons.

"You'll see that modern technology barely touched the place," she said. "Much of the equipment had been in use since the 1880s; why change, when it did a perfectly good job? Apart from the introduction of electricity in the 1920s, the place is effectively a time capsule of a working Victorian factory. Mind your footing."

Stevie led them down a spiral staircase into the factory proper. The atmosphere of age, dust and engine oil rose to enfold her, and she sensed the shades of workers. The visitors gazed at the engraved windows, pitted workbenches, shelves stacked floor-to-ceiling with thousands of die stamps. "Each time we do an inventory, every one of those items has to be removed, cleaned, and put back in the exact same position. See the oily overalls hanging up? They're just as the workers left them, the day the factory closed over thirty years ago."

The tourists murmured their interest as they spread out to look around. Light fell through a grimy glass roof. The place was far from pretty. Stevie felt a glow of pride in the knowledge that people were so genuinely fascinated by its history.

She pointed out a thick pane of glass set in the floor that revealed a huge sink full of sawdust in the cellar below.

"The water from all the sinks drained into that receptacle," she continued.

"Not a speck of gold was allowed off the premises, not even gold dust on the workers' hands. At the end of the year, they'd burn the sawdust and retrieve a lump of molten gold worth several hundred pounds. Just from hand-washing!"

The group expressed delight. Stevie powered up the fan belts that drove every machine in the factory. Sound filled the space, like a small aircraft taking off.

"Imagine this noise all day long." She raised her voice to be heard. "Grinders and polishers whirring, die-cutters thumping. It would have been deafening."

It was then, as she turned around, that she saw Adam.

He was standing at the back of the group, his complexion ivory against the sable of his hair and coat—unearthly because he'd appeared from nowhere. He was so still and watchful that he might have been one of her apparitions. As she caught his eye, he looked straight at her with an unapologetic, purposeful expression. His grey irises held flashes of green she hadn't noticed before.

Stevie stumbled over her words for a few seconds. Recovering, she carried on as if she hadn't seen him. The officious part of her mind wondered if he'd actually bought a ticket.

She operated stamping and punching machines, inviting everyone to try so they could see it was not as easy as it appeared. Sitting at an ancient workbench, she demonstrated how the jewelers had welded components, holding a pipe in their mouths to control the blowtorch flame with their breath. She described finishing processes involving chemicals that exposed the workers to poisonous fumes all day long.

"And this is where they made their pots of tea," she said, indicating a tiny side room. "When the premises were first reentered, after standing deserted for years, containers of cyanide and sugar were found side by side. You didn't want to upset the lady who made the tea."

There was a ripple of shocked laughter.

While she answered questions, Stevie stamped tiny cats from a sheet of brass to hand out as souvenirs. Finally, she ushered the group through a door that led back into the gift shop, reminding them of the café . . . Mundane concerns circled her mind at double speed while she was sharply aware of Adam lingering, waiting for her.

He smiled as she turned to him. She went hot with nerves. First impressions could deceive, but he looked even better than she remembered. She'd found good looks usually accompanied by a large ego, an undeclared wife and family, another girlfriend or an appalling personality—if not the full set. Adam seemed different. His eyes shone with genuine warmth and interest. There was an earthy, reassuring quality to his beauty that made her want to forgo all the preliminaries and fling herself on him.

Some woman must be very lucky. Or some man.

None of this showed on her face—she hoped. She cleared her throat, folded her arms. "You found me, then. I'm a bit startled to see you."

"I went to the counter and asked for you. The lady there said I could wait, or I could catch the guided tour if I ran. I think she was joking, but I bought a ticket anyway."

"I hope you thought it was worth it."

"It was fascinating," he said sincerely. "I thought making jewelry would be a relaxing, creative occupation."

"Not here, it wasn't," said Stevie.

"More like a sweatshop."

"Well, it was a job. They were skilled workers, and very loyal. Many worked here for decades."

"If the poison fumes or the cyanide in the tea didn't get them," he said dryly.

Stevie wasn't sure what to say. Attraction aside, she was uneasy about the fact he'd turned up without warning. "If you're here to ask about Daniel, I'm sorry," she said. "I'm still none the wiser. You?"

He shook his head. "Nothing. I hoped . . . I can't explain. I felt there was some connection that would make sense if only I saw you again."

He hadn't mentioned the triptych, so she assumed he hadn't seen it. "Did you look in the side room off the gift shop?"

"No, I came straight to find you. Why?"

"You'd have seen a piece of Daniel's work in there. *Aurata's Promise.* He sent it to me before he vanished, with no explanation."

Adam's eyes sparked. "Why didn't you tell me?"

"Any reason why I should?"

"I suppose not, but from my point of view—yes, every reason. Can I see it?"

"Can I stop you?" Finding no grounds to refuse, she gave a resigned smile. "Yes, of course." Stevie held the door open. "Shall we?"

As she led him past the shop counter, she was aware of Fin turning her head to watch them. Stevie glanced back to see Fin wide-eyed, mouthing, *Who is he?* She gave an apologetic shrug in return.

Apart from Alec grumbling over the workbench, the exhibition room was empty. A couple of visitors browsed the gift shop, but the rest were in the café. She saw Ron hurrying back and forth in his green apron with trays full of tea and scones, and a line of customers waiting at the café counter. He shot her a glance, indicating he could do with some help.

"Alec, could you go and give Ron a hand, please?" she said.

Alec gave her a long-suffering look over his glasses. "I can only do one thing at once, you know."

"Forget the lathe. Customers come first. I'll be there as soon as I'm free."

"Yes, ma'am." He strode off, wiping oily hands on his trousers.

Stevie sighed. "He thinks I boss him about. I keep trying to get it through his head that we all do the same duties, male and female alike—anyway, never mind that. Daniel's triptych." She indicated the threefold panel standing on a side table. "There it is. Take as long as you like. Tell me what you think, after."

Instantly transfixed, Adam moved close to the triptych as if he'd forgotten she was there. Fin called from the shop, "Stevie! Phone call for you!"

She rushed to join Fin, found her trying to serve customers and operate the till one-handed. Stevie took the handset from her and shut herself in the back office.

The caller was Jan Lindeman. Stevie hadn't expected to hear from her again.

"Hi, I thought you'd like to hear a snippet of info. I was talking to Sarah, the potter who works in the studio next to mine, yeah? Apparently Dan told her something. He said that he'd found a buyer for all his paintings."

"*All* of them?"

"Yeah, sounds a bit wild, doesn't it? Before you ask, he didn't say who. But that makes it unlikely he couldn't pay his rent, doesn't it?"

"Unless the buyer let him down," said Stevie, recalling that Frances had said the same thing and dismissed it as a delusion. Uncomfortably she thought, *Surely he wouldn't kill himself over that, would he?*

"The other thing is that Dan had a regular visitor who he'd let in, even when his Closed sign was up. I don't know if this guy was the mystery buyer."

"What did he look like?"

"Not like he had any money. When Sarah described him, I realized I'd met him. Spiky platinum hair—a bit like mine, only much more of it, the bastard. Brown overcoat . . . handsome in a craggy sort of way. Maybe thirty? Hard to tell. Six foot or so, not overweight but muscular rather than skinny. His eyes were unusual: one blue, one green. Oh, and he had a pierced ear. I remember, because he bought a single steel earring off me. It was a panther in two halves, so when you put it in, the panther looks like it's jumping right through your earlobe."

"How long ago did you see this guy?"

"At least a month. Sorry, that's all. If I'd known that Dan, the idiot, was going to vanish, I'd have paid more attention."

"So would we all," said Stevie, sighing. "I think the mystery man was called Oliver. Daniel's landlord had seen him, and so had his mother. I've a horrible feeling . . ."

"What?"

"That this Oliver might have been a drug dealer. Don't repeat that to anyone, because I could be wrong."

"Understood, but it might explain Daniel's erratic behavior." Jan spoke thoughtfully. "The only other thing I know is that, the day he vanished, a courier took a load of crates from his studio. I phoned the courier firm, but they flat refused to tell me details: customer confidentiality."

"That's frustrating," said Stevie. "But thank you so much for trying, Jan. I won't let this go. I need to see his mother again, for a start."

"Good luck, yeah? From what Dan said, she sounds a bit scary."

The call over, Stevie put down the phone and wiped her greasy palm print from its casing. Any scrap of knowledge helped, but should she tell Adam?

Next, she dived into the café to help cheery Ron and grumpy Alec for fifteen minutes. Gradually the place emptied out.

In the exhibition room, Adam stood gazing at the triptych as if he hadn't moved.

Twilight was gathering outside, a gale whipping rain against the windows. "Sorry about that," she said. "We have sudden influxes, and it's all hands on deck. Winter; everyone wants hot drinks and huge amounts of cake. Well? What do you think?"

No reaction. Then he gave a small start and turned to her. He appeared mesmerized, his eyes glassy.

"I know this," he said at last.

"How do you mean?"

He hesitated, then indicated the image of the auburn-haired goddess. Behind her, a translucent city hovered like flame on the mountainside. "I saw this on the website. But I don't mean I know the paintings. I mean I recognize the actual scenes. The people. Everything. But it's impossible."

Adam seemed shaken. Stevie paused, reserving judgment on whether he was, after all, deranged. "They look like fantasy scenes to me. What is Aurata promising, exactly?"

"I really don't know," he said. "Did Daniel ever talk about his inspiration?"

She sensed steel behind his unassuming manner. For whatever reason, he wasn't going to let this go. "Not recently." She took a breath. "When we were at college, he said his ideas came from me."

"In what way?"

"He couldn't explain. He said . . ." Long-ago conversations resurfaced, turning her warm with embarrassment. "He said I made him think of mermaids, and dryads dancing naked in the woods." *Oh god, did I say naked?* she thought, wincing. "Erm, and pagan deities and pre-Raphaelite maidens . . . that sort of thing. But I'm sure those images were in his head without any help from me."

"Was his work similar in the early days?"

"Yes, but it developed and changed, obviously . . . This is all too strange, Adam. I still don't know who you are, or why you're so interested."

"I'm sorry. It's hard to explain and I seem to have lost the art of conversation."

"You're doing okay," Stevie said tartly. "Have you been in a monastery? That might account for you going all *Da Vinci Code* on me."

"All what?"

"Oh, dear. That was a weak joke, but you talk as if you've been living on some remote island. You need to give me a clue, or we'll never get anywhere."

He looked at her for a good five seconds. "I was in Scotland."

"Well, that explains everything." Stevie rolled her eyes.

She heard a stifled explosion of laughter from Fin in the gift shop. Stevie couldn't blame her for listening in; she would have done the same. Every small sound echoed off the hard floors.

Adam smiled too, lips pressed together, eyelids lowered. "I'm not trying to be difficult. If only I could ask Daniel in person . . ."

"If only."

"If he knew Rufus, it would make sense. There's no other way he could have heard about such scenes to paint them."

"Who is this Rufus?"

"My brother." Adam spoke very quietly. "I need to find him, but I don't want him to find me."

"Huh?"

His smile twisted. "I know. Madness. I should go, and not inflict my problems upon you."

"Is Rufus dangerous? I'm not sure I want to be involved with this. I might put the triptych in storage until Daniel eventually shows up to take it away."

"No. Let me buy it," said Adam.

Stevie coughed in surprise.

"I can pay by credit card. How much? I'll take the work away, and it won't be your problem anymore."

"That's not the point. Danny left no instructions to sell it. My problem isn't his artwork, but what's happened to *him*. And you, asking odd questions you can't or won't explain."

"I'll go." His tone was apologetic, but this wasn't the response she'd hoped for. "You're absolutely right, Stevie. Thank you for showing me the work, anyway. I'm very sorry to have troubled you."

A clamor of voices rose as the remaining visitors left. Fin called out, "I'm putting up the Closed sign, Stevie, okay? Filthy afternoon: no one else is going to come in now."

"Thanks, Fin," Stevie answered. Turning back to Adam, she asked, "So, have you traveled up from London? What time's your train back? You can get the light railway back into town and it's only a short walk to New Street Station. Quicker than taxi."

"It's all right." Adam gave her a sad, enigmatic smile and turned to leave. "Goodbye, Stevie. It was nice to meet you."

No, don't go yet, she thought helplessly. *Damn.*

He glanced back as Fin let him out. Cold wind clawed through the gap, then sucked the door shut behind him. Stevie realized he was looking back for a last glimpse of *Aurata's Promise.*

After he left the museum, Mist walked towards the center of Birmingham. Within a couple of blocks he'd left the Jewellery Quarter behind and was treading along dreary, wet streets lined with shuttered shops and offices. Sleet stung his face. The cold was nothing compared with his long trek in the north, but that experience now seemed unreal. The longer he spent in the surface world, the more sensitive he became to physical discomfort. Cars hissed through puddles, splashing him.

He groped for the Dusklands, the first flimsy layer of the Otherworld, but there was nothing. The Duskland realm was patchy and capricious. In some places the Aetheric atmosphere lay as thick as honey; in others it was barely there, blown away like cobwebs.

Mist understood now that, when he first rose from the sea in a golden sunset, he'd emerged into a warm Dusklands cocoon, protected from winter. Without that comfort, the real world was raw.

He walked until his way was barred by a concrete river: the multiple lanes of a busy main road. Heavy traffic crawled in both directions. He could see his hotel on the far side, a bland modern building six stories high. Mist stopped on the curb and gazed up at the lighted windows, wondering how best to reach it without making a suicidal dash between vehicles. Needles of ice spiraled against the lights.

He knew he had no choice but to take the pedestrian detour. He hurried through an underpass with graffiti-scrawled walls and the stench of a public toilet. Strange, he felt as jumpy as a human. If he encountered a gang of thieves, he was ill-equipped to defy them. He was unarmed, and had no special fighting skills. Vanishing into the Dusklands didn't seem to be an option. And he knew he could die . . . The thought of another grueling journey through un-life and human pain to reach this point once more appalled him. So, for these few seconds, he felt very scared.

At the end of the tunnel, a homeless man lay dozing. He uttered a grunt of surprise as Mist dropped a ten-pound note onto his chest. And Mist hurried away, feeling guilty that he was prepared to offer money, but nothing else.

Reaching the other side, he entered the hotel where he'd taken a room for an indefinite period. He'd come here only because of Stevie and the tenuous link to a long-lost world. He had nowhere else, no other clues to follow.

Juliana had told him to get a cell phone, but he hadn't done so. It would be a spider-silk connection to her that he didn't want, because—as much as he loved her—she could not walk into the treacherous unknown future with him.

The hotel was pleasant enough: bland, modern and clean, used mostly by business travelers. Potted plants softened the atrium, and he could hear generic, soothing jazz issuing from the dimly lit bar. A handful of men and women made their way towards the restaurant, all dressed in crisp suits, with laptops grasped under their arms or small shiny phones in their hands. A chirpy blond receptionist was welcoming a young couple at the desk.

Mist took the elevator to the fourth floor and entered the comfortable, clean, characterless room that he'd checked into a couple of days earlier. There were two queen-size beds, a table and chairs, a desk and several lamps. He'd never experienced a modern hotel. He was fascinated by this unfamiliar, curiously sterile environment with its television, coffee-making equipment, a handy folder detailing all the services the hotel offered, and a sign promising Wi-Fi access. He'd also been puzzled to find the Bible and two other religious texts in a bedside drawer. Mist couldn't square the juxtaposition of startling new technology with a belief in supernatural agencies.

There was something touching, he thought, in the way that humans could assimilate so many apparently incompatible ideas without blinking.

Although he'd learned that his surroundings were typical of any hotel almost anywhere in the world, they were new to him. He'd spent some time in Juliana's old-world Scottish manor after existing for many years betweenworlds with Rufus, and before that, he'd lived a brief human life at the start of the twentieth century. Adam Montague's time had been one of candlelight and breaking ice on the water pitcher before he could wash . . . of reading the Bible until he knew it by heart, of prayer and belief torn away in the trenches of the Somme, amid mud and shellfire and all his friends dying around him.

Between then and now, the world had become an alien planet.

Mist opened the minibar and took out a tiny bottle of brandy. Each day, a housekeeper he never saw would restock the bar and place clean glasses on a tray. He removed the paper cover from a tumbler and poured in the liquor. The taste reminded him of Juliana, who had a weakness for brandy and used to give him a shot when he—as Adam—had struggled with the tangle of madness and confusion caused by Rufus. The memory of her kindness steadied him.

He stood at the window, watching traffic pouring along the road in rivers of white and red light. Double glazing reduced the sound to a muffled roar. On the far side, in the direction of the Jewellery Quarter, there were derelict buildings on overgrown plots, huge advertisements on billboards. Amid this ugliness, a handsome red-brick church stood proud, a remnant of the past that he, or rather Adam, remembered.

Life out there looked dirty, hard-edged and desolate. Here he was, watching from a plain, anonymous room. He had no family, nowhere to call home. Surely other Vaethyr—Aetherials who chose to live on Earth—didn't feel this sense of alienation from the mortal world? If they did, why did they stay?

There seemed no way to survive except by partaking in the same drab slog as humans. Jobs, cars, credit cards. Alcohol to damp the pain. Everyone needed a home to live in and yet houses and even apartments, paradoxically, were virtually unaffordable. He certainly stood no chance of buying one himself, not even on Juliana's platinum credit card.

Why would any Vaethyr live here, when they had the Spiral?

Yet when Mist thought of the Otherworld, he knew he had no home there, either. He'd never properly lived there. Boundry, a self-contained bubble on the edge of the Spiral, didn't count, since it had been a sort of halfway place created by Rufus and his entourage in the Dusklands. A pleasant refuge for Rufus, but a prison for Mist.

Thinking of Rufus, and the way he'd clung on to Adam for all those years, Mist wondered if his brother had simply been lonely. Afraid of being utterly alone in the bleak place that the human world had become?

Mist laughed off the thought. Sentiment. Rufus, afraid? Never.

There were pleasanter memories . . . the two of them strolling through the great cities of Europe during the time of the Renaissance as if they owned the world, their hostilities on hold. But Rufus had an unfortunate compulsion, the worst. An addiction to cruelty.

"Where are you, you bastard?" he murmured. "Juliana's right, I should forget you and walk away. And spend the rest of my existence looking over my shoulder? Cheers, Rufus." He raised his glass to the night. "Apparently I'm as sad and demented as you are."

Something was happening, though. Portrayals of his parents and sister, of Azantios and an ancient sacred object, the Felixatus, did not appear for no reason. This was not Rufus's modus operandi—but if not him, who was responsible?

Mist lay down on the bed and thought about Stevie Silverwood.

He knew he'd handled their meetings appallingly. She thought he was weird, mad or possibly dangerous; that had been clear in her eyes. In his place, Rufus would have spun a plausible tale and charmed her to pieces. Mist lacked that ability, didn't even try. Any talents that Rufus possessed, Mist rejected. Still, he was shocked to find himself so rusty at the simple art of communication. His encounters with Stevie had been disastrous.

She had asked a very good question about the triptych: What did the title mean? What *was* Aurata's "promise"? He had no idea. Perhaps Stevie could have helped him to work it out.

He wished she were lying on the bed beside him. But only to have someone to talk to . . . He pushed his hair off his forehead, rubbed his eyes. Who was he fooling? Yes, to talk, but he couldn't ignore the heat of arousal he felt when he thought about her. He kept drifting into mental images of her quirky, strong-boned yet pretty face, her natural grace and the flowing sea-colored dresses she wore. There was a lot going on behind her blue-green, smoky eyes.

Mist imagined the weight of her body gently shaping the mattress next to him, the amber ripples of her hair spread on the pillow, her warmth, and how sweet it would feel to touch her . . . He groaned.

If he wanted company, he only had to sit in the hotel bar for an hour or two, and eventually some woman would approach him. Once or twice, he'd come to close to succumbing to temptation. Humans found him attractive, but he'd never ruthlessly exploited them as Rufus had. There had been a bored, married woman, alone on a business trip. There'd been a talkative, over-groomed beauty that he, in his naiveté, hadn't realized was a call girl until she mentioned that she wouldn't expect payment as she was "off-duty"—and that besides, he was safe as long as her "boyfriend" never found out.

Mist made his excuses, and fled.

He sighed. He was lonely, but not desperate. Such encounters would have been sordid, worse than being alone.

Thinking back to Cairndonan, he remembered Gill, the young woman who'd helped Adam survive at his lowest ebb. Mist remembered her with deep fondness, but with no desire to seek her out. She had been Adam's lover, not his. There was a difference. Although he contained Adam's memories, becoming his Felynx self again had made Mist a changed individual. That aside, Gill and Adam had both acknowledged their encounter as sweet, healing, but short-lived.

Before Gill . . . there had been Rufus's wild mob of followers, who had pleasured themselves upon a confused, drugged, half-mad Adam until their attentions had become more torture than pleasure.

He shut his eyes, pushing those memories away.

Stevie was different. Was she Aetherial? It was hard to tell, because she seemed unaware of her own Aetheric radiance and apparently hadn't noticed it in Mist, either. It was bad manners among Vaethyr, if you weren't sure, to ask outright. He couldn't say, "Are you Vaethyr?" any more than one mortal would ask another, "Are you human, or some other bipedal species?" You were supposed to *know*.

For now, Stevie was an alluring mystery.

If ever she showed a glimmer of interest in return, it would be all too easy for him to fall for her. And if ever Rufus found out—*when* he found out, as he was bound to eventually—he would find a way to destroy her, as he had Helena. Just for the sheer mischief of it.

Helena. Mist shuddered. He couldn't place Stevie in such danger. Couldn't let it happen, ever again.

"*Mist . . . Mistangamesh . . .*"

He started awake, unaware that he'd fallen asleep. For a moment he thought there was someone in the room. No; the voice was calling him from a dream.

The subconscious vision shocked him. It was a dream he'd often had before—but the last time was several hundred years ago. His sister Aurata was standing in the midpoint of a whirling black-and-white spiral, in a strange watery-blue space like a flooded mansion. Her head was thrown back and she was simply calling and calling . . . and every time, as now, he'd woken to the painful knowledge that even if her soul-essence still existed somewhere, he had no way to reach her.

Stevie liked the end of the day, when everyone had gone home and she could make her final checks in peace. Factory secure. Till empty, and money locked in the overnight safe. Shelves fully stocked in both gift shop and café; floors clean, all lights and equipment switched off. All that remained was to arm the alarm, lock up after herself and walk the short distance to her apartment.

She paused to look at the triptych. In near-darkness Daniel's images looked unnaturally bright. She could almost see them not as paintings, but as windows.

She reached out, her fingertips hovering over the image of the flame-haired woman. If she reached any farther, surely her hand would pass through thin air and touch flesh. The idea gave her a shiver, thrilling but not altogether pleasant.

Why was Adam Leith so eager to buy the triptych? His evasiveness was infuriating. Daniel had claimed to have a buyer for all his work. *All* of it? Incredible, but . . . could Adam be the mysterious buyer?

Judging by the oddly impulsive way he'd made an offer, she doubted that he'd ever bought a painting in his whole life. Yet she could be wrong. Perhaps he had some kind of mental disorder.

With a jolt she remembered that, upstairs, the contents of the trash bags she'd taken from Daniel's digs lay in a sad pile on her bed, awaiting her attention. There was nothing unpleasant, just old clothes and a handful of store receipts. She would fold everything neatly and then—winter weather and Fin's willingness to lend her car permitting—take the stuff to Frances Manifold.

One last thing. She went to her workbench and switched on the lathe to check that Alec had made a proper job of replacing the motor. It seemed okay. She tidied the mess he'd left, putting her tools in their proper holders while resisting the temptation to sit down and reassemble the clock he'd been working on for weeks. She saw where every spindle and cog should nest, as naturally as a savant might recall facts and figures, so to leave it there unfinished was incredibly frustrating. Still, there was room for only one clock-repair genius, and if she completed his project for him, Alec would sulk for days.

The lathe was loud in the silence. She flicked it off and stood listening to the noises that the museum made at night. Pops and creaks and groans. Modernization was only a skin of plasterboard and paint; beneath, the old fabric of the building shifted, contracting as the night grew colder. Stevie wasn't the only one to have seen the ghostly forms of Mr. Salter or Mr. Soames treading the corridors.

"Anyone there?" she called out.

She listened for a response. Once or twice, visitors had almost been locked in, either because they were in the restroom, or nosing where they shouldn't be. No answer. Stevie had already checked. She refused to give in to her OCD tendencies and check again. She shook the bunch of keys in her hand, selecting the one she would need to lock the back door.

Something seized her from behind.

Powerful arms went round her, a hand groping to cover her mouth. It smelled bad, like iron or blood. By reflex she began to struggle with frenzied strength. She felt the flesh of her attacker's hand against her lips and she bit down. He gave a growl of shocked pain.

Stevie broke loose. Then a weight cracked onto her skull, and she hit the floor in a storm of black stars.

7

Avenue of Beautiful Secrets

That evening, Rufus and Aurata took a slow walk along the Viale dei Belli Segreti. Arm in arm, he let her lead him wherever she wished. He looked up at pastel facades, saw shadowy figures gazing down at him from the high windows . . . felt a chill running up his back.

"Cold?" said Aurata.

"This is an elemental place, isn't it? Somewhere for Aetherials to come and hide, when they're tired of full-on life. These houses . . . they're all full of specters. How can you live here? It's giving me the creeps."

Aurata grinned broadly. She kept her voice low as if they were passing through a graveyard. "Well spotted, sweetie. Yes, not all of us want to return to the Spiral or haunt a tree for five hundred years. They're mostly Venetian Vaethyr who prefer to haunt the place they love until they're ready for rebirth. And no, I didn't create this street myself. An old lover of mine brought me here, and when he faded into elemental form he gave me his house, Estel bless him. I like it here. Not that I'm a hermit; I'm usually working and traveling. But it's been a perfect retreat."

"A safe place for ancient artifacts?"

"Quite. The neighbors don't bother me and there is no crime."

Rufus nodded, sharing her amusement. "If only I'd known you were here! We might have met years ago. Mist, too."

She sighed. "As I said, I called, but only a few heard me. Veropardus, Slahvin—his assistant, when he was guardian of the Felixatus—and a few others who are not old Felynx but a new generation of Naamon blood who clearly feel drawn to me. They're my dear chosen ones. And now you're here, too."

"This old lover," said Rufus, "should I be jealous?"

Her laugh echoed off the sepulchral walls. "What for? You and I both worked our way through many willing companions, Felynx and Tashralyr, human and who knows what else. This particular man . . ." Her face went still, her eyes distant. "When I first woke and recalled the end of Azantios, I was deranged. I couldn't stop thinking about the power we conjured in the chamber, and the way the earth trembled and the fire blazed. When I heard of Mount Vesuvius erupting and burying Pompeii, I traveled there. That was where I met Diodorus, an Aetherial who took the guise of a mature and handsome Roman citizen with silver hair . . . He was the most wonderful, intelligent companion I've ever known. I became obsessed by volcanoes—and do you realize how many times Vesuvius has erupted? It's utterly awe-inspiring." Her eyes shone. "For several hundred years, Diodorus traveled with me all around the Campanian volcanic arc—that part of southern Italy, where the Eurasian and African plates meet, is the most thrillingly active area—and he had the patience to indulge my obsession until I regained something resembling sanity."

"So you think it's sane, to clamber around boiling lava fields?" Rufus shook his head. "You really are odder than I ever dreamed."

She only laughed again. "It was breathtaking. But Diodorus became tired. I could see him fading into elemental form and there was nothing I could do. So he brought me to Venice. It was in the middle ages, while the city was still evolving, but the Viale dei Belli Segreti was already there. I stayed with him until he faded entirely. And when he'd vanished, I grieved. I was angry . . ." She was talking faster now, becoming just manic enough to worry Rufus. "I knew I had a mission to fulfill. Diodorus was gone, but I wouldn't let sorrow destroy me. I used anger to inspire me instead. Oh, I went on many other travels, of course, not least to the Spiral that had once been forbidden to us. I sampled the chill of Sibeyla and the softness of Elysion, but only the fire of Naamon held my heart. Still, I kept returning here. I couldn't forget the Felynx. My heart always told me that there was unfinished business, something more to achieve."

At the end of the street, they stepped from Duskland Venice to real Venice. The atmosphere shifted and they passed through a veil of blue smoke into a bustle of humans and the noise of boat engines. Posters and graffiti appeared on the crumbling walls. Crossing endless bridges, they worked their way out of the back streets to the ageless grandeur of San Marco. They were both dressed smartly but discreetly in tailored jeans, black shirts and dark coats. Aurata wore earrings of red fire opal, the color of her hair. A wintry fog gave the city a mystical atmosphere. Rufus looked around at stunning churches, at café lights and shop windows full of Murano glass twinkling through the murk.

"It's very *Phantom of the Opera* tonight," he said. "I want a black cloak and a mask."

"You were going to tell me more about our brother?"

"I want to hear about your strange plans, and why your followers aren't here with you. What are they up to?"

She ignored the question. "You said that Mist died in Amsterdam, at the hands of a jealous husband? Why couldn't you save him?"

At that, Rufus felt a flash of anger. "Do you think I didn't try? His body bled out, and his soul-essence fled. Have you any idea how hard it is to carry a corpse, day and night, until you find a way into the Otherworld? I was distraught. I reached a portal which brought us somewhere into Elysion, and I found a healing place of blue stone, but he remained dead and began to decay . . . finally, a kind Aelyr maiden found us and said it was no good. His essence was gone, and his body would turn to dust. I had to let him go."

"I'm so sorry," she breathed. Rufus moved to the canal edge and watched some gondolas tied up and bobbing gently on the water.

"You know the rest: how hard I searched. Meanwhile, some fanatics from the Spiral Court decided to hunt me down, so I lived in hiding on the border between Spiral and Earth with some friends . . ."

"Your entourage," she put in.

"We were fugitives, but we still had fun, emerging from our secret pocket of the Otherworld to scare the locals . . . to perpetuate legends of the fair folk, encourage a little superstitious terror. They called us the Dubh Sidhe, dark elves—I like that, don't you? We'd kidnap someone, play with their minds, then return them to the surface world quite mad."

"Oh, Rufus. Unworthy."

"We were bored," he said, mock-defensively. "Anyway, that's how I found a divine young man, the absolute image of Mist. I snatched him from his human family and kept him for ninety-odd years."

"But you were mistaken?" said Aurata, her tone cool and shrewd.

Rufus felt pain in his throat, like claws. "I tried so hard to shock him awake. Extremes of pleasure, vile torments . . . everything I could devise to break down the dumb chrysalis and reveal Mistangamesh, the butterfly, inside. Nothing worked! Meanwhile, my obsession caused all my companions to desert me, out of sheer exasperation. I don't blame them."

"So you were left alone?"

"Apart from one beautiful, scared and mad human boy. Who died trying to save my life, which makes it all the more comically tragic. After all I'd done—still he tried to save me, without even thinking."

"He must have made a great impression on you," Aurata said thoughtfully, "for a mortal."

"Even now, I don't look back and see that I made a dreadful mistake. I just feel angry. Cheated."

Aurata was quiet, watching him. She looked so young; to outside eyes, they might have been a honeymoon couple in their early twenties. Still the spoiled yet innocent son and daughter of the Felynx Sovereign Elect, Poectilictis.

"Angry with yourself?"

"No, with him, for his muleheaded stubbornness. All the time, I suspected that he was playing me along, pretending!"

Aurata laughed. "If he was, that would be delicious. That would serve you right."

"Hm. I find humor in most things, but not this. How could I be so wrong?"

Delicately she cleared her throat. "If Mist wouldn't come back, it was because he didn't want to."

"Don't say that. No, go on, say it! I tried too hard. Mist is an idiot, always was. And I don't care anymore. I'm done with him."

Presently they climbed the long stairs of the Rialto Bridge and stood at the central balustrade, watching water traffic plowing below, the Grand Canal magnificent before them in its spooky cowl of fog. "You know, whether you made a mistake or not, we could probably still find him."

Rufus reacted with an angry hiss. "No, Aurata, forget it. I'm never putting myself through that again."

"What would you say, though, if you saw him?"

"Stop. I'd tell him to fuck himself on the Devil's pitchfork. I'd push him off the highest cliff I could find, since he seems to like that sort of thing. Aurata, I was as good as dead when you found me. I cannot go back to that state, ever again."

"And you needn't. We have each other now. Wouldn't you like to do something more constructive, more appropriately *Aetherial*, than selling guns?"

"Sounds promising. We could start with a gondola ride, then get drunk at the most expensive restaurant in town . . ."

"I meant a more ambitious, long-term project."

"Anything. As long as it doesn't involve tectonic plates."

"Sorry. It does in a way. How can you not be interested in the Earth's boundary places? Boundaries are where everything happens. Volcanoes, mountain ranges, mineral formations, rifts, earthquakes . . ." Her eyes shone pure gold. "Thresholds strain with pent-up energy. Also, they stand between Vaeth and the Otherworld . . . and what's the Spiral but an even more complex structure of energy layers and dimensions that we haven't even begun to understand? Forgive me, I'm ranting. But you'll understand, Rufus. You will."

"I don't want to understand. I want champagne. Shall we throw a party for our spectral neighbors in the Avenue of Beautiful Secrets?"

Aurata rested her head on his shoulder, exhaling. "You're a hopeless case," she said affectionately.

Rufus said in a low voice, "Do you know that you talk in your sleep?"

She looked up with a guarded expression. "So I've been told, on occasion. What did I say?"

"You were rambling about hiding something from profane human eyes, and being trapped by Sibeylan ice and glaciers. Was it a nightmare? What did you mean?"

"I don't remember," she said tightly. Her fingers dug into his arms, then released their hold. "It's nothing. Just my subconscious reminding me to be careful, because the fact is that when someone has a grand plan, there is always someone else trying to stop them. But I know how to protect my secrets, and, believe me, I am strong."

"I don't doubt that for a moment. Qesoth herself is on your side. You said so."

Her expression became a fierce smile. "Oh, you'd better believe it. So, drink in the sights while you can, because I'm only here to collect my precious Felynx artifacts. I'll be sad to leave, because this place was my sanctuary, but the next stage must happen elsewhere. And so . . ." With an angled hand, she mimicked a jet taking off.

"What next?" Rufus grinned, loving her spirit. "How long have you been planning whatever it is?"

"Oh. Only since the dawn of time, dear."

Stevie sat on the edge of a bathtub, swishing the water with her hand. The turbulence was hypnotic. She blocked the overflow with a washcloth and let the cold tap run until water began to slop over the side, pattering onto the floor and soaking her skirt.

She slid into the bath fully clothed, gasping at the cold. She let herself slip under to see how it felt, her hair drifting like weed. Like Ophelia in the painting . . .

She was drowning, being pushed deeper. Silver bubbles rose from her mouth. Above the rippling surface, a shape held her down and heavy hands were throttling her.

Darkness. She rose from the water as if she'd merely been sleeping. Her hands clawed at pillows of moss. She was in a swamp surrounded by tall thin trees. Silver birches trailed their slender branches on her head. She looked up through the trees and saw a glowing midnight sky with a steep jagged mountain rising black against it.

She could recall no past, no memories at all. Now she was running, terrified.

She climbed on all fours as the mountain became a city around her with streets like deep channels cut into the rock. Statues loomed, watching her from calm, blank orbs. Everything was black yet full of color, flashing with peacock blues and ruby reds that hurt her eyes.

Fleeing for her life, she was tumbling downwards through tunnels. With no more substance than a cobweb she could get no purchase on the stone steps. No one saw her, no one helped.

She emerged deep underground in a cavern. Green light rose from below to make rippling patterns on the ceiling. Water again. Terrified, she tried to crawl away.

No. No, *a voice echoed. You can't be here now. Go back,* go back!

A silhouette came drifting towards her with one palm held up, showing blood-red slashes inside the dangling sleeve. She shrank away. The time is wrong, *said the apparition.* Go back!

Stevie woke, blinded in one eye by an incredibly close, bright light.

The light dropped away to reveal a man in blue. Around him was a vague bustle of activity, laced with a musty smell of disinfectant. A hospital ward. Her head was exploding with every possible type of pain. A deep pounding headache, skull bones bruised and aching, soft tissues swollen.

"Miss Silverwood? Stephanie? Are you with us?"

The doctor in blue scrubs was young and dark-skinned with a dazzling smile. Her blurred eyes took a moment to unscramble the name on his ID tag. DOCTOR R. ARULANANTHAM, she made out, SENIOR REGISTRAR. She was in bed, propped up at an angle with a large pillow at her back.

"Oh, god, my head . . ."

"Try to stay quiet. You've been unconscious for a while."

"How did I get here?"

"Don't you remember?" The doctor sat on the edge of her bed, looking concerned yet cheerfully reassuring. "You arrived by taxi and told the receptionist that you'd tripped over your cat and banged your head."

"Did I?"

"And then you passed out."

She tried to gather her thoughts between throbs of pain. She'd been about to lock up and then . . . *Oh god, someone broke in.* Dim recollections returned . . . Rising to her feet in darkness with her head reeling.

Seeing that Daniel's triptych was gone.

Yet nothing else was missing. The display cases of jewelry were intact, the office door untouched. No broken glass, no mess. Her attacker must have come in through the back door, which she always unlocked in order to make a quick getaway once she'd set the alarm . . . only this time, she'd dawdled, checking the workbench and looking at *Aurata's Promise.*

As in a dream, she recalled making a logical decision not to call the police. *The break-in was my fault, the triptych my responsibility.* If she called the police, she knew the museum bosses would go into a mad flap and there would be days of questions, a huge fuss about security and insurance and all the rest. It would be in the local papers. She might even lose her job.

However, if she said nothing, no one need know. It was her task alone to discover who'd taken Daniel's artwork . . . and she had her suspicions.

All these decisions had seemed perfectly rational while she was making them.

So she'd left and locked up as normal—so she thought. Outside, though, she noticed that her ears were ringing and her skull threatening to implode. Hospital might be a good idea after all. Calmly she'd walked into the street and called a taxi. After that, events became blurred.

"Anyone we can contact for you?" asked Dr. Arulanantham.

"No. I live alone."

"Apart from the cat."

"Apart from the cat," she agreed. "It wasn't her fault, though. Also, I wasn't drunk. Neither was the cat."

The doctor chuckled, then asked if she knew the day and date and the name of the prime minister. She answered correctly, starting to feel impatient. "I know where this is going. I'm fine. When can I leave?"

He gave her a firm look. "Your CT scan was clear, but concussion can have nasty delayed symptoms, so we need to keep you in overnight."

"Oh, my god." She dropped her head back, wincing as the sore part hit the pillow. "Is that really necessary?"

"A nurse will wake you at regular intervals to make sure you don't fall unconscious, or develop any new symptoms." He grinned. "Relax, we aren't that scary. We'll take good care of you. You can go home in the morning, but you'll have to rest for a week."

"A week! No, that's impossible. I have a job, I can't . . ."

The doctor was kind but intransigent. "I'm sure your employers will understand."

Reaching up, Stevie found a dressing on her head. She could feel a distinct tender lump beneath it. The pain made her feel sick. Tears of delayed shock flooded her eyes. Anger too. How dare someone stroll in and attack her like that?

Of course I should have called the police, she thought in despair. *What was I thinking? Not thinking. Concussed. Acting on autopilot.* Yet she was still certain that concealing the truth was her only option.

"Where's my bag? Can I use my phone in here? I need to call someone." She would have to ask Fin to open up in the morning.

"No, complete rest for now. We can call them for you."

"No—no, it's all right. They might rush here, and I don't want that. I'll try first thing tomorrow."

Stevie realized, now she'd set her fake story in motion, that she would have to lie to Fin. To everyone.

Stevie dozed restlessly, woozy from medication. It didn't help that a nurse woke her every five minutes: so it felt, anyway. Opening her eyes to a bright and busy ward of white walls and blue bed-curtains, it took her a moment to recall why she was here.

Time was jumbled. The ward clock read nine. Nine! Panic gripped her, until she recalled waking at six-thirty with her mouth dry, her head pounding. She'd called Fin to explain—"I'm fine, no, please don't come to the hospital, they only kept me in as a precaution,"—then she'd had a cup of tea and fallen asleep again.

To her relief, she now felt better than expected. She began to sit up, reaching for a glass of water. Someone put the glass into her hand and she saw a visitor sitting beside her bed.

Her mouth opened in surprise at a tall, big-boned man in a thick sweater patterned with zigzags of red and green that tortured her eyes. His dark hair was shorn around a large bald pate, his large, handsome features finished by a neat beard.

It was Dr. Gregory, the psychologist whose email she'd deleted before Christmas. She'd been ignoring his emails for over a year, yet he wouldn't take the hint.

"What are you doing here?" she said, blunt with shock.

"I work here."

"I know. I meant . . ."

He gave the fatherly smile she remembered. "The registrar saw in your notes that I'd treated you in the past. You know with a head injury that amnesia can be a problem and, since you're particularly prone to the condition, you might need to be monitored more closely. Stephanie, I was dreadfully concerned to hear you've had this accident."

Stevie froze inside. A wall of denial sprang up. "There's no need. I bumped my head, that's all."

"And how are you feeling?"

"Not bad at all," she said, folding her hands on top of the sheet. She noticed that all her silver rings had been removed; she hoped they were in her bag. "It's good of you to come, but I'm fine."

He leaned forward, resting one elbow across his knees. "You haven't been answering my emails."

"No. I've been so busy."

"A head injury is a worry, because we still don't know what caused your original memory loss."

Dr. Gregory's kind yet probing manner, quiet voice and terrible taste in sweaters took her back ten years, to a consulting room in another wing of the hospital, where he'd tried to tease answers from a confused, introverted teenager—much to the frustration of Stevie's uncomprehending foster mother. And she did not want to go back there.

"That was an awfully long time ago, so I'd like to forget about it, if you'll excuse the pun."

He'd always been supportive. Stevie had liked him, but grown to dread his endless analysis, his "assessments," his refusal to let go of her case. Yet she could never tell him to get lost because . . . he was a doctor, and she was intimidated.

Now, though, she was stronger.

"I understand," he said. "However, I still think it's important we keep talking. You ran away from the problems before you'd fully confronted them."

She was silent for a moment. "That's up to me, isn't it?"

"Yes, of course. But . . ."

"I sorted myself out, Dr. Gregory. I have a job I love and I'm happy; I can't see how it helps to keep raking up the past. I'm a different person now. That's why I didn't answer your emails. I didn't mean to be rude, but I've moved on."

He gave his familiar, understanding sigh. "I respect that. My concern is that you are still burying things. One day they'll resurface and burn you. All I want to say is that, if you begin to experience problems, I'm still here to help."

"Thank you," she said, feeling guiltily grateful. "I know we didn't get to the bottom of my craziness, but our sessions weren't a waste. You helped me get into art college, and that changed everything. My only real problem now is that a friend of mine's gone missing."

"Daniel Manifold?"

A vein in her head throbbed. "How did you know?"

Dr. Gregory looked sheepish. "I know his mother. Academic lives cross quite a bit. Actually, I saw Daniel for a few months when he was much younger—this is confidential, but I know you won't repeat it—to assess him for possible clinical conditions."

Stevie focused, forgetting her own problems. "I knew he'd seen a psychologist, but he didn't tell me it was you. *Was* there something wrong with him?"

"'Wrong' is a subjective term. He was highly creative, with obsessive and manic traits towards the high end of normal. His father's early death exacerbated that, which is understandable. The main issue seemed to be a mismatch between his personality and Professor Manifold's view of how he *should* behave."

Stevie gave a pained smile. "That's exactly what I thought! Can you map out a definition of normal?"

"No such thing," he acknowledged. "Never in my life have I met anyone without some kind of neurosis, idiosyncrasy or borderline personality disorder—and I'm not talking about patients. As long as we can muddle along without harming ourselves or others, we're doing okay."

His words lightened her heart. What a revelation, that they could talk as equals. Quietly she confessed, "I still have the drowning dreams. I even had one last night, while I was out cold. And I still see apparitions—or migraine aura, as the doctors prefer to label it—but I'm all right. Any ghosts, I just say hi and carry on with my day. I think I'm doing quite well, considering."

He patted her wrist. "Sounds like you're doing wonderfully. So you rest now and do as the doctors tell you. Don't forget, I'm only a phone call away."

Dr. Gregory left. Stevie lay back, surprised at how tired the conversation had made her. She was glad, now, that she'd seen him. To learn that Daniel had also been his patient was an intriguing coincidence.

"I see things, as if the world's showing me hidden layers," he'd said, the first time they met. *"It's beautiful. That's why I wander off and stare for hours . . . but my mother thinks I'm mad. She's making me see a shrink. But I just like to really look at things, you know? Does that make me nuts?"*

"No, Dan," she said softly to herself. "Maybe Frances needs counseling, not you."

Stevie was finally discharged at midday, arriving home by one o'clock. In the taxi she pulled the bandage off her head; they'd shaved a tiny strip and put stitches in, but she arranged her hair to hide the injury. She paid the taxi driver and entered the museum to find the shop quiet. Fin was manning the counter, Ron chatting to her. Stevie began glancing around for disturbances she'd missed the previous night, telltale signs that might give the lie to her story.

"Hey, boss," said Fin with a concerned look. "How are you? What the hell happened?"

"I'm fine. Like I said on the phone, I tripped up and banged my head."

"You want to take more water with it, girl," said Ron. He gave her a hug with one arm around her shoulders, which she found embarrassing. She eased herself free.

"Yes, thanks, Ron. I thought they'd give me a quick checkup and send me home. Honestly, I'd never have gone in if I'd known I'd be there all night! So sorry to call you before the crack of dawn, Fin."

"No, don't be daft," said Fin, walking from behind the counter to join the hugging. "You did the right thing. Actually, Alec opened up because I had to get the kids to school. Are you sure you're all right?"

"Positive. A bit tired. Sore head. No lasting damage."

"Well, you'd better take the rest of the day off. You needn't think you're working."

Stevie thought of her empty apartment. She didn't even have a real cat waiting; only a small leopard-like phantom that was hardly a proper pet. The thought of spending the afternoon lying down depressed her. "What else will I do?"

"Well, I don't know," said Fin. "Lie on the sofa eating chocolate and reading a good book? I forbid you to work!"

Stevie smiled. "Okay, well, I need a shower and fresh clothes. And some lunch."

"It's a start. By the way, why did you take the triptych off display?"

The question hit her like ice water. Goose bumps crawled over her skin. She couldn't remember what she'd decided to say.

"Hello, Earth to Stevie? Delayed concussion?"

"Er, sorry, but I'd forgotten I'd done it. I—I suddenly felt weird about the artwork being on show while Daniel's missing, so I took it upstairs. I'll ask his mother if she wants it back. I need to see her anyway."

Her stomach was a tight ball of guilt as she told the lie. Fin only shrugged and accepted her word, which made Stevie feel worse. "Okay. Whatever you think best. I assume you'll want the loan of my car again?"

"Yes, that would be great—if you don't mind?"

"No problem, as long as I get fuel money and a bottle of wine like last time?" Fin winked at her. "I was going to say, 'Knock yourself out,' but, er, not such a great choice of phrase. You can borrow it, but *not today*. Don't even think about driving today."

"Even I am not that daft," Stevie retorted. The thought of a hot shower and food began to cheer her up. The jangle of the shop bell was her cue to leave. "Oh, by the way, I'm in love."

Fin's eyebrows rose. "Don't tell me: gorgeous doctor!"

"Absolutely. The guy who treated me, Dr. Arulanantham—he was so nice, and incredibly cute. He's from Sri Lanka. He's only a bit taller than me, so I wouldn't be able to wear high heels, but that's okay. He'd be worth it."

"You gave him your number, right?"

They were laughing as Stevie felt a presence behind her, saw Fin's gaze drift over her shoulder. A soft voice said, "Hello, Stevie." She turned, found Adam there.

For a moment she thought she might pass out again. If he'd attacked her last night, would he have the nerve to come back the next day? She had no idea. And she'd lied, so she couldn't yell for help—could she? She felt herself dissolving, losing all sense of what was true.

She didn't yell. Instead she looked coolly at him as if nothing had happened. From long practice, she could hide her inner turmoil. Usually.

"What brings you here?" she said, her tone casual.

"I heard what happened. I came to see how you are."

"Heard, how?"

Fin said, "He called earlier, so I told him."

"Oh, well, I survived, as you can see." She glared into Adam's eyes, trying to discern whether her suspicions were founded. She couldn't talk plainly to him in front of anyone else, but was she safe alone with him?

He looked worried, but that was easily faked. "How are you feeling?"

"Slightly shaken up. Starving. Otherwise, good."

"Can I take you to lunch, then?"

Stevie moved away from the counter, away from Fin's attention. "Why?"

"I'd like to talk to you."

She hesitated. Surely he wouldn't attack her in broad daylight, in public? "All right," she said. "I certainly need words with you."

She led him along the curves of Vyse Street towards a wine bar near the handsome Chamberlain Clock. The day was dry, cold and grey. For a while Stevie was tight-lipped; she didn't know what to say. She was slightly scared, too, but mostly puzzled, with a large dash of anger. Adam was silent. There was hardly anyone around. A couple in winter jackets and scarves were working their way from one jeweler's window to the next, looking at engagement rings. The security man outside the diamond merchants' looked bored and cold. She waved, and he saluted back.

"I didn't think I'd see you again," she said at last.

"I didn't mean to come back, but . . ." Adam let the sentence hang. "Can I ask why you took the triptych away?"

She looked sideways at him. "Do you seriously expect me to believe you don't know anything about that?"

"What do you mean?"

"Someone sneaked in last night and stole it. They hit me over the head first."

He stopped and swung to face her. "My god, Stevie. Why didn't you say? No one at the museum told me."

"That's because I didn't tell them."

"Why ever not?"

Her hands were cold. She pushed them into her coat sleeves. The coat, her thrift-shop find, was faux ivory suede with fake-fur trimmings, a hood and a waist-hugging belt; she'd liked it for its Russian winter fairy-tale style. "Complicated. But partly because I thought it was you. *Was* it you?"

"No!" His eyes grew wider. "How could you think that?"

"But who else was interested? Look, acres of jewelry in all directions. It's fairly safe here—there's a police station around the corner—but occasionally there's an attempted break-in, like any inner-city area. Thieves want gold, platinum, money. They're not going to run off with a bulky wooden panel. You tried to buy *Aurata's Promise* and I said no. So you took it anyway."

"No." He was adamant. "I give you my word I did not do this, Stevie. Why would I come back to see you, if I had?"

"I don't know! To make yourself appear less guilty?"

As soon as the words were out, she regretted them. She didn't want to believe Adam was capable of attacking her, then brazenly returning to pretend innocence. Yet she wasn't *sure.* That gnawed at her.

She had an idea. "How's your hand?" she said.

He looked puzzled. Before he could respond, she seized both his hands and inspected them. They were beautifully shaped, with long fingers—naturally, since he was so damned perfect—and they felt warm in her cold grasp. No teeth marks, no bruises.

Embarrassed, she let go. He inspected his hands for himself, front and back. "Why would there be anything . . ."

"Because I bit you. Correction, I bit whoever attacked me. Which apparently wasn't you."

"No, of course it wasn't." He looked horrified. His reaction appeared so genuine that she finally believed he wasn't acting.

"But who would take the panel, and nothing else?"

"Rufus," Adam said gravely. "Stevie, I'm so, so sorry."

The wine bar was a cavernous space with a partly glazed ceiling, ferns cascading down red-painted iron pillars. There were wooden floors, tables and chairs made from reclaimed materials. It had once been a factory, now renovated to a trendy mix of old and new. Stevie chose a table in a quiet corner, and let Adam go to the bar to order food and drinks. He came back with two tall glasses of fruit juice; she used hers to wash down painkillers.

Seeing her swallow the pills, he repeated, "I'm sorry." His complexion was deathly pale.

"If you didn't whack me, stop apologizing."

"But I've brought this trouble to you."

"Or Danny has, by sending me the wretched thing in the first place."

"He wouldn't deliberately endanger you, would he?"

"Not in a million years," she said. "Not the Danny I knew, anyway. Of course, he probably wasn't in his right mind when he sent it."

A waiter came with cutlery, napkins and a bowl of black and green olives. She thanked him, and began to devour the olives, gasping at the delicious burst of salt and oil on her tongue. "These are amazing. Try one. God, I hope they're quick with the sandwiches. I'm famished. Oh, and you have to call an ambulance if I drop unconscious or start acting weird." She licked the juice off her fingers. "This isn't me being weird, by the way. This is normal me."

"Stevie." He fixed his gaze steadily on her. She was fascinated by the way light and shade brought out different colors in his eyes. Now his irises were deep silver-grey, laced with leaf-green. "You seem . . ."

"What?"

"To be recovering quickly."

"I know. I'm supposed to take it easy, and I will, but I feel fine. Even the bad head's bearable."

"And that's characteristic of . . ."

"Being minutes from dropping dead?"

"I wasn't going to say that." He broke the gaze. "Stevie, are you *sure* you don't know Rufus already?" He sat back, continuing the discussion with himself. "But if you did, you wouldn't admit it. I might have walked into a trap; I gave you a name that he'd recognize. But if you knew him, he wouldn't need to steal the painting."

She sipped her drink. "I'm going to call the paramedics for *you* in a moment, Adam. I swear I don't know anyone who could conceivably be Rufus. You're not making sense."

"I know. I'm sorry."

"What can I say? I didn't fake being attacked. I'm not in league with Rufus. But I still have *absolutely no idea who you are*. How about telling me your real name?"

"Mist," he said softly.

"Missed what?"

"No, it's my name. M-i-s-t. Mistangamesh."

"Sounds . . . I don't know. Greek?"

"No. It's an old family name. My true name."

A shiver went through her. She remembered the fairy-tale premise, that to learn someone's true name was to gain power over them. Not that she believed in magic, but all the same, to offer a true name meant something. Willingness to be vulnerable?

One of them must start. Mist was gentlemanly enough, or desperate enough, to take a risk and go first.

"Daniel's art." He leaned forward, resting his elbows on the table. "He shows people and places I haven't seen for years. I know it's hard to believe, but please bear with me."

"I'm listening."

"It's been thousands of years since I saw them." He spoke so softly, she wasn't sure she'd heard him right. "Aetherial, Aelyr, Vaethyr or Felynx; we were all of those. Do those words mean anything to you?"

"I'm not sure." A faint, uncertain memory stirred. "I don't think so."

"They all name a race already here, long before humans arose. We were of the Felynx, a branch of Naamon Aelyr that lived on Earth, although I couldn't show you where on the map. There were plains, mountains and forests surrounding Azantios, the city in Daniel's painting, but Rufus brought it all to dust. He and I escaped and survived. I couldn't forgive him, and neither could I let him loose. He takes destruction with him wherever he goes. I spent centuries trying to stop him but . . . a time came when I gave up. I escaped. He became obsessed with finding me. Now I'm in the impossible position of trying to find him, without him ever realizing that I'm there, watching."

"I'm sorry, can you take it from the top? You lost me at 'before humans arose.'"

He looked straight at her. "You heard what I said."

"Well, the words went in, but . . . This sounds like the way Daniel used to talk on his flights of fancy."

"And he's painted what I'm describing. But that's impossible, unless he actually was one of the Felynx himself."

"As in . . . thousands of years old?"

Perhaps it was the strong painkillers that allowed her to take in his story without judgment. The sandwiches arrived, giving her a moment to breathe.

How to react? She already knew that Mist was terrible at lying. There was an innocence about him that inspired trust . . . that, or he was a madman who'd bopped her over the head and now sat insisting that his fictional, psychotic twin was guilty.

"Erm . . . I'm as sure as I can be that Danny's human. Perhaps it's coincidence that his scenes and figures look familiar to you. He has quite an imagination."

Mist disregarded her remark. "Occasionally, Aetherials can be reborn in human form. It happened to me. I can't make sense of it."

"That makes two of us," said Stevie. "I want to help you, but this is getting us nowhere." She took a large bite of her sandwich.

"Have you heard of Dame Juliana Flagg?"

She swallowed hard to avoid spluttering bread, reached for her drink. "Yes, of course. She's a sculptor, isn't she? This is an odd turn in the conversation."

"Are you all right? Don't choke."

"There was a documentary about her last year. She'd been out of the public eye for ages, then made a big comeback with this amazing group of sculptures. But what's she got to do with this?"

"I know her. She would vouch for me."

Stevie's eyes widened. "How? You mean like, phone her up and . . . ?"

"Yes."

She wiped her fingers on a paper napkin, reached into her bag and passed her phone across the table. "Go on, then."

He didn't touch the phone. "Look up the number for Cairndonan House on her website and dial it yourself. Otherwise I could be phoning anyone."

"True. I think you're smarter than you make out."

Her phone was old, but capable of web-surfing. Soon she was looking at a tiny photograph of Cairndonan House, familiar from the documentary film. She dialed, switched onto speakerphone, and waited. An antipodean-accented male voice answered briskly, "Yes, Cairndonan?"

Stevie felt nervous. Surely Dame Juliana couldn't be more intimidating than Frances Manifold? "May I speak to Dame Juliana Flagg, please?"

There was a very soft, long-suffering huff at the other end, as if he fended off scores of cheeky callers every day. "You can leave a message, or I can put you through to her secretary. Who is it speaking?"

"Stevie Silverwood. She won't know me, but . . ."

Mist spoke over her: "Colin, tell her it's Adam, as was. Plus friend."

There was a muffled clatter, as if Colin had dropped the receiver. "Adam, bloody hell, is that you? Dame J. told me she found you, but I didn't believe her! Hang on, mate, she's right here."

A moment later, a female voice emanated with a tinny hiss from the handset, like an old gramophone record. "Mist, my dear? And who is Miss Silverwood?"

The voice was unmistakable: smooth and plummy, yet warm. Stevie lost her composure.

"Er, I, I'm here with Mist, or Adam, and . . . Well, it's been a weird few days and he's telling me that he's thousands of years old with a bad brother called Rufus. I'm so sorry, you're the most famous artist in the country and I'm talking rubbish. Please excuse me, Dame Juliana. Perhaps he should explain?"

"Oh my lord, Mist, what's happened? Are you all right?"

"Yes." He leaned over the phone, speaking softly. "Something's going on. I'm not sure what it means, but I wanted Miss Silverwood to hear, from someone she will believe, that I'm telling the truth."

"About Rufus?"

"And everything else. Boundry. The Dusklands, the pathway from Sibeyla to Naamon, the fact that you saw it all with your own eyes."

"Are you sure that you want her to know?" said Dame Juliana, quiet with shock. "She's not one of Rufus's henchmen holding you at gunpoint, is she?"

"Nothing so dramatic," said Stevie. "We're in a wine bar."

"You want me to tell her everything?" Juliana gasped. "Good heavens, who is paying for this phone call?"

"Me, but it doesn't matter," Stevie said quickly.

"No," said Juliana. "It would take all day. He can tell you himself. I will say just this: that Mist is who he claims, and that I saw it all with my own eyes. Seen it, lived it, sculpted it. Oh—and if he puts his trust in you, young lady, you had better prove worthy."

The hiss cut off abruptly. Stevie wasn't sure if the connection had broken, or if Juliana had ended the call herself.

"Wow," she said. "That was really her. Dame Juliana Flagg!"

"Yes. She was wonderful to me." He looked steadily at her, his eyes as green as the ferns above them. She felt a shiver, remembering that Mist's aim was not to befriend her, but to hunt down his brother.

"So you now have license to tell me absolutely anything, and I have to believe it?"

"Only a little at a time." He smiled. "It's more a jigsaw than a narrative."

"Give me the basics, then. Who are the Aelyr? What are you?"

"An older race. We evolved from energy, rather than from flesh. That's what our legends say, at least. The world is porous to us; we can move into realms that stand sideways to everyday reality. And we're chameleons, able to adapt our form to our surroundings in order to fit in."

"An older, wiser race that's passed beyond the circles of the world?" Stevie tried to stay cynical, but she was captivated. Mist's quiet, unassuming manner suggested he was stating plain facts.

"I don't know about wiser. Nor are we really any more powerful than humans, otherwise we'd have taken over the world, wouldn't we, rather than living in secret?"

"Would you?"

"Perhaps, if we had the will. However, with certain exceptions, most Aetherials prefer to live peacefully and stay out of trouble."

"And humans would know you as what? Faerie folk, demons, were-creatures?"

"You want to put a label on us, but we're none of those. We're simply ourselves. And we live too long. I think that the more we mix with humans, the harder it is for our minds to cope with near-immortality. So we have dormant phases, or we turn into semi-sentient energy forms. Sometimes we die, only to resurface in another incarnation. It can be difficult to hold on to our memories and identity. Or it can be impossible to shake them off."

"That sounds . . . frightening."

He looked intently at her. There was no enchantment to compare with that of the most beautiful, sexy eyes she'd ever seen. She had to look away, wishing there were a vaccine against the effect he had on her. "Stevie, are you *sure* you've heard none of this before?"

"I don't think so. But it's making me feel weird . . . like I'm going to wake up in hospital again, any second."

Mist sat back, reminding her of Dr. Gregory when—after an exhausting therapy session—he would lean back and say, *"I think that's enough for today."*

"Let's finish our food, and I'll walk you to the museum. I can see you're tired. Forgive me; I talk to no one for years on end, then I don't know when to stop."

Luckily, I like the sound of your voice. She took another bite, preventing herself from saying this out loud. At last, with only a crust and a few strands of salad left on her plate, she said, "Well, we've made a start. I really should go home and rest."

"Can I see you again?"

"I'm assuming you mean that in a strictly business-like, let's solve the mystery, sense?"

Mist coughed. "Yes. Yes, of course."

"Good. Just making sure. We can talk some more in the car tomorrow, if you like. I need to see Daniel's mother, so you may as well come with me."

8

Azantios, Falling

The day was brittle, frozen white under a pure blue sky, hedgerows stiff with frost. Mist was in the passenger seat beside Stevie, telling stories that conjured distracting images while she tried to concentrate on the icy roads. These narrow lanes hadn't been salted and she'd felt the car slide too often for comfort.

"Daniel's representation of Azantios was uncanny," Mist told her. "The city was like a haze of pale gold flames cloaking red mountains. The Felynx race originated in Naamon, one of the Otherworld realms, but they quarreled with the ruler, Queen Malikala, and went into voluntary exile on Vaeth. Earth, I mean. There they founded Azantios. Not by physical building work, but by manipulating the fabric of the world and the Dusklands."

"Magic?" she put in.

"We wouldn't call it that. Aetherials pull energy and matter around by working in groups we call webs. That takes planning. It's not easy."

"And this was how long ago?"

"I don't know," Mist said ruefully. "My estimate is at least thirty thousand years, and of course the Felynx had established themselves thousands of years before I was born. I can't even tell you what continent we were on. With unchallenged arrogance we took Vaeth to be ours. We were barely aware of human tribes, regarding them as on a par with animals. They were terrified of us, and kept away. We thought the Felynx ruled the world."

"A nonhuman empire that vanished long before recorded history began?" Stevie envisioned angelic beings drifting through a spiderweb of streets and felt a shivery mix of awe and unease. As to whether she believed him—she suspended judgment.

Mist's tone was matter-of-fact. "My parents were Poectilictis and Theliome of House Ephenaestus, effectively king and queen through an esoteric election system. The palace where we lived was extraordinary, like a citadel spun from gold and silver glass. Of course, it seemed normal to us when it was all we'd ever known. In the great hall, my mother and father sat on high thrones, like pharaohs of later ages; but they weren't dictators. They were respected and loved, chosen to govern for their wisdom."

"Did you look as you do now?" Stevie asked. "Human-shaped, I mean?"

Mist hesitated. "I struggle to remember their faces. Their ceremonial forms were dark and cat-like, with narrow golden eyes. Yes, we walked upright—but we could change form to please ourselves. Azantios existed partly in the Dusklands, but we were sun-loving creatures, preferring warmth and fire. We revered fierce animals such as eagles and wild cats. Our tradition was to take on the characteristics of lynxes, their grace and beauty."

"And the hunting instinct?"

"Actually, we were gentle. Yes, we had a high opinion of ourselves, but we lived peacefully, extending our city, growing fruit and grain, falling in love, squabbling, creating art and poetry, holding great celebrations beneath the stars. We had conflicts, but generally life was good. We didn't know how fortunate we were."

"Garden of Eden," said Stevie. She caught her breath as a van came towards her too fast, shimmied on a patch of ice and missed her by inches. "Fucking idiot!"

"Are you okay?" Mist touched her arm.

"Yes." She exhaled. "We're nearly there. Go on."

"It was more like a fool's paradise," he murmured. "We're long-lived, but my parents would have stepped down eventually. Poectilictis nominated me his heir."

"So you would have been a sort of king? Wow, Prince Mistangamesh. I didn't know I was traveling with royalty."

He gave a soft laugh. "You're not. It wasn't like that; I'd have had to be formally elected, but my father considered me responsible, fair-minded, dutiful, everything a ruler needs to be. But Rufus—Poectilictis didn't trust him. He viewed his second son as feckless and self-centered—which he was, actually, but the question is, did Rufus go off the rails because he couldn't stand not being favored? Or was it the way he was born? I didn't want Rufus to be jealous of me, but I wasn't going to step aside to please him. As a result, he devoted most of his time to causing trouble."

"What about Aurata?" Mist said nothing. Stevie pushed him. "Come on. Why wasn't she considered a potential heir to the throne of Azantios?"

He was silent for a few seconds. "She was. We would have been expected to marry and rule together."

The car wavered as Stevie failed to slow down for a bend. "Oh. Incest? That's a bit . . . ancient Egyptian, isn't it? Keeping power within the royal family?"

"I suppose so, but the Felynx didn't see it as wrong. Aetherials aren't prone to genetic defects. Incest isn't common among us, but it's not taboo, either."

He sounded a touch defensive, she thought. He continued, "It hasn't always been taboo in human societies, either, but even when it's almost universally forbidden, it still happens."

"Fair enough. That's true."

"And Aetherials are very much more relaxed about such things."

"Clearly."

"I never slept with my sister, if that's what you're wondering."

"Oh. Right. Good."

"Rufus did, constantly, and as blatantly as possible."

Stevie's eyes were as round as saucers as she tried to keep the car steady. She glanced at him and saw that his lips had gone white. She was caught between disgust and the urge to laugh. "Why? Not just to piss you off?"

Mist grimaced. "Well. Partly. As I said, we weren't straitlaced about such things, but it was still enough to cause raised eyebrows because we were the rulers' offspring, and expected to behave with more dignity. Rufus was trying to make me jealous, by proving that Aurata preferred him to me. And it did piss me off, as you put it. Not because I wanted to be with Aurata—I truly didn't—but because of his attitude, which you could sum up as poisonous mockery."

"And how did Aurata feel about it?"

"Oh, they were as bad as each other. I think either of us could have ruled successfully alone, but together—whether we'd had a true marriage or a platonic partnership—it would have been disastrous. She thought I was too placid, and I thought she was too domineering. I didn't want to go against our parents' wishes, nor did I want to step aside for her. Poectilictis made it very clear that it was my duty to replace him. However, Aurata knew I didn't want to marry her and she took my reluctance as an attempt to exclude her from power."

"Was it?"

"If I'm honest, yes. It may sound arrogant, but if the Felynx wanted a peaceful reign, I had to do it alone. So she and Rufus teamed up against me. However, Aurata had a sweetness in her character that Rufus lacked. I think they genuinely loved each other, in their perverse way. And I loved them both, although we had strange ways of showing it. The Felynx were highly civilized, but complacent. We thought our civilization was eternal. I was blind, not to see the depth of resentment that Rufus had built up against our father." Mist sighed. "Or I saw, but didn't take enough notice."

His words slowed, as if following his thoughts into a private mire. "There can't be many things better designed to turn sons and daughters against parents than for the children to discover that their parents have lied to them."

"Mist?" Stevie said cautiously. "Can we finish this later? We're here."

She felt the car skid as she pulled up, the front wheel bouncing off the ledge of frozen grass that lined the lane. Their breath clouded the air as they got out. All around, the trees were leafless and salt-white, shedding a fine rain of frost. Stevie watched a couple of ducks slithering comically along the iron surface of the stream.

As Mist set foot on the road, he slipped and flailed madly before saving himself by grabbing the car roof. Stevie couldn't suppress a grin. "Careful," she said. "Work your way around to the grass. We should have brought ice skates."

She held out her gloved hand and he took it, his bare fingers white with cold. Grass blades broke like spun sugar under their boots. The earth beneath was rock-hard.

They crunched their way up the gravel drive, Stevie carrying Daniel's belongings packed in a large sports bag. Professor Manifold opened the front door. She was wearing a thick sweater that hung on her bony frame, with brown slacks and furry slippers resembling Eskimo boots. Her hair was limp, her face drawn tight and bloodless. Humphrey the spaniel came bounding out, barking excitedly at Mist, who stared as if he'd never seen a dog before.

"Hello, Stephanie and er . . . Mist, is it?"

Stevie had told her on the phone that she was bringing a "friend," even though the truth was that she still barely knew him.

"I'm pleased to meet you, Professor Manifold," he said, low and polite.

The professor pinned him with a sharp stare. "So, I understand you don't actually know Daniel? You can't shed any light?"

Before he could answer, she stepped back to beckon them in. "I'm sorry, I'm not giving you a chance, am I? It's so difficult . . . Do come in. It's not much warmer inside, but I'll get the fire going."

"So you've still heard nothing from him?" Stevie asked.

"Obviously not."

The house felt even gloomier and colder than Stevie recalled. Darkness massed in the stairwell, seeming to watch and move like an observant predator. It gave off a faint, unpleasant scent, like cold metal. She felt the shift of reality that presaged one of her episodes, as if a vast serpent was circling the space above their heads . . . With all her will, she shook it off.

The only spark of life was Humphrey, running around the big living room with a ball in his mouth. Frances kneeled down by the fire grate. Her hands shook as she tried to light matches, swearing under her breath as they broke or sputtered out. Mist crouched beside her and rebuilt the bird's nest of crumpled newspaper and firewood into a neat stack. He took the matches and soon the paper was lit, flames licking the wood. He began to add coal.

Frances let him take over. "You have the magic touch," she said. "I'll put the kettle on."

Stevie hung up their coats and followed her into the kitchen. Frances had known she was bringing her son's belongings, but when she saw the bag, her face turned grey.

"This is horrible." She took the burden and placed it on the kitchen table, resting both hands on top. "Like receiving someone's possessions after they've died. It's too real."

"It's only a few old clothes," said Stevie. "It can't be everything he owned. There's no wallet or passport."

Frances snorted. "That appalling landlord probably took anything of value." Slowly she undid the zipper and took out a stack of paint-blotched shirts and jeans, using both hands as if lifting a small child. The look on her face was ghastly. Behind her, the kettle began to hiss and rattle on the stove.

"I felt the pockets from the outside, but didn't stick my hand in. I thought you should do that, not me. Oh, there's an old sketchbook in there, too, from the studio."

Frances Manifold said nothing, only stood with the clothes in her arms, eyes closed. Stevie felt a dangerous surge of tears. She hurried to rescue the kettle and busied herself assembling teapot, cups and milk on a tray. She had to hunt for sugar. There seemed to be almost no food in the cupboards.

Finally Frances spoke, her voice hoarse. "Who's the man with you? Boyfriend? I didn't take in a word you said on the phone. My fault, but it's hard to concentrate these days. Please, tell me again."

"He's not my boyfriend." It was agony to witness Frances's pain and suppressed anger, but Stevie had no idea how to soothe her.

She'd worked up a plausible story in her head, but now couldn't get the words out. Telling the full truth was impossible, especially about the theft of the triptych.

"I bumped into him at the empty studio. Mist had wanted to see Daniel's work. We got talking, and he agreed to help me look for him."

All true, but unconvincing.

Frances placed her son's clothes on the table and was feeling gingerly into pockets as if expecting to find wraps of cocaine, or worse. All that came out was a piece of lined paper, folded in four. Frances looked at it, frowning.

"A shopping list," she said. "Milk, bread, tinned tuna . . . No fruit or veg. Typical."

"He always ate healthily at college," said Stevie, only to fill the silence. "He loved vegan stuff, like tabbouleh. No wonder he was as thin as a pole."

The professor stared straight through her. The look was hostile, almost unhinged. Stevie withered inwardly. *No. Steady and calm. I can handle this.*

"One thing I found out," she said. "Daniel apparently knew a guy called Oliver?"

"Oh, him." Frances's mouth pulled down as if reacting to a foul taste.

"He's the one Daniel brought here once. A sleazy-looking specimen with bleached hair. He didn't look like any kind of art lover to me."

"Who do you think he was?" Stevie asked.

"I believe he was providing Daniel with the illegal substances he stupidly thought he needed in order to work harder. Yes, Oliver was the subject of our most spectacular argument. The last argument, in fact. But the police can't trace him. They thought Daniel might have gone abroad, but there's no record of him leaving the country."

"Unless he got a fake passport," Stevie murmured.

"That's speculation," Frances said through her teeth. "I need facts. Facts."

"Can I ask you something?" Stevie kept her tone quiet but firm. "Do you automatically think the worst of Danny's friends?"

"Oh, for goodness' sake." Frances turned away, as if to dismiss her question as childish. Stevie was determined not to back down.

"Please. You never liked me, either. Was I rude? Badly dressed?"

"I didn't dislike you." Frances folded her arms, cleared her lungs with a low, rattly cough. Color crept into her gaunt cheeks. Embarrassment, or annoyance. "You were too polite, if anything. Too eager to please."

"I was nervous."

"Of what? You weren't right for Daniel. I was hardly going to encourage you."

"Maybe that's true, seeing as we broke up, but all the same—what made me *not right*? This is all connected," Stevie persisted. She found a packet of chocolate-chip cookies and arranged some on a plate. "Frances, I can't help unless you're straight with me."

"Very well, if you insist." Her arms were folded tightly around herself and her expression was barren. "As with Oliver, there was something dishonest about you."

"Dishonest?" All her breath rushed out.

"Evasive, then. Disingenuous."

"I—I never told you any lies. Why would I?"

"Well, I don't *know*," Frances said in a tone of exasperation. "It's more what you omitted to say. Don't forget, I've worked with students for many years and I've seen every shade of fakery; nothing gets past me. My son had problems, and the last thing he needed was an equally damaged girlfriend."

"*What?*"

"You did ask." Frances sighed through her teeth. "Since you won't come clean, I will. When Daniel was about sixteen, I took him to a psychologist, Dr. Gregory. I know you were seeing him, too."

Stevie felt as if she'd been punched in the gut. "How? Dr. Gregory can't have told you! That's a breach of trust. He wouldn't!"

"He didn't," Frances cut her off. "It was your then-foster-mother. On one occasion, I happened to sit beside her in the waiting area; she seemed a decent type, harassed, not terribly bright and enormously indiscreet. She regaled me with her concerns. You were the most difficult charge she'd ever had; you'd been found wandering the streets, you were virtually feral, no one could identify you, and you were severely disturbed, to the point of destructive behavior such as flooding the bathroom—not to mention physically attacking her son." Frances's face tightened. "I saw you emerge from the consulting room. Daniel was skulking in the hospital shop at the time, so he didn't see you. I thought no more of it until a couple of years later, when he brought you home."

Stevie fought for words. "But that—that was private. You don't know . . ."

"*Two* people with psychiatric issues hardly made a healthy combination. Perhaps I judged you unfairly, but I had to put my son first."

"So you wrote me off as damaged? I cared about Daniel. All I care about now is helping you find him. You don't actually know anything about me!"

"That's rather the point," Frances said frigidly.

Dumbstruck by a mixture of fury and shame, Stevie slammed the plate of cookies down on the tray, and walked out.

Outside, Stevie leaned against the side wall of the house, staring at the frosted garden. Trees and shrubs sparkled like a magic forest. Within seconds she was shivering. The cold made her head ache. She folded her arms around herself and blew out a stream of condensed breath.

After a minute, she heard the crunch of footsteps and Mist appeared. He leaned on the wall beside her and said, "What are you doing?"

"I don't know," she said tersely. "I just can't talk to her."

"I overheard your conversation." His tone was mild and apologetic.

"Oh, great. Now you both think I'm some kind of delinquent nutcase. I shouldn't have stormed out, but she's impossible. We're trying to help her, yet all she can do is drag up horrors from ten years ago? She condemns me for not telling her stuff that she knew all along?"

"She's upset," said Mist. "I'm sure she didn't mean to hurt you."

"But she's right. I have been dishonest by trying to cover up my past. I thought I had a right to keep my problems to myself, but the prof doesn't see it like that. She has a mind like a scalpel. She labeled me as broken and deceitful, and that really stings. But you know what? I pushed her to tell me why I wasn't good enough for Daniel. If I couldn't take the answer, I shouldn't have asked the question."

Mist leaned on the wall beside her, listening so intently that he might have been Dr. Gregory. She hugged herself a little harder. His coat hung open like a dark wing and his warmth shielded her left side. His irises were pale, reflecting the frosted world in miniature.

"Please come back inside. You're frozen."

She didn't move. "Mist, I need to understand what's happening. It's not just her. It's you, too. All the strange things you've told me . . . it's making my head hurt."

He blinked, his long eyelashes coal-black against the pale eyes. He was all contrasts: soft sooty blackness and ice, warmth and remoteness.

"I'm as confused as you, Stevie. If this is connected to Rufus, maybe he's already watching me and I've led his followers to you, which is why you were attacked. My fault." He briefly closed his eyes. "And if that's the case, I'm so sorry."

"Rufus has *followers*? Like a rock star, you mean?"

Mist grimaced. "He attracts people, and uses them. They worship him, run around doing his bidding, and the more he abuses them the more they love him. But what can he want with Daniel?" His eyes narrowed. "I'm sure Professor Manifold is hiding something. Stevie, there's a bad presence in the house. Didn't you feel it?"

"Oh." The ground swayed beneath her. "Yes, I noticed a shadowy shape in the stairwell above the hall, but I see apparitions all the time. I assume it's my brain playing tricks."

"No. I think that when you see things, you're probably seeing into the Dusklands."

"Am I?"

"Whatever's in the house is real, and menacing. It's some kind of malign elemental that's been drawn here for a reason. Whether it's followed us, or was already here, I'm not sure. Finding out is more important than tiptoeing around Professor Manifold's grief."

"Mist, you sound a bit crazy. And possibly, underneath your friendly act, as ruthless as your brother."

That made him pause. "I'm trying to put things right," he said tightly. "All Rufus can do is destroy."

"And for you, this is all about Rufus," she stated. "For me, it's about Frances and Daniel. I don't care how eccentric he was, I loved him. I still do."

He gave a slight smile. "Oh, I thought you were in love with the wonderful Sri Lankan doctor?"

He was teasing her. The nerve. "Shut up. That was wishful thinking."

Mist moved closer to her, slid one arm around her shoulders so she was inside his coat. "What are you doing?" she gasped.

"Trying to stop you shivering."

His warmth felt wonderful. She could feel the lean strong lines of his body through his thick sweater and dark trousers, and he smelled subtly delicious, like clean cotton and shampoo. She kept still, trying to uncouple her mind from her body's pleasurable reaction.

He said, "There's only one way to persuade Frances to open up, and that is honesty. We need to place all our cards on the table, or whatever the saying is."

"I'm not even sure what our cards are."

"You go first, Stevie. Explain why you were secretive in the past and try to make peace. If you speak plainly, then we both can."

"You make it sound easy."

"Is it so bad?"

"No, but it's *private*."

"I need to know what it is she's not telling us. For her own sake, as much as ours," he went on. "You don't want to leave her alone with that shadow presence, do you?"

"Good god, no, of course not, but what can we do?" She stood back in shock, using the movement to free herself from the all-too-pleasant embrace of his coat. "You aren't seriously going to tell her what you told me in the car, are you? How will that help?"

Mist looked thoughtful and somber. "It's a risk. Either she'll think I'm mad and throw us out, or she'll admit she knows something. I don't know if she'll listen, or if I can trust her. Or if you're ever going to stop glaring at me."

"Am I glaring?" She lowered her gaze. "Sorry."

"I promise I won't overwhelm her. If she has a question, I'll answer it. I know everything I've told you sounds incredible, and I feel I'm trying to rush you into believing me before you're ready. You don't *have* to accept what I say, even on Dame Juliana's word. Just . . . bear with me?"

"That's exactly what I'm doing." With all her heart she wanted to believe him. His fluent, undramatic narrative had sounded true, but there was still no guarantee that he wasn't the most charmingly smooth con man she'd ever met. She inhaled, letting the wintry air cool her emotions. Her anger at Frances and her feelings for Mist fell away. "The way you talk about Aetherials and suchlike is highly plausible, even to an average skeptic like me. But I'm warning you, you'll find Frances an infinitely tougher audience. Still, nothing ventured . . ." She smiled, and was gratified to receive a warm, bright smile in response. "Are you ready? Come on, Mist, let's do this."

Humphrey came running to meet them, his tail wagging so hard that his whole body was in sinuous motion. Frances Manifold was poking listlessly at the fire. The living room felt warmer, the drab walls mellow with creamy-orange firelight. Humphrey sat down at Mist's feet, gazing upward and making tiny jerks as if to plead in vain, *Let's play!*

Frances straightened up and said, to Stevie's surprise, "Are you all right, my dear? I don't blame you for walking out: I deserved it. I'm so sorry. Please come and have some tea while it's still hot. It's all my fault."

"What is?" asked Stevie.

"That Daniel went. I should have kept my opinions to myself. He was fragile. He must have felt I was suffocating him."

That, Stevie suspected, was close to the truth.

Awkwardly, she and Mist sat on a sagging couch with the professor facing them across a low table. Frances was like a wraith haunting the deserted shell of a house. Her spaniel pushed his tawny head into her hand as if to anchor her to life.

Stevie poured tea, trying to regain her poise. Her hands, by a miracle, were steady. "Can I explain why I was seeing Dr. Gregory?"

"You needn't."

"I'd really like to. Frances, I couldn't tell you about my background because I don't remember." Stevie took a breath. "I was found wandering in the countryside on the outskirts of Birmingham. Even that's a blur."

Frances's forehead wrinkled with doubt. "Stephanie, I know Dr. Gregory. He's a decent, professional man. He told me true amnesia is a myth. You must have memories, but you've blocked them out, for some reason."

"That's what he told me, too, but the effect is the same. It's called psychogenic memory loss. They estimated me to be about fifteen. The police took me to a psychiatric ward, where an array of doctors and social workers spent months trying to discover my identity. Nothing. So I was put with various foster families, who couldn't cope with me because I kept doing unhelpful things like flooding the bathroom."

"Why?"

"I didn't mean to be troublesome, but I had a fixation with water that I can't explain. It's blurry. I was frightened. In the foster homes, I often got pestered by older boys. I avoided being assaulted or raped, only because I fought back so hard I left bruises. Then they'd turn on a crybaby act, and I'd get the blame and labeled as aggressive. I don't want pity," she added sharply. "I'm stating facts. They sent me to school, but I felt too old to be there, out of place. Eventually I ran away, and found a job waitressing, earning enough to rent a tiny room. It was like . . . relearning how to live, I suppose. That was when I met Daniel. I must have been seventeen by then and I wanted . . . to be a normal person."

As she spoke, Mist was turning the pages of Daniel's sketchbook. He even studied the old shopping list, smoothing it flat on the coffee table.

"You remembered your name, though?" Frances put in.

"No, I chose my name. Stephanie, after a policewoman who was kind to me, and Silverwood because my first memory was of silver birch trees around me. That was my new identity."

"It's not easy to function without a birth certificate."

"I know, but not impossible. They sorted new documents for me."

Stevie described meeting Daniel, and how they'd started talking. "He was so happy about going to art college, absolutely glowing. He helped me produce some tolerable artwork, and Dr. Gregory wrote a persuasive reference. I was awarded a sort of vocational, give-her-a-chance place, thanks to my tough start in life. The first year was hard. Then I switched to the jewelry and metalwork course, and never looked back."

Frances made a *hmph* noise of acceptance. "Well, I'm glad they were more charitable than me."

"I can't emphasize enough that Daniel helped me to rejoin the human race. After college, I found jobs managing art materials and jewelry stores. I fell in love with the Jewellery Quarter and the museum, and made myself so indispensable that I ended up running the place."

"Quite a story," said Frances, her voice very soft.

"So all the bad stuff was twelve, thirteen years ago. My past is not who I am."

She stopped, finding it hard to catch her breath. Her memories—not least the missing ones—still opened a pit of fearful emotion inside her.

"Stephanie," said Frances in a small, dry voice, "truly, I'm sorry. I'm controlling, overprotective and intolerably overbearing. What you went through was dreadful. I should have been more understanding."

"It doesn't matter. The point is to clear the air and be honest. Mist thinks he knows—"

Humphrey barked. Cold air moved through the room, strong enough to shift the coals in the grate and nearly extinguish the flames. Again Stevie sensed the intrusive, writhing snake shadow. The fire recovered, but the spaniel continued growling at nothing. Stevie and Mist exchanged a quick, dark glance.

"I swear this bloody house is haunted," said Frances. "Sometimes I'll enter a room and see Daniel's father standing there, as clear as day, but he does *not* indulge in cold drafts and door-slamming antics. As if my nerves aren't shredded enough. Humphrey, silence!"

Without reacting, Mist pressed his fingers to the shopping list Frances had retrieved from her son's pocket. Stevie looked sideways and read the last few items out loud. "Toothpaste. Detergent. Bleach."

"I know," Frances said in an arid tone. "What single young man thinks to buy cleaning products? He was strangely domesticated, more so than me. Oh, I mustn't say *was*! He *is* domesticated. But it's just a list." She paused to cough. "What of it?"

"A name," Mist said softly. At the bottom of the page, a word had been neatly printed with a different pen, and a curved arrow drawn above it. "Poectilictis."

"What does that mean?" asked Frances.

"Poectilictis was the name of my father." Mist frowned, rubbing his fore-head. "How could your son possibly have known it?"

Her thin eyebrows rose. "I have absolutely no idea."

"And this." He showed her the sketchbook page with a pencil drawing of a carved stone disk. "What was his source for this object?"

"Oh, good lord." Frances's voice was croaky. Her face turned bone-pale. "You'd better come upstairs and take a look in his room."

It felt strange to be in Daniel's bedroom again. Stevie recalled times they'd spent on the narrow bed; usually talking, but occasionally—if his mother happened to be out—naked under the covers. Standing here beside Frances, she turned warm with embarrassment.

Nothing appeared to have changed. There was a bookshelf with a couple of worn teddy bears on top, a chest of drawers supporting a glass-fronted case containing fossils, *Doctor Who* figurines and some small sculptures Danny had made.

Mist went to the glass-fronted case and laid his hand on the door. Stevie saw his breathing quicken. "It's here," he said. "May I?"

"Please, go ahead." Frances waved a resigned hand. "You're so polite. It seems bad-mannered to disbelieve the tales you're telling me."

On their way upstairs, he'd told her only a bare outline of the Felynx story. That he came from a prehuman, lost city, Azantios; that he was trying to find his brother, Rufus, who might be the source of Daniel's ideas; and that he would not be offended if Frances didn't believe him.

Far from challenging him, Frances simply listened, uttering an occasional, wet cough that made Stevie worry that she'd got bronchitis. Perhaps she lacked the strength to argue, or even to concentrate fully on what he was saying.

He opened the door and took an object from the middle of a glass shelf. It was a thick disk of quartz, eight inches across and three deep. And it was heavy, from the way Mist lifted it in both hands. Stevie couldn't recall ever seeing it before, except in the sketchbook.

For long moments, he was so intent on the object that he seemed to have forgotten the others were there. Stevie looked over his shoulder. The disk was whitish and translucent, like rainbow moonstone, carved with stylized, inter-locking images of leopards and birds.

A color-changing sheen danced through the crystal, blue-green chased by fiery orange. Mist turned the object over and over between his hands. His ink-black eyelashes were wet.

"Professor, can I ask how Daniel found this?"

"He didn't. I unearthed it a couple of years ago. Fossils are my thing, not man-made artifacts, so I passed it to the archaeology bods at uni. They concluded it's what they call a UCSO, an 'unidentified carved stone object.' Possibly a forgery—you know, like the crystal skulls that turned out to be fifty and not five thousand years old, or whatever the figures were? So I kept it. A curiosity. I've never seen it change color before."

She sat down on the edge of Daniel's bed, fingers worrying at the edge of the duvet.

"And where did you find it?"

"On a dig in the States. We took some students on a field trip to Nevada. Why?"

Mist ran his fingertips over the carvings. "I recognize it. This is part of an item I thought was lost thousands of years ago. It's only the base, but still important. This might be the connection."

"So you found it, Frances, and Daniel made drawings," said Stevie. "Perhaps all the images and names are on it, in tiny detail, and that's how he came across them."

Mist was shaking his head. "No, they're not. But he might have picked up some kind of resonance from the stone."

"Resonance?" Frances moistened her lips, looking paler by the second. "What on earth are you suggesting?"

Mist sighed, "I don't know." His expression became apologetic and confused, which made him look less otherworldly and more endearingly human.

"No, let me clarify," said Frances. "Daniel didn't draw the UCSO after I brought it home. He was drawing it for years before I found it."

"*Before?*" they said together.

Stevie and Mist went still, waiting for her to continue. "He began after he met you, Stephanie. He also made some sketches of a distinctive landscape like you see in cowboy movies: desert scrub, mountains and buttes. I thought nothing of it, until I was actually in Nevada. One evening, I climbed the shoulder of a hill and saw the exact landscape Daniel had drawn. I assumed he'd seen photos in a magazine."

Frances broke off, wheezing slightly. "Normally I'm the most skeptical old curmudgeon on the planet. It was an ordinary dig, hot and tiring. I spent most of trip supervising students, helping them to identify fossils in the shale, to tell their ammonites from their cornellites. Strange things do not happen to me."

"Except this once?" Stevie asked softly.

Frances seemed irritated that she had to confess. She described waking in her tent to a strange glow and looking out to see the sky filled with golden columns; knowing she was dreaming, but stepping outside anyway.

The light resembled the aurora borealis, she said, but the fiery towers rose from earth to heaven all around her, as if she walked through curtains of light.

"I woke to find myself in the open, lying in a small ravine. In my hand was a lump of stone. I rubbed off the dust and dirt to reveal this carved tablet . . . exactly like the ones in Daniel's drawings."

"You saw Azantios," Mist said softly. "Did you find any ruins?"

"No ruins. Only crumpled rocks. The works of nature, not man."

"Of course." There was a trace of sorrow in his voice. "The city's fabric dissolved into the Dusklands."

"I've no energy to decide whether I believe your theories or not," Frances said thinly. "The experience shook me up quite severely. Visions of long-lost alien cities do not happen to cynical old bats like me. I may be in denial, but that was why I didn't want such things happening to Daniel. It's not pleasant. People lose their minds over less."

Mist pressed on, "Did Daniel consciously know what he was painting, or was he simply a cipher? It feels like there's a force trying to reveal Felynx secrets, and an opposing force trying to suppress them. Perhaps not Rufus at all."

"Who, then?" Stevie asked. Mist gave no answer.

Frances looked so exhausted that Stevie decided they should leave. There was no easy way to tell her that an intruder had taken *Aurata's Promise*, and no need to unload more stress onto her.

She'd no sooner made the decision than Mist said it anyway. "Someone found out Stevie had Daniel's remaining work, the triptych, and stole it." He touched the stone tablet. "Whoever it was may come for this, too. If they are not already here."

The pale furrows of her face deepened.

"Well, take the damned thing away, then," she said. "I don't care if it's genuine or priceless. I want no more of this. I want my son back, full stop." Her voice grew hoarse and ended on a rattle. A couple of coughs became a violent spasm that shook her until her eyes streamed and blood sputtered from her mouth. Stevie supported her bird-thin form with one arm and thrust her cell phone at Mist.

"Call an ambulance."

9

Fela and the Lie

Stevie dropped Mist near the city center at his request, and she was glad. Exhausted, she couldn't face any more intense conversation. She needed solitude. As she pulled up in front of the museum, she noticed with horror that it was six o' clock. Fin was standing in the doorway, looking distinctly irritated.

"Stevie!"

"I know, I know. It's unforgivable. I'm so sorry—it's been a nightmare. The roads are icy . . ."

"You could have phoned."

"I didn't think." Stevie hurried to hand over the car keys.

"I tried to call you, but it went to voicemail. I was worried!"

"Fin, I apologize with all my heart. Daniel's mother is really sick. We had to call an ambulance and they took her to Derby. She's got pneumonia. And I had to find someone to look after Humphrey, her dog—that's all she was fretting about in the ambulance—so I had to go back to her house. Fortunately one of her neighbors took Humphrey in. Bloody hell, what a day."

"My god, is she going to be okay?"

"I hope so. It's probably the best thing for her, because she wasn't looking after herself properly, but she's in a bad way. Now I *have* to find Daniel, in case . . . Anyway, Fin, I'm sorry."

Fin sighed. "It's all right. Andy picked up the kids, and you're okay, thank goodness. But honestly, Stevie, we can't make a habit of this. Next time, get a taxi or hire a car . . ."

"Or grow wings," said Stevie. She pushed a twenty-pound note into Fin's hand, vowing to add a large box of chocolates and a bottle of wine. "It won't happen again. You have my word."

"You're forgiven. I hope Daniel's mum gets better soon. Now go home, and don't you dare show your face at work before Tuesday. Doctor's orders, not mine, remember?"

Stevie had no answer. Cold and tired, she waved Fin off, then made her way around the building and up the steps to her front door.

Alone in her apartment, Stevie felt jumpy. In the four days since the theft, she hadn't felt safe anywhere. Yet the intruder had taken what he wanted and gone; surely there was no need to break in again? Mist had taken the mysterious stone disk, but would that put *him* in danger instead?

She firmly suppressed her fears. Her door was securely locked. She refused to feel vulnerable.

Supper was a microwave-heated shepherd's pie, a wrinkled apple and a glass of cold white wine. She tried to watch television, but could only fret about Frances. She might have collapsed anyway, and not been found for days—yet Stevie couldn't help feeling that the stress of their visit had tipped Frances over the edge.

In the corner of her eye, the small uncanny leopard lay flicking its tail. "Oh well, you save me a fortune on cat food and vets' bills," she murmured.

On a sudden thought, she jumped up and grabbed her laptop. Swiftly she typed a new regime for locking up the museum. From now on, no one must close up alone. She was more worried about her colleagues than herself, but she'd have to introduce the system subtly, so as not to arouse their suspicion . . . She saved the document, then opened the web browser and made a fresh search for Daniel.

Nothing. His profile had vanished from the Jellybean Factory website. Even the thumbnail of *Aurata's Promise* had been replaced by a red X. She groaned.

"What are we going to do, puss?" she said sideways to her companion. "Three more days before I'm allowed back to work."

Three days to find Daniel and tell him, "Cut the diva act and get back here *now* before your mother dies."

With a sense of urgency, she opened a new blank document and began typing Mist's story. He'd told her more on the journey back, and she wanted to record it before she forgot the details. The keys rattled under her fingertips. She knew that for every sentence Mist uttered, there were several pages unspoken, with a mass of mental footnotes. His shadowy, otherworldly grace lent credence to his words . . . while Daniel, who'd been lovable, shortsighted, and as mad as a box of polecats, was as plainly human as could be.

So how the hell had he painted Mist's life story, without ever meeting him?

Mist walked around the city center for a while, to avoid his empty hotel room. The stores were shut, the pubs and bars busy. Coarse de-icing salt crunched under his boot soles. At least he knew that Frances Manifold was safe from the entity that had been prowling her house. The presence, he suspected, was some form of barely sentient hunter, trained to sniff out a very particular trail: the aura of items or people connected with Azantios. Which meant that *someone* must have sent it.

In his coat pocket, the base of the Felixatus felt heavy and warm, tingling with its own life. He sat down on a wet bench and closed his eyes . . .

Mistangamesh looked up at the sun, seeing its brilliance dimmed to a flat white disk by veils of orange dust. Azantios lay behind him. From the viewing platform—a high natural ledge of rock—he surveyed the realms of the Felynx. In the far distance, mountains plunged towards steamy blue-green forests, wetlands and lakes. Closer lay a tumbled red landscape of canyons and tall, sculptural rock formations: Fire Valley, they'd named it. All around him, the ledges and slopes were covered by a shifting mass of Felynx, proud and beautiful in shimmering garments, their striped cat faces crowned with shining manes of hair.

Rufus and Aurata were with him, all three dressed in finery befitting their status as members of House Ephenaestus. This was a special day marking the climax of the racing season. The ultimate race was in progress. The air shimmered with heat and excitement.

The runners were all Tashralyr, a different clan of Aetherials who dwelled in the distant wetlands. They'd inhabited this area even longer than the Felynx, and generally the two clans had little to do with each other. The Felynx kept to their great city and the Tashralyr lived wild, but they had an interest in common: the Tashralyr were natural athletes who loved to race. Over the centuries, the Felynx had grown fascinated by their sport and were now enthusiastic spectators, placing bets, and even sponsoring their own favorites.

The event was in three parts, a race devised long ago by the Tashralyr for their own pleasure and now regarded by the Felynx as a thrilling yet deadly serious entertainment. First, the competitors swam across a vast blue lake. Next they undertook a grueling climb to the peak of a tall red hill. At each stage, weaker entrants were eliminated. Last, only the toughest remained to race flat-out around the challenging terrain of Fire Valley.

Now a sandstorm came pouring towards the spectators. The cheers of ten thousand Felynx rose in a roar. From the center of the cloud, the runners surged like a single, undulating fleece. The Tashralyr ran on all fours, their long legs a blur, paws barely skimming the ground as they flowed towards the finish line. Orange dust caked their silvery fur. Felynx race officials stood waiting at the finish line: a golden thread stretched between two spires of rock.

The favorite, Karn, was in the lead. Rufus pushed forward to cheer him on. Mist, caught in the moment, shouted for his own runner.

"What a surprise," Aurata said over Mist's shoulder. "Karn always wins."

"Because he has the best patron!" Rufus retorted. "Of course he's unbeatable. He's mine."

"Unbeatable, only because there's no competition," she said, giving Mist a smile behind Rufus's back.

"Jealousy doesn't become you, sister," said Rufus. "It's not my fault you have a nose for also-rans."

Karn was two lengths ahead of the pack when a dark muzzle drew alongside his paler one. Another Tashralyr was gaining. Then—impossibly—beginning to pass him. The cheering swelled, stoked to a climax by surprise. The outsider broke the finish ribbon, winning by a full body length.

"Who's that?" yelled Rufus, outraged. "Who in the name of all the stars is that?"

"I don't know," said Aurata, "but I lay claim. From now on, he or she is *mine*."

And she was off the rock and running downhill through the crowd, her fiery hair streaming. Rufus and Mist followed her, the Felynx crowd parting for the scions of House Ephenaestus.

Down in the valley, they entered the competitors' enclosure—a natural hollow in a canyon wall—where only athletes and their patrons were allowed. The Felynx race marshals let them through with respectful nods.

Stragglers were skidding in, panting for breath, while a crowd formed around Karn and the unknown victor. Mist congratulated his own runner, Tamis, who'd made a respectable third. He watched the exhausted Tashralyr beginning to unfold from their running form—long and lithe, silver fur dark with sweat, flanks heaving—into bipedal shape. Stretched feline heads flattened, manes became hair, paws morphed into hands. They kept the subtle grey coloring that distinguished them from the bright red-golds of the Felynx.

"Who is the winner?" Aurata called out.

One of the marshals said, "Her name is Fela."

"Let me congratulate her. Does she have—Fela, do you have a sponsor? I don't care who they are, I'll buy them out."

The calm face looked into Aurata's and smiled. "No, Lady Aurata, I have no patron."

"Well, now you do. We thought Karn was unbeatable. Why have we never seen you before?"

"It was my first race," Fela said modestly. "Karn is my friend. He encouraged me to enter."

"A decision he no doubt regrets," said Mist. He observed Fela's quiet pride and Aurata's swift claim of ownership: he saw Rufus with his arm around his own competitor's shoulders, Rufus glowering, Karn merely resigned.

"What went wrong?" Rufus demanded. "That was quite a loss of form."

"No loss of form," Karn answered. "I swam, climbed and ran as hard as I have in my life. Fela pushed me to the limit. She was better, that's all."

"Oh no, not good enough. We can't let this happen again, can we?" Rufus grinned menacingly at Karn, kissed him on the cheek. "Defeat is not in our plan, is it, my friend?"

Strange days, Mist reflected on his cold bench. *We may not have enslaved or abused the Tashralyr, but still we used them for entertainment . . . as if they were racehorse and jockey all in one being. Or as traveling acrobats visiting a royal court . . . to be feted one moment, discarded the next.*

He remembered the parade back to the palace. Fela, Karn and Tamis, wreathed in flowers, were borne high by the Felynx crowd. Sunlight shone through the dust as it settled like layers of glowing lace. Beneath a bright turquoise sky, the spires of Azantios shone yellow, orange and diamond-white, reaching up to the heavens as if weightless.

Mist trailed behind his brother and sister, amused in a jaded way by their endless bickering. They tried to bait him into taking sides, but he stayed aloof. Let them behave like children if it pleased them.

"How dare you snatch Fela from under my nose?" said Rufus.

"Dear Rufe, you have no automatic right to pluck the finest fruit," Aurata replied. "You have Karn, who has won and won to the point of tedium. Until today."

"He should have warned us about Fela."

"You are such a sore loser. Don't take it out on poor Karn." Aurata put her hand through her sulking brother's arm. "Don't discard him. I know what you're like. Don't boot him out of your patronage—or out of your bed—over one small *defeat*."

"Ah, sister. Are you interested in this Fela purely for her athletic prowess, or for other reasons?"

"She is very lovely," said Aurata, eyes narrowing. "And now she is *mine*. Remember that, Rufus. No trespassing."

Mist sighed to himself. While his brother and sister played their games, he never forgot that, if all went as planned, he would become Sovereign Elect. That meant no wild behavior to embarrass Poectilictis. He'd had only a very few, discreet lovers, and certainly had never taken his athlete Tamis to his bed. Aurata and Rufus cordially despised him for being straitlaced, and punished him by teasing, goading him, and worse. And he couldn't deny that, sometimes, their casual malice hurt.

On glowing evenings like this, however, they forgot such pettiness. Rufus and Aurata slipped their hands through Mist's arms, and the three of them drifted up the steep winding ways towards the palace with a huge train of followers, anticipating the evening of celebration, drink and pleasure ahead.

They were happy. The Felynx lived in a golden dream that could never end.

"There can't be many things better designed to turn sons and daughters against parents than for the children to discover that their parents have lied to them."

Stevie rapidly typed Mist's words. On the drive home, he'd explained what he meant.

"The lie was this," he told her. "No one told us that the Spiral existed. We, the Felynx, were given to believe that Azantios was everything. No one explained that we were exiles from the Otherworld, a vast Aetherial realm that was as much our birthright as that of other Aelyr."

He described Earth, or Vaeth, as a closed globe, while the Spiral was a ragged, ever-changing structure like the whorls of a snail shell. The two formed a double kingdom of outer and inner worlds, joined at powerful nodes of energy. Aetherial evolution was mysterious. First came the serene entity known as Estel the Eternal, then the sentient energies, Qesoth and Brawth, followed by the primal Estalyr, and then their descendants, the Aelyr in their various forms.

"We were told only the evolution part," said Mist. "Other realms were never mentioned. Only three people knew the truth: my parents, and Veropardus, the Keeper of the Felixatus.

"We were complacent," he added ruefully. "Vulnerable, because we had no predators and therefore no natural defenses. Death was rare to us, more a transformation in which the individual fades into a different state . . . but if we couldn't enter the Spiral, where did our lost ones go?"

He'd left the question in the air, although Stevie knew it was connected to what he said next. From Mist's description, and from the image in Daniel's triptych, she visualized the Felixatus as a mechanism of nested globes and lenses, its purpose unknown. "The tallest spire of the palace contained a chamber where the Felixatus was kept, pointing at the stars like a telescope," Mist went on. "Veropardus wasn't a priest, as such, because we didn't worship gods. He was the guardian of our sacred mysteries."

"But why did they keep you in the dark?" Stevie had asked as she drove.

"We were curious, of course. Poectilictis would have told me, as his heir, when the time came. I was content to wait, but secrets drove Rufus mad. He argued constantly with Poectilictis. Our mother would try to make peace, to no avail. Anyway, something changed. Rufus illicitly entered the Felixatus chamber. Somehow, he discovered the truth. He told Aurata first, and they both came to me raging that the whole Felynx race had been lied to."

Mist turned the stone disk over in his hands, and half-smiled. "Actually, it's all written on here, if you know how to read the symbols. Our founders, the first of the Felynx, had been expelled from the Otherworld. They'd quarreled with Queen Malikala of Naamon, who ruled the entire Spiral for eons, refusing to accept her authority. She could have destroyed them. Instead they agreed to exile on Vaeth, on condition that they never crossed back into

Naamon again. So they settled in a place with no portals nearby, founded Azantios, and let the Felynx multiply in ignorance.

"I've learned since that there were Aetherial settlements all over Vaeth, like a fine silver cobweb. Those societies rose and fell as successive ice ages engulfed them. Their inhabitants hibernated as ice elementals until the world warmed again. Then they'd find their cities long gone, swallowed by jungle and rain forest, and they'd move on. But in the golden age of the Felynx, we knew none of this."

"You must have had some suspicion . . . ?" Stevie put in. Mist shook his head.

"We lived in a layer of reality between the Earth proper and the Dusk-lands, but we took that for granted. It didn't mean we suspected deeper realms . . . or other secrets to do with what we actually *are*." Mist hesitated, apparently deciding not to expand. "When Rufus found out, he was furious. If you consider yourself a privileged member of the master race, as he did, you might feel entitled to be omniscient."

"And what about you? Were you furious, too?"

"No. I assumed Poectilictis kept our history secret for good reasons. I trusted him. He was a good man."

He fell silent, plainly struggling. He flicked moisture from his eyelashes, and continued. "I wanted us to talk calmly in private. That wasn't Rufus's style; he had to create a drama. He accused our parents of betrayal. He in-sisted that access to the Otherworld was our birthright. He worked himself into a fair rage, while our father answered coldly that the secret had been kept for our own protection. If the Felynx began finding ways into the Spiral, it would breach an age-old agreement and might even cause a war. Rufus countered that it was humiliating to live as exiles, that we'd a right to enter Naamon. The debate went on and on.

"However, Rufus lacked power. He could send rumors running through the city, but if he was hoping for a rebellion, he was disappointed. Poectilictis was loved, Veropardus respected and feared, while Rufus merely had a repu-tation for causing trouble. Which some enjoyed, but no one took seriously."

"What about Theliome? You don't mention her much."

"Oh, she was very much loved too. She was formidable in her day, and also the kindest person I've ever known. But I think she'd grown tired by this stage. She was nearly ready to transform into an elemental state, and was only waiting for Poectilictis to join her." Mist fell quiet for a time.

"If my questions are painful, I'm sorry," Stevie said softly.

"No, it's a relief to talk about it. Theliome may have been tired, and in the process of detaching herself from us—but, gods, she still had strength."

Stevie thought of the god-like statues, side by side in the ruins of Azantios.

"So Rufus was angry: not much change there," Mist continued. "But then someone was murdered. Not Felynx, but an Aetherial of the Tashralyr *eretru* who lived down in the lakes and forests. We let them alone and saw no reason to enslave them, but when they came among us I suppose we treated them as . . . not inferior, but different, unsophisticated. We were refined city dwellers, and they ran wild in the woods."

"You were royalty and they were commoners?" said Stevie.

Mist groaned. "No. Yes, in a way, but it was more complex than that. They were athletes and we revered them for it, although it was obvious they could live quite happily without our attention. Anyway, this particular Tashralyr was a celebrity among us. When the body was found, it was an immense shock, because murder was almost unknown. For various reasons, Rufus was the obvious suspect. No one wanted to believe that he was guilty . . . so Poectilictis asked him outright, '*Did you do this?*'

"Rufus didn't answer. I've never seen such a look of hatred as the one he gave our father at that moment. The same day, he vanished.

"A bare few weeks later, a barbaric army invaded Azantios. We were unprepared, unarmed. Rufus had gone out among the primitive human tribes and gathered them all together; they must have seen him as a god stepping among them. He'd told them that we were vulnerable and ripe for the taking. And then he led them against us. They sacked the city, slaughtered hundreds of Felynx in the streets, set our homes afire. By the time the invaders broke into the palace and entered the throne room, Poectilictis and Theliome were seated in their thrones, waiting . . . already dead."

Stevie had frowned. "But when you say dead . . . how? You use the term rather loosely."

"I mean that their soul-essences had departed, leaving empty shells for the barbarians to find. They sacrificed themselves. They deliberately vacated their physical forms in order to use their soul-energies against the barbarians."

Daniel's triptych. He'd perfectly captured the invaders' death-by-terror as they confronted the towering god statues, while the citadel crumbled around them. And the carved symbols in the pillars seemed to convey a message, if only she could translate them.

Stevie got up and prowled the apartment—pacing from the cramped living area to her bedroom and back—as she recalled the end of Mist's narrative, and his pallor as he told her. His horror was raw, as if these events had happened yesterday.

Her spectral cat jumped onto her shoulder as she paced, as if to comfort her. It was weightless, but she could see it from the corner of her eye.

"It was too late for us to save ourselves, but Azantios held what you might call a self-destruct mechanism. Of course I tried to dissuade my parents from self-sacrifice, but their plan was set. My last words to my father were a promise that I'd never rest until I'd hunted Rufus down. Then Aurata, Veropardus

and I, with several others, barricaded ourselves in the Chamber of the Felixatus, and we worked a tenfold web to cause an earthquake that brought the
city down upon the barbarians' heads. We destroyed Azantios, rather than
let them take it.

"I crawled out of the ruins alone. Aurata and Veropardus died, along with
thousands of others. I don't know why I didn't perish with them. If their
soul-essences escaped and found their way into the Otherworld, to this day I
don't know. I never saw them again. Some days later, though, Rufus found
me. He was crazed. We both were. Was he sorry? He barely possessed the
intellect to grasp the enormity of what he'd done. Should I have killed him?
Yes, but I couldn't.

"You need to understand that these questions weren't important, because
when the ashes of the holocaust settled, we had nothing left except each
other."

Stevie knew there was more to the story, but Mist was beyond telling it.

She heard nothing from him over the weekend, but was so busy she
barely noticed. Twice a day she called the hospital to check on Frances; her
condition was poor, but stable. She phoned every acquaintance of Daniel she
could think of, without result. She visited her foster-grandmother, Nanny
Peg, and sat reading to her and holding her fragile hand—an activity that
warmed Stevie's heart, until Nanny Peg had turned to a nurse and said without guile, "Make this woman shut up."

Oh well. Oh well. Stevie bit down hard on tears and gently kissed Peg as
she left.

Very early on Tuesday, infinitely relieved that her sick leave was over, she
made her rounds of the factory. She said good morning to the unseen workers, then wandered through the upstairs gallery with a duster, cleaning
fingerprints from the glass domes that protected her beloved skeleton clocks.
Each one was a feat of engineering in its own right. One day she'd wrest
control of her workbench from Alec and begin a grand project of her own.
Just a dream, but it was heaven to be back.

Stevie was counting money into the till when Fin arrived early, looking
harrassed.

"Have they told you?"

"Good morning to you too. Told me what?"

Fin gave a pained grin. "We have to close on the dot of four. Trustees'
meeting. I wish they'd give us some notice."

"Oh, great," said Stevie. "They'll want quarterly figures, a breakdown of
visitor numbers, all the usual stuff—do they expect it out of thin air?"

"We'll do our best," said Fin. "They might at least bring you a bunch of flowers for your bad head. It's wonderful to have you back, by the way."

They bantered easily as they got ready to open. Soon Ron was there ready to greet visitors, and Margaret on café duty. Alec arrived late and ensconced himself at the clock-repair bench without a word to Stevie. Surely he wasn't still sulking from last week? She didn't care. It felt so good to return to normal that she floated on happiness.

All day the ghost cat sat on her shoulder, peering through the waves of her hair. Unsettling, but Stevie kept reminding herself that no one else could see it. The hours passed swiftly. With a pang she realized she'd barely thought about Daniel.

Since there was no boardroom, as soon as the museum shut at four they pushed furniture together in the café to create an official-looking table lined with chairs. She was helping Margaret to make tea and coffee as the trustees filed in: descendants of the Soames and Salter families and officials from the city council including her nominal boss, Ruth, the senior curator. Fifteen in all. A frantic effort between Stevie and Fin had produced the statistics they'd want to see, and she'd written a rushed but enthusiastic report full of ideas for the museum's future.

The trustees would not wrong-foot her with an unexpected meeting. Stevie was ready to greet them with refreshments, figures and a broad, friendly smile.

Her palms turned clammy when her smile was not returned.

"Sit down, Miss Silverwood," said one of the Soames grandsons, a florid man in his sixties. "The rest of the staff, would you mind waiting outside?"

Out went Fin, Ron and Margaret, radiating curiosity and tension. Alec, last to leave, folded his arms over his belly and gave her a flat, smug smile. Alone, Stevie sat in the spotlight of the trustees' kindly but grave attention.

"Is there a problem?" she asked.

Mr. Soames sat forward. "It's come to our notice that you had quite a nasty accident on museum premises. How are you feeling?"

"Perfectly fine, thank you." Out came the lie again. "I was in my own front room. I'm not planning to sue for compensation, if that's what you're worried about."

"Well, no, that would be a legal matter. Our concerns arise because sharp-eyed Alec claims there were signs of a break-in, the night you went to hospital. On opening up, he found the rear door unlocked and the alarm not set. Also, there were blood spots and scuff marks on the floor in the events area. A piece of artwork was missing. He claims, too, that his workbench had been disturbed and tools taken."

Stevie sat frozen.

"All we're asking, Miss Silverwood," said Mr. Soames, clasping his plump hands, "is whether you heard or saw anything suspicious that night. Did you forget to set the alarm and lock up? Did the break-in occur after your accident—a coincidence—or were the two events connected?"

Stevie shifted, felt blood rising in her face. Fifteen pairs of eyes brimmed with curiosity. On her shoulder, the spectral cat snarled softly.

"Take your time," Ruth added gently. "All we're asking is that you tell us the truth."

A knock at her front door made her start. "Stevie? It's only me. Can I come in?"

Stevie opened the door and let Fin over the threshold. "What's going on? You came out of the meeting as white as a sheet."

"I've resigned," said Stevie.

Fin sat on a sofa arm, looking shocked. "I know, they told us, but why?"

"I had no choice. I lied, and put everyone in danger. I didn't trip. Someone broke in and hit me."

She explained. When she'd finished, Fin was gaping. "But—but surely there's no need for you to leave over this? They can't sack you for being a victim of crime."

"That's not the point. I should have called the police, but instead I tried to cover it up. I know Alec was only doing his duty, telling them his suspicions, but he's never approved of me and now he's got his way. He's levered me out." She stopped, strangled by the tears that she'd managed to hold back until then.

"I wondered why he had that smug look on his face! The old git!"

"It's not his fault. He did the right thing."

"But . . ." Fin foundered. "You live over the shop. They can't . . . this is awful. They can't really make you resign, can they?"

"No, but my position's untenable. Improper conduct, they said. And they're right. I lied about something really serious. It could have been any one of us who got attacked. Someone might have died. That's why I have to go. I have two weeks to vacate my accommodation."

"Oh my god," said Fin.

Stevie sat down and wept, unable to hold back. How pathetic, that the museum had become her entire life, her home, the only security she'd ever known. The truth was, she'd only ever been a tenant. The enormity of loss began dawn on her. The future had dissolved from steady, reassuring routine into a fog of nothingness.

Fin touched Stevie's hand. She asked softly, "Stevie, what actually is going on with you? You were always rock-solid. Ever since the triptych and your strange-but-gorgeous new friend turned up, you've been all over the place."

Stevie gave a weak smile. "You wouldn't believe me."

"Oh yeah? You should hear the tales my children spin."

"No, it's too weird. You'll think I'm crazy."

"I've heard weird and crazy stuff in my time. I keep an open mind."

"Not this strange."

Fin's gaze grew firmer, as if she took this as a challenge. "All right. When I was at university, I met a girl called August, a history student. She was meant to be studying the twelfth century, but instead she became obsessed with the story of King Richard III to the extent that she was actually living it. Or rather, living a sort of parallel-world version of history that was equally real. She confided in me because I took her seriously."

"You mean you humored her?"

"No." Fin looked as serious as Stevie had ever seen her. "I believed her. It was so real to her that I felt it too. August spoke about entering other realities. She talked about dark, slithery forces attacking Richard, trying to blacken his name. I don't mean the Tudors making him out as a villain; I mean something deeper. Those malign intentions were embodied in a person who was a dark force in his own right. Someone snaking through the night, whispering in one ear after another. She called him Dr. Fautherer; a name you won't find in the history books. The way she described him sent shivers right through me. I felt it too. I physically sensed this force myself, and it terrified the crap out of me."

Stevie felt a horrible thrill, recalling the shadow that haunted Frances Manifold's house. And the unseen museum thief, who'd been invisible but solid enough to put her in hospital.

Fin added, "Either my eyes are going funny, or you've had a little cat-shaped cloud in your hair all day."

"You can see it?"

"I'm not claiming any psychic or witchy powers. Maybe it's a reaction against my parents' Catholicism or maybe it's my Celtic blood, but I've always taken deep interest in the occult side of life, folklore and old gods and faeries and all that. I've heard many stories from sensitive people who've had glimpses. My friend August actually *touched* it. I've always sensed the same aura around you. They say the Otherworld has many layers and different aspects, some benign and some dangerous. So tell me."

Stevie put her hands to her face in prayer position, stifling a laugh. The world was falling apart in every direction. She'd assumed that she had Fin's measure; a straightforward, mainstream mother with a lovely husband and a cozy two-child family. Not an offbeat bone in her body.

How bizarre, that your perception of someone could change so abruptly. Stevie blinked. She'd got Fin completely wrong, only seeing what she expected to see. Fin the everyday mom had morphed into Fin the wisewoman.

She said as much, and Fin raised her eyebrows. "Who says I can't multitask?"

"If I tell you . . . it won't make much sense."

"Give me a try. 'There goes a woman with problems of an interesting nature,' I thought the very first time we met."

In as few words as she could manage, Stevie told her about Daniel's artwork, Mist's story and her own. At the end, she spread her hands and said, "Can you help me?"

Fin pulled a rueful smile. "This is out of my league. But you need to know that you can talk to me, and that there are layers to the world we can't explain. It follows that there's a good chance you're not crazy. I kind of envy you, actually."

"Don't," said Stevie. "I'm scared."

"You're bound to be. Seriously—at the risk of sounding like a rubbish fortune-teller—you're going on a journey. You've no choice, Stevie. The silver pard is a clear manifestation of the Otherworld." She indicated the phantom cat. "The main thing to accept is that entering the Otherworld is about transformation. It's a journey you embark on only when you've lost everything."

Stevie shuddered. The room felt like a fridge. "What happened to your friend, August?"

"She . . . we lost touch." Fin gave a small, regretful shrug. "I like to think she found her way into the world that had so enthralled her."

Snow was falling as Mist left the Jewellery Quarter station and turned down Vyse Street. As he came in sight of the museum, he saw Stevie. She was standing under a streetlight, staring upwards at white flakes whirling down through the glow. She wore her pale Russian-style winter coat, her hands buried in the white fur cuffs. The hood was up, so all he could see was the tip of her nose. Snow had settled on the hood and on her shoulders, and there were no footprints in the whiteness around her. She hugged herself and stood motionless, as if she'd turned to ice and didn't care.

He hadn't meant to come back; he knew his presence might draw danger to her. Yet they were tied together in some unfathomable way and here he was again, as if he'd known in his core that something was wrong.

"Stevie?" he said. "Why are you out here?"

She looked at him with wide, blank eyes. Her face was a porcelain oval, haloed by white fur and wavy amber strands of hair.

"The snow's so beautiful." She spoke faintly, as if in surprise. "I've nothing else to do, and nowhere to go."

Mist held out his hand to her. "That's not true. Come with me."

10

Helena

Daniel woke with the sun in his eyes. Thin curtains filtered the light, shifting in a slight breeze to give glimpses of bright blue sky and striped desert.

He looked at Oliver sprawled beside him in the king-size bed, his white-blond hair splayed on the pillow. Lying here in a luxurious log house with molten sun touching their skin, he reflected that the miserable London winter seemed a lifetime ago.

Daniel remembered how freaked out he'd been as he prepared to leave his studio for the last time . . . no, beyond scared: floating in a different reality. Utterly burned out. He had been serious with the blue nylon rope. Even now, he didn't know what he would have done if Oliver had not arrived at that moment.

Oliver had saved him. Yet it was Oliver who'd driven Daniel to the brink in the first place. It was all very well vanishing to start a new life, but you couldn't leave behind your own brain with all its fears and obsessions.

His lover woke up with a sleepy smile and reached for him.

Oliver's eyes were different colors, one blue, one green. He was almost albino, with white-blond hair, pale brows and lashes, his elongated face pale like the inside of an oyster shell. There wasn't a hint of fat on him, but enough muscle to make him as stocky as a boxer. In contrast, Daniel felt ugly, with his skinny frame, sand-brown untamable hair and crooked spectacles. He'd grown quite a beard over the last few weeks, too. Couldn't be bothered to shave. Oliver—smooth-chinned although Daniel had never seen him use a razor—had expressed no opinion on the beard.

"What are you thinking?" said Oliver.

"That I really should call my mother, after all."

"No, you shouldn't." Oliver rose over him, pinning him down with his hands on Daniel's upper arms. His face was changeable, according to the light. In London's gloom, he'd looked quite lined and rough like a handsome gangster. In Nevada sunlight he lost ten years, his face as smooth as an angel's.

"Come on, we've been through this. You said she was suffocating you. A controlling harridan who's undermined you all your life. You had to make a clean break."

"Yes." Daniel called to mind the reasons he'd left; their arguments, her disapproval, her attempts to change him. Would Frances have been so sour if his father hadn't died? He had no way of knowing. He thought, *Probably I'd have had both of them on my back.* The note he'd left was ambiguous, by intention. Let his mother think he was dead; he doubted that she'd even care. "I know. A moment of sentiment. Stupid."

"Let's have no more of that. No weakness. You've cut the apron strings. Now you're free to be yourself."

"Yeah." Daniel felt a smile forming. "Free at last."

"And you have me to thank for that, don't you? You've nothing to worry about except your work." He touched Daniel's forehead. "I wonder what else will emerge from that vision factory of yours?"

"Don't know. An icon of you, I think. Saint Oliver."

"Flatterer." Oliver's mouth came down on his, stifling any reply.

The phone rang. Oliver leaned over to answer it, then rolled out of bed and quickly dragged on the jeans and white T-shirt he'd left crumpled on the floor the previous night. "It's the front gate. I'll go down and see what they want. You stay where you are, relax."

Daniel lay back with his hands under his head, trying to do as he was told. He should be happy, but doubts gnawed relentlessly. Oliver had been fretting about the missing triptych, *Aurata's Promise.* It must be held up at Customs, he'd said, or lost. If the crate didn't turn up soon, he'd sue the carrier.

Daniel dared not tell him that the triptych was never going to arrive.

From the moment they'd met, Oliver had overwhelmed him—with attention, enthusiasm, sheer physical presence, everything. Only twice before in his life had he experienced a flash like that. The first was when he'd met Stevie; the second, when his mother brought home her "unidentified carved stone object," an artifact he'd seen in dreams for years. Each flash was a channel opening in his brain to let signals come pouring in on a beam of white light; scenes, images, names. He couldn't interpret their significance, yet he had to paint them, like a medium conveying messages from the Otherworld.

"That's all I am," he'd told Oliver. "A medium."

He'd been struggling with his career. Supernatural beings depicted in the style of Byzantine saints were too esoteric for most art buyers. His technique of layering gesso and tempera and gold leaf onto wood was painstaking, too slow to be commercially viable. Caffeine and speed helped him work long hours, only to crash him into paranoia. Although the Jellybean Factory was a prestigious location, he could barely cope with the harsh reality of paying his rent. Soon he'd have to vacate, and then what?

He'd be a failure, as his art teachers had predicted. His mother would roll her eyes and tell him to get a proper job. Daniel would rather be dead. The point was not only personal ambition, but the deep certainty that *the world must be made aware of these hidden mysteries.*

He couldn't explain why, except in the vaguest terms: that a nonhuman history had been lost; that it was rising again, and this meant danger. Or wonder. Both, in fact. Yet he couldn't make anyone *see.* Often he felt like a madman, talking to himself.

Then Oliver had walked into his studio. Rock star, or crime godfather; he had that air of power about him. Not a man who'd tolerate the word "no."

He'd found Daniel's work on the Internet, he claimed. For an hour he paced, looking intently at every panel. How did Daniel know about these things? What other ideas were in his head, waiting to emerge? Daniel answered as best he could. The conversation continued into the evening, like a police interrogation. Oliver's face was granite-hard with a mix of suspicion and gleeful curiosity.

"Icons for the New Age? What you've created here is incendiary, and you don't even know it," Oliver said at last. "I want your work."

"All of it?" Daniel was caught between flattery and pure shock.

"Every piece. And I want more. You won't turn down the offer I'm prepared to make. Half a million dollars, down payment. You need drugs, alcohol, anything else to get the visions flowing? You need your rent paid? You've got it."

Daniel was struck dumb.

"There'll be conditions, of course. You need to take certain pieces off display immediately. And I want to watch you work, which means just you and me. No visitors. Consider me your patron, and yourself in the position of a court artist. It's one hell of a privilege."

Mesmerized, Daniel fell. Within days they became lovers.

Daniel had never understood himself to be gay until then. Of course, it helped explain why his relationships with Stevie and other girls had foundered. He'd never even fantasized about his own gender—but Oliver was different.

A strange, feverish time ensued. The memories ran together like wet paint. He'd always worked hard, but with Oliver there, he couldn't stop. Artists were supposed to leave their studios by nine each night, but he was adept at sneaking back in to work until dawn. Oliver supplied him with remarkable drugs he hadn't known existed, but they only opened a channel for the new visions that flowed from Oliver. As with Stevie, Daniel only had to look into his eyes and pictures came. *Aurata's Promise* was one of those works.

When first Oliver saw the triple image of regal statues in a ruined palace, a priestly figure contemplating a globe-like mechanism, and in the center an auburn-tressed beauty pointing to heaven and hell against the background of a city in flames . . . he went ominously still.

Things changed swiftly after that. He told Daniel that it was time to leave.

He instructed him to ship all his work to a certain address, produced reams of fake ID documents and booked first-class tickets to Los Angeles.

Daniel, delirious with exhaustion and fully under Oliver's spell, went along with him.

A corner of his mind argued in a small, clear voice. *You've sold out. You have literally sold yourself. Buried your work in a private art collection for money, like some kind of rent boy. How does that square with warning the world?*

Hence the moment with the rope.

"No one must ever see my artwork except you?" he asked on the flight, too late.

"And I'm paying you handsomely for that privilege," Oliver agreed.

"It's not about money. It's about forging a reputation as a serious artist. I'm not there yet, and I never will be if no one sees my work."

"But this is infinitely more important than *you*. As I've told you, what you are painting, my dear friend, is too dangerous to be seen. This isn't just my opinion, but the judgment of the higher authorities to whom I answer. Don't you understand that you are portraying the end of the world?"

Those words had hung in Daniel's mind ever since, terrifying. Oliver overpowered him. He was so beautiful, and so strong. You couldn't defy him, any more than you could defy a god.

Yet Daniel had committed one small act of defiance. He'd sent a secret cry for help to Stevie. She would know what to do.

Perhaps he and Oliver were both insane. The icons were only pictures. He'd let himself be brainwashed, purchased at a rich man's whim, all because he wanted to escape his mother . . . who, after all, wasn't evil or cruel, only aggravating.

Ten minutes later, the bedroom door opened and Oliver came in, gripping a folded wooden panel between both hands. He held up the Gothic point beneath his chin and opened the side flaps, displaying the blazing colors within.

"Look, it's here!" said Oliver. "*Aurata's Promise*. Finally!"

Daniel couldn't speak. He felt blood drain from his head, churning through his veins like cold acid.

"What's wrong?" Oliver still grinned, but his warmth turned to feral menace. "You've gone white. Would you care to explain why you shipped this work to a friend of yours, and not to me?"

Mist brought Stevie to a square box of a hotel beside the expressway—or distressway, as the locals termed it—that encircled the city center. She must have passed the hotel scores of times without noticing. It was a prosaic setting for a creature of glamorous, mystical descent . . . yet what had she expected? Unless he melted literally to mist each night, he must be staying somewhere.

She felt disoriented. It seemed so wrong, going to his room as if they'd met in a bar and were heading for an awkward one-night stand. Neither spoke as they took the elevator and emerged to walk along a carpeted corridor to his door. The room was spacious, with two queen-size beds and a small breakfast table. Stevie went to the window and looked out at a river of cars, brought to a standstill by the modest snowfall.

"I shouldn't be here," she said.

"I'm glad you are," he answered. "I mean—not glad you lost your job. I feel it's my fault. But speaking from a purely selfish point of view, I'm glad you're here." He added quickly, "I'll book you a separate room. I'm sure the hotel's not full."

"Oh—thank you. I'll pay for it myself, of course. But can we sort it out later? I can't think straight."

"You look frozen," said Mist. He adjusted a control on a heating unit and she felt warm air blowing around her. "Sit down and rest. I can make coffee, or order room service?"

"Anything hot is fine. Or something stronger, I must admit."

She removed her coat, while Mist got the coffeemaker going. When she turned around, he was placing several miniature bottles on the table.

"Oh my god, don't take stuff from the minibar!" she exclaimed. "It costs a fortune. So they say, not that I've spent much time in hotels. They completely rip you off."

He half-smiled, unconcerned. "I know. It doesn't matter. My expenses all go on Dame Juliana's credit card."

Taken aback, she glared disapprovingly until he added with a rueful smile, "I know how that sounds, but one day, when I'm a position to pay her back, it won't be the end of the world that a drink has cost me six pounds instead of three. Don't worry."

Mist brought her a mug of coffee and tipped brandy into it. She sat with her hands wrapped around the mug, thawing out. "This world is virtually impossible to live in if you have no identity," she said. "I should know."

"I suppose there are ways to fake it without human help, but I'm out of touch," he said. "There are networks of Vaethyr living among humans. Perhaps I should have sought them out, but I was afraid Rufus might find me." Removing his walking boots, he sat on one of the beds and leaned against the headboard. Stevie sipped her fiery coffee. Neither of them was inclined to make conversation for the sake of it, and this felt comforting.

Within minutes, she felt the brandy reaching her head. She went to the other bed and reclined on the quilt, propped up by fat pillows. "I was looking at the triptych, just before it was stolen. While I was standing in the street this evening, it came to me that some of the symbols carved on the pillars were *arrows*. As in pointers, not weapons."

"Meaning what?" Mist looked intrigued.

"All I can make of it is this. Aurata's standing there with her orb, pointing at a molten crack in the Earth. The arrows seem to indicate that this not just something that happened in the past. It will happen again in the future."

"Great goddess of the Cauldron, I hope that's not true," Mist exclaimed in soft astonishment. She left him in thought for a while, then prompted him to go on.

"You got as far as the earthquake," she said. "Can you tell me more? I've been writing it all on my laptop; I hope you don't mind."

He laughed and shrugged. "I'd rather know more about you." He rested with a hand in his disarrayed blue-black hair. He had the carved disk under his hand and was tracing the carvings with one finger. Stevie saw trails of color following his fingertip like fish in a pond.

"Everything I told Frances, that's all there is."

Mist looked at her with clear disbelief, but didn't press her. "All right."

"So you carry on . . . if it's not too difficult?"

"You're easy to talk to and the pain is very well-worn, so I'll try."

He was in the chamber with nine others arrayed in a circle, the tenfold web a cat's cradle of green fire streaking between their hands. In the middle glowed the Felixatus, emitting a hum like a mass groan of pain. Aurata's face was dust-streaked and bore a look of stony fear he'd never seen before. But there was strength there, too. Like their mother, Aurata was a powerful web-weaver who kept her talents quiet.

"This is the beginning, not the end," Veropardus kept saying, glaring straight at Aurata across the circle. The energy lines deformed the fabric of the Dusk-lands until it began to tear apart, pulling reality itself out of shape.

He hadn't known how powerful Aurata was, until this moment. Then the combined force of his parents' energy surged in like a fireball, turning the web to dazzling gold.

He cried out, knowing they were dead.

The ground trembled, rising like the backbone of a huge beast shouldering its way out of the earth. He tasted dust and sulfur. Everywhere, the towers of Azantios were toppling, the air shuddering with thunder and with human screams.

Mist screamed too. The tenfold web broke apart and vaporized. Its creators fled. He yelled but they didn't hear him. He saw Aurata brought down by a pillar, saw Veropardus racing away through clouds of dust and falling rubble until the ground itself crumpled beneath them.

Mist fell and fell, as if down a long shaft full of smoke, until debris buried him. His hand closed on something cold and smooth, like glass. Then the universe shut down into blackness.

"I don't know why I survived to crawl out, when the others did not," he told Stevie. "I came round with part of the Felixatus in my hand, the lens from the top. I assumed the rest was destroyed; it's incredible that Professor Manifold found the base. Anyway, Rufus and I were in such deep shock that we did little but survive like wild cats for countless years. Ice ages carved the land into different shapes, humans began to migrate and develop settlements. Aetherials came out of hibernation. We began to find each other. That was when Rufus and I discovered we'd been born too late for the *truly* golden age of the Aelyr, a time before Malikala arose, and when the Earth and Spiral were more closely entwined, porous to each other."

"And dinosaurs roamed the Earth?" said Stevie.

He laughed. "Never saw a dinosaur. My guess is that our ancestors were still in primal energy forms that far back. Now the Felynx and other lost peoples are only remembered in fragments of folklore. We disdained violence, so we were bad at fighting. No wonder we lost our grasp on the world. The long, stretched-out lives we lead, versus the hot, aggressive energies of humans and their sheer overwhelming numbers: we stood no chance. So we gradually slipped away into myth.

"Still, Aetherials always continue in one form or another. When Rufus and I finally found a way into the Otherworld, we learned there had been changes. Malikala's rule was over. Azantios was not the only city to have fallen to humans. Many displaced Vaethyr formed an army to invade the Spiral, led by one Jharag the Red, and there was quite a battle between Vaethyr and the Aelyr who didn't want the Earth dwellers back. A peace agreement was reached, but to stop any future conflict, all portals between Earth and Otherworld were concealed and put under the control of the Great Gates. We could pass in and out but it wasn't easy, and it was near-impossible for humans. Ironically, for all Rufus's rage, we found we preferred life on Vaeth. It was what we were used to."

"Did you really manage to forgive him about Azantios?" Stevie asked.

"No. That was too great a disaster for anyone to forgive. We fought and separated more times than I can count. Still, humans were becoming interesting and we were drawn to them out of sheer curiosity. We changed physically, to fit in among them . . . I could tell endless stories of Uruk, Egypt, Rome, India, Renaissance Europe, but let me just say that a pattern emerged. The Felynx doesn't change its stripes, and Rufus entertained himself by stirring up all the chaos and misery he possibly could."

"Trying to control him can't have been much fun."

"Sometimes it was," Mist said darkly. "I'm ashamed to admit it, because my last promise to Poectilictis was that I'd stop Rufus. But I'm not the paragon my father seemed to think I was. I should have destroyed Rufus, but I couldn't."

Stevie bit her lower lip. "And now you don't want to confront Rufus, because he . . . killed you?"

"Not by his own hand, but effectively, yes. Not only me, but a woman I loved. It was her death I can't forgive."

"What was her name?"

"Helena."

"Helena," she echoed softly. "She sounds like a goddess."

"She was human. No chance of rebirth."

"Some humans believe in reincarnation . . ." She exhaled. "Sorry, that verged on flippant. Can you talk about it? If not, say so and I'll shut up."

Mist lay back with one arm under his head. Stevie was a motionless shadow on the other bed, reclining on her side with her hair falling beautifully around her. Her blue and green dress was a patchwork of tie-dye print and lace panels, elegantly outlining her long, curvy body. The handkerchief-points of the hem revealed her bare feet and ankles. Only her eyes were animated: gleaming with interest, reacting to everything he said.

"We were in Amsterdam, Rufus and I, in the mid-seventeenth century. The Dutch Golden Age, as they called it later. It was a time of incredible change and energy, and Rufus always had to be at the heart of things. It was a tolerant city for its time, wealthy and no longer subservient to religious restrictions. Have you been there?"

Stevie looked mildly surprised to be asked. "No, but I've seen it in lots of photos and films. A very handsome, quirky city, isn't it? I expect it's changed hugely since your day."

"Have they filled in the canals with concrete or knocked down the beautiful houses?"

"Of course not. You'd recognize the older areas. I'm trying to imagine what you saw, the streets full of traders instead of tourists. Their clothing. I'm seeing paintings by Breughel and Vermeer, lots of gloomy hues. Was everything tastefully grey and sepia in those days?"

Her tone made Mist laugh. "I remember a bright place. Many of the buildings were brand-new."

He described barges plying the Amstel river, great ships bringing cargoes of spice from the East Indies. When he closed his eyes, the scenes came to life. Magnificent churches and lavish new houses, canals everywhere like curves of shimmering green silk.

"Those were wonderful years. We weren't forever fighting each other, don't think that, but we were always outsiders. Other Aetherials blend in with humans. Rufus and I, though, because we came from the early days, we stayed on the fringes, playacting at being part of life. Which is a shame, because the mortal world is so fascinating, always changing."

"It sounds as if Rufus played a bit too hard, to compensate."

"And my attempts to reason with him only egged him on. Often I'd give up and walk away for a while. I still had the Felixatus lens. Amsterdam was full of scientists and I wondered if someone could help me discover what the lens actually was. There was a man called Jaap de Witt who'd made a fortune from trade and now devoted his time to experimenting with microscopes and telescopes. So I went to his house with the lens to ask for his opinion."

"Wasn't Aelyr scientific knowledge more advanced?" Stevie opened two more brandies, tipped one into his glass and the other into her coffee mug.

"Not really, no. Why bother inventing the Archimedes screw, or penicillin, or electricity, when we could spin what we needed from the fabric of the Spiral itself? We interact differently with the universe, without putting names and labels on everything. There's no real need for technology in the Spiral. The ancient skills still work, so our priorities are different.

"Science fascinated me, because humans evolved knowing nothing. Instead they had to find out for themselves, describe and explain the world through painstaking experiments. Often they got it wrong, but when they got it right—I can't describe the exhilaration."

"You sound like a seventeenth-century geek." There was a smile in her voice.

Mist responded with a soft laugh. "I don't know where I've heard the term 'geek' before, but it doesn't sound like a compliment. I wanted to *learn*, rather than rollick around seducing people and upending their lives, like Rufus. Aetherials think they know everything—maybe some do—but humans don't, so they take the trouble to find out. Jaap de Witt was part of that early movement."

Mist tasted the atmosphere, as if he were still there. Jaap de Witt's house was in the Grachtengordel, part of the new ring of canals and streets built for wealthy merchants. He made his way through Dam Square past the Nieuwe Kerk, threading between crowds of traders and citizens, then walking cobbled paths beside the canals. Rows of tall, grand houses rose on either side.

Young elm trees lined the bank. Fashionable couples were promenading; a coach-and-pair passed over a bridge, their reflection rippling in the water. Mist found the house of Jaap de Witt and looked up at its large windows set into pale brown brick. The neck gable that surmounted the roof was tall and curvaceous, embellished with carved dolphins and seashells.

Mist rang the doorbell and waited, feeling the hard smooth curve of the lens through the silk pouch that contained it. The last surviving part of the Felixatus. The day was warm, spring sunlight glistening. Presently a housekeeper with her hair tucked under a white cap answered, and led him inside to a reception room. Narrow at the front, these Dutch houses were cavernous inside, all treacly wood and luxurious furnishings.

Presently Jaap de Witt glided in to greet him.

"What did he look like?" Stevie put in. "I want details."

"A neat, upright man with a pointed beard, greyish complexion, narrow eyes. Aged about sixty. He carried himself like a priest on the lookout for heretics. I see him vividly, because his was the last face I saw for three hundred years."

To that, Stevie said nothing.

"He was flattered by my sincere interest in his work, not to mention the chance of a free research assistant, and he invited me into his laboratory. As soon as we entered, I saw Helena. His wife."

"Oh," said Stevie. "Oh dear."

Mist sipped his drink, trying to push away memories away in the vain hope they'd become mere words, not burning emotions.

He described the musty, chemical smell of the laboratory, with its molasses walls and black-and-white tiled floor, benches arrayed with instruments, shelves stacked with bottles of chemicals, poisons, floating animal fetuses. Amid this surreal space, Helena was outlined by a red-gold aura from the fire. The fine downy hairs on her neck were filaments of flame. He took in the neat outline of her bodice and long skirts; the perfect shape of her head clasped by shining golden hair, her sharp profile and her cool, intelligent eyes. Her creamy skin glowed as she turned towards him with a soft smile.

A single look. Both were lost.

"She was many years younger than him," Mist went on. "It was a common situation among humans: a girl from a poor family, married off to a rich merchant in search of a young pretty wife. She had no choice. She considered it her duty to obey her parents."

"Who cared nothing about her happiness, obviously," said Stevie.

"I'm sure that wasn't the case. They had different values. Helena had dignity, a quality of gracious acceptance. She wanted to support her family, because she loved them. She wasn't a woman that any husband would dare to bully. And de Witt treated her with respect, as far as I could tell. Theirs was a working partnership. He loved her in his way, or was certainly proud to possess her. It was his third marriage and he was childless, so all his hopes rested with her. However . . ."

Stevie was watching him with a cool expression that reminded him of Helena. He anticipated a dry remark about an ill-considered affair. She only waited for him to go on.

"Once we saw each other, if was as if her husband ceased to exist. Not that we could do anything about it. I was almost never alone with her. We were never more intimate than a stolen kiss—the sweetest moment ever tasted—

but this bond was always there, burning between us, while her husband continued, utterly oblivious to it." He sighed. "It was torment. Torment. I don't know what we thought could happen . . . A few weeks of study, then I'd be gone and we'd be nothing more than a sweet memory to each other. That aside, I had the matter of the Felixatus lens."

Helena's eyes had opened as wide as her husband's as he unwrapped the heavy crystal from its silk. They thought it must be a jewel from the ancient world, created from an unknown mineral. "I worked with them for a few months," Mist went on. "We made lenses from molten glass and built instruments. Every new project was an experiment. It was quickly obvious that Helena was the true scientist of the pair. No one said this aloud, since de Witt must be the acknowledged genius. Helena had the ideas and he took the credit, but she never protested. We'd just smile at each other behind his back.

"Those few weeks were magical. Agonizing paradise. I don't know how long I would have stayed, or if one night we'd have run away together. No, she wouldn't risk her family's fate with a reckless love affair. Perhaps the pleasure lay in imagining what *might* be.

"Then Rufus tracked me down. With his usual charm he insinuated himself into the household, and laughed at my private pleas for him to leave. He saw immediately the feelings between Helena and me, a perfect lever for blackmail and torment. Unfortunately, de Witt fell under his spell. I wouldn't make promises about wondrous discoveries, but Rufus had no such scruples. He promised de Witt the Earth. A cure for every plague, incredible inventions that would ensure his fame for eternity. I watched de Witt growing excited and greedy and frightened, all at once. He was beginning to lose his mind . . . similar to what I suspect happened to Daniel."

Stevie raised her head, frowning. "Rufus drove them mad, for the hell of it? Daniel as well as Jaap de Witt?"

"The thing is that de Witt was already afraid that other scientists would mock his inventions, or worse, that the Church might condemn him. Amsterdam was fairly liberal, but he was still a believer. Certain religious doctrines insisted it was heresy to magnify the stars, or the microscopic parts of insects."

"My god. It's hard to imagine the struggle scientists had, when they could be burned at the stake for suggesting that the Earth goes round the sun," Stevie put in. "Unbelievable. D'you know, people are still arguing about evolution to this day? To think they were risking their lives, just by *looking* at the world."

"Almost every investigation into the fabric of nature brought unwelcome attention from that quarter. Even though Amsterdam was more tolerant than many cities, de Witt was nervous. I don't blame it all on Rufus, but he didn't help. He threw the household into disarray, flirted blatantly with Helena, trying to take her from me—and did so right in front of her husband. De Witt was a very controlled man, but you could see him tightening like a spring.

"Meanwhile, we made a makeshift telescope to see what the Felixatus lens might show. De Witt was the first to look through it. The only one, actually. He turned as grey as iron, and then he smashed the telescope to pieces with his bare hands.

"It took Helena awhile to coax out of him what he'd seen. Another world, he said. The stars were all wrong. There were things *inside* the lens. Living things, specks of light that must be tiny demons. It followed that Rufus and I had brought him something devilish, and that perhaps we too were demons or witches of some kind."

Mist rubbed his eyes. The memory of the end still made his breath quicken with dread. "What happened to the lens?" said Stevie.

"Oh, it was undamaged. I think Rufus took it. He's always been pleased by snatching things from me, as if we were still squabbling children. Well, there was a leaden atmosphere the next day. Naively I thought we could smooth things over. But Rufus remained as provocative as ever and eventually Jaap de Witt blew up. I never knew such a stone-cold man could erupt with such violence, literally turning scarlet like a volcano."

"You have to watch the quiet ones," Stevie murmured.

"He accused Rufus of an affair with Helena. Rufus was shaken, but also gleeful, because he lived for melodrama. He answered that de Witt should be looking at me, not at him.

"Our silence declared us guilty. We were both paralyzed, Helena and I, and de Witt had a huge knife in his hand—some kind of kitchen knife the size of a small sword. There was chaos and shouting. I felt the blade go into me. Then I saw it go into Helena as I tried to protect her. She bled to death in my arms. It took seconds. De Witt stabbed me again, in the throat this time, and I followed her."

Stevie made an incoherent sound, struck wordless by horror.

"To Rufus, this was all great sport," Mist went on. "That's what he does; walks into a peaceful domain and destroys it. He sees people's weakness, or happiness, and snatches it away. He didn't mean for me to die, because what sport am I to him, dead? However, since he rarely thinks five minutes into the future, it didn't occur to him that the upright Jaap de Witt would seize a weapon and stab his own wife in the stomach and then, as she bled in my arms, kill me too."

"Oh my god," Stevie said very softly. "What happened to you after that?"

"It's hard to describe. My soul-essence was severed from my body . . . A long time later I was in a kind of forest lit by dim blue starlight. I felt as if a thousand years had passed, as if I'd always been here. It wasn't unpleasant. I felt peaceful for a long while, but then I remembered . . . Helena. And all that had passed between Rufus and me.

"I came to a pool in a wood. All I had to do was touch the water and I would begin to spiral outwards again, towards a new life. But I didn't. I turned away from the Mirror Pool and drifted away. I decided to remain elemental until I finally dissolved into the Spiral itself. However, the Spiral seemed to have other plans. Or my *fylgia*. I don't know."

"Your *fylgia*?"

"The shadow twin of our soul-essence. It exists in the Spiral and anchors us there."

"Like the subconscious?"

"In a way." He looked at the cloudy cat on her pillow, a *fylgia* if he'd ever seen one. "Are you sure you don't know this already?"

"Why would I?"

"The gap in your life before you were fifteen?"

"No. Ghastly childhood trauma or a neurological condition—move along, nothing to see here. Don't spin this web of weirdness around me."

"Too late. I think you're already part of it, Stevie."

"But we're talking about you. What happened next?"

"You know the rest. I drifted back to consciousness as a human named Adam, who had stern parents and wonderful sisters. I survived the First World War, only to be snatched by Rufus and driven mad all over again."

"I'm so sorry," she said. "About Helena, and everything. You've been through hell."

"I don't want pity. I'm just glad to have found a friend to tell," he said softly, pushing the Felixatus disk under his pillow. "Talking of unconsciousness, we should get some sleep. Did you realize it's past midnight?"

"Too late to get another room."

"I don't mind, if you don't? Two beds, plenty of space. And it goes without saying, you get first turn in the bathroom."

"Thanks." She began to rise, then asked, "By the way, what happened to Jaap de Witt?"

"Oh. According to Rufus—and I checked the historical records—he was arrested for murder, declared insane, spent the rest of his days as he awaited execution babbling about demons and other worlds. That's why I think that Aetherials . . . although we are not demons or devils or vampires . . . are still too often poisonous to humans."

Stevie lay on her back, trying to sleep and failing. The darkness was gemmed with tiny red and green lights on the smoke alarm, heating unit, bedside clock. Had she thought that she and Mist would end up in bed together?

Had she even wanted it? It wouldn't be the best idea, when you were upset, confused and slightly drunk.

The subject of their conversation, anyway, had dampened any such urges. Yet it would have been so easy.

They were both alone, with a shared experience of being tipped into the world from nowhere. Mist seemed gentle, trustworthy, more than happy in her company . . . and all too attractive. His face and hair and strong, lean body demanded to be touched. Was the feeling mutual? He certainly looked at her a lot. His gaze didn't feel intrusive, only warm and sad. And he didn't hesitate to wrap his arms around her when she was shivering, or upset . . . at the slightest excuse, in fact. Still, he'd made no moves towards seduction. Either that showed a respectful, chivalrous streak, or it meant he wasn't interested in anything beyond friendship.

Which was fine. It was difficult to feel passionate when you were jobless, homeless, gutted. She knew it could happen that you met someone and slid into each other's embrace because the mutual pull was irresistible. Perhaps it could have happened with Mist . . .

But now she saw that he was still in love with Helena.

One look and we were lost. Smiling behind her husband's back. It was agonizing paradise. A stolen kiss, the sweetest moment ever tasted. Torment, torment.

Warmth faded inside her, extinguished by a tiny snowfall of realism. She had to be practical. His sweetness was illusory; the truth was that they barely knew each other.

Her love life since Daniel had been a halfhearted mess. A few times, she'd been on dates with men who seemed perfectly nice, as fresh and open to possibility as any sixteen-year-old . . . only for him to spend the entire evening moaning about his ex-wife and custody of the children, or rhapsodizing about football. She lacked the patience to pretend that this was not an instant turnoff.

Then, when she brushed them off, they'd be puzzled and complain she was cold.

No one came without baggage. Mist did not have baggage so much as a fleet of long-haul trucks. By contrast she was traveling light. Weightless. No past of significance, not even a family to complain of.

She turned on her side—facing away from him—and found a tiny face looking straight into hers. The astral cat lay on the pillow beside her, swishing its tail. Stevie lay looking into its eyes. Its body shifted like faint, glowing fog, but this was the first time she'd seen it so clearly.

She heard Fin saying, *"The silver pard is a manifestation of the Otherworld."*

So what are you trying to tell me? she thought, and realized she was already asleep, sliding into dreams of glistening green water . . .

Stevie woke abruptly.

The room felt wrong. There was no light at all, only a blue-blackness that seemed to swirl violently like a gale. She heard the sounds of a struggle. Shuffling footsteps, grunts and cries, a heavy object crashing to the floor. She felt movement all around her, yet she couldn't see a thing.

"Mist?" she called out.

It had to be a nightmare, but she couldn't wake up.

She curled against the headboard as pressures whirled around her. Like strong winds, they stopped her breath. She felt the entire room tipping. Again she caught the metallic stink she'd noticed in Frances's house, and when she'd been attacked in the museum.

Stevie got up, reasoning that if she was on her feet she might be able to see, or at least defend herself. The whole space was turning inside out like a twisting doughnut with no end or beginning. It kept turning and turning, and there was nothing to fight.

A solid force that felt like a body colliding with hers slammed into her, sending her reeling against the bed. Now she saw the diffuse outlines of the room, but no sign of Mist. She caught glimpses of shadow, flashes of light. When she half-closed her eyes, the flashes resolved into two dim figures in frantic struggle.

One of the figures was feathery and pallid, the other long and reptilian . . . she got only impressions that were too vague to make sense.

"Stop it!" She tried to shout but her voice failed. "Mist?"

A voice came, "Stevie, help me . . ."

It emanated from the paler figure.

She reached out and touched flesh. Her hand, too, was transparent. She jumped back as the two specters rolled across the bed and hit the floor, the snake-like one rising on top. The paler shape cried out.

Stevie opened the bedside drawer, seized the Gideon Bible and brought it down hard on the scaly skull of the attacker.

She heard a grunt of pain and then something rushed through the room. A door opened and slammed shut. The world shook itself. A light came on and reality coalesced around them. Stevie was standing at the end of her bed, Mist down on the floor at her feet. The bedside lamp revealed a room that appeared to have been ransacked.

"Mist?"

She helped him up onto his bed and he sat there, gasping. There was a red welt on his cheek. His eyes were cloudy with shock, and bloodshot.

"What the hell was that?" she said. "You look dreadful. Are you all right?"

"Yes, I'll live, but . . ."

"What was it?"

"I don't know yet. Did it hurt you?"

"No, only scared the hell out of me." She had another flashback to her unseen attacker at the museum. "*Fuck* . . ."

"Whatever it was, it's taken the last of the Felixatus," said Mist.

11

To the Labyrinth

"What the bloody hell—?" said Rufus.

He leaned on the cab door and stared up at the scene they'd left behind the day before. San Marco Square with the Campanile tower standing against a bright blue sky. The Doge's Palace, a gondola drifting beneath the Rialto Bridge . . . all the famous landmarks of Venice grouped together in chocolate-box perfection. The buildings were spotless, the water as clear and brilliant as a swimming pool.

"It's our hotel," said Aurata. "The Venetian. Wait until you see inside."

"Oh, funny," Rufus said. He broke into laughter. "Brilliant joke. They built a Disneyfied copy of the real thing? You're priceless, Aurata."

She joined in his amusement, both of them helpless for a few minutes. "I thought you'd appreciate it. Welcome to Las Vegas."

Shining marble halls with elaborate ceilings brought them to the hotel registration desk. Music from *The Phantom of the Opera* pumped through the sound system. Presently they were settling into a large suite with a sunken seating area, views of Caesar's Palace and other legendary hotels, and of the dusty-brown mountains that encircled the city. The room had the biggest bathroom Rufus had ever seen, replete with gold taps, marble and mirrors. Aurata managed to cram their valuables—the ancient book of Veropardus and boxes containing parts of the Felixatus—into the safe. Then they showered together, and swapped rumpled traveling clothes for smarter attire. Aurata had a taste for bright red dresses and jewelry that clashed with her hair. Rufus chose a crimson shirt with his dark suit, just to clash a little more.

"You like?" she said.

"You, or the hotel?"

"Everything. I thought you'd be asking more questions."

"I'm going with the flow. I like surprises."

"I hope you'll like this one. I need a hair salon. My hair's a mess and I want the short sleek look for a change."

Aurata took him down to the "Grand Canal Shoppes," a labyrinthine pastel mockup of Venice rendered in astounding detail. The effect was softly lit, opulent and atmospheric, although he could have done without costumed actors bursting into song every few minutes. Rufus loved the squeaky-clean fakery as much as he'd loved the decay of the real place. They bought ice cream from a gelato store and roamed the streets beneath a domed plaster sky, watching real gondolas plying a fake canal. Shoppers browsed expensive gift stores; diners sat on terraces drinking cocktails. Rufus curled his tongue around the delicious cappuccino-flavored ice as he took in every pillar and arch and icing-sugar facade.

"This is incredible," he said. "Only in America. I thought Las Vegas would be wall-to-wall sleaze."

Aurata slipped her hand through his elbow. "You need to catch up with the world. The Strip is all glitz and showbiz these days."

"But there are seedy areas, right? We have to see the nasty end of town before we leave. Where's the casino, by the way?"

She pointed at the smooth cobbled pavement. "Next floor down."

Rufus sighed. "I could make a fortune here."

"What, gambling?"

"God, no," he said. "As a prostitute, of course. I'd be the hottest transvestite hooker in town. Ladies welcome too; I don't discriminate."

She shook with laughter. "You are absolutely serious, aren't you? I know you. You'd do it, for the hell of it. But we're only here for two nights. I wanted to have some fun with you, because things will be serious again soon enough."

"Damn. Not long enough to build a solid client base." He rushed onto a bridge and leaned on the side rail to watch activity on the canal. "Marvelous, the way the gondoliers pole the boat and sing cheesy operetta at the same time. Can we have sex on a gondola?"

"Only if we want to get thrown out," she said. "They let people get married on them, although even in Vegas they might draw the line at brother and sister."

"Never mind. I'll steal you a diamond ring anyway."

"Isn't it killing you, not to ask where we're going?" She pulled him towards the crowded main square, her voice taking on the serious tone he associated with her "Dr. Connelly" persona.

"Yeah, but I like suspense."

"It's all about remaking the world. Reclaiming what we lost when Azantios fell. The pent-up energy between the plates of the Earth's crust is apocalyptic, and it's deeply connected to the boundaries between Earth and Spiral . . . I've so much to tell you. There's something incredible in motion."

"I don't like the sound of this. Does it involve me being sacrificed to atone for all my crimes?"

"No, idiot. It involves you helping me."

He paused to look at a robed man pretending to be a statue. His face and hands were painted silver to match his shiny silver garments. "Aurata, I've got a confession to make."

"What's that?"

He gave her a helpless, pleading look. "I'm shallow."

"I never guessed."

"As shallow as that fake lagoon. I don't care about these deep, dark mysteries and apocalyptic cosmic plans of yours. I wish to fritter my life away. You want to know why I destroyed Azantios? It's because I knew I wasn't fit to rule the place, but I didn't want anyone else to, either. There's brainless immaturity for you."

Aurata turned him to face her. "This is not news to me, Rufe. It's your ruthless cunning I need."

"But you know . . ." His voice became quiet and hard. He had to make her understand. "You do know that it wasn't me who murdered your pet? Fe—"

"Don't say her name." Aurata pressed a finger to his lips. "She's nothing. Prehistory. But yes, I know it wasn't you."

"Thank goodness. You're the first ever to believe me. I know it was only one death among thousands, but I hate inaccuracy."

"Rufe, you were a delinquent boy waiting for an excuse to—to set fire to your own house. If being falsely accused hadn't set you off, it would have been something else. You always wanted to shake up the world, didn't you?"

"I was bored. The Felynx were stagnant. Perhaps you and I should have staged a coup against the dull, safe rule Mist was planning, but even that didn't seem enough."

"So imagine forging a realm to make Azantios look like a flea bite, only this time completely ours. Doesn't that appeal?"

He decided not to mention her nocturnal murmurings about Sibeylan glaciers, since she barely seemed to remember them. "Well . . . put like that, yes. I'm interested."

"Every time Vesuvius and other volacanoes erupted, I kept returning there—until I realized, that was what Azantios had needed. More than an earthquake. Molten dissolution."

"Errr . . . that's still not sounding like fun."

She put her arms around his neck and kissed him. The silver statue pursed his lips and made a smooching noise. Rufus gave him the finger.

"I promise you," whispered Aurata, "there will be more fun than you can imagine."

Stevie and Mist took a train from Birmingham to Leicester, then a taxi to the village of Cloudcroft. They'd checked out of the hotel and were now effectively homeless. Her life was in a shoulder bag; a few clothes, some personal effects and her laptop. She tried not to think of what she'd normally be doing now: guiding a tour group, chatting to visitors . . . Staring out of the taxi window as suburbs gave way to rural roads, Stevie wondered how much stranger this adventure could become.

Yesterday's events cycled through her thoughts. Disbelief that she'd lost her domain, the museum; the nightmarish attack in the hotel by some unseen, slithering force . . . Perhaps fear or grief would come later, but right now she was too shell-shocked for emotion.

The road narrowed, climbing steadily as the landscape changed to a mix of farmland and rocks thrusting from rugged hills, dead bracken spilling over rough granite walls, gnarled bare oaks. Leicester had been damp and slushy, but here on the high ground of Charnwood Forest, the scenery was white with freezing fog. She couldn't foresee the next ten minutes, let alone a future.

"This reminds me of the Scottish Highlands, on a small scale," said Mist. Neither had spoken for a while. "I can imagine Aetherials living here."

"And what are you going to say, assuming we can find them?"

"I don't know, but I'm sure Peta Lyon will help us." Peta was Vaethyr, he'd told her; an artist colleague of Dame Juliana, who'd helped Mist-as-Adam. "If she's even home yet."

The taxi driver hummed along to jaunty bhangra music on the radio, and showed no sign of interest in their conversation.

"Might Rufus have come here?" asked Stevie.

"Anything's possible. If he sent the shadow elemental to attack us, he must know where I am, so there's no point in trying to hide."

"I keep telling you not to be afraid of him, but after last night, I don't blame you. What was that thing?"

"I'm not sure. Strange beings emerge from the Otherworld, and Aelyr themselves go into different forms. It reminded me of a *dysir*—a sort of elemental guardian—but much nastier."

"Why did it steal the UCSO from you, but not from Frances?"

"It was a disembodied being, sniffing around blindly for Felynx objects. All I can think is that when I touched the object, I made the Elfstone resonate in a way that allowed the creature to locate and physically touch it."

"Ugh," she said. "Like the Nazgul in *The Lord of the Rings*?"

"I wouldn't know," he said. She explained, and he pulled a horrified face. "Well, let's hope it wasn't a demonic wraith-king," he said wryly. "I don't know what level of conscious intelligence it had, but that doesn't mean it wasn't an Aelyr of some kind. If you think about it, what is consciousness anyway? What does it mean to be alive, or to be reborn? When I was elemental, I was conscious, but I had no thoughts or emotions. When I was Adam, I wasn't myself. I was him, and he's still part of me, but he's not *me*. All that connects us is memory."

"It's memory, then," said Stevie. "I went to see my Nanny Peg—well, she's not mine, but she was the only one of my last foster-family who liked me—and she's got Alzheimer's and doesn't know who I am anymore. Is she still herself? Her body's there, but her mind isn't. It's memory. Your personality's no more than a cobweb without it."

Mist tilted his head to look at her. His eyes were shaded by the black fall of his hair. "What does it mean to be conscious at all?" he said. "Events are happening on the other side of the world, or the next street, the next room, and we've no idea what they are. People are living lives of which we're entirely unaware. We've no more knowledge of them than we have of daily life before we were born. We might as well not exist as far as those people are concerned. We could be dead, or unborn. And they to us; they'll never know what we're going through, or what we're talking about."

"I don't what you're talking about, half the time," Stevie said with a grin.

"Oh yes, you do. The Aetherial quality of being semi-mortal—I can't call it immortal, because nothing can last for eternity—and all our phases of living for eons, turning elemental, then returning to life again . . . Please don't think that death means nothing to us. Being violently evicted from your body is never fun. Nor is being trapped inside while your wounded flesh heals. Humans find eternal rest, or perhaps a timeless afterlife as some believe. But we never know what's next, who or what we'll be, if we'll forget bliss or remember pain . . . That's not easy to bear. If we're reborn with no memory of our previous existence, what proof is there that we're the same being? None. And if memory does return, still no proof that we haven't absorbed energies from some other Aetherial, or even from a human. Adam's still alive, but only through me. What does it mean?"

"Aetherials are fluid, not here-and-gone like humans?"

"Yes, but . . ." He tipped his head back. "I don't know. But . . ."

"What? You've been giving me strange looks ever since we met. Come on, say it."

"All right, at the risk of giving offense by stating the obvious . . . Stevie, I'm certain you're Aetherial. Are you pretending not to know? I believe that's why you came out of nowhere with your memory blurred. These things happen to us sometimes. It happened to me. I know how it feels, how frightening it can be."

Her breathing grew faster. He'd tried to say this to her before, she knew, and every time she'd pushed the idea away. "It's no good asking me that. You might as well say, 'I'm certain you're really an octopus, or an Egyptian deity.' I don't know how I'm meant to feel different. I'm still just me. I know I'm loopy and damaged, but everyone's damaged in some way. Aren't they?"

Mist made no immediate response. Then he said, "I've brought nothing but trouble to you."

"Can't argue with that." Again the thought of her lost career pierced her. "But let's say you're right? What makes us forget?"

"Time. Changing form from physical to spectral and back again. Perhaps it's a kind of protection, to forget horrors so we can make a new start. Or the unfathomable nature of the Spiral." He paused. "Regaining the memories can be more frightening than losing them."

"So I'm in denial."

"Possibly." He gave a slight smile, a hint of warmth that always disarmed her.

"But you're not looking at me and seeing exactly who I am, and why I'm like this?"

"No. I'm not psychic," he said. "I can't hack into you as if you were a computer. You have a certain energy that I associate with Aetherials. And sometimes a small cat shape on your shoulder, which suggests a *fylgia*, though I've never seen one attached before and I don't know if that's good or bad."

"God, you can see that?" She gasped, briefly speechless. "Fin saw it too. I feel like I'm going round with a tattoo saying 'Weirdo!' on my forehead. Honestly, Mist, enough. I need a drink."

"I can ask the driver to take you back to the station," he said in a neutral tone.

He was giving her a genuine choice: to walk away, if she couldn't take it. That startled her more than anything else he'd said, made her slightly angry too.

"Right. You can't seriously think I'd come this far and not carry on?"

He gave his irresistible smile. "You need a drink. I can see a pub."

The driver left them on a snowy village green in front of a pub called the Green Man. The slate roof was white with frost. Buttery light glowed from small leaded windows. Mist and Stevie wove their way between snowmen and giant snowballs, entered a cozy bar with a fire blazing in a grate and low, beamed ceilings. A handful of customers turned to glance at them. People always looked twice at Mist, but she noticed they seemed to be scrutinizing her with equal interest.

Stevie sat in a booth and let Mist go to the bar, where he ordered two bowls of soup and two brandy-and-gingers. She heard him ask the barmaid, "Do you know Peta Lyon?"

"Yeah, everyone knows Peta," the woman replied. "Haven't seen her around for a couple of years though. Think she went off traveling."

"Oh." He gave a quiet sigh of disappointment. "Would you know where I can find her family?"

"Put it this way, I know where they live, but I can't give out people's addresses to strangers. Sorry, duck."

Mist took a piece of paper from his pocket. "Actually, I have her address, but I don't know my way around."

The barmaid glanced at it, nodded. "Woodhouse Lane. When you leave the pub, turn right, go up the street for a couple of hundred yards, turn right again. The village only has about five roads anyway, so you can't get too lost."

"Thank you," said Mist, and came to Stevie with their drinks. She sipped the fiery liquid and looked into the log fire, grateful for this moment of warmth. It was definitely a good idea to eat before they began exploring.

"What are you going to say to Peta's family?" she asked.

"I'm not sure." He sat back, long legs extended, boots crossed at the ankle. "I don't know if she told them anything about me—about Adam, rather—or about Rufus. I won't reveal details about Daniel's disappearance, or who I am, or the fact that something's happening but I've no idea what it means . . . What the bloody hell am I going to say, in fact?"

Stevie grinned. His air of self-containment was usually inviolable. When he had a moment of utter helplessness, she couldn't help but find it endearing.

"I'm sure we'll think of something," she said. "Improvise. That's all I'm doing, at the moment."

The house was nothing special; a plain, brown brick box constructed be-tween the wars, softened by a garden full of shrubs and conifers all grey with frost. A tall, intimidating woman answered the door. She wore her thick coppery hair in a messy updo, and was dressed in overalls covered in paint splotches.

"Hello?" Her voice was attractively husky. "I'm in the middle of decorat-ing, so if you're selling something or recruiting for a cult, the answer's no."

"I'm a friend of Peta's," said Mist. "You must be her mother, Mrs. Lyon?"

She'd begun to close the door on them, but stopped, looking intently at Mist. "Yes, I'm Catherine. I'm afraid she's not here. Gone backpacking with her friend Gill, presently tiger-spotting in Bhutan, I believe."

"Is there any way I can get in touch with her?"

Catherine Lyon paused, weighing him up. "Only if I email and ask her to contact you, but we sometimes wait weeks for a reply or phone call. Anything I can help you with?"

"I'm Mistangamesh," he said quietly. "This is Stevie. I don't know if Peta would have mentioned me, but she knew me as Leith, or Adam?"

Her eyes opened wide. "Oh, my goodness. Yes, but aren't you supposed to be . . . ? Oh. Come in."

She let them in as far as a carpeted hall. Framed photographs were grouped on the walls: pictures of Catherine with a smiling, academic-looking hus-band, numerous photographs of five different girls with the same startling red hair—Peta and her sisters, Stevie assumed. Through an open doorway, she glimpsed a large living room covered in white sheets with a stepladder in the center. A miasma of emulsion paint hung in the air. For a Vaethyr family, the household was strikingly normal.

Then she saw a framed sketch drawn in colored pastel, signed by Peta and dated two years earlier. It was a seascape with a figure rising like Neptune from the waves. Its face was Mist's face.

Stevie's mouth fell open. *Oh, gods, not more of this!*

"Forgive the intrusion," said Mist. "I don't know what I expected Peta to do, really. It's only that she knows me . . . I'm lost. She might have had advice, or an opinion about . . ."

"An Aetherial situation?" Catherine kept glancing from him to Stevie and back. Her demeanor was thoughtful and reserved. "Oh, she always has an opinion. Yes, she told me about you, and Boundry, and the trial of Rufus Ephenaestus . . . I can't claim she told me *everything*, but she told me a fair amount. So, you came back after all! She'll be so happy to hear it."

Mist shook his head. "No, don't tell her. Not yet, anyway—I'd rather explain face-to-face. Anyway, if she's not here, it doesn't matter."

"What's wrong?" Catherine pulled a rag from her pocket and began rubbing at the dried paint on her hands.

Mist gave a wry laugh. "I'm not actually sure."

"Clearly something's very wrong. Two Aetherials turn up . . ." She looked at Stevie. ". . . one with her *fylgia* hanging around her, which is not supposed to happen."

Oh no, not another one, Stevie thought. Glancing down, she saw the whitish form of her leopard winding around her feet.

Mist ignored her comment. "A friend of Stevie's went missing, and I suspect my brother Rufus has taken him, and he could be in danger. But I'm out of touch with the Aetherial network. I don't know where to start."

"You've come to the right place," said Catherine. "Cloudcroft, I mean. There's not much I can do personally to help you. I'm working on a long-term project mapping all the little ways in and out of the Spiral around the British Isles, which is fascinating to me but probably not much use to you. I've heard nothing of Rufus beyond what Peta told me. So, I'm going to suggest you go straight to the person with his finger on the esoteric pulse, as it were. Go to Stonegate Manor and ask for Lucas Fox."

"Who's Lucas Fox?"

Catherine blinked. "You really have been away, haven't you?"

Following Catherine Lyon's directions, they took long chilly walk, past the Green Man again and towards the far end of the village. It was like walking through a Christmas card, thought Stevie: granite walls, thatched cottages nestled beside stone houses, windows shining yellow against the winter gloom. Passing the last of the houses, a big, friendly looking beamed place named Oakholme, they continued up a winding, unlit lane to the wide gateway that Catherine had described.

Huge chunks of granite flanked the entrance to a driveway that curved up the side of a hill and passed out of sight. A small sign on the left-hand gatepost read STONEGATE MANOR. The wrought iron gates stood open. There was nothing to say either Welcome or No Entry! The lane and the fields beyond the hedgerows were deserted and desolate. She felt the temperature dropping, even as they hesitated.

"Come on, then," she said. "What are you thinking?"

"That it's a long, cold walk back into the village if there's no one in. Did the pub have bed-and-breakfast? You must be cursing me for all this."

"Honestly, I'm tougher than I look." She tugged his arm and they began to walk up the drive. "If there's no one here, we'll hurry back to the pub, warm up again, and call a cab. It's not the end of the world."

Mist sighed. He put his arm around her, in his companionable way. "Every time I knock on a door, I have a vision of Rufus answering and standing there laughing at me. Hands covered in blood." Stevie was about to reply with a witticism when he added, "*Her* blood."

He meant Helena.

Her words died in her throat. They walked in silence. Presently she said, "Peta's mother saw my *fylgia* too. Why?"

"The *fylgia* is like a thread or an anchor that connects us to the Otherworld. It's rare to see it. For some reason, yours has come loose and is following you around."

"That doesn't sound good." She shuddered. Mist was like a shadow guiding her into the underworld. She'd never felt so physically cold, nor so mentally unsettled in her life, yet she kept walking.

"The *fylgia* is meant to be an inner guide, the source of our deepest wisdom."

"Mine never says anything. It only looks sideways at me, like it's waiting for me to understand something I don't get yet."

"That's what they do. I've never seen mine—though I've sensed it once or twice—and I think Rufus's must have slunk off in disgust centuries ago. I've no answer for you."

He spoke in a distracted tone, his fingers tightening on her shoulder. She assumed he was thinking about Helena and Rufus. As the slope rose, a landscape of wooded hills and dead bracken unfolded around them, shrouded in wintry fog.

At the top of the hill loomed an impressive manor house with granite walls and a slate roof: almost a fortress. There were lights in the lower windows, an outside lamp illuminating a turning circle of gravel where a couple of cars were parked. Stevie let out a cloud of breath. These signs of modern civilization reassured her slightly, but Mist's expression was set and his eyes cold.

"Don't worry," she said. "I'll knock. If Rufus answers, I'll knee him in the groin and as he goes down, you get him in an armlock. He won't stand a chance."

"This isn't funny."

"I'm not joking," she replied thinly.

They reached the portico that framed the front door. Stevie gave three knocks with a brass stag's head and stood back. It was near dark, the sky thick with snow. One of the double doors opened and a slice of light fell across the step. A young woman peered through the gap. Slim and bright-faced, she had glossy brown hair swinging around her shoulders, silver eyes. She was dressed casually in black jeans and a thick plum-colored sweater.

"Hello," she said cheerfully. She opened the door, beckoned them in. "You must be Stevie and Mist? I'm Rosie Fox. Come in, we've been waiting for you."

Entering Stonegate Manor was like stepping back two centuries into a baronial hall, full of ghostly undercurrents. The house had the eeriest atmosphere Stevie had ever experienced. The air was full of crackling energy layers, like her "migraine" moments, but definitely not inside her head this time.

Rosie led them through the vestibule into a great hall two stories high surrounded by galleries on the upper floor. There was a vast stone fireplace at the far end surmounted by a coat of arms. Although a fire blazed in the grate, most of the heat was swallowed by the cavernous space. Rosie led them briskly across the hall into a cozier living room, full of warm light from a log fire. The far wall had French windows giving a view of a wild-looking rock garden edged with rhododendrons and birch trees. Rosie walked across and drew a pair of old-fashioned, flowery curtains.

"Sit anywhere," she said. "You both look frozen. It's a nightmare trying to keep this place warm in the winter. Can I get you a drink? Hot chocolate?"

"Thanks, that would be wonderful," said Stevie. "How did you know we were coming?"

"Catherine Lyon phoned us." Rosie grinned, eyes shining. Stevie, despite being chilled to the marrow and as wary as a cat thrown into a haunted house, couldn't help warming to her. "Nothing supernatural about it. Not yet, anyway."

"She told us to come and speak to Lucas Fox."

"My brother," said Rosie. "Yes, Sam's gone to get him; this house is so ridiculously big, you can lose people and wander round for an hour trying to find them. I swear it's bigger inside than out. I still get lost. Sam grew up here—he's my partner—and even he gets confused sometimes. Parts of Stonegate drift off into the Dusklands, so it's not always very . . . stable. But really, it's not so bad when you get used to it."

"Thanks for asking us in." Stevie felt warm enough to take off her coat at last. "You must wonder what we're doing here. I'm not sure myself, yet."

"What did Catherine say?" asked Mist, color returning to his face.

"Not much," Rosie said gently. "Two Aetherials in distress, seeking help. That's what we're here for. Back in two minutes."

She took their coats and left the room. Stevie sat in a high-backed armchair. Mist paced around, glancing outside through the curtains, looking around at the cream-colored walls and framed prints, mainly of Pre-Raphaelite images.

Stevie said, "She's the third person . . . What are people seeing in me that I'm missing?"

"A similar aura to the one you *didn't* see around Rosie Fox."

"Is it something you learn, like bird spotting?"

"In a sense."

"Mist, are you okay? Are we safe here? Not that I know what safe means, anymore."

"Well, we'll find out." There was a sharp look in Mist's eyes that she hadn't seen before, as if he was rediscovering his strength, like a knight strapping on one plate of armor at a time. She pulled a calm veil over herself, remembering the feral Stevie who'd fought off teenage molesters.

"We're not defenseless," she said firmly.

Rosie returned with two men, the blonder one carrying a tray of mugs. Both males were a couple of inches short of Mist's six foot, and both attractive in different ways. "This is Sam," Rosie said, "and this is my brother Lucas. Stonegate is Lucas's house, but we're staying here too, because the place is so darned big."

Sam looked like a fighter; lean and muscular with a face that was a strong-boned, rugged work of art. His shortish hair was brushed back, golden-pale with dark roots. His eyes were a piercing blue-green beneath thick eyebrows that retained a demonic quirk despite his bright, friendly grin. He wore a charcoal sweater and blue jeans. If Stevie had been expecting Vaethyr to dress up like medieval royalty, she was disappointed.

Lucas reminded her of Mist. He might have been Mist's brother, a couple of years younger. The greatest difference was his air of innocence. Unlike Mist, she guessed, he had not been torn apart and remade several times over. Not yet.

They exchanged handshakes and greetings. Stevie was relieved to find them so approachable, yet she sensed the soft-footed padding of creatures that could only be seen from the corner of the eye. These creatures were far bigger than her supposed *fylgia*, and dark, like Rottweilers. Mist sensed them too; she saw his uneasy glances.

Lucas noticed too, and said, "Don't worry, they're my *dysir*. Elemental guardians. Like a guard of honor, but they only turn nasty if there's a real threat. I've even given them names. More than most Gatekeepers have bothered to do."

"Did Catherine Lyon tell you who Luc is?" Rosie asked.

"Gatekeeper to the Great Gates between the Earth and Spiral realms," said Mist. "Was she supposed to give out that information?"

Lucas shrugged. "Most Aetherials know. It's not the best-kept secret. Anyway, I'm just a glorified security guard."

"More than that," put in Sam.

Stevie expected someone in such a position of responsibility to be older and more powerful in appearance than Lucas. Still, he compensated with an alertness that suggested he took his duties very seriously indeed.

"Are the Great Gates easy to sabotage?" Mist asked.

"Not really. Their function is to oppose sabotage. They're to keep the realms from launching attacks on each other—and the ways are well guarded."

"Not foolproof, though," said Mist.

"No, but they're not meant to be prison gates," said Lucas. "Why?"

Mist leaned on the back Stevie's chair. "I'm looking for my brother, Rufus. A notorious troublemaker. He thinks I'm dead—twice over, if not more— but there's a possibility he's found me. I'm sorry to be so vague."

"I think this story might take awhile to tell," said Stevie.

"Are you talking about *the* Rufus Dionys Ephenaestus?" Lucas frowned, staying on his feet while Sam handed out mugs of chocolate. "We heard about him, partly from the Lyon clan and partly from Iola . . ."

"His girlfriend," said Sam.

Lucas shot him a look. "When it suits her. Iola's part-elemental. She comes and goes according to her own inner voice, but she keeps an eye on the Otherworld for me, while the *dysir* mainly watch this place."

Rosie sat bolt upright, nearly spilling her drink. "You're Rufus's brother? Part of the Felynx *eretru* of Azantios? I only know this stuff because my father's an historian in his spare time—but they vanished so long ago, no one's sure if they were real, or an Aetherial myth. So you're . . . Mistangamesh?"

"I'm amazed you've heard my name. Yes. Azantios was real."

"That's incredible. You're the oldest Aetherial I've ever met, to my knowledge." Rosie gave a rueful smirk. "Sorry, that sounded gloriously offensive by human standards. You know what I mean."

"He is wonderfully well preserved," said Stevie, daring to tease Mist. She shot a glance over her shoulder at him; he returned a look of mild amusement.

Sam said, "Well, my grandfather Albin looks younger than I do, which is downright disturbing."

"According to my dad, the fount of all knowledge," Rosie said, "we only have a struggle with this age thing because of trying to juggle our human lives with our Aelyr side. Who knows how old any of us are, really? When an Aetherial is born, apparently, we spread out to all points of space and time. So none of us are any older or younger than the others, on the Aetheric plane."

"Hey, I like that," said Sam.

"Was it even grammatical?"

Mist, staring at Sam, said, "Wait—did you say that your grandfather is called Albin? From a noble Sibeylan house? He looks as if he's made of ice, covered in swan feathers? Bright blue eyes . . ."

Sam pointed at the center of his own forehead. "All three of them? You've met him?"

"Briefly. He played a major part in putting Rufus on trial before the Spiral Court. Rufus slithered away, as he does, while Albin seemed to have got on the wrong side of everyone. I don't know what went on behind the scenes. We were told it was a political clash between those who want to keep free access between Vaeth and Spiral, and those who want to seal off the Spiral forever."

"Figures," said Sam. "Albin's a monster. Seriously, he's a complete bastard. Did a great job of screwing up my father and he'd do the same to us, if he could."

Lucas's face was a mix of quiet anger and fear. "You don't need to remind me about Lord Albin," he said softly. Looking at Stevie and Mist, he added, "Albin tried to stop me becoming Gatekeeper, because in his twisted vision there should be no Gates and the Spiral should be cut off from Earth completely. I wasn't told a thing about Rufus's trial until afterwards, still less about Albin's part in it. I try to put him out of my mind, but the truth is that I have no idea what he might be up to in the Otherworld, or whose ears he's whispering in. Not that I've any sympathy for Rufus, but I was glad to hear that Albin lost that battle . . . because who knows what power Albin would have gained, if he'd won?"

"And I don't think he was the sort to give up easily," said Mist.

Lucas sighed. "True. Please, tell us your story. We might be able to fill in the gaps for each other."

"We'll feed you," Rosie said with genuine heart. "It goes without saying, you can stay over. We'll warm up a spare bedroom for you."

"Er, two rooms," Stevie said, and felt her face turn warm. Fortunately no one noticed. Their attention was on Mist as he gave a shorter version of the events he'd described to her.

As he spoke, she was aware of unusual energies around her, as if she'd developed a new sense for the unseen. She noticed soft bluish veils washing around the room, the *dysir* prowling or lying down, and pale golden auras around everyone, even furring her own hands. Now and then she saw these auras infused by different colors, as if betraying emotion. Her *fylgia* clung to her knee. For the first time, she realized it was *purring*.

All this felt weird, but not unpleasant. She was growing used to it.

"Whatever Lord Albin has done," Mist said when he'd finished, "I doubt it included the genocide of an entire civilization." He was sitting on a sofa by then. To Stevie's distress, he bowed his head and wept. "To lose something as precious as Azantios—I begged my mother and father to flee as the barbarians came, but they would not move. They gave up their life-essences to help us destroy the invaders; either way, the city was finished. My father told me to help weave the tenfold web, so I obeyed. The last promise I made was that I'd hunt down Rufus. I still owe my father that. I forgave Rufus too much in the past, but no more. This time it must end."

Lucas put a hand on Mist's shoulder, only to be shrugged off. Stevie's heart ached. Mist didn't deserve this pain.

Eventually Sam spoke. "So you're up against an enemy you can't see and can't find?"

"An enemy solid enough to have attacked both of us," Stevie put in. She elaborated on her own experience, filling out the parts Mist had skimmed over. "He, or it, was determined to take both Daniel's work and our piece of the Felixatus. So if you can give us even the tiniest clue as to what's happening . . . we're desperate. Aside from anything else, I'm really frightened for Daniel. His mother's so ill that I'm terrified I won't find him in time."

Lucas walked back and forth, arms crossed. "Being Gatekeeper doesn't grant me a magical overview of the realms, unfortunately. We've heard nothing of this. We enter the Spiral, of course: usually the nearest realm, Elysion. We've noticed nothing unusual. Have we?"

Rosie and Sam shook their heads. They sat close, her hand resting on his thigh.

"Iola's been deeper in, and reported the usual ebbs and flows; energy surges, the landscape changing, or an *eretru* creating a new small realm for which you hope they've got the Spiral Court's permission," Lucas went on. "Nothing especially worrying. We've heard nothing of Rufus Ephenaestus since his trial failed. Nothing of Lord Albin, either. To be honest, I really would like to know where Albin went."

Mist had composed himself, his eyes red-rimmed but dry. "Albin was associated with a sect who'd isolated themselves in Sibeyla, devoted to keeping the Spiral pure, whatever that means. I think he broke with them, though."

"Not extreme enough for him," Sam said sardonically. "He's probably in a cave surrounded by Nazi memorabilia. Rufus sounds Albin's absolute opposite. Can't see them becoming best mates."

Rosie said, "We'll do anything we can to help—not only for you two, but for the sake of the Otherworld itself. The bigger picture, so to speak."

"We need to find Rufus and Daniel, and what's left of the Felixatus too, I think." Mist added, "I'm sorry to unload this onto you."

Rosie waved away his apology. "Don't be daft. We're so grateful you came. We depend on Aetherials reporting any weirdness to us."

"And it's my duty to know," said Lucas. "One thing I've learned since I've been in this role is how infinitely precious and fragile the Spiral is. Aetherials wove it, Aetherials can tear it apart like a spider's web. Don't underestimate the threat to the Otherworld of the sheer *mind power* of a determined enemy. There are checks in place, such as the Spiral Court and the Great Gates, and the fact that the realms can only be manipulated by groups of adepts working in webs. But it's not enough. If a primal power such as Brawth arose, it might shred the Spiral into the Abyss in a day. What we'd lose is beyond measure. I can hardly bear to think about it, but I do, every hour, every day."

"That seems an awful burden to carry," Stevie said softly. Lucas responded with a faint smile, resigned.

"Look, whatever's happening, we'll crack it," said Sam. "I like a challenge."

"Don't you just," Rosie said with a private glance. "Here's a thought, Stevie: Have you got an email address? Maybe Daniel's tried to contact you."

"He hasn't so far, but it's worth a try." Stevie pulled her laptop out of her bag. "D'you have Wi-Fi?"

"Yes, but the signal's a bit dodgy. You'll need to come up into the library."

Leaving the men in the sitting room, Rosie took her across the great hall and up a broad staircase. Upstairs, wide corridors led off in several directions. Stevie felt a fresh wave of the eldritch atmosphere: corridors stretched at impossible angles and eerie coldness pricked her skin. She observed, too, how much warmth and life Rosie, Sam and Lucas brought into the forbidding house.

To have such a family . . .

The room resembled an old-style public library, with rows of bookshelves and a large table, the musty scent of old books. The only sign of modernity was a modem winking in one corner. Stevie sat down and booted up the laptop.

"The house belonged to Sam's father, Lawrence Wilder, who was Gatekeeper before Lucas," Rosie said. "Well, strictly speaking it belongs to whoever is Gatekeeper. We don't like Lucas being here—our parents have a perfectly lovely house down the hill—but he has to, for tradition's sake. Stonegate Manor's a dreadful old pile, really. It's haunted me all my life. I'm not crazy about living here, either, but Luc's much happier with company and basically . . . I want to keep him from turning into Lawrence."

"Why, what happened to Lawrence?"

Rosie paused in thought. "He was driven crazy by loneliness. That was part of it. Having Albin as a father didn't help, of course. And in case you're confused, I probably ought to explain that while Sam and I are not related, Lucas is half-brother to both of us. Lawrence had, er, a thing with my mother. It's not secret, but it is a bit of a touchy subject. Just so as you know."

"You don't need to explain," Stevie said, pretending not to be intrigued. She trusted Rosie and it was a good feeling. "They both seem lovely."

"They are, in their different ways. Luc's stronger than he looks, but he worries himself ragged, especially when Iola keeps vanishing into the Spiral. Sam's wonderful, with a wicked streak—heaven help anyone who threatens me, Luc or the rest of our family. He's the very man you want in a tight corner."

"How did you meet?"

"Well." Rosie blushed. "The full version would take all night. The short version is that we were next-door neighbors, give or take half a mile. We've always lived in Cloudcroft, pretending to be human but actually Vaethyr . . . our act is pretty seamless now. What about you, though?"

Stevie checked her email. All spam, apart from a message from Dr. Gregory. Holding her breath, she opened it; he'd visited Frances in hospital, he said. She was still very poorly, but stable. Stevie let her breath go.

"I've told you everything. People keep insisting I'm Aetherial and it's starting not to seem so far-fetched anymore. The whole 'appearing from nowhere and not knowing who I am' experience has sent me nearly mad at times. I hate it, but what can I do?"

"A similar thing happened to a friend of mine. She was convinced she was human, then discovered otherwise. Of course it freaked her out. It's bound to. It's rare, but maybe more common than we realize."

As they spoke, Stevie ran through one search after another, trying to find some recent trace of Daniel. "I wonder about Danny," she said. "Perhaps he's a reborn Aetherial too? How else could he have channeled all those visions?"

"It's possible, but there are some humans who are hypersensitive to Aetherial energies. They might become witches or psychics or visionaries. Or be locked up, if they're unlucky. We call them *naemur*." Rosie leaned on folded arms on the table. "It sounds like Daniel may have had that gift, or misfortune."

Frustrated, Stevie entered "Danifold" as a domain name. A cloud storage site appeared, containing private files, accessible only by password. She bit the side of her lip. Remembering the name on Daniel's shopping list, she typed in "Poectilictis." *Incorrect password*, came the message.

Then she remembered the curved arrow drawn over the word, and tried again, backwards. "Sitcilitceop."

The folder opened to reveal a list of digital image files. She clicked on one, and up came a painting in Daniel's distinctive style; three silver creatures were chasing on all fours across the foreground, and standing on a hill above them was a red-haired figure with her hands outstretched like a saint giving blessing. Aurata again.

"Yes," Stevie said, amazed. "He left me the password! Look, Rosie, all his artwork must be on here." She opened one after another, seeing a dozen scenes that Mist had described from his life. Aurata seemed to feature more than anyone else, which might indicate that Rufus was still obsessed with her memory. "This is unbelievable."

"And a text document," said Rosie. "SS.doc. Updated yesterday. Your initials, no?"

"Oh my god." Stevie's hand shook and she fumbled to get the mouse pointer in the right place. The document opened to show a letter.

Stevie I'm so sorry. How did he get the triptych from you? Should never have sent it sorry sorry. He said I'm painting the end of the world but he won't explain what he means but it's forbidden knowledge. Something's happening. No one knows but you and me. He brought me to Nevada a house called Red Cedars in Jigsaw Canyon. It's like a fortress. He's furious, won't let me go. I'm so scared now. Can't explain more, I'm so afraid but tell mum I'm all right.

The message ended abruptly, as if Daniel had been interrupted. Stevie sat back, pushing her hair off her clammy neck.

"Nevada?" she said. "That's virtually on the other side of the world."

"You can reply to him," said Rosie.

"How?"

"Just write a new document and upload it."

"Yes, of course, I didn't think." She placed her fingers on the keys, then let them fall. "No . . . it's obvious he's in danger. What if Rufus, or whoever's holding him captive, finds out he's communicated with me? What can I say? 'Come home, your mum's in hospital,' or, 'Hang on, we're coming to get you'? If the captor sees it, Dan could end up in even worse trouble."

She closed the document and pressed Delete. "There. If he looks again, he'll know I've read it. I hope."

Rosie pressed a warm hand on her shoulder. "At least you know where he is."

"I have to fetch him." Stevie groaned. "But how can I go to America? I'm not sure I've enough money to book a flight, let alone hire a car. I haven't even got a passport! He said it's a fortress and he's scared. What the hell am I going to do?"

"Deep breaths," Rosie said firmly. "I said we'd help you and I meant it. You know there are ways to travel other than crossing the Earth's surface, don't you? Aelyr ways."

12

Waterfall Dreams

An overnight snowfall was melting as they climbed the hill towards the Great Gates. Lucas led the way, Stevie and Mist following with Sam and Rosie behind them. Grass squelched underfoot and a damp cold breeze sighed past. The landscape was desolate; bare trees, brown bracken and rocks pushed out of the colorless grass.

They were dressed as if for a camping trip in thick clothing, heavy boots and waterproof jackets, with small rucksacks to carry essentials. Stevie, who loved her bohemian dresses and jewelry, felt odd in jeans. She was nervously excited. It was so good to feel they were doing something—and she couldn't believe the generosity of Lucas, Rosie and Sam in agreeing to guide them. Her *fylgia* was on her shoulder, barely visible.

Luc had explained that there were shortcuts. A path that lay across the Earth's surface, linking two distant parts of the Otherworld, was a *conlineos*. One that led through the Spiral, linking far locations on Earth, was an *anti-lineos*.

Mist had nodded, as if this made perfect sense.

Their combined confidence buoyed Stevie's mood. She'd replied to Dr. Gregory's email, *"Tell Frances that we've heard from Daniel, he's alive and we're trying to find him. Give her my love. She has to hang on."*

"I thought entering the Otherworld would be more exotic than this," she remarked.

"It's as exotic as you like, on a celebration night," said Rosie, "but for a journey, it's best to go commando."

Sam burst out laughing. "Rosie, you do know that 'going commando' is slang for not wearing underwear?"

Rosie giggled. Even Mist smiled. "Well, I'm not wearing any," she said.

"Works for me," said Sam.

Before they'd set out, Lucas had argued that there was no need for Sam and Rosie to come, that he could guide Mist and Stevie perfectly well without an escort. Sam had flatly told him he had no choice. They were coming, whether he liked it or not, partly because there was safety in numbers and partly because they didn't want to miss the adventure. Lucas had acquiesced with a show of reluctance, but Stevie suspected he was more grateful for their company than he'd admit.

Stevie could see nothing that resembled gates. At the peak of the hill there was a dip in the ground, and on the far side a huge outcrop of weathered, cracked granite tilting out of the earth. As they descended into the dip, its bulk towered over them.

"These rocks are remnants of a long-dead volcano," said Luc. "Apparently the Aelyr decided it was the perfect disguise for the master portal."

They climbed to the roots of the rock. Stevie placed a palm on its cold, granular, age-old surface. Then Lucas raised both hands and drew down the Dusklands around them, the first layer of the Aetherial realms. The atmosphere turned a fluid blue and became full of moving shadows. The outcrop itself changed. It grew bulkier and dome-like, shining with runes that sparkled and flowed over the surface like projected light.

"We'll go in through the Lychgate," said Lucas, pushing his hand into a crack barely eighteen inches wide. "We open the grander ways only on special occasions. But the Lychgate's always open, so any Aetherial can come or go as they please."

"Not very secure," said Mist.

"It's not supposed to be," said Lucas. "That's the point. I'm only here to keep an eye on things, not dictate who goes in or out." He exchanged glances with Sam and Rosie. "The hundreds of hidden portals across the world are all controlled from the Great Gates, and it's my job to keep them open. Or to close them all, if there's a major threat of some kind . . . but let's hope it never comes to that."

The crack in the rock looked like nothing unusual to an untrained eye. Lucas pushed his way into the darkness. Stevie followed, then Mist, with Rosie and Sam behind them. The walls squeezed her and a chill crept over her skin: instant claustrophobia. The air smelled of deep caves.

Lucas said over his shoulder, "Stevie, have you got a brand?"

"D'you mean a flashlight?"

"No. Brand, as in a symbol burned into your skin."

The question startled her. "Not that I'm aware of. It's a bit late to strip and examine myself, isn't it?"

"Oh, I don't know," said Sam with a smile in his voice, adding "Ow!" as if Rosie had inflicted a light physical rebuke.

"I should have asked before," Lucas went on. They were pushing their way through a narrow, curving passage that made her think of the entrance to a burial mound. "When a Vaethyr born on Earth enters the Otherworld for the first time, they're likely to meet a band of hunters called Initiators who insist on branding them with a spiral mark. It leaves a scar."

"As if we're cattle?"

"Pretty much. It's part of initiation. It's a weird old Aelyr tradition, as if to say, 'We know who you are and we claim you.'"

Rosie said, "It's an honor or an assault, depending on your point of view."

"But how will they know I'm unbranded?" Stevie felt a rising tingle of dread.

"I don't know," said Lucas. "They just do."

"Does it hurt?"

"Well, yes, it stings like hell," said Rosie. "And it can give you a load of strange visions, too. That's part of the initiation ritual."

"I haven't got time for all that," Stevie said brusquely, alarmed.

"I know," said Lucas. "If a band of Initiators scents you, though, it's going to be fun trying to escape them."

"Should we even be doing this?" She glanced around at Mist. "No, I'm not going to let it stop me. If they catch me, they catch me."

"It will be all right," said Mist, touching her shoulder.

"How do you know?"

She heard Sam laugh. "He doesn't. But don't worry, we're veterans at this stuff; we'll do our best to keep you safe."

For a time they followed a curving labyrinth. Stevie kept feeling symbols carved into the walls. Then a fragrant draft blew towards them and a triangle of cobalt light appeared.

Lucas led the party out onto a slope of lush grass that plunged towards a forest. Trees as tall as sequoias swayed like a sea in slow motion against a sky whorled with stars. There was no snow on this side. In contrast, the air was warm and deliciously scented with pine resin. It smelled like incense. Stevie felt light-headed, overwhelmed by the subtle unfamiliarity of this new realm; the scents and deep oceanic colors and the astonishing whirlpools of stars.

They'd stepped from a fissure in a rock that, looking back, appeared far smaller than the one they'd entered. Trees and brambles embraced its flanks. A path wound downhill and curved out of sight between the tree trunks, subtly shining like a snail trail, or dew.

Stevie's four companions formed a protective diamond around her, with Lucas leading the way down the path. Luminous dust swirled around their feet. Stevie realized that the light came from clouds of tiny fireflies.

"Why is it always night here?" said Rosie. "I swear, every time we come through, this part of Elysion is always dark."

"It's the Aetherial realm showing off," said Sam. "Creating the right atmosphere to intimidate the newcomers."

"Is he always so cynical?" said Mist.

"Oh, yes, Sam can be relied upon for it," said Lucas. "That lack of respect is really going to land him in trouble one of these days."

"What d'you mean, one of these days?" said Sam. "I've not only got the T-shirt, I've got certificates and medals and a prison record to show for it."

At first, Stevie thought she was all right. Then, with every step, she grew more light-headed. The others were looking all around as they went. There was no obvious sign of anyone following. The forest surrounded them in all directions, rustling with an eerie life of its own.

The trees themselves were sentient, she suspected. The very ground beneath their feet reacted to every footstep.

The whole Spiral is alive and aware.

This knowledge filled her as if she'd always known it. The firefly light of the path was hallucinatory. Elysion became distorted, as if seen through water. Her companions' voices echoed but she could make no sense of the words . . . She wondered if, despite their protection, the Initiators had branded her already, their attack stealthy and invisible.

Now Sam and Rosie were helping her to walk. They all seemed to be half-floating, as if wading along the bottom of a lake. She struggled to keep her feet. She saw unexpected movement out of the corner of her eye, and she heard Mist's voice murmuring in concern, fading . . . A dark figure flitted past her into the trees, vanishing.

She was aware of a commotion around her, raised voices. All she heard clearly was Rosie asking, "Where is he?"

"Never mind." Sam's voice, strong and determined. "Keep going, Luc. Just keep going."

Stevie found herself being carried down a steep slope defined by a rock wall on their right and pale birches on the left. Above, the sky shone with rivers of stars. These celestial bodies emitted a sound like rushing water.

She tried to cry out, but couldn't make a sound. Elysion was wondrous, terrifying. They were sinking into an ultramarine gully. She made out a shape, some kind of building in silhouette, a cottage . . .

Her companions helped Stevie over a threshold. The vast, underwater blue world was replaced by a golden-ivory cell: a room aglow with firelight.

Her dizziness began to recede. Strength returned to her limbs and her tongue felt as if it might eventually work again; but for now she was speechless, disorientated. Sam helped her to sit down on a soft mound. The floor was carpeted with soft dry moss, more like a meadow than a normal floor.

"Are you okay, honey?" Rosie asked, kneeling beside her.

Stevie looked around. The fey room was odd but not alien. Mossy mounds and cushions surrounded a low round table like a solid disk of lapis. Containers on a long wooden worktop and a water pump indicated that this was a kitchen of a kind. She saw Sam, Lucas and someone new, an angular yet graceful woman in a long plum-colored dress. This woman had long, crinkly black hair around a striking face that was all bones and hollows.

But where was Mist?

Stevie caught her breath, her heart rate rising as she tried to process his absence. No . . . she looked over her companions again, very carefully, in case it was a trick of her disordered mind. There was only Lucas, Sam and Rosie, and the witchy inhabitant of the cottage. All had grave expressions that perturbed her even more.

At last she managed to speak. "Where's Mist?"

Rosie placed a steady hand on her arm. Sam and the woman withdrew to murmur in a corner. "We're not sure. Try not to worry."

"Not sure? What happened? I—I don't feel right."

"The first time in the Spiral can be very weird," said Lucas. "I should have warned you, Stevie. It affects some people more strongly than others."

"Did the Initiators come after us?"

Lucas shook his head. "No, we didn't see hide nor scale of them, for a change."

"So where's Mist gone?"

A pause. Rosie answered, "We don't know. I'm sorry. Entering Elysion seemed to affect him strongly too. You didn't notice?"

"I saw movement . . . I was too confused to understand what was happening."

"Mist seemed to panic a bit," said Rosie. "He stared to change physically, like he was taking on an Otherworld form. That could be what spooked him. He just ran, like a horse bolting. When we spend a long time in the human world, our Aetherial aspects can come as a huge shock. Terrifying, even."

She glanced at Sam, who added, "Not many of us are privileged to be all-powerful or all-wise, unfortunately. We muddle along as best we can."

"Is it a long time since Mist was in the Spiral?" Lucas asked.

"I'm not sure." Stevie tried to recall what he'd told her. "He spent some years trapped in a corner of the Otherworld, but he was human at the time, or believed himself to be. Before that, he was in elemental form for centuries. And before that, he was mostly on Earth, I think. I really don't know. It's complicated."

"Perhaps I should have chained us all together." Lucas sat on another mound, facing her. "The last thing I expected was for Mist to plunge into the forest and vanish."

Stevie recalled a shadow fleeing, voices calling after him. Caught in a whirl of dizziness and double vision, there was nothing she could have done to stop him.

"Oh my god," she gasped.

"Try to stay calm." Rosie pressed her arm. "Sam was going to follow him, but we decided it was more important to get you here safely first and worry about Mist afterwards."

"I'm sure he can look after himself," Sam put in. "By the way, this is my mother, Virginia. Mum, our new friend Stevie."

"It's a pleasure to meet you," said the woman, shaking Stevie's hand with a quick warm grip and kissing her cheek. She smelled like the forest itself; of herbs and rich resins, like incense. Sam's resemblance to her was obvious in their strong bone structure and striking eyes. Virginia had an air of cool power that was reassuring without being overfriendly. She gave Stevie a long, appraising look. Stevie averted her gaze as if to shield herself. It seemed everyone she met felt the need to stare at her, as if she were some bizarre specimen that defied explanation.

"Sam's told me a little of what happened." Virginia moved to a side table, poured liquid into a blue stoneware goblet and brought it to her. "You're obviously in shock. The Spiral will do that to newcomers. Just sit and rest for a while."

Stevie took a sip. Sweet, fragrant fruit juice moistened her tongue. "We have to find Mist. He wouldn't disappear for no reason. A creature attacked both of us on Earth, and it might still be hunting us."

"We'll go and search," said Sam, looking at Rosie. The two of them went straight out, leaving Stevie alone with Lucas and Virginia. She felt numb, almost inert, not knowing how to react to anything.

"Are you hungry?" asked Virginia.

"No, thank you. I couldn't eat."

"Try something light." She brought a plate of round white cakes to the table. "You'll feel better, I promise."

Stevie took a cake and nibbled the edge. A delicate taste like rice milk and rosewater melted in her mouth. It took no effort to eat after all, and Virginia was right. The grounding effect of food and drink was magical.

Lucas said, "Where's Lawrence?"

"Not here, I'm afraid." Virginia sat down on the hearth, crossing one bare foot neatly over the over, the hem of her plum dress falling across her ankles. "He went to Tyrynaia a few nightfalls ago."

"Is he coming back?" Lucas sounded startled.

"Well, I surely hope so. However, it's a journey that takes time and I'm not expecting him home in a hurry." Turning to Stevie, she said, "It's a kind of pilgrimage, you might say. Tyrynaia's the oldest Aetherial city, and can be found only if it wants you to find it. The deeper into the Spiral we travel, the harder it can be to come back. Lawrence didn't share his reasons for going, and I didn't ask; it's a very personal matter to each Aetherial."

"He must come home," Lucas said fervently.

Virginia smiled. "Don't look so worried, Luc. You seem to think you still need his guidance, but it's obvious you're managing perfectly well on your own."

"I was thinking about you, Mrs. Wilder." He gave a wry smile, and again Stevie thought how much he reminded her of Mist. It must be an Aetherial trait, that alluring dark-and-pale beauty. "Still, you're right; I do rely on him too much. I try not to come here more than a twice a year, but still . . ."

"Perhaps that's part of the reason he went. He trained you. Now it's time to trust your own instincts."

"And I do," Lucas said softly. "But it's reassuring to know that you're here."

Stevie remembered Mist's fight with the shadowy attacker. Chills feathered her skin. Was it still following, lurking in its own dimension? Paranoid, she looked around, but the room remained steady, golden, safe.

"Do you feel ready to talk?" Virginia asked Stevie. "No rush."

"No, I'm all right." After a couple of deep breaths, she explained, in as few words as possible, how she'd met Mist and who he claimed to be. Virginia listened with wide eyes and parted lips.

"And you had an artifact from the time of the *Felynx*?" she said as Stevie finished. "I wish Lawrence could have seen it. So old, it must have been mined in Naamon itself. Even among Aelyr, the Felynx were thought to be mythical. Certainly extinct."

"Mist seems to think that he and Rufus are the only survivors. Now he's certain that Rufus is on the loose and planning something appalling."

"The Felynx. Creatures of fire," Virginia said softly. "Well . . . it's possible that if Rufus feels he's not answerable to the Spiral Court's authority, he might embark on a drastic rampage of some kind."

"How d'you mean?" Lucas sounded alarmed.

"He might want revenge on Albin. Fire against ice, anarchy against restriction. It's about balance. Brawth rose . . ." Virginia paused. "You know our creation story, don't you, Stevie?"

She gave a small shrug. "Mist told me a bit. I'm happier with science than myth. Qesoth was a vast fire elemental and Brawth was her shadow, her adversary?"

"No one knows if those tales are factual or symbolic, because the paradox of the Spiral is that, sometimes, we make things real by imagining them," said Virginia. "Even humans can do that, to an extent. However, as ideas and as energies, Qesoth and Brawth are absolutely real."

Stevie pulled her jacket around her shoulders. "Because Aelyr *imagine* them to be?"

"In a sense. Energy is real, after all. Storms and torrents. The sun's radiation. Winter and summer. We call Brawth the shadow giant from the beginning and end of time. Not so long ago, Brawth rose—or an *idea* of him rose, with the same devastating effect—and very nearly brought an end to the Spiral and Vaeth itself."

"That was a fun evening," Lucas said dryly.

"The Earth nearly ended?" Stevie's eyebrows rose. "And I didn't notice?"

"It was early May, only a few years ago," said Lucas. "You might remember massive thunderstorms, power cuts, trees all over the road . . . that sort of thing?"

"Oh . . . but weather happens. Everyone got up the next day. The world didn't end, did it?"

"No. Brawth was made dormant again, thanks to the bravery of certain individuals." Virginia gave Lucas a warm, meaningful look. "My concern is that an opposite force might rise in response, in the sort of automatic way that a pendulum swings. Qesoth might well rise in her turn. The Felynx were said to be closely aligned to her, being creatures of fire and sun. So, if Rufus is planning mischief, he might find a heavyweight power on his side."

"I don't think Mist has even thought of that," Stevie said uncertainly.

"We should warn them," said Lucas. He'd gone nearly grey.

"Warn who?" Stevie asked.

"Everyone. All Vaethyr and Aelyr. Tell the Spiral Court . . ."

Virginia was shaking her head. "Tell them what? Luc, I'm only speculating."

"But if there's a rising threat, I need to know. Am I expected to defeat it on my own? I can't do it. I'm not Lawrence!"

"Lucas," Virginia said firmly, "Lawrence didn't act alone. You know that. No one expects you to take sole responsibility. You're an employee of the Spiral Court."

"But I'm the Gatekeeper." His breathing quickened. He looked so concerned that Stevie wished she knew him well enough to put her arm around him.

"Yes, just that. Not Lord Protector of the entire Otherworld. We have to consider various possibilities without scaring ourselves to death."

"I know." He took a long breath. "But how can I think of everything? Even Iola can't be everywhere at once. No wonder Lawrence . . ."

He stopped, but Virginia finished for him, "Went a little mad?"

"In any case," Stevie put in, "warning people about things that haven't happened yet could be dangerous. Daniel was taken because his paintings were supposed to be leaking secrets. Which means *someone* must be able to interpret the hidden messages he was channeling."

"Channeling from where, though?" Virginia said, frowning.

"Allegedly, from me." Stevie sighed. "I don't know how, because I'm the 'Eternal Sunshine of the Spotless Mind,' like that film where they got their memories wiped."

She was quiet, remembering the previous night when they'd all looked at Daniel's paintings on her laptop screen. Mist had barely spoken, only stared with moist eyes at images of his parents and their Felynx courtiers, lined up like stylized angels. He and Rufus—feline, not quite human, but still recognizable—had appeared in some of the paintings. *But*, Stevie thought again, *why were there so many of Aurata? Why was she so prominent, much more so than her brothers or parents? And what the hell was her "Promise"?*

After an hour or so, Sam and Rosie returned, looking grim and disheveled. "No sign," said Sam. "We'll try again when it gets light."

Rosie touched Stevie's shoulder. "Try not to worry about him. Easier said than done, I know."

"He might find his way here, anyway," said Virginia. "Come on, make yourselves at home. Sam will help me get a meal ready, won't you, love? You'll stay the night, I hope. We'll talk things over until the picture seems clearer."

Stevie stood up, restless. "No. I mean—please, stay and eat and talk, whatever. But I can't just sit here. I need to find Mist."

She let herself out of the cottage, crossed a lush garden and entered a meadow beyond. The landscape was soaked in deep ultramarine twilight, the sky ablaze with constellations she'd never seen before. Every detail felt heightened, more intense than on Earth. Elysion's beauty was surreal and intoxicating. Stevie found herself on the bank of a wide, shallow stream that gushed noisily along the valley floor. In front and curving to her right, cliffs protected Virginia's domain.

She called Mist's name, but heard no answer. She turned and walked upstream until she came to a waterfall that plunged down a high rock wall.

Stevie stood on the large smooth stones that edged the waterfall basin and stared into the churning water. The sight disturbed her, yet she couldn't move away. Water equally scared her and fascinated her. She remembered nightmare times in her foster homes, when she'd filled bathtubs to overflowing and climbed in to see how it might feel to drown . . . without the faintest idea why she'd felt the need to do so.

Her *fylgia* stood at her feet, one paw raised and its muzzle aimed at the pool, like a pointer dog. Cool spray chilled her face. The sheer energy of cascading water electrified her. She stared and stared into the pool, hypnotized.

Someone moved softly alongside her. "Stevie?" Virginia said from the gloom. "It's all right, the others stayed inside. You really shouldn't be alone."

"I don't know what to do." Stevie watched the roiling water. "My dear friend Daniel's in danger. I have a gaping hole in my identity. I've lost my job, the only thing that kept me sane. Now I've lost Mist, too. I've no idea what's going on or what I'm supposed to do about any of it."

"Let's start with what I see."

Her matter-of-fact tone arrested Stevie. "Okay, go on."

"You're Aetherial. It's a gracefulness, a glow, a look in your eyes as if you're harboring unearthly secrets . . ."

Stevie laughed. "I wish."

"My dear, you're not the first person I've met who's Aelyr and yet absolutely unaware of it." Virginia sat down, tugging Stevie's arm so she sat with her. Spray sifted over them. "I chose to live here in Elysion, but as time passed, I started to forget I'd ever lived on Earth among mortals. I had a vague memory of a husband and sons, but it became distant . . . as if it happened to someone else. Imagine, forgetting my own family! But this can happen, and it's disturbing, if not downright terrifying."

Stevie had a sudden memory of Nanny Peg, looking up with clouded eyes to ask, "Are you one of the nurses, dear?" Tears stung her eyes.

"Your memory came back, though?" she said. "Like being reborn?"

"You could say that. We're lucky to get chances that mortals rarely get. Second, third, fourth chances . . . Are you all right?"

Stevie wrapped her arms around her bent knees. Her hair slid forward to shroud her. "I'm trying to stay calm, but I'm scared to death."

"I know. That's the flip side of being semi-mortal. It's as if we can't keep up with ourselves. We're constantly being dangled over the void of the unknown."

"It's the water." Stevie looked up, and let her gaze drop with the torrent into the foaming basin beneath. The depths appeared bottomless, glowing deep green as if lit from below, all too welcoming. "I've always had a thing about water, like a phobia, except I can't tear myself away from it."

"Melusiel," said Virginia, nodding.

"What do you mean?"

"You know the Spiral's divided into five realms? Asru for the spirit, Naamon for fire, Elysion for earth, Sibeyla for air, Melusiel for water. Like the primal elements, although more complex in reality. All Aetherials have an affinity, which is usually but not always connected to the realm they were born in. Everything about you suggests your origins are Melusiel."

"Is that good or bad?"

"Neither. It's a clue to your nature, that's all."

"Why does water frighten me, then?"

"That I can't answer."

"It's like an urge to stand on a cliff edge even though you're frightened of heights. Which I am, incidentally. Also I'm not keen on centipedes, and as for *millipedes* . . . I think it's that whole segmented invertebrate thing that gives me the creeps."

Virginia interrupted, "Changing the subject is not going to help. Let's think about water. Relax and see what comes into your mind."

"Are you trying to hypnotize me?"

"I'm trying to help. Often a light trance will dissolve memory blocks."

"But I'm afraid to remember." She was trembling. Her heartbeat felt like an earthquake.

"I know." Virginia placed a gentle hand on her spine.

"I'm afraid I might dive in and never come back up," said Stevie.

"Is that what you want to do? Go into the pool?"

"Yes. I feel as if I'll die if I don't plunge in there. But that's insane. I'm not going in; it's dangerous and I'll drown."

"Can't you swim?"

"I don't know. I doubt it. I've never tried, because of this phobia."

"Well, you can hang on to the rocks."

Stevie gasped. "Aren't you supposed to dissuade me?"

"No," Virginia said coolly. "If it's what you need to do, then you must."

"I can't," Stevie whispered. "But . . ."

Fear rushed through her, louder than the waterfall, as she rose to her feet and threw off her jacket, her boots and clothes and underwear. She stood on the lip of the pool, not caring that she was naked because there was only Virginia to see her. The next she knew, she was leaping feet-first towards the center of the pool; and then she was underwater, pushed down and down by the water's force, the torrent roaring in her ears.

She was sinking into green glass, air bubbles rising from her mouth and nose. Complete terror filled her. Panic. She was drowning. Down and down through an infinite lake. She clawed the water, desperately trying to scramble upwards. No revelations came, no *fylgia* to guide her, only the knowledge that she must resurface or die . . .

A shape came snaking towards her through the emerald gloom. It was blue-black yet iridescent, some kind of serpent—no, more of a seahorse, covered in scales that flashed purple and red and orange, adorned with fronds and tendrils like a leafy sea dragon.

Its sinuous form flowed over her, touching her, gripping her with its tail wrapped around her left thigh. She arched her back, helpless. She felt its muscular scaly length pressed along her stomach as the seahorse head swung close to her face. Entwined, the two drifted along the lake bed. She put her arms around the creature, in some vain hope that it would carry her to the surface. The spokes of its ribs pressed into her. She was aware now that she'd stopped breathing and was yet still alive, calm and numb and resigned. She looked into the leafy dragon's black eyes, saw its mouth gaping to reveal fangs—and then it struck.

She felt two needles pierce her collarbone. A convulsion of pain and ecstasy made her arch like a bow. Loss of consciousness came as a blissful release.

Was it possible to live in two worlds at once, without attracting jealousy? Fela had little ego, but even the wildest of Tashralyr could not have resisted basking in triumph. She enjoyed her short time of glory, of walking proudly through the lanes of Azantios with Karn and their fellow athletes, wearing garlands of victory. They were paraded at palace gatherings, their silver-grey forms conspicuous among the gilded Felynx, their silken fur adorned with finery sewn from watery silks and silver mesh. Aurata was always there as her patron and protector. Rufus was never far away with an entourage of his own; yet he was always glancing at his sister with Fela; wanting what he could not have.

And Mistangamesh . . . he haunted the edge of the crowd, looking troubled. Sometimes he was with Poectilictis, sometimes alone or in a small group. When Fela saw his friends around him she felt strange, because they were close to him in a way she could never be. To Aurata and Rufus, she was a coveted plaything. To Mistangamesh, though, she was nothing, because he didn't play such cruel games. He moved in a higher circle that barely overlapped with hers.

When the races and the parties were over, Fela would go home to the quiet, watery lands of her own *eretru*, and try to live among them as if nothing had changed. Karn had been like a brother to her. He was a good and kind Tashralyr, but even his heart was not great enough to resist envy when she began to outrace him every time. They drifted apart.

Her own people were different with her now. Not openly hostile, but less welcoming. Many resented the Felynx with their power and pretentions, so Tashralyr who associated with them were viewed with suspicion. Even life among her fellow athletes was no easier. They were too competitive; their admiration of her prowess soon soured to jealousy. She thought of running away, but to where? In any case, Aurata would not let her. And she'd grown attached to Aurata, in an uneasy way.

Fela thought that she'd rather become a gracious loser than an outcast. Pride, however, would not let her. While she was racing and winning—and basking in the adoration of the Felynx—only then was she truly alive, and in ecstasy.

One misty evening she was alone, slipping between ferny trees down a long gully that led to her favorite lake. She paused, watching vapors drift thickly over the swampy ground at the lake's edge. Then she heard someone call her name. "*Fela?*"

At first she thought it was Karn. She heard the call again, emanating from the heart of the swamp. Was someone in distress? Curiosity led her on, one paw after another.

"Fela!" Still faint yet distinct, the voice lured her. She crossed the swamp, stepping on spongy green cushions of moss. The water was only a paw's depth below her. Otter-like, she was a creature who lived beside water, not in it. She knew there were water-breathing undines who lived in the depths, but they were shy beings, rarely seen. To them, Fela was an intruder. In her four-legged form, she had waterproof fur, but no gills, nor any other means to breathe underwater.

"Fela, I must see you!"

Fainter now, and farther away, the voice was imploring. Male or female, she wasn't sure . . . could it be Mistangamesh calling, wanting to see her in secret? The thought crossed her mind because he'd tried to speak to her in the palace, to warn her away from his sister and brother, but Aurata had scolded him and swept Fela out of his sight.

Now hope and curiosity drew her. She had no reason for suspicion. Although Aetherials had their differences and conflicts, there was rarely violence.

"Fela?"

Vapors thickened and the swamp spread all around her. She was no longer sure of her way back.

"Who's there?" she called.

Something reared out of the water and seized her. She was pinioned, turned over, and forced down into the swamp. All turned to confusion. She felt herself being pushed underwater, the surface closing over her face. She held her breath and struggled, but a dark shape of terrible strength was holding her down without mercy. She saw the surface rippling above her head, distorting her killer's shape, saw the last of her breath escape in a string of glassy bubbles.

Darkness carried her down.

13

Persephone's Chamber

"Is there anything else?" The voice issued from a silhouette standing against a dim green light. She glimpsed a long black dress clinging to a curvy figure, a veil of raven hair . . . Virginia? *"There's something you've left out."*

Fela was tumbling downwards through channels of wet black rock. She wound between the feet of the living but no one saw her. Reduced to a pale soul-essence, she darted like a terrified cat down convoluted walkways and terraces, descending long flights of steps deep into the city's secret heart, down into cellars that became caverns and tunnels, a ghostly streak against dark rock. She had no idea how she'd come here. There was nothing in her mind but fear, and the terrible cold reek of water drawing her like gravity into the deepest subterranean caves of the underworld.

Daniel sat in the workroom and began a new drawing. He felt compelled to work, even though his right eye was swollen shut and his left arm aching where Oliver had twisted it and thrown him down. His kidneys throbbed. His skin was a tender mass of bruises beneath his clothes. Still the visions kept coming.

The huge floor-to-ceiling window gave a breathtaking view of blue sky, red rock studded with cactuses, and a distant glint of barbed, electrified fences. The house ranged over four stories, poised on the hillside above Jigsaw Canyon. The workroom they'd given him was bigger than his London studio, yet took up only a corner of the second-lowest floor.

There were at least thirty Aetherials living here, sharing duties of security and housework in echoes of a religious commune. Like Oliver, they tended to stay in human shape, with a dress code of dark, smart suits for male and female alike. Oliver still hadn't properly explained who they were, beyond describing them as "staff."

Whose staff, though? Daniel wondered. Oliver was firmly in charge, but had an air of tense hyperactivity about him that suggested he was managing a business rather than simply living here. He seemed to have no family, and was not the relaxed, wealthy head of household that Daniel might have expected. Sometimes they would all vanish into a private room and he'd hear eerie chanting. If this was a cult, Oliver must be their leader . . . but he acted more like a commandant than a serene guru.

Daniel had learned the hard way not to ask questions. The response was either silence or rage. His duty was to work, and keep his mouth shut.

Swiftly he sketched a body floating face up, like Ophelia drowning. He added the hint of shady figures retreating in the distance, their crime complete. The colors in his mind were grey and aqua.

"What the hell is this?" Oliver said over his shoulder.

Daniel started violently. His nerves were on fire.

"I-I-I don't know. Murder, perhaps . . . I keep telling you, I only see things. I don't know what they mean, I never have."

Oliver ripped the page out of the sketch book and shredded it.

Daniel recoiled in shock. "What are you doing? You said paint whatever I see!"

"Not that one."

"So now you're censoring me? Why have you changed your mind?" Daniel cowered after he spoke, waiting for a blow. He hated himself for the reflex, but he'd never been the fighting type. When his lover turned from mentor to monster, he had no defense. His awe of Oliver was collapsing into plain terror.

Oliver grabbed his hair and jerked his head back, sneering at Daniel's gasp of pain. "No. I said I want to *know* every detail that you're channeling. I decide whether it's fit to be seen by my . . . colleagues, or better buried. If you think *I* am harsh, believe me, there are higher powers whom we truly do not want to displease."

If Oliver answered to unseen superiors, it might explain his own manic tension and his impulse to take out his frustration on Daniel . . . or it might simply mean he was mad. Daniel understood now that Oliver was eventually going to kill him. He would squeeze out every last drop of inspiration, then throw away the husk. What was to stop him? This was a stronghold, with no escape, and nothing beyond the security fences but miles of desert.

Worse than this was his fear of dying without ever learning the truth. He'd painted otherworldly beings and then discovered they were real. That knowledge was enough to drive him insane. But never to learn what was going on, what Oliver *needed* from his work—the frustration was unbearable.

He'd no way of knowing if his panicky message would reach Stevie. It was unlikely. He'd had only five minutes on an unattended laptop to write the document and pray that no one saw it. Oliver had made him set up the secret file storage, apparently so that unnamed absent "colleagues" could view the images.

For Daniel to add a personal, subversive message was a mad risk. As smart as Stevie was, there was little chance she'd ever see it. Now, for her own safety, he hoped she hadn't.

All this flew through his mind as Oliver gave him a painful upside-down kiss then let go, shoving Daniel away from him with such force that he slipped off his seat onto the floor. As he got shakily back to his feet, he saw that Oliver was holding a familiar stone disk between his palms. With a menacing smile he asked, "D'you recognize this?"

Daniel stared in horror at the familiar carved object that he'd last seen in his display case at home. He couldn't breathe. "How the hell did you get that?"

"The question is, why didn't you give it to me when you had the chance?"

"It's my mother's. If I'd known it mattered to you . . ."

"Well, my good assistant Mr. Slahvin is attuned to sniff out artifacts such as this, and the triptych, and bring them to me. There's nothing you can hide from us. *Nothing.*"

"Did he harm my mother, or my friend Stevie? If I *ever* find out he hurt them—"

"You'll do what?" Oliver laughed. "Don't worry. People only get hurt if they defy me. Stop fighting me, Daniel, you dear fool." Oliver regarded him with an expression of glowing, cruel-to-be-kind love that rendered him helpless.

"I'm not fighting." Daniel's voice came out as a husky whisper. "I want to make you happy. But this is not what I expected."

"I don't care what you expected. Most artists would kill to be given a studio like this and the promise of great rewards in exchange for indulging their talent all day. Yet you're complaining?"

"No. You're missing the point. This can't work." Daniel pulled at his own hair and glared up at Oliver. "You're angry because I'm not painting what you want to see!"

"That's what you think?"

"Yes. You described me as a 'court artist.' That means you want flattery. You want me to produce a happy ending of some kind. But I can't. I don't see one. I see betrayal. Some kind of fire goddess, and the Earth in ruins."

Oliver hissed. For a half-second, Daniel saw him as a savage lynx-faced being who might have stepped from one of his paintings. "Just paint the truth. Suppose the fire goddess is on her way? We need to prepare for her arrival."

"How?"

Oliver pointed at *Aurata's Promise.* "Read my mind. Paint her again, in a posture of triumphant glory. I know you can do it."

"What if I can't?"

"As I said, no one needs to get hurt. However, if you continue with tricks like sending paintings astray, forgetting to give me sacred artifacts, or trying to send pathetic little secret messages to your friend Stevie, it will be a very different story."

Daniel froze. Oliver's tone was soft and dangerous. "There's little chance she will have seen it. But suppose she did? Do you really suppose she would attempt to find you? All you'd achieve is to put her in the most incredible danger. Had you thought of that? Is it what you want?"

Daniel couldn't answer. Of course he'd had those thoughts, so chilling they kept him awake at night. He braced himself for a physical blow, but Oliver only stood towering over him like a white-gold angel, laughing and laughing at him.

The deepest chamber was a black obsidian cave, dappled with watery light from below. Fela slunk in, clinging to the contours of the cave-wall until she found a recess. There was nothing left of her but an indistinct, whitish shape the size of a lynx. She pressed her elemental form into the angle where floor met wall, wishing herself invisible.

Whoever she'd been before was lost. All she knew was that her soul-essence had been severed from her body: that she was dead, or worse: suspended in some strange half-death.

This echoing black space that rippled with reflections was her last refuge, a cave beyond the world.

The source of the glow was an oblong hole in the cave floor, perhaps fifteen feet wide, like a large sunken pond. The ever-moving light made the chamber seem full of water. She imagined she lay at the bottom of a lake, all breath and life crushed out by the water's weight.

Fela became aware of a figure moving around the chamber; a female silhouette with raven hair falling loose. She turned, revealing a lovely, ageless face with bright skin. The long pointed sleeves of her dress brushed the ground and were lined with blood red.

The splash of red made Fela tremble. The dark maiden looked at her with grave, kind eyes of darkest purplish brown.

"Welcome, Fela. I'm Persephone. I like that name best, of the many given to me. You're safe here."

Fela dared not believe it.

The jade glow transfixed her, mysterious and ineffable. Water had become an element to dread. A mesh of soft blue-green radiance reflected from every surface, creating an ever-lapping hypnotic rhythm.

Meanwhile Persephone swept the shiny-dark surface of the floor with a twig broom, then lit candles in niches around the cave walls. After a time she spoke again. "Fela, my dear soul. No one will disturb you here. Speak or be silent, as you wish."

She hesitated, tried to speak and was surprised when a rusty whisper came out. "The water . . . what is it?"

"It's Meluis, the underground lake. It shines always."

"Make it stop!"

The dark maiden blinked. "I can't, but it won't harm you. Most find the light soothing." She held out a hand. "Come and see."

Persephone's voice was steady and mellow, but Fela's dread was strong and she clung to the cave wall. "No," she said. "No."

With a grave look, the maiden nodded, and turned away.

Fela crouched in her niche. Slowly the fear sank down inside her: still there but quiet, like a steadily beating heart. As helpless as a wounded animal, she closed her eyes and went into a dream-like trance. She heard a stream of soft words. Even when she realized she was speaking her own thoughts, she couldn't stop.

Aurata leads me into the citadel amid a laughing group of Felynx. I'm used to the soft waterways of the wetlands, to solitude and twilight, so I'm overwhelmed. The Felynx are creatures of the sun and the stars; the Tashralyr dwell in the dusky, damp forests. We are not enemies. We simply coexist, fiery sun and remote shadow. Yet . . . who can resist the temptation of being cheered and celebrated for our speed, taken among the golden ones and celebrated, almost worshipped—if only for a year or two?

Aurata and her brothers are so beautiful. They seem to delight in my innocence, my wide-eyed stares at every new sight. Because I'm unused to holding a two-legged shape like theirs, I feel insubstantial, like a creature of rippling silk amid their golden solidity.

Aurata takes me through one vast hall after another. There seem to be no walls, only columns holding up ceilings of light and gauze. I'm dazzled. The palace is cream and pale gold, with splashes of ruby-red and turquoise. Dozens of beautiful wildcat masks turn to stare as we pass. I walk taller, reminding myself that Karn and Tamis and I are here to represent the Tashralyr, and for that reason I feel proud. We move among the Felynx with all the grace we can gather, like columns of cool water sliding between them.

I look around in wonder at the Audience Hall, at the high ornate chairs on a dais beneath a high canopy like a starry sky. "This is where our parents, the Sovereigns Elect, sit to preside over Azantios," Aurata tells me.

The thrones are empty, but later I see Poectilictis and Theliome in person: two tall figures robed in stiff garments striped with red, black and gold. Their faces are covered by dark lynx masks with golden eyes. My heart races with excitement. They are gentle rulers, yet still remote and awe-inspiring.

Their offspring, Rufus and Aurata and Mistangamesh, greet them with graceful bows. I echo the gesture, spreading my palms and inclining forward over my pointed toe. I didn't expect to be so moved by their presence, yet I am.

They've held their position longer than I know, but they won't be here forever. One day Mistangamesh and Aurata will take their place. What kind of leaders will they make? Mist is not full of laughter and sardonic wit like his brother and sister. He stands aloof and watchful.

The first time Aurata brings me here, I find Mistangamesh at my shoulder—first congratulating me on my victory and then murmuring a warning. "Be careful of my brother and sister. They will play games with you. I'd urge you to flee the palace now, if you would—but if you stay, be wary."

His concern touches me. More than that: his kindness is a jewel in my heart that will stay forever.

Soon I discover what he means. If Aurata leaves my side, Rufus is with me at once, flattering and cajoling. He is the most beautiful of the Felynx, but I'm afraid of him because I've heard tales. I fear that if he can't seduce me away from Aurata, he might try to lame me instead. More than once, Mistangamesh physically drags Rufus away and warns him, angrily, to let me alone. He already has Karn—and others—but he wants everyone.

Sometimes Aurata takes me to her bed. I find this pleasurable but awkward, because we can never be genuinely intimate as lovers, friends or sisters. She keeps herself closed away; a stranger. I am her plaything.

Mistangamesh is different. Whenever he's there, my gaze is drawn to him. He appears lonely. He has a paler complexion and darker hair than his siblings, as if there is more water than fire in his soul-essence. Does he have many lovers or none? He is a mystery. I shouldn't even contemplate the question.

My time of glory is brief. After I win the greatest race of the following season, there is a vast celebration and I drink too much spicy wine. Aurata is missing. Needing fresh air, I become lost in the endless halls of the palace and Rufus appears at my side, all smiles and flowing russet mane. He tries to kiss me, but when I push him away he only laughs. It's something else he wants. "Come with me, swift Fela, to a view a sacred sight that few are privileged to see."

I know him well enough by now to be impudent. His one good point is that he never takes offense. "Please, my lord Ephenaestus, stop," I whisper. "From what I hear, half the population of Azantios is familiar with the sight."

Rufus throws back his head in delight. "I'm not referring to my personal attributes, as pleasurable as I'm sure you'd find them." He puts his lips to my ear. "I'm talking about the sacred heart of the Felynx."

He guides me up secret, winding ways to a spire at the summit of the mountain. The topmost chamber is covered by a crystal dome, and in the center, the Felixatus stands on a column the height of my chest.

I see spheres within spheres, with a web of metalwork securing the structure to a base that is carved with Felynx symbols. The mechanism shines so brightly that I can't look away.

Then I understand. The Felixatus shines with the soul-sparks of a million Felynx. They are falling into it like dust from the stars as I watch.

Rufus is talking, though I barely hear him. "This is a place so sacred that the only ones allowed to set foot here are my parents and the Keeper, Veropardus. So consider yourself privileged, little swamp dweller. You're standing in the holy of holies."

I wonder, then, why the chamber isn't guarded. "Where is Veropardus?"

"He's busy in bed with my sister," Rufus replies with a mixture of resentment and glee. "She lured him away. That's why I knew there'd be no one here."

I walk towards the Felixatus. The soul-light dazzles and mesmerizes. I hear Rufus exclaim, "No, don't touch it!"—too late. I lay my hands on the casing and at once I know.

Everything.

I must have cried out because he demands, "What is it? What are you seeing?"

Rufus looks shocked and angry . . . more so when I begin to tell him.

Fela drifted, half-dreaming. From her low angle, the glowing pool was fore-shortened to a green slot in the flat black floor. By its radiance, she saw a man lying along the far rim. His arm was curled under his head, his face hidden. She quailed to see him lying so close to the lip, as if he'd fallen carelessly asleep on the edge of a cliff.

Then she saw a tremor in his shoulders. He was weeping. For a long time, Persephone watched over him, but asked no questions. Then he began to murmur of a broken heart. Persephone tended gently to him as he poured out his sorrow.

"Is it so wrong, to want oblivion?" said a new voice, female. A woman had joined them, sitting on the edge with her feet dangling in the green light of Meluis. "I am Aelyr. I cannot die. Not properly, at least; not finally. I could slit my own throat and bleed out my life—but my soul-essence would still be aware. Is there no respite from consciousness? I don't want to continue in-definitely! I don't desire one life after another. Nor do I want to fade into the Spiral, part of a sentient mass that never rests. I dread it."

The man said, "To merge with the forces that created us—what form of being could be more blissful?" He frowned. "It's natural."

"Am I the only one who feels this terror?" the woman asked. "I feel ashamed."

Quivering, Fela murmured to herself, "You're *not* the only one. Being torn out of yourself and dropped into darkness . . . What could be more horrify-ing? Who would *not* be afraid?"

Only Persephone seemed to hear, and gave her a quick, kind glance. Fela understood, without being told, that this was a place where no one would be judged.

"No shame. Never feel that," said Persephone.

"But what does it mean to exist forever?" the woman implored.

"What does it mean to exist without love?" the man countered. "You're asking for an answer no one can give."

"I know there's no answer." Her voice was calmer, and she pressed the man's hand with her own. "I can bear it, as long as we can bring our pain here, where no one judges us. Persephone's acceptance is everything."

The man said, "Good Lady Persephone, have you no advice? Won't you stop us wallowing in misery, and thrust us back onto the path of shining Aelyr perfection?"

"There are countless others to do that," she answered wryly. "This is a place where nothing is demanded of you. That's all."

"There must be more."

"Only if you need more."

With a start, Fela awoke properly. She had a lingering impression that many others had come to confess their fears and sorrows while she slept, but they were all gone now. Only the dark maiden remained.

Fela began to edge across the cave floor, which was smooth and cool beneath her outstretched form. She felt as if her skin were stretching, cracking to reveal new flesh. Anxiety rose but she pushed herself forward inch by inch until her head crested the lip of the fearful lake.

An arm's length below the edge lay a body of aqueous light without boundaries. The surface glittered. The first few feet were transparent, but the deeper down the water turned opaque like cloudy emerald, hinting at unimaginable depths, unbearable weight.

Terror surged and choked her.

She imagined falling in, sinking forever through a fissure in the underworld into an ocean abyss, eternally drowning but never dying . . . She jerked in a spasm of horror. Her form was changing, unfolding. She tried to scream. Only a rasp emerged.

Panic unraveled her. She knew she'd been lured into the desolate marshland and betrayed. She remembered a powerful force pushing her down until water closed over her face. The last silvery bubbles of her breath rushed up towards the surface and murky green water swallowed her . . .

Then the dark maiden was there, holding her. From a position high on the cave ceiling, she watched herself screaming in Persephone's arms.

Persephone steadied her as she sobbed. Fela thrashed as her feline form changed, her limbs straightening, fur turning to smooth skin, hair flowing from her head. All her terror and confusion flowed into Persephone, who absorbed it all into the endless shadows of her being.

At last Fela lay still across her lap, exhausted. She was now a slender, pale girl, silver and pearl within a cowl of shimmering mist. An orphan soul.

Presently she said, "Someone lured me into the swamp and drowned me. I was . . . murdered."

Persephone asked, "Do you remember why?"

"No. I try, but there's nothing there."

"Your body died on the surface world, then something blocked your soul-essence from finding its way to the Mirror Pool. Yet you forced a way into the Spiral and came to me instead. That shows great determination."

"Or despair. Blind instinct brought me here. I wasn't conscious."

"Well, that's how Aelyr find me. Fela, if you can't recall the past, let it go. You can enter a new existence and leave the old one behind. Forgetting can be a mercy."

Fela was quiet for a time, her thoughts burning. Then she said, "No. I need the truth." She tensed, seeing a flash of city spires, feeling herself on all fours, her long strides eating the ground. "I was an athlete. Whom did I offend?"

"Perhaps no one," said Persephone.

"But I need to know . . ." A fresh urgency seized her. "What if others are harmed, too?"

The maiden's face was full of concern, but no pity. "Is that your responsibility?"

"Yes! I can't turn away and pretend it doesn't matter. It does. It's vital." She pulled herself from Persephone's arms and knelt facing her. "What should I do?"

"It's not my purpose to tell you that, but I can suggest a choice."

"Please."

Persephone pointed at the cave ceiling. "You may go out into Asru and haunt some tree or hill until you're ready to begin your Spiral journey out-wards towards rebirth."

"And if I do that, I'll forget?"

"Very likely. That would be the easiest path." She pointed down at the lake. "However, if you want the hard path, a way to resolve the wrong done to you, you can leave through Meluis."

Fela recoiled. "I used to love the water. Now it terrifies me. I'm afraid of drowning. Again."

"You won't drown. All the streams, lakes and seas of the Spiral flow into Meluis, even the Mirror Pool itself. It's not water you need to fear, but what lies beyond. Are you ready to face whoever took your life? To relearn truths so painful your mind has wiped them away?"

Fela was quiet. Fear and doubt pinched her. "I must," she said.

Leaning down, she made herself look into the bright water of Meluis. The turbid, cold scent of water flowed up and the sound of its lapping filled the cave. Fish slid through the shallows, their scales flashing with rainbows. Now and then a leviathan would surge up from the deeps and vanish again.

The idea of following those great fish into an unknown realm filled her with dread. She saw her own reflection swimming up to meet her: a soft pale shape, undulating and re-forming. As she reached down, her twin soul reached up towards her.

Fela rose to her feet and said, "How do you bear this? Always being here, and people endlessly spilling their misery into you?"

Persephone opened her arms. Fela saw that the lining of her sleeves had changed from blood-red to spring green. "Pain exists in time, but my sanctuary is timeless. I'm always here, always the same. If you come again, you may not remember this visit. And I . . ." She smiled sadly. "Much as I'd wish to do so, I may not remember you either. So, take courage now." She indicated Fela's ghost-self in the water. "Your *fylgia*, your shadow soul, will guide you."

She took a last look at the guardian in all her dark splendor. Her arms were half-raised, her palms open in blessing. Then, like a swimmer poised to race, Fela focused her full concentration on the waters of Meluis.

In Persephone's chamber all fear dissolved. Raising her arms, she took a last breath and dived—unleashed herself like an arrow into the green-glass depths.

14

Circles and Sacrilege

Stevie surged upwards, powered by the force of her companion's fins. Entwined like a single entity, they torpedoed through fierce clouds of bubbles. She felt her head break into the air, felt the waterfall's weight splashing over her. They kept rising, as if thrown by a wave right out of the water to land painfully on the flat stones of the bank.

There they lay, gasping.

Stevie saw the sea dragon changing. Leafy fins were reabsorbed. Its vibrant, fire-laced blue-black hues leached away to ivory as the sinuous body smoothed and flattened into human form. The seahorse head tipped back, metamorphosing until she found herself looking into Mist's stricken face. Only his eyes stayed the same, black orbs wide with shock.

She was changing too. One outflung arm was coated in dewy fur . . . then it was suddenly her own pallid, human arm again.

Too weary for speech, they lay side by side, panting. Their naked bodies streamed with water, as if they were made of ice and dissolving.

Virginia had gone, but she'd made preparations for their return. Two dark blue towels, as big as cloaks, lay folded on the dry grass. Stevie sat up, racked by a violent coughing fit. She was aware of Mist wrapping one of the towels around her shoulders. The fabric was warm and delicious against her chilled skin. She huddled inside, coughing and shivering.

When she could breathe again, Stevie looked at Mistangamesh. He sat wrapped in the other towel, squeezing water from his hair. The brief sight of him naked would have been thrilling, if she hadn't been too exhausted to appreciate it. Her experiences replayed through her mind but she felt weirdly calm now, all emotion spent. She understood . . . not all of what she'd seen, but most of it.

When she managed to speak, her voice was croaky. "Well, I found you."

"You were looking for me?" He seemed disoriented. His black eyes were lightening gradually to their familiar grey-green.

"Of course, but I wasn't expecting to be . . . ambushed."

"I'm so sorry." His head dropped. "I've changed into my Otherworld form so rarely, I'd almost *forgotten*. How could I forget?"

"Forgetting seems to be part of our condition."

"Stevie, are you hurt? How are you?" He moved so their shoulders were almost touching. She wanted the physical comfort of his arms around her, but they both held back. What had happened was too raw. He'd sunk serpent fangs into her. After that, you couldn't simply . . . hug someone, as if nothing had happened.

"Wet. Shaken up. I feel as if someone's blasted my brain out with a flamethrower. But yes, I'm all right." She touched her collarbone. The small double wound flared with pain. "You bit me!"

"I know. Unforgivable. There seemed a good reason at the time, but now—gods, this is dreadful. I don't make a habit of it, and I'm sure I'm not venomous . . . If you never come near me again, Stevie, I wouldn't blame you." He rested his head on his knuckles. "I would never have wanted you to see me in that form. I didn't want to frighten or hurt you . . . nor see that look in your eyes."

"What look?"

"Shock, horror . . . however you'd describe it."

"Well, it *was* a shock. You didn't warn me."

"How do you tell someone, 'Oh, by the way, my Otherworld form is a scaly salamander thing—wouldn't you prefer to go out with a nice predictable human?'"

Despite herself, she smiled. "You're under no obligation to explain your secret propensities to me. And I had no idea we were 'going out,' as you put it."

"No. Er . . . slip of the tongue."

She let the remark pass. "I certainly wasn't expecting to be carried off by . . . whatever you were."

"It's an altered state of consciousness," he said softly. "I acted by Aetherial instinct. And you were in the same state."

"Yes—I get that now. But I'm new to it. It was . . . a hell of an experience."

"I wouldn't frighten or upset you for the world, Stevie. This is horrible. This is why I wish that I could have stayed human, or dead, or both."

"Don't say that. Mist?" He looked up, his eyes raw. Resting her hand on his shoulder, she said gently, "You startled me, and I was shocked and not happy to be bitten—but you know what? I'll get over it. The important thing is what we both learned. You saw what I saw, didn't you? We were together in the visions."

"Yes, but only fragments. You'll have to tell me what they mean."

She looked down at the place where the serpent's fangs had struck. The swollen double puncture made a figure eight on her left collarbone: a small infinity sign.

"I think this is what I received instead of a branding. You were my Initiator."

He closed his eyes in pain for a moment. "Then the Spiral itself used me to initiate you." Pressing one palm to the rock, he added, "The ground feels solid but it's full of capricious energy swirling around, doing what the hell it likes with us. The Spiral used me."

"Maybe, but it couldn't be any other way, could it? It had to be you, because we knew each other all those thousands of years ago. I was Fela."

Mist nodded. He was troubled, and she knew why. "Do you remember . . . ?"

"Everything," she said softly, "except who killed me."

As they walked back to Virginia's cottage, they reconstructed events. Stevie asked him to speak first and he did, while she listened in numb silence.

One day Fela was a star among the Felynx; the next, she vanished. Afterwards, said Mistangamesh, all he knew of her death was that her body had been dredged from a swamp. Fela, a strong swimmer, had obviously not drowned by accident. There were injuries on her throat and a rock on her chest to weigh her down. Azantios went into a state of shock at the news. Murder was almost unknown among them, accidents rare, suicide alien.

Aurata was inconsolable. Why would anyone murder a being of such grace and talent as Fela—except out of jealousy?

Perhaps it was another Tashralyr, a jealous rival. Or was the murderer a Felynx patron, furious about having to watch his own champion repeatedly humiliated? A notorious malcontent . . . such as Rufus?

Then a witness came forward, claiming he'd seen Rufus walking back from the Tashralyr wetlands that night. The witness was a respected member of the Sovereign Elect's staff, an assistant to no less than Veropardus himself.

No one dared accuse Rufus directly, but rumors ran wild. He reacted with outrage. Poectilictis and Theliome called their son to them and asked him, quite gently, if the rumors were true.

"I was there," Mist told Stevie. "I can't forget the look in his eyes. He didn't answer, didn't say a word. His eyes burned, as if he simply couldn't believe his own parents would ask such a thing. He told me, much later, that it was the final insult. He turned and marched out of the hall. It was the last we saw of him, until he led the invasion."

"I can't say if it was Rufus or not," said Stevie. "All I saw was a shape. But I know why . . ."

Tears flooded out of her. She put her hands over her face. They'd reached the edge of the cottage garden, so Mist drew her into the cover of soft foliage among fruit trees and bushes. "I'm here," he said, letting her weep without trying to soothe her out of it.

"I'm not crying for myself," she said. "It's what I learned. All those Felynx souls, held prisoner."

Briefly she told him of her time in Persephone's chamber. "My memories were muddled, but I saw myself back in Azantios again. I was in the palace, after I'd won my last race. I had too much wine and I got lost and Rufus found me."

Mist groaned.

She gave a shaky smile. "You were always in the background, watching. So like Poectilictis, but without his confidence—your strength was more subtle. I remember how you physically dragged Rufus away from me at times. Protecting me. I wish I'd listened. I was no one to you, yet you tried to keep me safe."

"And failed," said Mist.

"But you tried." She found it impossible to admit that his kindness had made it all too easy for Fela to start falling in love with him. "You couldn't watch me every moment, and nor could Aurata."

He looked sad and troubled. "I wonder if he killed you in anger because you rejected him? He was increasingly wild in those days."

"No, it was stranger than that. He took me to see the Felixatus."

Mist stared. "He what?"

"I know," she said. "The Felixatus was a sacred object that even he was not allowed to touch. He said that Veropardus was having an affair with Aurata and that's why no one was guarding the chamber that night. Although I don't know why someone else wasn't put on guard."

"The chamber was often left unguarded, because it was assumed no one would dare enter. We were trusted to respect the rules. And we did . . . except Rufus, of course."

"That was his game," said Stevie. "Sacrilege. He knew he had no business revealing the Felixatus to the profane eyes of a Tashralyr, so that's just what he did."

Mist gave a sigh, tinged with anger. "In hindsight, regarding the Tashralyr as 'profane' is the most disgusting idea, but that's how the Felynx were. I'm sorry."

"Don't apologize. The Felixatus was your hallowed object, not ours."

"Well . . . yes, you're right, but that was Rufus all the way through. Irreverent. A forbidden sanctum was irresistible bait to him."

Stevie said briskly, "And he was trying to impress me, seduce me and blackmail me, all at once. Fela wasn't stupid. She knew what he was up to."

"Did he succeed?"

"What, in seducing Fela? Is that your business?"

The sudden tension between them startled her.

"No. Well, yes," he said. "All I mean is that I knew he was trying to use you. I don't want to hear that he succeeded."

"He didn't," she said, nettled. "I'd never have left Aurata's patronage. I'd grown to love her, in a way. And Karn was my friend; I wouldn't betray him by replacing him as Rufus's favorite. No, I wouldn't have gone with him in a million years. Either way, Fela ended up dead."

Mist drew back, rubbing his temple. "Forgive me. Go on, tell me what happened."

"The Felixatus was dazzling, a globe of crystal full of stars. It was all held together by the most beautiful metalwork, with cogs and gears like the most perfectly engineered mechanism you could imagine. It was exquisite."

"I saw it, too," said Mist. "I think its purpose was only understood by its creator, who was long gone. I assume my father and Veropardus would eventually have told me what they knew, but events overtook us before they had a chance."

Stevie paused, arrested by vivid memories; the simple room with its polished marble floor and crystal dome, and the Felixatus sparkling in all its jeweled mystery. Rufus's hand on her arm; her inner panic as she wondered how to escape him . . .

"I went to the Felixatus and touched it. Even Rufus was shocked by that. Did you know that the inner sphere was full of Felynx soul-essences?"

Mist frowned. "Not at the time. Later, Rufus told everyone. While we had Frances's carved object, I could still feel their energy, even in the base."

"Well, it was my fault."

"What was?"

"That the truth came out. As soon as I touched the sphere, I knew. Hundreds of voices flooded into me, crying for help. And I told Rufus. I couldn't help myself. I was overwhelmed, and didn't realize I was telling him something he didn't already know. Later, I told Aurata, and she was equally shocked. I'd have told you too, if I'd known you better."

"About the Spiral?" Mist prompted her, as she stopped for breath.

"Yes. The voices spoke of another realm, kept secret from the Felynx because of a long-ago conflict. I don't think the Tashralyr knew, either, since it didn't mean a great deal to Fela. I don't remember anything being said about other realms; we just lived quietly around the lakes and forests. It obviously meant a lot to Rufus, though."

"I remember him raging," said Mist. "How dare our parents conceal the truth about the Otherworld, our true home? Who was this Malikala, who dared forbid the Felynx to enter? He confronted our parents, who insisted they'd done what was best. The Felynx couldn't reenter the Spiral without risking a war, so we sealed ourselves off. But there it was. Because Poectilictis favored me, and kept secrets, Rufus decided to bring down Azantios. Being accused of killing Fela sealed his decision."

"But that wasn't the whole of it." Stevie gripped his arms to make her point. "Aelyr and Vaethyr souls alike, when their bodies die, are set free drift wherever they choose. I think the same applied to the Tashralyr. But the Felynx weren't free. The Felixatus was being used to capture their soul-essences. They were all drawn in like, I don't know—like insects into a sundew plant."

"I know," Mist said stiffly. "Our father and Veropardus were forced to admit it. But there was a reason. Since we weren't allowed into the Spiral, they said, we were being gathered into the Felixatus until the Otherworld was reopened to us. It was only a matter of time. The Felixatus was meant to keep our spirits safe until then."

"Well, someone was lying." Stevie's voice rose. "Didn't you guess? The Felixatus wasn't a refuge. It was a prison. *Someone* wanted to keep control of the Felynx forever."

"No." Mist turned as pale as the blue-white lilies swaying in Virginia's garden. "We heard rumors, but Poectilictis would never have allowed such an atrocity."

She let her hands fall. "Well, you know your father better than I did. He was a good man."

"Yes, he was."

"Veropardus wasn't, though. What if he was capturing souls in order to seize power? I believe that's why Fela was killed," she finished. "She knew too much and, after all, she wasn't Felynx, only a marsh dweller."

"Rufus never said that the knowledge came from you."

"Well, he wouldn't. But it did. So it was my fault—his rebellion, the fall of Azantios, everything. All Fela's fault."

Stevie ran out of words. She felt drained. Where could her embryonic relationship with Mist go now? As strangers, in the guise of modern humans, they'd met as equals. As Aetherials, though, they'd been utterly different. Mistangamesh had been a prince of fire, Fela a creature of the wild. She might have adored him in secret, but she'd had to accept that nothing would ever come of it.

"No," he said. "It was all Rufus's doing. And ours, for being negligent. But absolutely not your fault, Fela."

"Don't call me that!" she flared. "I am not Fela. I have her memories, but I'm different now."

"I understand."

"Do you?"

"Of course. I lived as Adam for a century. Even with Rufus constantly in my face tormenting me, I couldn't rouse the slightest memory of being Aetherial. I know how it feels."

"All right, I can't argue with that. But I've no experience of being *born* human. All I recall is lurching out of a woodland, fully grown but mindless. I was only half a person."

"You will feel complete again. It takes time."

"I don't know that I want to. I'm Stephanie Silverwood now. I don't want to be Fela, I want to be complete as *Stevie*."

Mist, still pale, spoke without emotion. "Fela did nothing wrong."

"All the same—been there, done that," she retorted.

"Why are you angry?"

The question made her more furious. She controlled herself and tried to explain in a rational tone. "You didn't see the Tashralyr as equal. Why should you? The Felynx were the elite. You didn't care that we'd made a peaceful home on Vaeth eons before you arrived."

"We could be arrogant. I can't deny it."

"Oh, not you personally." She paused and spoke more gently. "You were different, Mist; you seemed kind, but we still never had a chance to make friends. I'm thinking of Rufus and his cronies, loving us for our entertainment value. Aurata was Fela's patron, as in *patronize*, or whatever word we used in a language I can't remember."

"I agree. Aetherials have no excuse take such attitudes," said Mist. "Yet why should we be egalitarian and perfect in a way that humans aren't? We're not angels. We're simply a different race." He lowered his eyes. "But I swear, I never looked down on the Tashralyr. They were magnificent beings. If I'm honest, I was a little envious of Aurata for having your companionship."

"Envious?" She was startled. When Mist didn't expand on the remark, she went on, "I don't know if this means anything but sometimes . . . Aurata would talk in her sleep. She'd say Veropardus's name, and mutter about being trapped inside ice, and needing to break barriers. I had no idea what it meant. Usually I'd be booted out of her bedchamber long before she fell asleep."

Mist exhaled, and spoke at last. "I'm not denying there was exploitation. The Felynx were like pampered cats, basking in the sun. However, I know how hard my mother and father worked to maintain that state of grace, and I was so afraid that, when my turn came, I wouldn't have the wisdom necessary to sustain it."

Stevie half-smiled. "I'm sure you would have. What would you have done about the Felixatus, though?"

"I don't know. It's academic, since it was lost when Azantios fell."

"Yes, it was gone, but it's come back to haunt us. I know how self-centered this sounds, but is it coincidence that I met Daniel, and suddenly all these fragments of the past are spilling out and *someone* is trying to suppress them?"

He met her gaze. His face and eyes, luminous in the sapphire gloom, contained a mass of thoughts she couldn't fathom but which she was sure were deadly serious. "You dived into Meluis, were lost for thousands of years, and emerged at a precise point in the modern world?"

"Give or take the ten years that I needed to acclimatize."

"It could be the Spiral pushing us around, or some deeper knowledge inside you that sent you where you needed to be. So no, Fela, I'm sure it's not coincidence."

"Great," she said thinly, "but if you call me Fela one more time, I'll kick you into that bramble hedge! I'm *Stevie!*"

A wedge of light fell out of the cottage. "Guys?" came Sam's voice from the doorway. The edges of his hair were a spun halo. "D'you know we can hear every word in here? How about you come inside and tell us all about it?"

". . . Meluis itself was a dream. Green glass, fading into nothingness. And then the Spiral spat me out." Stevie completed her tale, now dry and dressed and basking in the delicious heat from Virginia's fireplace. "All I remember is clawing my way out of a swamp, clinging onto tussocks of moss and tree roots. There were thin pale birch trees all around me. I dragged myself up off the wet ground as if I'd just been born. I had a human body, and I was soaked, with only my hair to cover me—that and a layer of mud. No memories. I slipped between the trees like a dryad, hiding when aliens in strange clothing went past. I realize now they were just ordinary people out walking. Some had dogs, and if the dog wasn't on a leash it would come bounding towards me—but the humans never saw me."

"You must have been terrified," said Rosie.

"And completely disorientated. I came to a field with a gate onto a lane. Someone had left a pile of garbage in the gateway—a horrible mess of truck tires, rubble and old clothes and furniture—and there was a dress: grubby white cotton with little flowers. I put it on and I started walking along the lane until the police picked me up."

Sam asked, "What did you tell them?"

"I had nothing." Stevie shivered at the memory. "Not even my name, age, where I was from, nothing. They took me to hospital, where I was washed and fed and examined. They questioned me for hours, then passed me to social services. I was put on a psychiatric ward for a few weeks, then into foster care while they tried to find out who I was, if I'd been attacked or drugged or suffered some trauma to account for my state. I hate to think about those days. All these strangers making a fuss over me, even though I was nobody to them. I started speaking after a few weeks, picking up the language and mimicking their behavior until I sort of fit in."

She briefly described the families who'd tried to care for her, but found her too disturbed. "I was obsessed with water, and kept leaving taps to run, playing Ophelia in the bath, and not really understanding why they freaked out when I caused a flood. I also had a habit of taking household equipment to pieces. I've only recently realized it was my way of trying to understand how the world worked. No wonder they kept taking me for psychiatric assessments!" Stevie grinned, amazed to find she could suddenly laugh about it. "I was pretty violent, too. Sometimes there were older boys in the family who would try their luck with me, not realizing how hard I could hit. The bruises were impressive enough to get me moved, at least four times."

"Wow, it sounds like a nightmare," said Rosie.

"For them as much as me." Stevie smiled. "In the end I ran away. I found a job and lodgings, and that was when I met Daniel. Everything changed then. He was someone I could talk to. He made me feel I was *real*, that I had a personality and identity after all."

As she spoke, it struck her powerfully that her companions accepted everything she was saying as though it were perfectly normal. Virginia seemed the archetypal wisewoman—a more down-to-earth Persephone—who'd heard scores of such tales. Dive into her waterfall and emerge transformed? The most natural thing in the world.

Virginia asked, "So, although you forgot your Aetherial past, Daniel picked up images from you?"

"Apparently, but not only from me. He's painted scenes that Fela couldn't possibly have known about, because she was gone by then."

"There's a name for humans who can channel Aelyr energies," said Virginia.

"*Naemur*," said Rosie.

Virginia gave her cool smile, tempered by a wink. "Thank you, Rosie. Now I know who to call if I need a quiz team."

Lucas asked, "Could Daniel have once been Aetherial?"

"I don't know," said Stevie. "It's a nice thought, but if he was, I'm sure I'd feel it inside. All I remember sensing from Dan was . . . humanness. I think he's exactly that: a wild, visionary *naemur*."

"And someone," said Rosie, "possibly Rufus, saw Dan's work and perceived it as dangerous because it would reveal Aelyr secrets. So they've won his trust and kidnapped him. Right?"

"That's how it looks," said Stevie.

Sam said, "Mum, have you picked up any insider knowledge? Is this anything to do with why Lawrence went to Tyrynaia?"

His mother shook back her crinkly hair. "I don't think so. I'm attuned to my little patch of Elysion, but the Spiral's deeper currents don't reach me unless they're extremely powerful. If you were attuned to every stirring, you'd go mad." A pause. "I often feel and see things that are . . . disturbing. But that's common, it's all part of the ebb and flow."

"Spiral weather," said Lucas.

"Quite. So I'm here to do what little I can, if only to offer shelter."

"You've done far more than that," Stevie said warmly. "Did Rosie tell you, we found an address? I don't know if it's genuine or a trick. And it's in Nevada, and I've got no passport and not much money."

"But like I said," Lucas interrupted, "why would Aetherials need passports?"

"Well," said Virginia, "because it's usually easier for us to hop on a plane than struggle through the coils of the Otherworld."

"Doesn't have to be. There are shortcuts."

"Oh . . . You're thinking *antilineos*?" Virginia's eyebrows rose. "I should get out more. I'm not aware of any path that leads from here to that part of the States."

"I'm not just thinking it," Lucas said with a grin. "I've got the route all mapped out. All we need to do is get to the edge of Melusiel and away we go."

"Luc's actually rather good at this sort of thing," Rosie said with clear pride.

"Well, that's what I'm here for." Lucas smiled. "Trust me, I'm a Gatekeeper."

15

Melusiel

The landscape of violet mist was more water than land, with placid lakes edged by reed beds, distant hills vanishing into the pastel softness of the clouds. The sky was low and full of rain, with no sign of the wondrous cosmos Stevie had seen in Elysion. Instead the Spiral turned fluid, awash in amethyst, lavender and grey: mournful shades that made her feel like crying, as if she'd come home without knowing it.

A night in Virginia's strange cottage—despite sleeping in a room that seemed to have no boundaries, on a bed of dried flowers, next to a cave with icy running water for a bathroom—had left her refreshed. When morning came, Virginia fed them and kissed them all farewell.

Lucas had again told Sam and Rosie that there was no need for them to travel all the way if they'd prefer to go home. The argument had been brief: they were coming, whether Luc liked it or not. Stevie was secretly, deeply glad of their company, and guessed that Lucas was too.

Lucas led the party through Elysion's lush greenery and oceanic forests for three or four hours. Occasionally they saw dark-clad figures running through the wildwoods in the distance. "They're Fheylim," Rosie said. "My uncle's of that *eretru*. They're a taciturn lot, but harmless as long as you don't get on their wrong side."

The border was surprisingly distinct. Elysion ended on a scarp of lush ferns and flowers. Below lay the violet water realm, exuding a cool scent of rain.

"The *antilineos* lies across Melusiel," said Lucas. "It should take us two days, maximum, to reach the portal that comes out somewhere in Nevada. Or California."

"Could you sound a bit more confident?" said Sam. "What you need is assertiveness training, mate. Convince *us* you know what you're doing, even if you don't. You do have some clue how *big* the States are, don't you?"

"Leave him alone," Rosie said mildly. "When's Luc ever led us wrong? I'd rather he was a bit cautious than insanely hot-headed. Mentioning no names."

Sam raised an eyebrow at her. "Hey, you can talk."

"Only two days?" said Stevie. "I thought the Spiral was big, verging on infinite."

"Yes, but because it twists around on itself"—Lucas demonstrated with a vague twirl of his hands—"and intersects with the Earth at various points, that creates shortcuts. Shortish, anyway."

"Not forgetting wettish," said Rosie.

Mist said, "We need a boat." It was the first time he'd spoken for a while. Since their experience at the waterfall, Mist had been very quiet. He barely seemed able to look at Stevie this morning, let alone speak to her.

She was concerned, and a bit hurt. Of course he was anxious about the journey and what might await them; that was only natural. Was his silence a symptom of delayed shock, from learning the truth about her origins? Was he disappointed that she'd once been Fela, and not a reincarnation of his beloved Helena? Perhaps his mood was due to something else entirely. Stevie sighed to herself, and let him be.

"Boat. Good point," said Lucas. "I should have thought of that. Vast tracts of water and only a few fingers of squelchy grass to walk along—trying to cross Melusiel on foot isn't the brightest idea."

They descended the scarp, working their way diagonally across the wide, concave slope with dark flint sliding under their boots. Stevie felt more than a change of climate or damp air on her skin; she felt a different energy, an indefinable shift of atmosphere, as she'd felt at Stonegate Manor.

"Why do we need feet, or boats?" said Sam. "C'mon, Mistangamesh—you spent half of yesterday as a bloody great water dragon. Stevie's apparently from a Melusiel-related clan. I'm sure the rest of us can manage with doggy paddle, or sprout a few fins."

"You are joking?" said Rosie.

"No, I'm suggesting we use our Aetherial attributes. Or wings! Who can produce wings? Come to think of it, we all can, if we revert to our most primal form. You ever done that? Become Estalyr? It's quite a wild ride."

"No," Mist said softly. "I don't believe I have. One transformation was enough for me."

Rosie was shaking her head. "Sam, it won't work. Becoming Estalyr takes a huge amount of group energy and even if we could, you know it makes us go strange in the head. The last thing we need is everyone heading off in different directions and vanishing."

"I'd rather not," said Stevie. "Change form and swim, I mean. I don't know why, but I need to stay . . . human-shaped for now. Feels more controllable."

"You may not be in the best place, if you like things controllable," Sam said dryly.

"I'm not a *complete* control freak."

"Didn't say you were."

"Okay, maybe a bit," Stevie allowed. "This is all new to me, but also very old, as if it happened to someone else. I feel . . . out of joint."

Rosie put a reassuring hand on her shoulder. "Don't worry, we all know that feeling. Practical point, we don't want to end up losing clothes and belongings en route, do we?"

The scarp flattened onto the wide, reedy bank of a waterway. Looking back, Stevie saw nothing beyond the edge from which they'd descended; only cloud vapor, concealing any hint of Elysion.

Sam asked, "So where do we get a boat from?"

"We'll ask the Halathrim," said Lucas.

Following Luc's gaze, they saw a handful of Aetherials sitting at the water's edge, barely visible amid tall reeds. Their hair was long and dull violet in hue, their skin the silver of rain. They turned to look at the newcomers with slow, sinuous movements like waterweed.

As Lucas approached, all the Halathrim slid into the water, leaving only fanning ripples behind.

"Wait!" he called. "I'm Lucas Fox, the Gatekeeper to Vaeth. Please, good Halathrim, we need your help."

A head broke the water. It was a female with a grey-green complexion, purplish hair floating around her shoulders. She appeared to be naked, although mostly concealed by the light-distortions of the water. Her body was strong and long-limbed and she paddled gently to keep herself afloat.

"Where are you going, Vaethyr friends?" she said.

She was a true water spirit, some kind of naiad. Stevie wondered if the Halathrim and Tashralyr were related in some way . . . if there were any Tashralyr left. Stevie felt no particular kinship to the naiad. Still, she seemed friendly enough, regarding them with calm green eyes. Other heads broke the surface as her fellows trod water around her.

"We're following an *antilineos* to another part of Vaeth," said Lucas. "Will you let us pass? We won't disturb you."

"Go wherever you wish. We don't own the realm. No one owns the Spiral."

That was a strangely obvious assertion to make, Stevie thought. Lucas said, "Could you help us find a boat of some kind?"

The Halathrim looked amused, as if pitying the land dwellers. "Obviously you don't need boats," Rosie said, crouching down beside her brother. "But we would like to stay dry, and there must be many Melusians who live beside the water, not in it." She indicated Stevie. "Our friend here used to."

The naiad smiled. "There are, although not close to this place. Still . . . I know where there's an old vessel abandoned in the reeds."

"As long as it's watertight," said Sam, adding under his breath, "Doesn't sound promising."

"Blessings of Estel the Eternal upon you." Lucas rose and bowed to the Halathrim.

Fine drizzle sifted from the sky as they waited. Sunlight appeared briefly, turning the glades to silver and diamonds. Soon the naiads returned, pushing a low, oval vessel that appeared to be tight-woven from reeds. A coracle, primitive and handmade. The Melusians pushed this floating basket hard into the bank and held it steady for the Vaethyr to step aboard.

Sam went in first, lending a hand first to Rosie, then to the others in turn. The vessel rocked alarmingly as they boarded. There was space enough for the five of them, with simple wicker seats across the front, middle and rear. Although the boat looked fragile and shiny-grey with age, it felt sturdy on the water once they were seated. Lucas took a position at the prow while Sam and Rosie sat on the middle plank, with Mist and Stevie at the rear.

There were four oars, long and spade-shaped. "I think I know how this works," Sam said, passing one each to Rosie, Lucas and Mist. "The person at the front has to paddle—sorry, Luc, did you think you were going to sit there with the wind blowing through your hair while the rest of us did the work? Person at the back steers. Rosie and I will row too, to add to the speed. This is going to be fun."

Mist took the steering oar. They pushed out of the reed beds, with the Halathrim helping to pull them into clear water. "Estel watch over your journey," said the female naiad. "Fare well."

The coracle rocked as the Halathrim let go, causing Stevie to gasp and grab the side. Rosie looked back at her with a smile. "I've realized who you remind me of, Stevie. You know the painting by John Waterhouse, *The Lady of Shalott*, where she's drifting away in a boat? You look just like her."

"More like the Bag Lady of Shalott," Stevie retorted. "Hold on, wasn't she floating away to her doom?"

"Ah. Not the best analogy," said Rosie. "But you do have the same great hair and nervous expression."

"Thanks, I think," Stevie said with a grimace. She saw the faintest smile touch Mist's shadowed face. What did the smile mean? That he was ready to talk to her again? "Look, I have a weird relationship with water and I don't want to sit here being rowed to a romantic death. I'm the relief oarsman, okay? As soon as one of you gets tired, I'll take over."

"It won't be Rosie," said Sam. "She's a landscape gardener. Arm muscles like an ambidextrous tennis player. Lucas, on the other hand, rarely lifts anything heavier than a magical staff. My money's on Luc giving up first."

Lucas, without turning round, showed Sam a finger.

Stevie grinned to herself. She couldn't express her relief at being in the company of these three Aetherials who were so down-to-earth and confident enough to make jokes while she was quietly terrified.

Soon the Halathrim were lost to sight and the wetlands became eerily empty. Violet waters slid by. The only sound was the splash of paddles in the water. They were passing down a long, wide channel between reed-beds that made Stevie think of the Florida Everglades that she'd seen on television . . . but those images had been green and blue and sunny, full of life, usually with a noisy fan-driven boat churning parabolas of spray. Here there was only purple-blue emptiness. A couple of herons skimmed across the waterway in front of them . . . then stillness fell again. Melusiel reminded her, too, of the marshes where Fela had lived . . . and drowned.

"Is this it, for two days?" said Sam. "This is like the canal boat holiday from hell."

"Worse," said Rosie. "At least canals have pubs."

"Can you two show the *slightest* bit of reverence?" said Lucas. "It's a magical pathway. Of course there are no fucking pubs!"

While they bantered, Stevie said softly to Mist, "Are you all right?"

He glanced at her. "Yes, why?"

"Because ever since . . . you seem worried, withdrawn. Not yourself."

"I know. I'm sorry."

She waited, but he said nothing more. "So what's wrong?"

At last looked directly at her. "Where to start answering that? Everything."

"Have I upset you? I know we argued a bit."

"You?" He looked surprised. "No, Stevie, no." He touched her hand, then was silent again, all his attention focused on steering as Lucas called out instructions.

Stevie knew the feeling of simply not wanting to talk, and worse than that, being *unable* to. It chilled her. She let him alone.

Wisps of fog drifted past, forming shapes that tricked her eyes into seeing spectral beings. Along the shore, ferny trees showed in silhouette against gold-touched cloud.

Some hours later, they steered into the edge of the waterway and pulled the coracle up onto the bank. There were no reeds to hamper them, only a mat of thick, lacy vegetation. About twenty feet inland, a ridge rose from the bank, clustered with outcrops of rock. Trees clasped the rocks with twisted roots. Their branches reached up like gnarled willows, glittering with leaves like tiny green coins, vivid against the dull lavender hues of twilight.

They found a sheltered place to make camp in a curve of the ridge. Then there was nothing to do but try to keep dry while they ate and rested. Sam, Rosie and Lucas were talkative. Mist added occasional remarks, but Stevie felt that all their talking had been done last night.

She removed herself from the group and sat on a rock, looking out at the softly mysterious wetlands. Rain misted down. A flock of small birds resembling egrets took flight. Most of them were white, but three were a startling bright red. The sight made her smile in surprise. She felt at peace, as if it would be easy to forget Daniel, Mist, Rufus and everything else, and remain here until she dissolved into the rain and trickled down to join the naiads in the lake where she could drift among the lilies without a care.

"Are you doing okay?" Rosie asked, sitting down beside her. She put a chocolate bar in Stevie's hand and added, "You didn't eat much. Have this."

"Yeah, I know. Thanks."

"The journey's not too awful, is it? I know they say it rains all the time here, like in Manchester or Seattle, but I like Melusiel."

"It's nice, actually, just drifting along. It's what we're heading towards . . ."

"Well, we'll do our absolute best to help. Don't worry. We've been through far worse than this, believe me."

Stevie again felt so glad of Rosie's company that she could have hugged her. Instead she held her feelings inside, unsure how to be demonstrative without looking like an idiot. "You didn't have to come with us, but I'm so glad you did."

"Oh, you'd have managed," Rosie said cheerfully, "but the more, the merrier. To be honest, Lucas isn't doing this out of charity. He's got an ulterior motive. He won't admit it, but I reckon he's looking for Iola. She's lovely, but *very* Aelyr. She keeps vanishing and he's always scared she won't come back. And he's also after news of Albin."

"From what I've heard about Albin, he's better left alone."

"True. He tried to stop Luc becoming Gatekeeper. It's a long, convoluted story, so let's just say, Albin is always trouble. They say he was never in his right mind after his wife Maia vanished, but I think it's the other way round; she went, because he's a cold authoritarian bully."

"Is Luc scared of him, maybe?"

"I think so. We all were. Albin needs cutting down to size in our minds, because he feeds on fear." They sat quietly, sharing the chocolate. Then Rosie said, "When you find Daniel . . ."

"*If* we find him."

"Have you ever wondered if you might get back together?"

Rosie's question took her aback. As if her strange rebirth had stripped her of social skills, she felt rusty at friendship, unwilling to confide. "Why do you ask?"

"There's affection in your voice when you speak about him. Sometimes we don't recognize what we really want until it's almost too late."

Stevie saw a chance to deflect the question. "Do you speak from experience?"

"Oh, I'm the queen of horrible mistakes." Rosie grimaced. "But we got there in the end."

"So everything felt right with Sam?"

"Oh, no. Everything felt wrong, *completely* wrong! We've known each other since we were quite young, and he was a nightmare—we couldn't stand each other." One side of her mouth curled up. "Then it turned out we couldn't keep our hands off each other, which caused even more problems. But it's so easy to form distorted ideas about people. He's not perfect, but neither am I. Underneath his bad-boy act, he's the bravest, most loyal person I've ever known. I've seen him *literally* sacrifice his life to save others. Being Aetherial, we got a second chance, and not a day passes that I don't give thanks for it. We argue like crazy, but never with any hard feelings, because we're sure of each other. It works, for some reason."

"It must feel good, to have that certainty."

"I'm so much luckier than I deserve. However, we were talking about you."

"You're shamelessly nosy," said Stevie. "You remind me of my friend Fin."

"Who's she?"

"A woman I worked with." Memories of the museum rose and choked her, as she recalled with fresh shock that she wouldn't be going back.

"You all right?"

"Yes." Stevie mastered her tearful moment. "Fin and I weren't that close, which was my fault really, but we got on well and she could always be relied on for common sense. When the strangeness started, I broke down and blurted it all out to her, and she didn't turn a hair. Talk about getting people wrong! I'd judged her as an 'ordinary mother of two' who was going to suggest I needed therapy. But no, it turned out she was grounded in all sorts of esoteric matters."

"Aelyr experiences?"

"I don't think so . . . related, maybe, although I don't know how. I'm starting to see layers in everything, and they all seem connected."

"Fin sounds interesting," said Rosie. "And what did she advise you to do?"

"To go with the flow. To accept what was happening instead of fighting it. So if I lost my job and went with Mist . . . it was meant to be."

"Wise woman."

"Literally, I think," said Stevie. "She had a definite touch of witchiness, like Virginia, although less full-on, of course. And like you."

"Ah, no, witchy wisdom is not my strong point," Rosie said with a grin. "But I'm quite good at gardening, and telling dirty jokes. It's the earth element in me."

"Is that really any more influential than a horoscope sign?" Stevie pulled her jacket closer, feeling coolness in the air.

"Good question. I'm sure there's *something* in it, simply because this is the Otherworld and we're part of it. Ideas that are vague on Earth have a life of their own here. But the rules don't bind us. You might be born to an earthy family of Elysion, for example, only to find your nature is more of air or fire. Or a mixture. Mist, for example. He came from the Felynx, an *eretru* of fire, didn't he? Yet he appears to have powerful watery leanings."

"I hadn't thought about it like that. Why, though?"

Rosie shrugged. "Who knows? Perhaps he felt different from his fiery family. Or because he's so clearly, madly attracted to you."

A small shock went through Stevie. She shook her head vehemently. "Oh, no, he's definitely not that. We're just friends."

"Right."

"Really."

"Are you sure? That's why I asked about Daniel. I wondered if you might be torn."

"There's nothing to be torn about." Stevie realized she was beginning to sound defensive. She didn't want to argue with Rosie. "It can happen that you like someone, but you can't do anything about it due to circumstances, and that's fine. Okay . . . I admit that Mist is easy on the eyes."

"He's gorgeous," Rosie teased. "I would, if I wasn't with Sam."

"Oh, yes?"

"Ah, now you're giving me a definite 'Hands off!' stare."

"No! Was I? No. The thing is, it's beside the point. If Mist looked like an orang-utan, I'd still help him. And he's on another planet, emotionally: still in love with a woman called Helena who died close to four hundred years ago. Nothing's going to happen. And I don't want it to; I'm not pining after him, if that's what you think."

"No," said Rosie. "Sorry, I'm being mischievous. Matchmaking is the most dangerous of games."

Stevie put her hands around her raised knees and stared through the glistening willows. The lake surface danced under the rain. "Yes, pinning all your hopes on romantic love is a great way to screw up your life. When I surfaced on Earth, I was totally alone and clueless. One of my biggest shocks was hearing all this strange alien music; I mean pop songs on the radio. Once I could decipher them, I was absolutely astonished to hear endless love songs where the woman loves her man so much she'll sacrifice *anything* for him. She's offering to completely lose her identity, merge her whole self into his. How is that admirable? And then all those defiant, angry songs stating, 'I can survive without you, just see if I can't!' when the singer sounds about ready to kill the guy and set fire to his new girlfriend. What's healthy about any of that?"

"Bloody hell," said Rosie. "That was quite an outburst."

"It made me realize that there are more important things than pairing up and trying to live out the wild expectations inspired by romantic songs. It's brainwashing!"

"Again, bloody hell," said Rosie. Then she gave an infectious grin, and they started to laugh.

Stevie added, "What I had with Danny was wonderful, a connection that made me feel *real*. He saved me, like a hand pulling me out of the ocean onto the safety of a ship. Yes, it was love, but neither of us needed it to last forever. And that's okay."

They sat without speaking for a while. She heard the men's voices murmuring at a distance. Eventually Rosie said, "I know what you mean, Stevie. I've suffered the whole romantic delusion business myself. When the real thing happens, though, it is quite nice."

"Well, I'm fine without it. All the same . . ." Her gaze drifted to Mist and she stared at him for a few seconds before forcing herself to look away. "God, why do things have to be such a mess?"

Rosie put her arms around Stevie, and kissed the side of her head. "Hey, it's all right. Plenty of time to sort it all out. You're not alone; we'll be with you all the way."

Stevie briefly returned the hug, breaking it before Rosie's sheer warmth and sweetness made her cry. She felt steadier. "I hope Sam knows he's the luckiest man in the world to have *you*," she said.

"Oh, I never let him forget it," Rosie answered cheerily.

Sheltering beneath the rocks on higher ground, Mist glanced at Stevie and Rosie and wondered what they were talking about. He was glad she'd moved apart. A cloud of darkness had settled inside him. He felt dreadful, but each time he tried to speak, he had no words to offer her. Nothing.

Fela, Helena: both had died—indirectly or otherwise—at his brother's hand and he, Mist, had done nothing to protect them. He couldn't let the same happen to Stevie.

A weapon against Rufus . . . that was what he needed. And this time, no mercy.

Sam and Lucas, who'd been at the water's edge looking over the lake, walked up to join him. "A thought," he said, as they sat down. "I know Lord Albin has been no friend to you, but he was part of the faction that tried to bring charges of treason and genocide against Rufus. He failed, but . . . he might become our ally, after all."

"Ally?" said Sam. "That would be more than out of character. That would be a bleeding miracle."

"Yet he's your grandfather."

"So? Like they say, you can't choose your family. Albin is a coldhearted, sociopathic bastard," said Sam. "He screwed with my father's head. No wonder my grandmother left him. He couldn't even get on with his own mother,

Liliana, who was Gatekeeper for centuries. She was held in great respect, plus she's a sweetheart. But Liliana was living on Vaeth, and Albin in Sibeyla, so perhaps he resented her absence or maybe he was born without a soul-essence, I don't know. I don't think he *was* born, but chiseled from a block of ice. There must have been a tiny strand of passion because he managed to get together with Maia for long enough to produce my father, Lawrence. Maia's long gone, though; even she couldn't stand Albin. He took her desertion badly. Any remnant of humanity vanished with her."

"What about Albin's father?"

"Y'got me there," said Sam. "Liliana was always alone. There was a rumor of a liaison with an Aelyr of Elysion, which would make Albin half-earthy and not pure Sibeylan after all, which knowing him would make him *very* unhappy. Hence the purist extremes."

"Perhaps that's what we need, to counter Rufus's extremes of mayhem and destruction. I'm certain he's planning something monstrous."

"And Albin's powerful, and hates him?" Sam's mouth pulled to one side. "Mist, mate, you've got to ask yourself, what would Albin's price be for helping us? You know the old saying: He who sups with the devil should have a long spoon."

Mist took this in, exhaled slowly. Since his leafy-dragon transformation, he felt colder and stronger. "I'm not sure that Lord Albin is still as powerful, after his humiliation before the Spiral Court. You're right, Sam. I have to deal with Rufus myself."

Lucas said, "One time—after the last big conflict was over—Rosie met Albin and he said to her, 'Are you so very sure that the *true* danger of the Spiral has yet shown itself?' You should ask her about it. We thought he was trying to unsettle us, because that's what he does. What if he really meant it, though? Perhaps he knew something. Maybe he knew that if Rufus was set free, he'd take his revenge?"

Sam spread his hand at Luc. "See, this is why we came with you, Mist. Not for a free river trip. Because Luc has an instinct for when something really bad is brewing."

Mist smiled with grim satisfaction. "Thank you for taking us seriously."

"So, when you catch up with this brother of yours," said Sam, "what are you planning to do?"

Mist answered simply, "I am going to kill him."

After few hours of uncomfortable sleep, they refloated the coracle and paddled out into the current once more. A hint of sunlight sprinkled the water with millions of tiny diamonds. Soon the lake narrowed into a gorge with high rock walls. The fabric of the rock was slumped like thick honeycomb toffee and pocked with small caves, making the walls appear full of mournful faces. The current built up and rushed their boat along the gorge in an exhilarating burst of white water.

Stevie suddenly knew there would be no going back—at least, not by this route.

The coracle spun and bucked alarmingly. They held on hard, fighting to stay afloat as they were flung down steep rapids: a slalom of rocks and gushing foam. Eventually the gorge spat them out and they surged into a vast, calm lake.

No land was visible in any direction. Wisps of fog hung over the water. "Okay, Luc," Sam gasped, pushing back his wet hair. "You're still sure we're on this *antilineos* that's taking us from A to B with no weird detours?"

"Yes," said Lucas. "I can tell we're moving in a straight line, even if you can't."

"Fine," said Sam. "Just checking."

Stevie looked down into the water. Instead of purplish murk, she was amazed to see green light rising from below, crystal clarity that went down and down, as if Meluis itself lay deep below the surface. The sight gave her a disturbing urge to dive in. It woke memories of Persephone's cave, of diving and swimming towards rebirth, and diving again into Virginia's pool to recapture her lost life.

In response to a question from Mist, Rosie was talking about Lord Albin. "Yes, I met him, and he did say those words, 'Are you *sure* that the true danger has yet shown itself?' I assumed he was trying to unnerve me, but we can't discount the possibility that he meant it. He might know there's a secret catastrophe on its way, but if we can't work it out in time—tough."

"That sort of cruel tease is just his style," said Sam.

"If there is a plan, it must be *his*," Lucas said bleakly. "You can look back and see his bitterness feeding on itself. Albin was jealous that Liliana skipped over him for the role of Gatekeeper and gave it to her grandson Lawrence instead. His wife Maia left him. Then his mother and son, too, deserted him for Earth. I don't see how Albin would ever have been satisfied with the Gatekeeper role, but he wanted it anyway, because he seems to want control of everything. Just because he's been quiet doesn't mean he's stopped plotting to sever the Spiral from Vaeth. Worse, he might want to destroy every realm except Sibeyla itself. He *won't* have stopped."

Sam added, "So the loss of a court case against Rufus and losing the support of a small monkish sect won't have dented his ambition?"

"It's unlikely," said Lucas. "He wanted to destroy the Gatekeeper—even his own son or grandson—and seal off the Otherworld forever."

"I concede," said Mist. "Albin doesn't sound the ideal ally against Rufus."

Stevie took in their words but could not tear her gaze out of the lake depths. Two fathoms below, she saw several Halathrim swimming the opposite way, skimming like torpedoes. They took no notice of the vessel above them. Their urgency alarmed her.

"Why are they in such a hurry?" she asked. The others looked down but no one answered.

Then Sam said, "What the hell is that?"

A blur blanketed the horizon, like a roll of white cloud. From its center, a needle-thin tower pointed at the sky. As they drew closer, the shape resolved into a land spur across their path, strange because it didn't seem part of Melusiel. The shoreline appeared airbrushed into the violet lake. Lights shimmered around the tower, a halo of ice crystals.

Rosie said, "Luc, is that meant to be there?" The coracle began to rock on a fan of waves emanating from the shore.

"I've no idea," said Lucas. "It looks like part of Sibeyla intruding on Melusiel. Weird."

"Can the Spiral do that?" asked Stevie.

"The Spiral can do whatever it likes," Sam said with a shrug. "Which isn't always a bad thing."

"But how?"

"As soon as you think you understand, things change," said Lucas. "Usually there's a clear boundary between realms, a definite transition. But the geography shifts around unpredictably, like weather systems on Vaeth. No one understands whether the Spiral's sentience makes conscious changes, or whether it's asleep and having restless dreams."

Rosie said, "But it's also a fact that webs of Aelyr can work together to create distortions. They can tap into the sentience and coax it to change. If some Aetherials wanted to create a Sibeylan spur across part of Melusiel, perhaps they could."

"But why?" Mist put in. "It would have to be an incredibly focused group of adepts, or a singularly powerful individual . . ."

Luc said, "What we're seeing may not even be solid, just a mirage projected from somewhere else. We'll row around and pick up the *antilineos* on the far side. But if the waterway's entirely blocked, we'll disembark, drag the coracle across, and continue on the other side—"

His words were cut off as a wave surged at them. The vessel plunged. Melusian water-beings were speeding upward from below, thrashing all around them. Webbed hands seized the sides of the boat, heads rose like seaweed-coated boulders.

More Halathrim. The attack took Stevie and the others by surprise and for a few wild moments they could do nothing but cling on. Her human self still rebelled at the idea of drowning, while her deeper self knew she could change and swim, and so could Mist, but what about the others? Powerful ropy hands pulled at the vessel, dragging them back the way they'd come.

Sam beat at the hands with his oar, trying to force them off. Rosie dislodged one of the Halathrim by jabbing her oar straight into its face. Stevie saw a change in Mist, his skin darkening and tendrils flowing amid his hair. He still had the steering oar, so she was looking around for some other weapon when Lucas yelled, almost screamed, "Iola! Sam, stop! Iola's with them."

A naiad surfaced, water streaming from long bronze hair. She looked like a beautiful statue, come to life. "Lucas," she gasped, gripping the front of the coracle as she tried to turn it, "Go back. There's danger here."

"What danger? Get into the boat."

"No, I'm safer where I am." She pointed at the white tower. "Turn away. You should know," she paused for breath, "he's growing too strong. You should be careful whose name you speak in the Otherworld, lest you summon them."

White hands came out of the water and seized her. Pulled under, she vanished in a mass of bubbles. "Iola!" Luc cried.

Dozens of pale shadows were rushing underwater from the direction of the island. Not dusky Halathrim, but a different *eretru*, a shoal of pearl-white serpentine creatures. The water exploded into foam. All around them, the Halathrim were under attack. The coracle tipped violently, spinning. Water slopped in and they began to sink. Stevie stared down into the water, saw scores of attackers all around them, pale and scaly with powerful tails and sharp fins slashing at their enemies.

Outnumbered, the Halathrim began to flee.

The pallid ones circled the boat like sharks, then rose up, their smooth reptilian heads and webbed hands bursting from the water to seize the sides of the coracle. The vessel tipped wildly, inches from sinking.

Sam, Rosie and Mist were all shouting, beating at the long pale hands with their oars. Stevie whirled her rucksack to catch one of them across the skull, to little effect. Unlike the Halathrim, these new creatures barely seemed to feel the blows but hung on with muscular power. One reared up and seized Mist's oar, forcing him to let go or be dragged overboard.

Stevie saw Mist's hands turn scaly for a moment, then revert to human skin. She felt a creeping, chilly power in the air—a force dampening their Aetheric natures and pulling them in like a magnet.

The coracle, although three-quarters awash with water, began to rise. The creatures were bearing up the vessel. They had full power now to upend it like a soup bowl and tip out the passengers at their whim.

"Stop fighting them!" said Rosie. "They'll capsize us. Sam, stop!"

Reluctantly he obeyed. Stevie clung to the sides, staring down at the pale forms in the water, their white scales ashimmer. She saw upturned snake faces with solid blue orbs for eyes. She held her breath, ready for impact with the water.

Iola's head broke the surface, yards behind. "Lucas!" she cried out, a call of despair.

"Go!" he shouted at her. "Flee, fast as you can!" He pointed at the tower. "Whatever this is . . ." He made some urgent signs at her, which she obviously understood. Dolphin-swift she dived, and was gone.

The coracle steadied. The serpent beings began to propel the vessel forward at speed. Stevie and Mist gripped each other. Sam was swearing under his breath. Helpless, they were carried to the island, effectively hijacked.

The island looked translucent, like a reflection or a mirage: one image laid over another. The greyish, frost-dusted rocks supported the tower—a slender spire of quartz—that rose like a white spindle to pierce the clouds.

Behind the tower, the sky held an impression of mountains, no more than chalk lines sketched on Melusiel's rain-heavy canopy.

Their captors brought the coracle to shore beneath the white tower. Despite their gossamer appearance, the rocks were real and solid. Some of the water dwellers clambered out, torsos streaming, tails bifurcating into legs. Dragging the coracle onto the rocks, they indicated Lucas's party to disembark. They had no choice. Many others still lurked in the water behind them.

"Just do what they want," said Lucas. "Fighting will get us nowhere."

"Who are they?" Rosie asked in a tone of strong suspicion.

"I don't know," said Lucas. "A misunderstanding to be sorted out, then they'll let us go."

"You'd better be right, Luc," Sam said with menace. "They'll have a hell of a fight on their hands if they don't."

"How?" said Stevie. "There's a power here constricting us to human form. Can't you feel it?"

Mist gave her a dark look. That was too uncomfortable a question for anyone to answer. She became aware of how very wet, cold and exhausted she was.

As they stepped onto the shore one by one, the air changed tangibly from the moistness of Melusiel to dry, sparkling cold. Snow lay like powdered sugar on the rocks. The structure before them might be a natural column of rock, or a tower carved from ice.

Stevie recalled Luc's and Rosie's hints that the Aelyr could shape the Spiral by power of will. So, if someone had *willed* the tower into existence . . . it would make sense that it could look both natural and Aelyr-made, existing in both states at once.

Looking up, Stevie saw a shape emerge from an embrasure near the very tip of the tower. Small as a feather at first, the shape drifted downwards to become a hawk, and then a winged angel, and finally, as it touched down on the shore, an Aelyr man in a cloak of feathers. Their aquatic captors parted to let him through, bowing in slave-like obeisance. He walked towards Luc's party, his hands open in greeting.

He was a swan-white man with three dazzling blue eyes, as Sam and Mist had described.

Albin.

16

The White Tower

The fire goddess is coming.

Daniel applied a priming layer of gesso to a fresh panel. His hands were shaking. At least he'd finally stopped passing blood. Oliver's second physical attack had been brief but thorough. *"Defy me again and I'll leave Slahvin to finish the job,"* he'd said casually. Daniel knew he meant it.

But the worst, the most horrifying thing was that he still loved Oliver.

Or was under his angelic spell. He couldn't tell the difference. Instead, bewildered, he pushed himself harder than ever to win back Oliver's favor. After all, many artists saw visions of heaven, of angels or hidden worlds, but how many lived the reality?

Daniel knew how privileged he was. And how heavy the price.

He was struggling to work. He couldn't eat or sleep or stop his thoughts whirling. Oliver had forbidden him to paint anything negative, but all his visions seemed malevolent.

Movement outside caught his eye.

He went to the huge window. Outside lay a vista of sand and rock, a barren estate of desert plants and razor wire. Farther away lay the rim of Jigsaw Canyon. All was scarlet, brown and dull gold. Against a rosy sky he saw a handful of figures, recognizable as members of Oliver's staff but dressed in robes of burnt orange, with tall headdresses on their flowing hair. He counted ten. They were performing a strange dance, very slow, with intricate hand movements.

Daniel watched, mesmerized. The air rippled above them—with heat haze or magical energy. One of his earlier icons showed a similar scene of creatures engaged in a mystical dance. He sensed the ritual might be a summoning . . . but of what, he had no idea.

When he saw the group returning to the house, he rushed back to his easel. Presently Oliver strolled into the room, removing an orange, dusty-smelling robe to reveal a plain white T-shirt and jeans underneath. Daniel trembled, but Oliver was in a good mood for once.

He smiled. "In case you wondered, we were rehearsing."

"Rehearsing for what?"

"You ask me that, when you've painted such scenes?" Oliver swept a hand at the back wall, which was covered with Daniel's artwork.

"I told you, I'm just a cipher."

"Be glad of it. This is not for humans to understand."

He clenched his teeth. "Oliver, you need to appreciate . . ."

"What?"

"That I can't see into the future."

"What exactly am I paying you for, then?"

Daniel gave a sour smile. "Paying me? I haven't seen a cent yet, not that it matters. I get it now. You're not using me as an artist, but as a kind of risk assessor. I see a vision of your plans, and if you don't see the outcome you want, you make changes. But what if I paint all possible worlds? How will you know which one is real?"

Oliver frowned at him. "What are you saying?"

"That I can see bits of your past, because it's already happened. But I can't see the future." Daniel stared at the blank panel on his easel, avoiding Oliver's stare. Physical blows might hurt less if he didn't see them coming. "What I'm picking up are *intentions*."

Oliver's hand landed on his back—caressing, not violent. "That makes sense."

"You believe me?"

He turned Daniel to face him by swiveling his chair. "Of course. It's a good thing, because the future can't be pinned down, can it? No sooner do you try to define an outcome than it changes. Just give me the most beautiful image in your head."

All gilded beauty and smiling white teeth, Oliver leaned in and kissed Daniel. He felt his doubts evaporating, wild surrender pulling him down . . . the sense of wonder he'd felt when he first met Stevie, magnified: and a sense of relinquishing free will, like an unbeliever falling to his knees before a vehement evangelist. Every time he began to doubt Oliver, this feeling would ambush his spirit all over again.

"There's nothing much left in my head," he said. "Visions of the fire goddess, blazing."

"Paint her in glory, then. Aurata enthroned. Daniel, I want you fully on our side, to be part of this. Don't you want that too?"

"Yes! About the triptych—I only wanted the world to know about this wonderful change. I made a mistake."

"You realize that not all Aetherials would think it wonderful? That's why it must be kept secret. We can't risk anyone trying to stop us."

"I understand that now. I'm sorry."

"And I forgive you." Oliver stroked Daniel's matted hair. "Oh, and the little message you left for your friend Stevie?"

Daniel went nauseous with terror, couldn't speak.

"I forgive you for that, too. If it brings the very people here who might have been a nuisance, you've done us all a favor."

"She won't have found it," he said.

Oliver only half-closed his eyes. "Probably not. We'll see. You're a mess. Why don't you go upstairs and shower and wait for me in bed?"

"I want the visions to stop," he groaned. "I'm exhausted."

"Oh, they'll stop soon enough," said Oliver. "The fire goddess is on her way."

The central eye was actually a jewel that appeared to be inlaid in Albin's skull, apparently as watchful as his true eyes, and as blue as the heart of a glacier.

"Oh, god," Rosie whispered.

"Fucking hell, this is all we need!" Sam spoke more audibly. His words reached Albin, judging by the tilt of the snowy head.

"But what's he going to do?" said Stevie.

"Probably nothing," Rosie answered. "But every time we're in the Spiral, Albin turns up. Well, not *every* time, but enough for it to be more than coincidence. How does he always manage to find us?"

"You heard Iola," said Mist. "Be careful what names you mention, lest you summon them. Perhaps you're always finding *him*."

Lucas frowned at him. "Why would we want to do that?"

"The same reason I want to find Rufus?"

"I wanted information about him, but not like this, not *now*."

Albin changed as he approached. He became column of white flame, with vast wings blazing. Stevie, transfixed, felt Mist's hand on her waist. Whatever was left of their fragile relationship, an instinct to protect each other remained. But what could you do against a blazing angel the height of a house?

It would have been a good moment to flee, except for captors preventing escape in any direction. These beings, presumably Albin's servants, stood motionless and alert. Out of water, their aquatic qualities diminished, scales fading to a smooth alabaster finish. They were like automatons. Their blankness horrified Stevie.

As if they have no will of their own.

She felt physically stuck to the ground as Albin bore down upon them, moon-white in the drifting vapor.

Then he was in front of them, in human dimensions but at least half a foot taller than Mist. Now he had a cloak of feathers, a pale hawkish face. The transition happened in a flash: a display of effortless power, designed to intimidate.

"The Spiral is such a small realm," Albin said. "Wherever I go, it seems one of you always finds me. Welcome, Rosie, Samuel, Lucas . . ." He turned his cobalt-laser eyes to Mist. "I seem to know you, too. From the trial. Your name is Adam? I took you to be human, but I see I was mistaken."

Mist said nothing. Albin turned to Stevie with a chilly smile.

"Someone new. Someone very old, yet reborn; it appears to me you haven't so much kissed the Mirror Pool as nearly drowned in it. May I know your name?"

Stevie saw a creature of ice. His face wasn't emotionless; arctic, yes, but burning with the controlled idealism you saw in the eyes of religious fanatics. Bone-chilling. He reached out towards her. For a moment, his hand was the head of a snake. She tried to suppress her instinctive recoil, but of course he noticed. Albin missed nothing.

"Stephanie," she said woodenly.

"Vaethyr." Albin uttered the word with contempt. "Never mind. No one's beyond hope. You are all welcome here. Won't you come inside for a while?"

Sam answered, "We'd love to, pops, but we're in a hurry, so no, sorry. Another time. Can we have our boat back, please? And call off your guards. What are they, anyway?"

Albin ignored Sam's disrespect. Stevie became aware that in addition to his pallid servants, the air, water and fog around them swarmed with translucent elementals: more of Albin's supporters, ready to act upon his signal. Did he even need such guards? His personal aura was irresistible, as if he'd thrown a chain-mail net over them. "Where are you going?"

"Nowhere," said Lucas, pointing to the lake on the far side of the narrow island spur. "*Antilineos*, back to Vaeth, gone. Soon be out of your way."

"Not 'nowhere,' then. Now I am really curious. Explain."

Sam stepped forward, hands on hips. "How about you explain how you've managed to park a piece of Sibeyla across the middle of Melusiel with a bloody great tower on it? You've creating an obstruction. I'm sure there's a Spiral Court law against this sort of thing."

"It's my home," Albin answered in a mild tone. "I move it wherever I wish."

"Is it on wheels, like a caravan?" Rosie said, staring upward. The white spindle shone, luminous against the steely sky. "How?"

"Come inside and I'll explain."

Mist shook his head. "No. We must go."

"But it's growing dark. I can see you're tired. You'll need to rest at some point, so it may as well be here."

Eerie gloom was gathering, as if Albin himself had willed it. He turned, beckoning. They followed the sway of his magnificent cloak; Sam, Rosie and Lucas first, Mist and Stevie hanging back. No one argued, not even Sam. That was plain sinister.

As Stevie began to walk, she felt pain piercing her left shoulder—Mist digging his fingernails into her. She opened her mouth to object, only to see that he wasn't touching her at all. Her tiny translucent *fylgia* was on her shoulder, clawing her.

Warning her, *Don't go in.*

Indicating the other three, Mist whispered in her ear, "Albin has their *fylgias* inside. That's how he's lured them here."

"What? How on earth could he do that?"

"I've no idea. If you and I can break past his guards, we could run."

"And abandon our friends? What's got into you?" she snapped, aggravated by the pain of the claws. She tried to pull the *fylgia* loose, couldn't grasp its ectoplasmic form. "You haven't been the same since—"

"We can't afford this delay!"

Mist looked nearly unhinged. Stevie wished, not for the first time, that they'd never begun this journey. "Look, either Albin's less scary than he looks and wants a friendly a chat with his grandsons—or he's dangerous. Either way, we can't let them go in there alone."

"I know," Mist sighed, relenting. "But can't you feel the power Albin's emanating? He wasn't like this before. Something's happened to him."

"Yes, I feel it. Like trying to walk in a lead suit." Stevie said nothing more. Mist was beginning to alarm her as much as the specters around them.

Albin led them through a narrow aperture: a tunnel that brought them to the interior of the tower. Inside, there was nothing more than a pale cave, rugged, empty and smelling of cold stone. He guided them to a stairway rough-hewn around the wall, upwards to a smaller chamber above. This was a hollow cone of quartz, lit by floating white spheres. There were no chairs, no furniture at all, only rocks to sit on.

Stevie touched the wall: polished ice. Wherever Albin looked, the walls reflected the concentrated spot of bright sapphire blue on his forehead. It was a jewel, but more than decoration; she had the horrible impression that it was the inner eye with which he saw the universe.

Albin smiled and swept a hand around the space. "I live simply, as you see. Sit anywhere you wish. You're wet and cold, I realize, but I have no means of warming you. I suggest you use your inner Aelyr resources to overcome the discomfort."

He spoke politely, but Stevie had never seen more frightening eyes. You saw that arrogance in the eyes of deposed dictators, who'd stashed away billions to furnish lives in luxurious exile. There was no luxury here, but Albin had exactly that martyred, unrepentant stare.

Stevie wondered what he lived on. Raw fish, lake water, pure air?

They found places to sit, forming a rough circle. Albin sat too, as if holding court. Sam rested his elbows on his knees, leaning towards him. "All right, Grandfather, what do you want with us?"

"To talk." Albin's tone was as downy-soft as his cloak. "To catch up on old times, and new. I never could make Lawrence listen to me, but I would rectify that. You are my grandsons, after all, and Rosie virtually a granddaughter to me. Adam here—"

"I'm Mistangamesh."

Albin stopped. Mist had actually managed to surprise him. "Indeed? So you're the brother of Rufus Ephenaestus, after all? What are your feelings towards him now—he who wrought such devastation on his own race, and yet got clean away with it?"

"My feelings are my own business."

"Have you seen him since?"

Mist shook his head. "Seen nothing, heard nothing."

"When Vaidre Daima set Rufus free, I wasn't the only one grievously betrayed by the Spiral Court and others I'd counted as allies. The Spiral itself was betrayed. I saw that I could rely on no one but myself. I work alone now. I've learned so much. Instead of trying to persuade Aelyr and Vaethyr to my cause, I looked into the Spiral itself. I learned so much about its moods and strange properties, the energies that some call *roth*."

"And are you happier?" said Rosie. She sounded sincere.

"Happier?" Albin blinked. "That would be strangely unambitious. No, my dear Rosie. I seek to be stronger."

"So is this your new power base, then?" said Sam. "Mobile headquarters?"

"If you like. Persuasion and politics haven't worked. The Spiral Court has had its own way for far too long. Power, however—that's the only answer. Force is the only language that most creatures understand, human or Aelyr. Wouldn't you agree?"

There was an awful silence. Albin's tone was reasonable, but Stevie saw apprehension in the faces of her companions, Luc's in particular. The pain in her shoulder made her wince. *Ease up*, she told her *fylgia*. *I get the message, and we will leave—but not yet. This is important.*

She said, "Any chance of a drink, Lord Albin? We are really tired. We brought supplies, but they're running low."

"Of course." He rose gracefully, his feathery cloak swaying. "How inhospitable of me." He left the chamber, heading downward.

"I wouldn't put it past him to poison or drug us," said Sam.

Stevie looked at him. "Really?"

"He puts curses on people, and the curses stick. Then he'll try to make out he's innocent, that it's all in the victim's mind. I'm telling you, he's an arch-manipulator. I wouldn't put anything past him."

Rosie dumped her backpack on the floor and distributed a sad, damp collection of cereal bars. "Let's eat and try not to get wound up. Yes, Albin can talk until he's persuaded you night is day, but I'm not afraid of him. Last time I saw him, we met as equals."

"You were Estalyr that night," said Sam. "It was a night of miracles. This is different."

"I'm still not scared of him!"

"Well, neither am I. I'm just saying, I know him. He mistreated and alienated my father, Lawrence. That *never* gets forgiven. It damaged all of us."

"I know." Rosie touched Sam's fingers. "But I saw another side of him that night."

"Right, grabbing you with his serpent hand and stating that everyone who disagrees with him is perverse and polluted? Charming."

"It was quite an argument," Rosie agreed, pushing her hair out of her face. "But mainly I sensed overwhelming loneliness."

"Of his own choice!" Sam rubbed his face. "Rosie, thousands of people suffer pain and loneliness. Most of us manage to deal with it. A few go crazy with guns. Some try to take over the Otherworld. It's not an excuse."

"I didn't say it was. But it's a fact that his wife swanned off into the Spiral and left him heartbroken."

"Nah," said Sam. "She left her *son*, my father, heartbroken. Albin has no heart. It's years, if not centuries, since Maia went. He must be over it by now. That was possessiveness, not love. He's had every chance in the universe to find someone else. He may have a dozen lovers, for all we know. His wife left him because he's a twisted psychopath, not the other way round."

Rosie tilted her head. "How would you feel if I left you?"

"How can you ask that?" Sam gazed back at her. "I'd be in pieces. But I wouldn't rest until I'd found you. I *definitely* wouldn't be venting my wrath on everyone around me, trying to punish the Spiral itself. He's insane. No, love—I know you've got the softest heart in the world, but come on. Don't feel sorry for him. He's a bitter, twisted lunatic."

"Who can no doubt hear every word we're saying," said Mist.

"Too bad." Sam shrugged. "He knows what we think of him."

Lucas added, "And now he's incredibly dangerous."

"He talked about the way we drift apart like galaxies because we live too long," said Rosie. "It chilled me to the core, even more than this place."

Mist spoke quietly. "Albin's whole purpose at the trial was to convince us that the Spiral should be severed from Earth, to stop maniacs like Rufus from running loose. He was defeated. His support collapsed."

"Not defeated, obviously," said Luc. "It's only made him stronger. He's gathering an army. I'm sure no one knows about this. Virginia can't have known or she'd have told us. Even Iola's only just found out."

"The signs you were making at her?" said Mist.

Luc's answer was barely audible. "Yes, to warn the Court. Or anyone. If she makes it. Do you really think Albin could take over the Spiral, bend all the realms to his will and seal the Gates?"

"No," Rosie said quickly. "Don't leap to the worst conclusion, Luc."

"Not that he couldn't cause hellish chaos trying, of course," said Sam.

"Exactly. And you do realize that he's taken us prisoner?" Lucas said grimly. "Since no one else will say it?"

"It will be all right," Rosie said. "He likes to play mind games, that's all. He never had any true power over us. We'll talk our way out."

Mist said quietly, "I don't think we are going to talk our way out of this. He may have had no power before, but he's got plenty now. Luc's right. You know he has your *fylgias*? Not mine and Stevie's: I don't know where mine is, but I don't sense it *here*, and hers is sticking fast to her. But yours were free in the Spiral, and he's captured them."

All three stared at him in disbelief.

"That's impossible," said Rosie. "We would have known."

"Would you, though? You might not feel a thing."

Long seconds of silence passed. Stevie saw that they couldn't accept Mist's assertion. Eventually Rosie spoke. "But the Spiral itself is sentient. If Albin's up to no good, the knowledge would pass through the ground. Surely the whole Spiral would know?"

"Unless Albin's found a way of sealing himself off," said Mist. "He might be powerful enough. Even Rufus hid from the Spiral Court for years, and he was an amateur in matters of energy manipulation." Mist stood up, moving restlessly around the chamber. "We can't let ourselves be side-tracked by this. We have to escape."

"I know," said Lucas. He drummed a rhythm on his knees. "But how can I leave Albin to his own devices? The Gates are my responsibility. I have to do *something*."

"Iola," Rosie whispered. "She'll get word out."

Sam said, "It's a fact that if Albin gets his way, we won't be able to leave the Spiral, or get back in again. No one will be going anywhere or finding anyone."

Albin returned, bearing a tray with six glasses and a decanter, all of cobalt glass clasped in carved silver. He filled each with colorless liquor, saw them hesitate as he presented the tray.

"Now you are not drinking? I promise, I wouldn't do something so crude as to drug you. Please. I am trying to make peace."

Cautiously, Stevie accepted a glass and took a sip. She tasted elderberry and lemon, with a warming tang of alcohol. Then they all took a vessel, except Sam, who swigged from a plastic bottle of orange juice, and fixed Albin with an implacable glower.

"Samuel?"

"It's all right. We'll manage with what we've got."

"I can see how tired and hungry you are. There's too much of Vaeth in you. Your bodies have forgotten how to survive without food and rest. If you'd surrender to the Spiral and become pure again, you'd know freedom from hunger and fatigue and pain. True freedom."

"What do you really want?" Sam said bluntly.

"The same simple thing that I've always wanted," said Albin with his icy smile. "Purity. I wish the Aelyr race all to be gathered back into the Spiral where we belong and all the gates and portals to be sealed. Stay with me, shake off your human camouflage, and become part of the true primal Aetherial race again. I wish fulfillment and happiness for all. However . . . I no longer see any way of achieving my goal, except by force.

"Make yourselves comfortable, if you can. Remain in this chamber until it grows light. Sleep for a few hours. It's all I can offer, but you are Aetherial and able to bear a little discomfort—unless living on Vaeth has left you *too* soft. It's living too close to the human world that drains us of our true abilities. So, am I powerful, or is it you who are weak?"

Sam gave a hard laugh and stood right in front of Albin, his arms folded. "One more 'puny humans' remark like that and we'll see who's weak. D'you know you're insulting the bravest and best people I've ever known? We're the only family you have; we might even have loved you, if you hadn't turned into this arrogant jerk. Who summoned Brawth and tried to blame it on Lawrence, your own son? And who risked their lives to lay Brawth to rest again, if not Lawrence and Lucas, Rosie and me? Answer that, and then tell me who's weak, *Grandpa*."

Albin's face flickered with rage, but he didn't take the bait. His voice stayed emotionless. "I'll leave you in peace to think on what I've said."

Mist drifted into uneasy sleep and dreamed about the scene that Rosie had described while they were in the coracle: Rosie in primal, winged, Estalyr form, Albin, a figure like a pale statue on the balcony of an alien city, his forearm twining around Rosie's like a snake.

"Don't be so quick to pass judgment," he'd said as she confronted him with his cruelty to his own son, his family. The snake-shaped hand reared and rubbed its dry cheek across Rosie's. "I tired of the game . . . Child of Vaeth, don't go back. You may not see your loved ones again, but you won't care. Caring is a curse, when we live too long, and spend eternity like galaxies drifting away from each other."

A cascade of strange feelings spilled through Rosie. A strange coldness tugged her heart, like a distant call, or something urgent she had forgotten to do. The urge to fly was irresistible. Time shifted and she was airborne again, Albin a small pale figure looking up from the pooled shadows below. "Lawrence locked the Gates to protect Vaeth from terrible danger." His voice was faint as the wind took her. "Are you so very sure that the true danger has yet shown itself?"

The dream changed. Mist was holding Helena as she bled and bled . . . only it was not Helena dying in his arms, but Stevie.

He woke violently, aching all over. A dim lavender glow showed the sleeping forms of his companions. Sam, nestled against Rosie, was as deeply asleep as the others, so their slumber couldn't be the effect of Albin's wine. In a trance he rose, and began to climb a stairway that spiraled up the wall to a higher room.

He found himself in the tower's highest chamber, a smaller cone rising to a pointed apex. There were narrow slits for windows, a stone shelf with a few items—reminding him of Jaap de Witt's laboratory—arranged in a neat row. Crystals, bottles, instruments of quartz and brass. The central space was filled by a long oblong block of lapis-blue stone, like a bier.

On this block, Albin lay asleep.

Mist felt no fear. Surely they were equals. How real was Albin's power? Rosie might be right, that Albin was a lonely eccentric given to dramatic posturing. And perhaps it was their own fault they couldn't match his apparent strength.

He looked out of an embrasure at a starry sky that seemed to belong to Sibeyla, not Melusiel. The landscape was a blur, the horizon curving in odd directions.

A cold voice said, "Did I not ask you to remain in the chamber below until light returns?"

Albin was on his feet. Mist turned to face him, unperturbed. "When dawn comes, you must let us go. I'm trying to find Rufus—to finish what the Spiral Court could not. In that regard, you and I are on the same side."

Moving beside him, Albin looked out of the narrow window at the dark landscape beneath his tall narrow spire. "Rufus is a spent force," he said.

"How can you know that?"

"My sight is clear, up here in the cold. I hold the power of one who's given up, lost everything. Every bid I made to seal the Spiral from the Earth, to sever those destructive connections, has failed. All the supporters I had on the inner council of the Spiral Court fell away. I had nothing. So I created my tower."

"It's impressive," Mist agreed.

Albin picked up a small orb of quartz. "Do you know what this is? In other versions of the Spiral, they call it an *anametris* sphere. It is used to open and close portals. The sphere won't work in our realm, but it must be useful to have such devices, literal keys to lock the Gates. Were you even aware that there are other Spirals, attached to other Vaeths? Other tribes of Aelyr, interacting with different worlds?"

"I never thought of it."

"No. Few do. But when I close my eyes I see them, like shifting, shimmering planes intersecting with each other. How can I hope to seal them all?"

"Why would you want to?"

Albin gave a thin smile. "Indeed, I can only concentrate my energies on my own realm. I come from a long line of pure Sibeylans, pale and ascetic, who consider ourselves the purest of all Aetherials, closest in spirit to the icy energies of the Spiral, of the stars themselves. My *eretru*, the senior House of Sibeyla, has long held and passed down the office of Gatekeeper, first appointed by Sepheron, whose mother, Jeleel, overthrew the tyrant Malikala, so-called Queen of Fire.

"However, there's a paradox. The office of Gatekeeper is an earthy one—in the elemental sense—to do with manipulating rock and matter. It has an intellectual dimension, too, of esoteric calculations, but that's more a matter of instinct than science. It's a role that involves dealing too intimately with Vaeth. And there's the biggest concern of all: that while the role of Gatekeeper is important, it cannot be seized or held. The unseen energies of the Spiral bestow or withdraw the power. Those energies are as moody as the ocean."

"Sam and Lucas mentioned this," Mist said evenly. "Your magnificent mother, Liliana, held the role, and was followed by your son, Lawrence. But you were overlooked."

"That's unimportant." Albin placed the *anametris* sphere back on its tripod.

"Is it? Weren't you jealous?"

His smile became a thin flat line. "I had a higher purpose. All that distressed me was that Liliana took Lawrence to Vaeth to train him. To corrupt him."

Yes, jealousy, thought Mist, *though he'd never admit it*. There must have been closeness between Liliana and Lawrence from which Albin was excluded. Perhaps he, by his cold nature, had excluded himself. "I wondered which came first. Did your anti-Vaeth philosophy make you an unsuitable Gatekeeper? Or was it being passed over that turned you against the system?"

"Don't try to analyze me," Albin said softly. "My reasons are far deeper. Indulging in such shallow speculation is entirely the wrong approach. All family ties are long severed and dead to me."

"Truly?" said Mist. "So Lucas and Sam could be just anyone?"

"Yes." A pause. "Although I admit that the connection amuses me. It would give me particular satisfaction to bend them to my ideals."

"Aetheric purity," said Mist, thinking that Sam was right. Whatever sadness Albin had endured did not excuse him turning into some form of Sibeylan fascist. "It's not true, then, that your father came from Elysion, nicely saturated in the energies of rocks and earth and trees? I picture him as an earth god: a big, laughing man all in gold and green, with a curling golden beard."

Albin's eyes turned to glass. He breathed out in a soft hiss. "You should know better than me, ancient Felynx, that blood does not equal affinity. You could be born of parents from Elysion and Naamon—clod-like earth and aggressive fire—who lived the basest, nearly human life on Vaeth, and yet if the spirit of a different realm called, you would fly home. The true Aelyr spirit can escape its binding roots, soar back to the Spiral and be purged of all contamination. Being Sibeylan—a creature of pure intellect, of ice and stars and all things celestial—is a state of mind, not a factor of birth."

"So there's hope for all the muddy, contaminated ones?" Mist glanced around the chamber, hoping for some sign of the trapped *fylgias*. He sensed nothing. "Even an anarchist like Rufus?"

Albin didn't react to his hint of sarcasm. "Yes, I'm certain that all Aetherials can achieve this state. I believe they *must*. And believing it, I've found a degree of equilibrium. Peace." Albin smiled, a genuinely warm natural smile—all the more unnerving for the words he'd spoken. "I don't know why it took me so long to see the light, but that's wisdom for you. A quality that takes many years to mature. Go back now and sleep, Mistangamesh."

"You are a fascinating man," Mist said softly, "and I must ask again one favor of you. Let us go on our way, so that I can destroy Rufus."

Albin only repeated, "Go back to sleep."

Stevie woke abruptly, aching to the bone. For a moment she had no idea where she was, and only faintly recalled some odd dreams. Then she saw the others waking, stiffly sitting up. The first brush of dawn light entered the chamber from the stairwell. Fully clothed, she felt damp and stale.

"C'mon, let's get going," said Sam. "I'm not listening to any more shit from Albin. If he's obstructive, we'll fight our way out. Change shape, use our fists—whatever works. Agreed?"

"I spoke to him in the night," said Mist. "I couldn't sleep, so I went to the top chamber and he was there. He told me about his ideas, and about Aetherial powers."

The other four gaped at him, astonished.

"But *I* was talking to him," said Stevie. "For ages. You weren't there. You were fast asleep."

"That's weird," said Lucas. "I went up and spoke to him, too."

Sam and Rosie were nodding, their faces a picture of shock and bewilderment.

"Looks like he had us all," said Sam.

They went down the stairway and through the lowest chamber, meeting no challenge. Albin was waiting for them on the shore outside, surrounded by his aquatic guards and hundreds of elementals, swarming thickly in the fog.

"Don't go," he said. "Think about all I've said, dear children. Leave behind all pollution and become pure Aelyr: part of the Spiral, as you were meant to be. It's who you really are."

He spoke so passionately that Stevie, for a moment, was tempted. What else did she have? *Daniel*, she told herself. *Frances, and my friends. For goodness' sake, Albin, get out of my head!*

"Come on, it's time to go," said Sam. "Grandfather, I'm asking nicely. Stand aside."

"Please stay."

"I'm sorry, Lord Albin," said Rosie. "You have your way of seeing things, but we can't share it. Sorry."

"You misunderstand. I'd prefer you to stay of your own volition, but you are staying here, in any case."

"Albin, please." Rosie's tone verged on anger. "We're your family. We're not doing any harm. We've got stuff to sort out. We'll happily come back and see you again—but only if you let us come and go freely."

"As if I am some befuddled old grandfather to be humored?" Albin's expression was intransigent.

"It's not happening," said Sam. "We're going."

"Nowhere," said Albin.

Lucas squared up to his grandfather with strength Stevie hadn't seen in him before. "You summoned Brawth! All along, everyone blamed Lawrence, and he blamed himself—but you did it, to torment and undermine him. I've always known it. The whole Spiral will know, unless you let us go *now*."

"You don't seem to understand," Albin said softly. "None of you can leave. You think I would let the Gatekeeper go? Let any of you go?"

He opened his hands, and the air began to ripple with lines of light, weaving a cat's cradle all around them.

Stevie found herself moving slowly, like a fly stuck in honey—and then unable to move at all. She was frozen to the spot. Cold air iced her skin. Albin's cage of light wound tighter and tighter around her: a horrible feeling of numbness.

She saw the same happening to Sam, Rosie and Lucas; saw them trying to move towards one another, ever more slowly as time seemed to slow down, their mouths opening to shout to one another but no sound emerging as they turned from flesh to quartz.

Stevie was paralyzed, staring through a glass pane at three statues, half-seen through drifting ice vapor. Time stopped and she was caught there, forever staring and horrified and not knowing why.

Movement. A dark blur . . . Mist was still moving. He struggled as if battling a hurricane. She felt herself pulled sideways, throbs of power shaking her. He was in his water-dragon form again, taller than Albin. She saw two figures wrestling briefly, one white, the other ink-blue and emanating orange crackles of fire . . .

There was a roar of rage. Albin? She saw Mist fall back. As he fell she felt herself seized by hands, or tendrils, that were muscular, irresistible.

She and Mist fell together and hit water.

Down, down they sank. She could move again and found she'd transformed by instinct into the new water-breathing creature she'd been in Persephone's cave and Virginia's pool.

Mist was beside her in seahorse form. Albin's slaves were in the water all around them, trying to herd them back to shore. They fought. Stevie felt parts of herself ripped off; saw fragments of her own fins and Mist's leafy tendrils floating around them. She saw blood in the water.

Another pulse of power from Mist shook the lake like a depth charge. Albin's creatures were thrown back. Then the two of them were surging through the water, free.

Rosie Sam Lucas . . .

She and Mist broke the surface and came up gasping into the soft air of Melusiel. Looking back, Stevie saw Albin's tower far behind them, no more than a pale needle on the horizon. She felt a current pulling at her. Even as she looked back she felt the pull of the *antilineos* taking them farther away from their friends.

"We can't leave them!" She coughed and gasped, pushing wet hair out of her face. Her skin felt reptilian, her hands abrasive on her scaly forehead.

"We have no choice," Mist said. His aquatic face was slate-blue, his voice gruff. Red-gold Felynx eyes burned into her. She wondered if this was truly Mistangamesh at all.

"Our friends—we can't leave them there!"

"We must."

He spun in the water and let the current take him. Stevie did the same. He was right. They had no chance against the pull of the water. They tried to join hands but turbulence pulled them apart and they surged helplessly on, the lake narrowing to a river, then to a channel and soon to frothing rapids that ended suddenly on the edge of nothing . . .

They were falling, millions of tons of water plunging with them.

Falling off the edge of the Spiral itself.

17

Desert Springs

Stevie was in darkness, lying on a hard surface. There was a glow far above her and dust sticking to her wet skin. She was soaked through, hair dripping, clothes hanging heavy with the weight of water. Every cell of her body hurt. She began to shiver with the wet, piercing cold.

As she lay there nearly insensible, fragments of memory assaulted her: being carried for what seemed hours along the raging *antilineos*: losing sight of Mist; plunging off the edge of the world in a deluge of foam . . . falling, falling . . .

Visions of Rosie, Sam and Lucas assailed her: imprisoned by Albin, turned to ice and stone. But now they were unreachable, somewhere beyond a cosmic waterfall, in another realm.

Our fault, she thought. *They came with us out of the simple goodness of their hearts and now they're lost and doomed and it's our fault, mine and Mist's . . .*

Her body shook but no sobs came out, only rasping coughs.

"Stevie." She felt warm breath on the icy whorl of her ear. "Stevie?"

She raised her head and there was Mist's beloved face above hers. His features were human again, shadowed with pain and shock as if he'd crawled from a shipwreck. She made out the dark bulk of a boulder behind him. The landscape felt stony and desolate. She was so cold that the water dripping from him felt warm on her skin.

"Are we back on Vaeth?" She used the Aelyr name for Earth; funny how fast she'd learned the habit.

"Yes, I think so."

He helped her sit up, wrapping one arm around her. They sat clinging together for a while, silent with exhaustion. They were on a flat empty plain with low hills in the distance, luminous with starlight. A pool of water gathered around them and soaked into the bone-dry soil beneath.

"No tears," he said, kissing her rat's-tail hair. "Aren't we wet enough already?"

"The others . . ."

"I know."

"We can't leave them there. We can't!"

"There's nothing we can do." His voice shook. "I would if we could, but it's too late."

"We've got to try. We can't abandon them."

"I know, but we have to help ourselves first."

"Yes. Okay." She forcibly gathered her thoughts. "First we need to find out where the hell we are." She began to stand up. Again the horror of Albin's attack swept through her and she stumbled onto her knees. "Oh my god, Mist."

"It's all right." He held her arm and they stood together, leaning unsteadily on each other. "There's no sign of the portal we came through, only a boulder that looks like every other boulder. We can't go back. We have to go on."

Looking up, she saw the Milky Way spanning the dome above them, ablaze with billions of glittering stars. The sight made her feel tiny, lost and desperate. "We'd better start walking," she said.

"Which way?"

"I don't think it matters."

There were stones beneath their boots, scrubby bushes catching at their clothes. She felt shocked relief that their garments had survived the ordeal, apparently having transformed to fur and fin and back again, as if altered reality acted on fabric as well as flesh. The subzero night did nothing to dry them out, but Stevie was past caring about her physical discomfort. She felt her jacket pockets; one small mercy, she'd remembered to close the zippers.

"I still have my wallet," she said, teeth chattering. "That's something. You?"

"Yes," Mist answered. "But money won't help us against Rufus, or find a way back into the Spiral."

"No, but it will buy practicalities like food and transport and accommodation, without which we'd be *totally* stuffed."

"I think we should avoid human habitation."

"Why? We're not wild animals. Even *finding* a human in this wilderness is going to be a miracle."

"We're Aetherial. We don't need them."

She looked at his stony profile and a chill went through her. "Mist, will you stop it? Maybe Albin's superhuman, but we're not. Have you forgotten you tried to walk the length of Scotland and woke up in a hospital bed? *We need help.*"

He closed his eyes, gave a faint sigh. "You're right."

After an hour or so, they reached a long straight highway that bisected the desert. A line of telephone wires dwindled into the distance in both directions. The road was empty, dark. Stevie's heart was too heavy to give the smallest twitch of hope. She guessed the road might continue for a hundred miles before it hit a town.

"Even if a vehicle comes past, we can't take the risk of stopping anyone," she said. "If the police pick us up, we're screwed. We've got no passports. If they find out we're here illegally, I don't know what they'll do to us, but it will totally wreck our plans."

"Now you see why I'm reluctant to ask for human help?" Mist looked up at the stars and said, "Let's try north."

"Is your Aetherial radar working? Can you sense Rufus, or even a small town?"

"No," he said. "But it's as good a direction as any."

They walked through the scrub, keeping parallel with the endless road.

The distant hills seemed barely to change position. Now and then a vehicle swept past, headlights dazzling—and then Stevie would think, too late, that they should take a chance and flag down the driver. Yet they didn't. The risk was too great.

They trudged on with the cosmos turning above them, dawn beginning to brush the horizon.

Stevie was asleep on her feet, hallucinating, so hungry that her stomach had contracted to a ball of pain. Her legs were agony, feet burning, her skin like ice. The thought of death seemed welcome . . . but where would she find herself next time? In Persephone's chamber again, or in another new, mad existence without memories? Would Mist be with her, or would she never see him again?

A voice reached her. Realizing Mist had stopped, she came out of her stupor to see an array of lights. There was a gas station a few hundred yards ahead, with rows of parked trucks, a big wooden building with brightly lit windows, a sign announcing MOJAVE MOE'S 24-HOUR DINER. An oasis.

"Oh, thank the gods," she gasped, pushing her still-damp hair out of her face. The ends were stiff with ice. "Sanctuary."

She pulled at Mist's arm, but he resisted her. "We can't go in."

Her exhaustion flared into rage. "We are going in that fucking truck stop if it's the last thing I do!" she growled. "You do what the hell you like. Find Rufus, kill each other, I don't care."

She hobbled away from him. It had been a mistake to stop; a minute's pause was enough to turn her legs to rods of red-hot iron.

Mist hurried after her. "Stevie."

"If you know what's good for you, you'll shut the fuck up and come with me."

"I'm with you," he said, his tone contrite. "It's just . . . we're a mess. I'm so sorry I brought you into this."

With a start, she realized that Mist was as scared as she was, if not more so. "Hey," she said more calmly. "It will be all right. If anyone asks, we'll tell them we're British tourists and our car broke down. And we have credit cards, which are waterproof, I hope. We can buy food while we sit and have a think."

She put her arm through his, feeling how cold he was beneath the damp jacket. She felt his heartbeat shaking his ribs. He looked as rough as she felt, but there was a fierce and desperate glow in his eyes.

"Ready?" she said. "Come on. Just try to act normal."

They crossed a wide parking lot and pushed open a glass door. Inside, heat enveloped them. The glare of fluorescent lights was dazzling. Stevie blinked, reeling from pure sensory shock. They were in a wide corridor with a convenience store on the right, a diner on the left, restrooms and some kind of amusement arcade at the far end.

There were perhaps twenty people in the place; enough to give a gentle air of activity, not enough for the open-plan space to feel crowded. No one seemed to take any notice of them. Stevie pulled Mist's arm and said, "Let's head for the ladies' and gents'. We can dry our hair and check we're not covered in dirt. Tidy up a bit. Look," she said, as they progressed. "There's a cash machine. See if you can get some dollars out, then go in the restaurant and order breakfast. Anything. I'll meet you in there. I've had an idea."

"What?"

"Just do it!"

In the restroom, Stevie washed her hands and face, looked at herself in the mirror. She saw a bloodless, haunted face staring back. She pinched her cheeks to raise color, tried to relax her expression and produce a carefree smile.

"Eugh," she said to her reflection.

She bent her head under the hand-dryer to fluff up her bedraggled hair, then removed her still-wet jacket and stood in the hot-air stream to dry her clothes as best she could. She estimated she'd have to stand there for an hour before she was bone-dry, but it was better than nothing. The hot air burned. She stopped when another woman came in, passing her with a quick "Hi" and a smile.

No one's interested in us, she thought with a wave of relief.

Emerging, she headed to the store and found a rack of road maps. California. Nevada. The West Coast. Arizona. Promising, but she didn't know which one to choose.

"Excuse me," she said to the assistant, a wiry dark-haired woman who looked as if she'd been on duty all night. A badge labeled her Glenda. "I need a map of the state."

"Sure, help yourself."

"The thing is, we're lost. Tourists. First time here. And, er, the map we had in the car wasn't that good and we've driven off the edge of it. The road went on forever. Could you show me where we are?"

"Oh—no problem, hon." Glenda, despite her weary demeanor, seemed pleased to help. "Where you from, Australia?"

"Er, no. England."

"Man, I always get those accents mixed up," she said, emerging from behind the counter. "You having a good trip?"

"We were, until we got lost." Stevie smiled, hoping she didn't resemble a grinning skull. "We're so glad to find this place, I can't tell you."

"So here we are . . ." Glenda unfolded a map of southern California and Nevada onto the counter and circled her finger over an array of intersecting roads and contour lines. The area looked a long way inland. Stevie was so pleased to find herself in a definite location, she felt like crying. "So you're near the top of the Mojave Desert, see, just inside the Nevada state line. Where are you headed?"

The question threw her. She stared at the map and picked a place at random. "Death Valley."

"Oh, you like the deserts, then?"

"Love them," Stevie said emphatically.

"They're pretty spectacular. Death Valley's amazing. The one thing you have to watch out for in the desert is freezing or roasting to death! We only do extremes. Did you know it was seventeen degrees around here last night?"

Stevie did a quick conversion in her head: that was about minus eight Celsius, well below freezing. "Really?" Trying not to look stunned, she refolded the map, grabbed some chocolate bars and paid for everything with her card, thinking, *If we weren't Aetherial we probably would have died.* "Is there a telephone I can use? My cell phone isn't working."

"Sure, go down the aisle past the restrooms, you'll see the booth on the right." Glenda added as Stevie thanked her, "You take care, now. Have a good trip."

Stevie hurried to the far end of the building again, realized she had no change, then saw that the pay phone accepted credit cards. She felt in her top pocket and extracted her poor notebook, which was swollen with water. The pages were close to disintegrating as she turned to the one she needed and read the blurred ballpoint ink.

"Any time you're in the States, call me," Fin's brother Patrick had told her on Christmas Day. But where had he said he lived? San Diego? San Francisco?

Hands shaking, she punched in Patrick's number.

The ring tone sounded for so long that her heart fell. Then a voice answered, thick with sleep. "Yeah?"

"Is that Patrick Feehan?"

"Yeah, speaking."

Her throat went into spasm and she could barely get any words out. "It's S-Stevie . . ."

"Steve who?"

"Stevie. Fin's friend. Christmas? Remember you said I could call you any time I was in the States?"

A pause. Her heart sank further. It was so easy, she thought, to say convivial things at a party that you didn't mean in the cold light of everyday life, and the slurred voice was grumpy with displeasure. "Yeah, but d'you know what time it is? It's six o'clock in the bloody morning! What, what . . . ?" She heard a rustle of sheets, as if he was trying to wake up.

"I know, I'm so sorry. I didn't mean to disturb you but I'm, I'm in a mess and I thought you might . . ."

"Where are you? Stevie, you sound terrible. Can you call the police, or something? I'm not feeling great . . . I'm really hungover and I'm s'posed to be at work."

She took some deep breaths. "I'm sorry, Patrick. No, I can't call the police. I know we barely know each other, but I don't know anyone else to call. I'm stuck in the Mojave Desert. I was hoping maybe you could come and get me. Really sorry."

"How the hell d'you manage to get stranded there?"

"I, er . . . it's complicated but I'm really desperate."

Another silence. "Shit. You know I live on the coast, right? I'm in San Luis Obispo."

"I knew it was San something."

"You're talking two hundred miles, minimum."

"That's okay," she said hoarsely. "We'll think of something else."

"No, wait." His tone changed. "Stevie, of course I'll come get you. Don't worry, that distance is nothing in the States. You need to tell me exactly where you are. Five minutes for shower and black coffee, and I'll be on the road. But you know it's going to take me three or four hours to get there?"

"That's okay." Tears ran freely down her cheeks. She told him the location, as detailed by Glenda. When she finished, she said, "There's a restaurant we can sit in. Thank you, thank you so much."

"What the hell happened to you?"

"Crazy story. I'll explain when you get here."

Slipping past the queue at the "Please wait to be seated" sign, Stevie found Mist in the diner. He was in a booth with cushioned seats and a red gingham tablecloth. Country music played in the background and the place had a nostalgic ambience that seemed to please the truck drivers and families who were slowly filling the place.

Mist looked up, his face pallid beneath unkempt raven hair. There was orange juice and coffee on the table. Stevie seized a glass of juice and drained it. Freshly squeezed, it was the most divine liquid she'd ever tasted.

"I asked for the best breakfast they make," he said. "The waitress grinned knowingly. Heaven knows what we'll get."

"As long as it's hot, I don't care. I found out where we are." She placed the folded map on the table. "And Patrick is coming to pick us up. We just have to wait."

"Who's Patrick?"

"Oh—you remember Fin at the museum? He's her brother. But he'll take a few hours to get here."

"Did he mind?"

"At first. He was no grumpier than I would have been, woken up by someone I barely know. But he's on his way."

Mist nodded in tired relief. "Stevie, thanks. I wish we didn't have to involve someone else. Again."

Rosie, Luc, Sam. Stevie shuddered. "I, I know, but even if they rented cars from here, which they don't, you can't rent a car without proper ID, like a passport and driving license. I know that much."

Breakfast arrived on huge plates containing omelettes stuffed with cheese and ham, hash browns and pancakes, toast on the side. Stevie's eyes widened. Surely there was enough here for four people who hadn't eaten for a week. She began to pick at the omelette, feeling guilty about eating while Rosie and the others were frozen, imprisoned, left for dead.

"Try to eat," said Mist. "We need all our strength."

"According to Albin, proper Aetherials don't need food."

"Albin is deranged."

"Do you know how cold it was last night? If we were human, we might have frozen to death."

Mist poured coffee into her mug. "That's our trouble. We're Vaethyr; Aetherial enough to survive hardships, but human enough to collapse in a heap at the end."

"So let's resign ourselves to needing Patrick's help."

"I should have come to terms with it by now." He gave her a wan but tender smile. "You're right, we would've been mad not to come in here. Forgive me for being stubborn."

"Forgiven," she said. "I've never seen such vast portions of food. I never thought I'd be in the States . . . mind you, I imagined a beach in California. Not this. I can't stop thinking about . . ."

"I know, but we won't help them by starving ourselves."

She obeyed, eating steadily until the plate was three-quarters empty. The overstuffed omelette was luscious; the pancakes, drenched in maple syrup, obscenely good. A waitress came past and refilled their coffee mugs, dropping half-and-half creamers on the table.

"You guys okay?" she said. "You need anything else?"

"We're fine, thanks." Stevie managed to produce a smile. Everyone was so friendly and solicitous. "Only . . . is it okay if we stay for a couple of hours? We're waiting for someone to collect us."

"Oh, you got car trouble?"

"Er . . . yes. Broken down. It's okay."

"No problem, you can stay right there unless we get super-busy. I'll keep the coffee coming. I thought you looked a little frazzled when you came in."

To Stevie's surprise, a huge man sitting a couple booths away turned to them. He had long hair straggling from beneath a cowboy hat, a wild mustache, forearms black with tattoos. "Hey, ma'am, I'm driving a tow truck. Can I look at your vehicle for you?"

The kindness of strangers. Stevie opened her mouth, speechless. Mist spoke first. "Thank you, but we ran off the road into a dip and it's a mess. You'd never find it, and even if we did, it would be impossible to pull out."

"It's all right, I've called my, er, my brother," Stevie added hurriedly. "He's on his way. But thank you so much for offering."

"Well, you all just let me know if you change your minds. You called the cops about the accident?"

"My brother is a cop," Stevie lied by reflex. "We're fine, but thank you."

He tipped his hat and turned back to his breakfast. Stevie and Mist stared at each other in vague alarm. It was so easy to become entangled in a mire of lies without even thinking. She prayed no one else would start asking friendly but awkward questions.

"Why did you say we ran off the road?" she whispered as the trucker left.

"Why did you say your brother's a cop?" he retorted. "I think we need to say as little as possible."

"I should have said you're a gambling addict who can't pass a slot machine without playing for hours while I sit stewing with frustration."

"What is a slot machine?"

"Didn't you see, near the restrooms, the arcade area with flashing lights? Never mind."

"I'm not averse to gambling," said Mist. "Perhaps I'll give it a try."

"Perhaps you're more like Rufus than you realize," she remarked.

His eyes narrowed, very dark. "Don't say that, even as a joke."

"It wasn't a joke. It was sheer nastiness, because I'm tired and pissed off. Sorry."

"You're angry with me?"

"Yes and no. Yes, because you saved me but not the others. No, because the situation was Albin's fault, not yours. I'm just . . . exhausted and scared."

"And so am I. Don't let's argue. I'd have rescued them too, if I could."

"And so would I." Stevie ate a piece of buttered toast and sipped her coffee. Guilty heaven. "What are we going to do?"

"Find Rufus, as we planned."

Mist's eyes took on a strange expression, cold yet burning. Stevie wasn't sure that he was entirely sane any longer. Any mention of Rufus made him look as driven as Albin.

"And Daniel," she said softly. She was silent for a moment, then added, "I feel terrible that Rosie and Sam and Lucas got involved."

He reached across the red gingham and gripped her left hand. "I know, but even if we could go back this minute, how could we help them? I don't even know how I got the two of us out. Albin had a hold over the others that he didn't have on you and me. I repelled his attack, grabbed you and jumped. It happened so fast."

"Well, Iola's on her way to the Spiral Court," said Stevie. "Let's pray to Estel—is that the goddess's name?—that she makes it. That someone can help them."

"Estel the Eternal," he murmured. "Not a deity, exactly, but she's said to be the very first of us. Which makes her goddess-like, I suppose."

"In the non-intervening sense?" She rested her head on one hand and stirred her coffee. "I don't know why people get so excited about gods, because they never bloody do anything."

Mist laughed, giving the quick, beautiful smile that made her heart twist. The smile vanished as fast, as if darker thoughts had snuffed it out. Through a window, she saw a police car cruising slowly across the car park.

"Mist," she said, "when we find Rufus, what are you actually going to do?"

He became very still and looked straight into her eyes. "I intend to kill him."

"Oh," she said. "Oh. In cold blood?"

"Not cold, when it's been brewing for centuries."

Stevie broke the gaze. She asked herself, *How am I supposed to travel with someone who means to kill his own brother? Will that make me an accomplice to murder? If I stay with him, it's like I'm condoning it. But I can't not go. If anything, I must try to stop him . . . or at least to rescue Danny. If he wants rescuing. If he's even there. If, if, if.*

"Has it occurred to you that Rufus is exactly who we need to help us against Albin?"

"I already asked for Albin's help against Rufus. He brushed me off." Mist shook his head. "It won't happen. Rufus never helped anyone but himself, in his entire existence."

"But isn't Rufus . . . unkillable?" She dropped her voice to a whisper.

"I can sever him from *this* life, at least."

"But you can't simply execute him. What if he kills you?"

"Then we'll die together."

Stevie stared, resisting a desire to throw something at him. "Will you please cut out the melodrama? Is it too much to ask that we sort things out in a civilized manner?"

Her heart jumped as she saw a policeman at the restaurant entrance, talking to their waitress. She heard the officer say, "Highway Patrol, ma'am. A truck driver flagged us down to report that a vehicle had skidded off the road into a ravine? He said the driver and passenger were here, waiting for help? British tourists?"

The waitress waved in the direction of their booth.

Mist's eyes locked onto Stevie's in mutual alarm. Before she knew what was happening, he was rising, grasping her elbow, and the world was rushing past in a strange shimmery blur. She heard the waitress respond, "That's weird, they were right there a moment ago."

They slipped out the rear entrance and paced around the parking lot, looking at the desert. Mist, acting faster than thought, had pulled her into the Dusklands as they fled the restaurant, and they were still hiding in that realm, which gave the world an eerie patina of ultraviolet tones. A sensation that Stevie previously dreaded as a frightening temporal-lobe storm, full of hallucinations, now felt welcome.

In the Dusklands, human eyes could not see them.

"Why did that truck driver have to call the police?" she groaned.

"I suppose he was trying to help," said Mist. The purplish light catching his face and ebony hair accentuated his unearthly beauty. His eyes and teeth shone very white.

"Did you pay, by the way?"

"I left a hundred dollars on the table. Was that enough?"

Stevie uttered a gasp. "About four times more than we actually owed. They'll be happy with that."

Twenty minutes passed before the patrol car pulled away. *Come on, Patrick, come on*, she thought, frustrated to know he would be at least another two hours. Shaken, they moved cautiously back to surface reality and went inside again to wait. In the store, they bought a selection of cheap T-shirts, jeans and sweatshirts—and a bag to carry their damp stuff—so they were able to change into fresh, dry clothes. She added toothbrushes and other basic toiletries, bottled water and some unhealthy-looking cakes that resembled yellow sawdust filled with shaving cream. Looking around at other travelers, who were peacefully choosing magazines and candy bars, she thought how comfortingly mundane this felt. She didn't want to leave. How wonderful, to feel normal and human for a while.

By now, a new shift of staff had taken over. Anonymity was restored, but she stayed on edge for the remaining hours. They spent awhile in the amusement arcade, gambling away twenty dollars and winning back twenty-two. Then Stevie noticed a small glass-partitioned room with a row of computers. She slipped in and paid for half an hour's Internet use, but was out again within ten minutes.

"Are you okay?" Mist asked. "You've gone pale. Was there an email about Frances?"

"Yes. She's still the same." Stevie took a deep breath and exhaled. "But it's Daniel; his file storage site has disappeared completely. Does that mean they found the message he left for me?"

"We've no way to find out," Mist said firmly. "Don't jump to conclusions."

"Well, what else could it be?"

"Perhaps . . ." He shrugged. "If Daniel created the site for *you* and got found out, yes, he might be in trouble. But what if the images were put there for some other, unknown person to look at? If they've seen them, the site wouldn't be needed anymore, would it?"

"Some accomplice of Rufus?" She shook her head, trying to blink away the gritty tiredness in her eyes. "Mist, my head will explode if we try to figure this out now. Believe it or not, I'm hungry again. Do you think it's safe to go back in the diner?"

This time they sat on stools at a long counter, drinking more coffee and sharing an enormous triple-decker of bread stuffed with chicken, bacon and lettuce. She was beginning to feel they were doomed to spend the rest of their lives at a truck stop, spirits in limbo. Then a hand came over Stevie's shoulder and stole half the sandwich.

"'Scuse me. I am fucking starving. You don't mind, do you?"

Patrick.

She'd worried that she wouldn't recognize him, but she knew him immediately: dark hair cut short, stubble darkening his pale complexion, a broad, good-natured face like Fin's. Stevie turned and flung her arms around him.

"Woah," he said. "I'm pleased to see you too. Bloody hell, what a drive. I didn't stop once."

"You look knackered." She released him, shaking with the urge to cry from sheer relief. "I can't tell you how glad I am to see you. You're a hero. Oh, this is my friend, Mist."

The two men shook hands. Patrick mumbled hello around a mouthful of food. Then he glanced sideways at Stevie with a brief widening of his eyes, as if to say, *Wow, where did you find* him?

Not noticing, Mist said quietly, "Thank you so much for coming."

"Honestly, I can't apologize enough," Stevie said. "We're stranded. I didn't know anyone to call, except you."

Patrick raised a hand to quiet her. "No apology needed. Any friend of Fin's, et cetera. But what the hell happened to you? No offense, you're still gorgeous, but you look like death."

"Thanks." Stevie found a smile. "You don't look too clever yourself."

He took another big bite of the sandwich, almost swallowing it whole. "Oh, that's not your fault. The reason I drank too much last night was because I had a stupid argument with the boyfriend. He wanted to go clubbing, I wanted to stay in, but he went anyway. He said I was putting him under too much 'pressure' and he needed to 'party.'" He mimed quotation marks and rolled his eyes. "I was in no mood for talking to him today, let alone working with him, so I'm glad you called."

"That's a shame," said Stevie. "Are you going to forgive him?"

"Yeah, I always do. Selfish scumbag!" Patrick exclaimed, loud enough to make nearby customers turn and stare. "Him, I mean."

"Er, I didn't think you meant me. Are you sure you're okay?"

"Absolutely. Sorry; no more outbursts, I promise. You must be desperate to get out of this place after sitting around for hours."

"You could say that. Don't you want a rest first?"

"Nah, bathroom break and I'm fine. What the hell happened to you?"

"It's a really long and unbelievable story." She exhaled.

"I'm not the police." Patrick shrugged, took her coffee mug and drained it. "Just tell me what you need to."

"We ended up in the middle of the desert with no passports, nothing."

His eyes widened. "You got carjacked?"

"No. I didn't say that. And please keep your voice down! Look, the important thing is that we desperately need to find a friend of mine, Daniel. We've got an address, but no way of getting there."

"Short of stealing a car," Mist put in.

Patrick glanced at him with a slight smile. "Don't worry about a thing. I'll take you."

"Are you sure? We'll pay for your fuel, food, everything."

"Never mind that. Where d'you need to go?"

Stevie moved plates aside and unfolded the map on the counter. She pointed at the location of the truck stop, then slid her finger north and east across the contours of Nevada. "Here, somewhere. Jigsaw Canyon." Patrick studied the map for a moment, then nodded.

"You do realize what distances are like over here? There's no way we'll be there before nightfall, and you both look bushed."

Seeing Mist's slight frown, Stevie asked, "Do you want to arrive after dark, all three of us falling over with tiredness, not knowing what we're going into?"

"No," said Mist. "That would not be the best idea."

"So what we'll do," said Patrick, "is go as far as we can today and find a motel for a good night's sleep. We'll set off first thing tomorrow, all fresh and bushy-tailed in the morning, ready to meet your friends."

"Sounds good," said Stevie.

Patrick tapped the map, looking pleased with himself. "Oh, yeah. I know exactly the place to stop. You'll love it. Get ready to meet the Big Red Buddhas."

The motel was basic, a bit scruffy, but not the sort of place to demand the passports of foreign visitors. Patrick booked two double rooms, not even asking Stevie if she and Mist wanted to sleep separately. She didn't argue. She had an intuition that, if Mist had his own room, he might vanish in the night and find his way to Jigsaw Canyon alone.

She wanted to keep an eye on him.

The room was large but threadbare, last decorated sometime in the early seventies. Still, it was clean, and the plumbing worked. The view outside was of a dusty road, a mountain, and the sign: BIG RED BUDDHAS MOTEL. Stevie couldn't see anything to love, but didn't care; they'd driven for four hours, by which time she could have fallen asleep on a boulder.

They'd told Patrick the bare minimum about their search for Rufus and Daniel, adding that they'd been waylaid and robbed by someone they should have been able to trust. She felt guilty about the white lies, but Patrick was accepting. He kept putting up a hand and saying, "It's fine, only tell me as much or as little as you want. I'll get the full story when you're ready."

Stevie and Mist lay on the bed together, clothed, their bodies apart, curled up facing each other. He stroked her cheek and hair, the touch of his fingers soothing, almost unbearably so. From each fingertip waves of warmth spread through her. She wanted more, wanted everything, but knew it wasn't going to happen. She tried to ignore the hot ache of frustration that threatened to dissolve her. Did he feel the same? She kept her eyes firmly above his waist, in case his feelings were physically evident. Or not. Iron self-control or brotherly indifference? She preferred not to know.

It was pointless. Nothing was going to happen, because they were both floored by exhaustion, and by all the other barriers between them: their friends, in Albin's cold prison; the taint of Fela's memories; Mist's obsession with Rufus . . . And Helena, bloody Helena, the immortal icon raised to sainthood by being both perfect and dead.

She stamped on the unworthy thought.

There was so much still to talk about, but neither spoke. They only gazed at each other with the unspoken question, *What the hell is going to happen to us?*

Stevie fell asleep. When she woke, she was alone.

Judging by the light, it was late afternoon. The world outside looked rosy, the sky deep blue. In a rush of anxiety, she got up, checked she had her room key, and went outside. The day's warmth was beginning to fade, and there were only a few cars parked alongside Patrick's Chevy Impala. She made her way along a walkway past reception and down a set of steps until she found herself in the grounds that lay behind the building.

An alien landscape.

A gentle rocky slope led to an area where steam wreathed the ground, rising from plates of flowstone stained red, yellow and copper-green. Hot water bubbled and popped from vents. She saw, roughly a hundred yards away, a cluster of bulbous shapes about eight feet high.

The formation looked like three fat red buddhas, squashed together.

There was a path winding to the area with a small wooden sign stating the obvious: TO THE HOT SPRINGS. Smaller lettering explained that the "buddhas" had been formed by dissolved minerals being forced from deep in the earth's mantle to pile up into bizarre sculptures on the surface. Halfway down the path, she met Patrick walking back up. He had a towel wrapped around his waist and his hair was damp. "Hey," he said, "Mist said you were fast asleep, but there's nothing to revive you like bathing in a thermal pool. Ever tried it?"

"No." The prospect of soaking her aching body in hot water was irresistible. "So this is your surprise?"

"Yes, isn't it incredible? I once came here with—" Patrick closed his eyes.

"The selfish party-loving scumbag?" Stevie suggested.

He gave a soft growl. "I *will* stop being mad with him by the time I get home. Healing waters are great for gaining a perspective on your troubles, so you *have* to go in, Stevie. You'll find towels down there."

"I was looking for Mist, actually."

Patrick hooked his thumb over his shoulder. "Yeah, he's still soaking, if you can spot him through the steam. Mist in the mist."

Stevie went on until she reached the buddhas and studied them in delight. The rounded formations were shiny-red, with steam sputtering from blowholes. Scarlet and yellow mineral stains gave them an unreal appearance. All around them lay shallow pools, terraced at different levels. Steam rose from milky green water. Each pool was bounded by a lip of flowstone stained with iron and sulfur. She felt as if she'd stepped onto another planet.

The water reminded her of Persephone's cave. And as always, she felt a thrill of fear and fascination . . . *But it's just hot water*, she told herself. There was going to be no Aelyr transformation this time, no revelation, no reincarnation.

There was no one around, so she stripped down to T-shirt and panties, and slipped into the waist-deep water. The miasma of sulfur was strong, but bearable. The hot water felt delicious on her aching body, thick and silky with dissolved minerals. The infinity-sign scar on her collarbone stung a little. Above her, the triple geysers hissed and spat like boiling kettles.

She swam slowly through the jigsaw of pools and found Mist around a curve beneath the buddhas. He was resting against the lip of the pool, arms outstretched, head tipped back and eyes closed. His body was as lean and beautiful as she'd imagined, although less pale. There was a hint of Felynx gold in his skin tone. She found a place to settle a few feet away so as not to disturb him. Sinking down until the water reached her chin, she released a sigh of bliss.

Mist started. His eyes came open, as green as the water.

"There you are," he said. The weariness in his face smoothed away when he looked at her. His gaze softened.

"You should have woken me up."

"Patrick knocked on the door, but you didn't stir, so I left you to rest. Feeling better?"

"Yes, lots. Physically, at least." She stretched her legs and arched her back. "You'd think I'd be absolutely sick of water by now, but this is different. It feels wonderful. You?"

"Same. Nothing is forgotten, Stevie, but Patrick was right about us needing rest and a night's sleep. I should've learned my lesson by now."

Stevie smiled. "I think he fancies you."

"Well, he's not having me on the rebound," Mist replied equably.

His tone made her laugh. "I hope he kept his hands to himself."

"He did. He was a perfect gentleman."

"Maybe . . ." she began. She swished her feet in the water, unable to finish the sentence.

"Maybe what?"

"If you had a wild night with Patrick, you might feel more diplomatic with Rufus in the morning. Joke! Not very funny. Sorry."

"A wild night playing cards is as far as he'll get with me." Mist looked into her eyes with tender amusement, making her flustered with no effort.

"Sorry, that was a really inept bit of teasing," she sighed. "I'll be honest. What's bothering me is the thought that you are actually intending to kill someone."

"I know," he said.

"And I'm sure you'd prefer not to have me at your side, trying to prize your finger off the metaphorical trigger."

"I don't know what will happen, even if we find Rufus."

"I'm worried that you might set out on your own, in some misguided attempt to protect me while you fight things out with him. Which I can understand—but I am part of this, as much as you are."

He interwove his fingers with hers. She couldn't help drifting towards him as the silky water carried her along the pool rim. "Yes, you are. More than you know."

"What don't I know?"

"That you're right: in an ideal world, it would have been me and him and no witnesses." Mist pulled gently and she slid closer to him along the smooth rock. His arm went around her shoulders. "But it's only through you that I have a chance of finding him. And if you hadn't come with me, I would have fallen apart by now."

"Me too," she said.

Their lips brushed. She hadn't expected or intended that, but it happened without either of them pausing to think. Mist's thumb gently stroked her initiation scar. He kissed her again, in earnest this time. She was so startled that she pulled back for an instant. Then she responded, tasting salty minerals on his tongue. Her self-control melted.

Their limbs entangling in the warm buoyant water was the most erotic sensation she'd ever felt. Her breathing grew fast and ragged as she felt him responding. His palms slid down her back, pressing her body firmly to his.

"Oh, god," she gasped, very softly. Mist said nothing, only gazed into her eyes, while his chest rose and fell rapidly under her hands. For a moment she thought that one of them should say, "Stop," before this went any further. Neither did and then it was too late.

Flimsy fabric was easily pushed aside as she wrapped herself around him. All rational thought deserted her. The melting, honeyed heat overwhelmed them: nothing else mattered but to express that they'd wasted too much time, should always have been together. She gasped in amazement at the most divine sequence of sensations she'd ever experienced.

The swell of their movements sent up waves that surged across the surface, bouncing off the lip of the pool to return and create a frothing tide around them. Their pleasure swept to a peak so intense that Stevie thought she might actually pass out; she wanted to laugh and cry at the same time, but couldn't even take a breath.

She collapsed onto his chest. Mist clasped her hard against him, still moving to draw out the last throbs of bliss, his open mouth pressed to her hair. They lay in the water, half-floating, panting with astonishment.

"Oh my god," she groaned. "I didn't mean to do that."

"Neither did I."

"Oh dear. Too late now. The heat and steam sort of . . . melted my common sense."

"And mine." He caressed her face. The ends of their hair drifted in the water. "Not that I haven't wanted to, from the first moment we met."

"I never guessed. I thought . . ." She stopped herself from saying, *that you were going to stay tragically in love with Helena forever.* No doubt he still was; one episode of impulsive sex did not change that. "You're so self-controlled. Aloof, even."

"Perhaps on the outside, but it's not how I feel. You know that."

I like you so much, Mist, she thought. *Damn, I like you far, far more than is safe.* She couldn't put this into words, either, so she lightly bit and kissed his neck instead.

He groaned. "Stevie, you don't know how much I've wanted to be with you. I thought I was strong enough to resist, but clearly I'm not. Anyone I'm close to, Rufus sees as fair game. People who come too near the Felynx get burned by us. Everyone I love . . ."

"Steady on. Don't start throwing the 'L' word about. We got carried away, that's all. And it was amazing . . . but if you want to pretend it never happened, that's fine."

He tipped his head back, moisture shining on his face. "Do you?"

"No," she said. "I'd be quite happy to stay wrapped around you like this indefinitely. But we have other things to worry about. Other people."

"If I had power equal to Albin's, I would know what to do, but . . . I've put you in danger."

"No," she said. "Don't ever think that."

"But it's true."

"No, it isn't! You don't have to keep repeating the past. Do you think you're my guardian? News, Mistangamesh. I'm not gentle Fela anymore, I'm not Helena, and you are not the flaming prince of Azantios!"

She gripped him tightly as she spoke. His eyes widened as steaming water sloshed around them. "So I'm wrong to want you kept safe?"

"No. All I'm saying is that we are equal partners. If I'm in danger, I put myself there. If something happens to me, *it is not your fault.* Tell me you understand what I'm saying."

His expression became firmer. "Yes, of course. Equals. There is still a thing called loyalty that means I'll give my life to protect yours."

"Likewise. I'm as Aetherial as you are. I learned so much from Rosie, from Persephone and Virginia, even from Albin. And from you. We're in this for each other."

He stroked her shoulders, hands sliding down to grip her upper arms. "Then you will understand that . . . whatever feelings we have now, and tonight, tomorrow we may have to push all that aside?"

"And be warriors? Yes. I'm ready."

"Then we'll need every scrap of Aetherial strength we possess."

"Mist, you're stronger that you know. And so am I." She breathed onto his neck. Above them, the swollen red buddhas spat steam into the air. "Look, since we can't undo what we've just done, shall we go back to our room get carried away some more?"

Daylight was creeping between the curtains when Patrick began rapping on their door. "All right, chaps, are you awake? Time to go, as soon as you're ready."

After a quick hot shower, and hurriedly dressing in their brand-new sweatshirts and jeans, they were on the road again. Stevie sat in the front beside Patrick, Mist in the backseat. The Impala was spacious, comfortable and, Stevie guessed, could not have been cheap. For breakfast, they sipped water and ate the yellow cakes she'd bought at the truck stop, which were as nastily sweet as they looked.

The landscape rolling past was desolate yet captivating, with brownish-red expanses of desert, clumps of dry scrub, cactus and dramatic Joshua trees. After the lush green of England, it was as strange as the Spiral. Stevie followed their route on the map, to ensure that Patrick's GPS was not leading them astray. In any case, there were only a few narrow roads to choose from across a vast wilderness.

They saw a right turn ahead, little more than a dirt track vanishing up into the hills. Patrick slowed down and stopped so they could read the signpost.

"Jigsaw Canyon Trail," he said. "Is this it, kiddies?"

Stevie glanced back at Mist. His eyes were glassy and he didn't return the look. Fear settled inside her. "This is the place," she said.

18

Jigsaw Canyon

The track snaked upward through forest, bringing them onto the high flank of a hill. A dramatic view opened to their left. In the far distance, reddish mountains rolled away towards a vast horizon. Much closer lay the ragged edge of a canyon, snow-dusted. The floor was too deep to be visible from their position, but they saw the tops of spectacular rock formations striped with scarlet, yellow and orange; pinnacles carved into fantastical shapes by erosion. There were columns, spires, and a great arch leaping out from the rim.

Every sight took Stevie's breath away. All was softened by a reddish haze. It was difficult to judge distance, but the far wall—with sandstone layers like rippling bands of toffee—appeared to be only a few hundred yards away.

"It's not exactly the Grand Canyon," said Patrick, "but it's pretty amazing, isn't it? Apparently the wilds have loads of these little ravines. I've never heard of this one, so I'm guessing it's not open to the public."

"What wouldn't I do to be a real tourist, free to explore," she said with a sigh.

Mist said nothing. Memories of the night before—of being seduced by the sensual heat of the thermal pool, and later twining naked on the bed, so enraptured with each other that she hadn't even noticed the lumpy mattress, only the smooth muscular warmth of Mist's body, until they'd drifted asleep in satiated exhaustion—she put firmly from her mind. No affection today. Business as usual.

Several hundred yards ahead, and at a higher elevation, a grand and solitary log house jutted from the hill. The place looked contemporary and impressive, constructed of red cedar over four levels. The front wall was all glass, fitted seamlessly to form one gigantic window from roof to foundations.

Patrick pulled the Chevy into the side of the track and stopped. Between them and the house there stretched a double fence, with spikes along the top and warnings to trespassers of death by several thousand volts. Closed-circuit

TV cameras swiveled on top of posts. Inside a tall steel-barred gate waited four men in dark suits and sunglasses. One of them was speaking into a walkie-talkie.

Stevie was certain—from every American TV drama she'd ever seen—that gun holsters would be hidden beneath the jackets.

"Holy fuck," said Patrick. "Were you expecting this? I thought we were coming to someone's house. This looks more like . . . Waco, or something."

"What's Waco?" said Mist.

"Nothing," Stevie said hurriedly.

"Well, it was a place in Texas where this religious cult—"

"Patrick!"

"Okay, I'm just saying. Or a film star's place. Anyone rich would have security around their property, right? It's perfectly normal."

"Are you sure you've brought us to the right place?" asked Mist, leaning forward between the seats.

"You gave me the address. According to Stevie's map and my GPS, this is it. Why don't we pull up to the gate and ask?"

"Once we're in, we may not be able to get out again," Mist said matter-of-factly.

"If they even let us in," said Stevie.

Patrick drummed his fingers on the steering wheel. "Let me know what you want to do, guys. Are you sure about this?"

"No," said Stevie. "I was picturing a rural lodge of some kind."

"Let me go in alone," said Mist. "Patrick, I'm not dragging you into this. You can take Stevie away and then I'll know you're both safe."

"Oh, no way are you going in without me!" she exclaimed. "Did we not have this conversation yesterday?"

Patrick spoke over her. "Look, you've got me really worried now. If it's dangerous, I'm not going to abandon you. D'you want me to call the police?"

"No!" they said in unison.

"Well, the 'Men in Black' have seen us, anyway."

Four pairs of black shades were fixed on them. The steel gate stood ajar. One of the men spoke into his radio while another was walking steadily towards the car.

Stevie saw that they were all Aetherials.

The revelation took her by surprise. She wasn't sure what changed; the world made a subtle shift, the light deepening to reveal four faint auras, hints of unhuman grace and different, barely visible shapes cloaking the men. She was seeing them through the Dusklands, the first Aetheric layer of altered reality.

"I can't turn back," said Mist. "If Rufus is in there, I must see him. Stevie, please go. I don't care if I escape, but you have to."

"Right," she said angrily, "because you're going to kill each other, end of story? Have you forgotten that I'm here to find Daniel? And that we still need to rescue our friends? Mist, if you die, I am going to kill you myself!"

Patrick laughed. She added, "I'm not joking. Every time he comes back to life, I'll kill him again. For eternity."

"You two are crazy," Patrick said, eyebrows raised. "Hey, I'm keeping an open mind. Fin has a nose for weirdness and I believe what she tells me because, well, she's Fin. But seriously, if there's going to be murder, I'm out of here. I don't want to be an accomplice! No way am I spending the rest of my life behind bars. I prefer to choose my boyfriends, thank you very much."

"There will be no murders," Stevie said firmly. "This isn't a spy film. We're just going to talk."

"Well, I hope so," said Patrick. "As long as you know I won't do anything heroic, like cut through the electric fence, kill all the guards and rescue you?"

The security man reached them and tapped on the window. Patrick pressed a button and the glass slid down. A sharp-chinned, impassive face looked in. He wore a tag naming him as Mr. Slahvin, Head of Security.

"Can I help you, sir?" The Aetherial spoke in a velvety tone, exactly as a security guard should sound. He carried off the part to perfection, but Stevie saw the shimmer of his Otherworld form: a bluish aura, with hints of black and red. She caught a familiar, faint but menacing metallic smell that made her freeze inside.

"Erm . . ." Patrick gave a cheesy grin. "We might be lost."

Mist rolled down his own window and leaned out. "We're looking for Rufus Ephenaestus and Daniel Manifold."

"And who would be looking for them, sir?" the guard asked without any overt reaction.

"Tell him it's . . . Adam Leith. And Daniel's friend, Stevie."

Mr. Slahvin grinned. His short white teeth looked to her as if they belonged to a nonhuman creature, perhaps some exotic fish or eel.

"Mist," she whispered, trying to convey that she knew his smell and his aura, that this was the same malevolent being who'd stolen the triptych and the carved disk . . . but she couldn't make her mouth work, and then it was too late. The guards all seemed to be smiling as they murmured rapidly into their walkie-talkies.

The huge steel gates began to swing open. "Drive on up, sir. They've been expecting you."

"How can they be expecting us?" Stevie said anxiously.

Mist watched the scenery slide by as Patrick's car climbed the hill: bare rock, scrubby trees, clumps of startling yellow and purple flowers. A black limousine followed, Mr. Slahvin at the wheel. To their left, a view of the

canyon and mountains unfolded into the cyan sky. The far peaks were patched
with snow. Mist felt nothing; he dared not allow himself any emotion. He let
his ancient Aetherial core rise to the surface, the same exiled, elemental self
that he'd been while the human Adam had dwelt in his body.

He must become nothing more than a cold intelligence, like Albin.

When he didn't answer, Patrick said, "The security man probably just
meant they're expecting you because he'd radioed up to the house."

"No, it can't be that simple," she said.

"Lucky you've still got your getaway driver, then," Patrick said dryly.

"You should have stayed outside the gates," said Stevie.

"No chance! Miss this? I'm too nosy."

"Mist?" Stevie touched his arm. "Did you hear me? Is it what I think?"

He stirred out of his thoughts, and replied, "If you think that they saw
Daniel's message to you, and guessed you'd come—yes, I imagine so. They
tracked down the triptych and the Felixatus base, so obviously they knew we
were together. Rufus wasn't especially smart, but he obviously has support
staff who are."

He saw anxiety in her face. For the hundredth time he regretted bringing
her, but pushed the regret away. Two things mattered. First, to destroy Rufus,
and then to get Stevie and Daniel out alive.

She said, "The shadowy thing that sniffed us out—it was Mr. Slahvin, I'm
sure. Didn't you sense it? His smell?"

The idea shook him, but as soon as she said the words, he knew she was
right. "I felt something odd, yes. He'd have to possess a very unusual talent,
to shift form so drastically and travel so swiftly, but it's not impossible. Gods.
I sense he was one of the Felynx . . . and there must be others in there."

"I wish I knew what the hell you two are talking about," said Patrick, "but
it beats sitting at a stupid computer all day."

"Will they know I was Fela?" she asked, ignoring Patrick's remark.

"Possibly . . . but I doubt it. Why?"

"Because I don't want to be labeled. I'm not her anymore! Please don't tell
them."

"I won't, but don't you want to know who drowned her? If it *was* Rufus . . .
it will be a shock, to say the least. Are you ready for that?"

"No. Of course I'm not. But he might be more shocked than me. To be
honest, I'm not even thinking about it. I'm here for Daniel, and that's it."

He gripped her hand briefly, reminding himself that she was Aetherial.
We're in this together, equals, she'd said. And he thought, *If the worst happens, if
she dies . . . I'll die defending her. Perhaps our soul-essences will stand with Rufus
before Estel the Eternal, and Estel herself can judge what becomes of us.*

———

At the house, Patrick was taken away by two Aetherials—copper-haired women in smart black skirt-suits—with promises of coffee and food. Stevie expressed concern, but Mist murmured, "We've no reason to believe they won't look after him properly. He's not involved in this. Don't worry."

There were Aetherials everywhere, to his surprise. The house was spacious with a touch of faded glamour, all cedar-paneled walls and lush brown carpeting, with a huge stairwell leading up and down, broad corridors branching off to other rooms. Everyone seemed swallowed by the space, like staff dotted around a hotel. Mist felt their eyes on him and Stevie, distant and curious. He wondered who these Aetherials were, and why they were here.

Mr. Slahvin was formal and polite, revealing no sign of the monstrous form that had previously attacked them. He showed them into a vast living room and withdrew. Mist looked around at a vaulted ceiling supported by redwood beams, light fixtures made from stag's antlers, a massive stone fireplace. The far wall was a floor-to-ceiling window giving a panoramic view of the canyon and mountains beyond.

A man stood waiting to meet them. Not Rufus.

Mist didn't recognize him. Tall and stocky, he was casual in jeans and a white shirt, his handsome, narrow face topped by spiky white-blond hair. A stainless-steel panther jumped through one earlobe. He held a fully human shape, but Mist saw the glow that betrayed his Aetherial nature. His aura was reddish with flashes of silver. The man didn't smile, but his odd eyes— one green, one blue—opened wide. He regarded the visitors with the controlled attention of a hawk on a post.

"Lord Mistangamesh?" said the blond man. "Is it really you?"

"As you can see." Mist opened his hands slightly. "Should I know you?"

The male walked forward, stopping an arm's length from them. "I'm Oliver. You don't remember me? We have all changed, of course, but I thought you would see beneath the surface. I knew you at once."

"I don't . . ."

To Mist's astonishment, Oliver gave a shallow, stylized bow. With that gesture, everything changed. They could have been standing in a chamber filled with starlight, bearing the elongated faces of lynx deities, their bodies clothed in weightless silks and jewels and pale gold fur . . . Their forms had long since mutated to echo those of humans, but the bow was all it took to ignite Mist's memory. He knew the deference of a high-ranking Felynx to one even higher: the heir to Poectilictis himself.

"Veropardus?"

"The same, my lord Ephenaestus."

He flashed back to those last moments in the chamber. *Their hands weaving a frantic web to destroy the invaders. Earthquakes shaking the ground, their web torn apart as walls tumbled and fire roared through the city. Distant screams.*

*The Felixatus was falling apart as Veropardus and Aurata fought for possession . . .
And Mist was trying to drag them to safety, yelling at them to follow him . . . then
fleeing for his own life, their figures fading to shadow in clouds of dust as the chamber collapsed and his world went black . . .*

That was the last he'd ever seen of Veropardus and Aurata. The memory
was so sharp that he could smell the stench of fire.

He remembered—later—clawing at rubble, weeping on his knees in the
dust . . . not yet understanding that the Dusklands had been torn away by
the catastrophe, that there was now only the plain Earth around him, that
the Felynx civilization was gone, erased. There was nothing left but a single
component of the Felixatus, a smooth cold lens in his palm.

"I can't believe it," Mist said softly. "We thought everyone was lost, except
Rufus and me."

"Most Felynx perished, it's true, their essences crushed or burned out of
their bodies. It was a form of mass death; a tragedy. But I came back, as you
see. My soul-essence was powerful enough to remember who I'd been, and to
hold true."

Mist stared in disbelief. Veropardus, Guardian of the Felixatus, had been
a priest-like mystic whom he'd never really known or trusted. To find him
standing here in modern dress, with a haircut that would not have disgraced
a rock singer, was beyond belief.

One thing was the same: the mismatched eyes with their sharp, dutiful,
measuring gaze.

He hid his reaction and spoke steadily. "So do we address you as Veropardus, or Oliver?"

"Oliver will do. Here we are in the modern world. Your companion?"

"I'm Stephanie Silverwood," she answered. Mist was aware of her at his
shoulder, radiating nervous warmth.

"Well, I am delighted to greet you both. Please relax. You look anxious,
and there's no need. What brings you to us?"

"I've reason to believe Rufus is here." Mist kept his expression stony, his
tone neutral. "Is he?"

"He might be."

"What's that supposed to mean? Surely you're not acting as his henchman?
I seem to recall that you hated him."

Oliver turned at an oblique angle, as if to defuse confrontation and invite
them deeper into the room. "What Felynx in their right mind didn't hate him?
He destroyed Azantios. Still . . . time passes. Aetherials evolve. Things change."

"What things have changed?"

"I have no strong feelings about Rufus anymore. His time is long over."
Oliver moved towards the window-wall and Mist followed, Stevie close beside him. The vista glowed red. The canyon's surreal geology was astounding.

"Is Rufus here or not?"

"Yes, he's here, Lord Mistangamesh."

A violent shock ran through Mist, electric waves of dread. He'd always been too slow to anger. Through his passivity, he'd let Rufus get away with murder, patricide, genocide and more. After all Rufus had done, Mist had nothing left for him but pure rage. And yet . . . he still felt afraid.

It was almost a phobia. He knew Rufus's seductive poison. Mist had tasted freedom, but he feared that the moment he saw Rufus's beautiful, ever-smiling face, the same old venom would be pumped into him and he'd fall, drugged once more into stupidity.

No. Not this time. It was time to avenge Helena, Poectilictis and Theliome, Adam, and all the others whom Rufus had tricked and destroyed: the entire Felynx race.

"Then where is he?"

"It's a big house," said Oliver. "And here's the thing: He doesn't actually know you are here. He arrived only a few days ago. He's still settling in."

"Settling in? I don't understand. I assumed this was his house. You seemed to know we were coming, and yet Rufus doesn't?"

"Not yet." Oliver gestured at a bank of luxurious leather seating. "Why don't you sit down, enjoy the view? Would you like tea, or something stronger? We've a lot of catching up to do. And you're here as our guests, so please make yourselves at home."

Mist remained on his feet. "Is Rufus a guest, too? Not a prisoner?"

"No, not at all." A glimmer of a smile touched Oliver's mouth. "Only if he misbehaves, but he won't. We're trying to make peace, to put the past behind us. Aren't you in favor of that?"

Mist glanced at Stevie. Her eyes were large, glistening with wary puzzlement. "I'm all in favor of peace," he said quietly. "I've known little enough of it, thanks to him."

"Sit down. As soon as you're ready, I'll let Rufus know you've arrived."

As Oliver turned away, Stevie said, "Wait. Did Rufus bring an artist called Daniel Manifold here?"

"No," he answered. After a pause for a slight, self-satisfied smile, he said, "I brought Daniel here myself."

"You're the mystery man from London," she said flatly. "Is Danny all right? What's happening?"

"Ah, what isn't happening?" Oliver looked at her with his head slightly tilted. His unreadable gaze and oblique manner were becoming more familiar to Mist by the second. There'd always been a calculating quality to Veropardus he'd been unable to fathom. "So many questions! He can tell you himself."

Mist saw excitement rush through Stevie, almost lifting her off the floor. "Can I see him?"

Oliver raised a patient hand. "Yes, soon. He's working. Again, please relax. There's no cause for concern. Everyone will be pleased to see you."

Mist said, "It's hard to relax with so many armed guards about the place."

"All Aetherials. They're for our protection, including yours. It's normal security."

Mist let the remark pass. Slahvin's aura had reeked of malevolence, not safety. Nothing felt normal. "So Rufus had nothing to do with Daniel coming here?"

Oliver shook his head. "On the contrary. Rufus was rather shocked to see the subject matter of Daniel's paintings. Even delighted, in his perverse way."

"And did Rufus tell you that he thinks I'm dead, *truly* dead?"

Oliver became still. His voice fell. "He's reluctant to talk, but the story came out, yes. First, that you were the unfortunate victim of a jealous husband. That he later found you in a human incarnation, stubbornly refusing to admit your true identity, before dying by violence yet again. Rufus was grief-stricken."

"Grief-stricken?" A cynical laugh broke from Mist. He remembered Juliana's words—*Rufus went to pieces. He was insane with grief*—but he'd never believed it.

Oliver's cool eyes showed little reaction. "From what I hear, he's been a walking ghost ever since. Distraught, bent on self-destruction . . . He's changed. That's why I've managed to find some compassion for him. I would never condone any of his misdeeds, of course, but the desire for revenge seems pointless now. However . . . here you are, after all!"

"What are you implying?"

"That Rufus was right. It *was* possible for you to come back. All he had to do was to stop struggling so desperately to find you—and you came straight to him. I think there's a lesson for all of us somewhere in that."

"You make it sound easy. It was not easy."

"Are you ready to see your brother now?"

Mist drew a thick breath. "What will you tell him?"

"Well, if I tell him it's you, he won't believe me. I'll simply say there's a visitor for him . . . and let him see you with his own eyes."

Oliver repeated his quick, graceful bow and left the room. Minutes passed. Stevie touched Mist's arm and said, "What are you going to do?" but he shrugged her off, isolating himself. He was so tense he could barely move. All his senses seemed to be shutting down.

Become a marble statue, like the one he had once inhabited . . . it was the only way to face this.

"Mist?" she murmured. "We'll all keep calm and it'll be fine, okay?"

He didn't answer. She moved away from him, towards the windows.

There were voices, coming closer. Mist heard the unmistakable, melodious, slightly sardonic note of his brother's voice. Oliver reappeared, and at his side was the so-familiar sight of Rufus, slim and graceful, with brown-red hair rippling to his waist.

He saw Rufus freeze, saw his face open wide with incredulity, saw his eyes turn to liquid glass . . .

"Who the hell is this?" said Rufus.

Silence. Eventually Oliver said, "It's Mistangamesh."

Rufus began to shake his head, lightly at first then harder and harder. He backed away towards the fireplace. "No. No, it's not. Who is it? Impostor!" Hand shaking, he pointed a finger at Mist. "Get him out of here. What sick joke is this?"

"Truly, it's him," Oliver said calmly.

"No. No no no. Get him out!"

Rufus was shouting. Mist felt a smile spreading over his face. He stood quietly, opening his palms. "It's me. Isn't this what you wanted?"

"No. You're out of your mind. You're dead! Who's responsible for this? What the hell—? Take him away. It's not him, it's not, it can't be . . ."

Mist was astonished by Rufus's crazed rambling. Until the moment they saw each other, he hadn't known how he would actually feel; hadn't expected vehement denial verging on hysteria from his brother; hadn't expected to feel nothing in return but a sense of cold, faintly amused despair.

Then Rufus seized a long, heavy poker from the fireplace and rushed him, his face set in a snarl. He swung the iron rod like a sword at Mist's head. Mist flung up his hands and the poker slammed into his palms, stopped in its trajectory.

His ice-cold thoughts ignited into red fire.

No longer could he hear Rufus's voice through the rushing of blood in his skull. His fists were clamped tight around the rod. He lunged, and the next moment, Rufus was pressed back against a wall and Mist was forcing the thick shaft of the poker across his throat, squeezing, crushing . . .

Rufus struggled. His hands also gripped the poker, resisting, but he could not dislodge his brother's death-lock. Rufus's angelic face turned ugly with rage: hideous, shiny-crimson and bloated. A thread of blood ran down his neck, oozing from broken skin. Voices cried out in the distance but all Mist could hear was the rasp of Rufus's mockery.

"You idiot, you can't kill me! I can't die, in thirty thousand years I've not been able to die!"

"Let's see."

Mist pressed harder. Rufus began to laugh. His eyes bulged and his face turned purple as he fought for breath—yet he was laughing. The mixture of amusement and agony horrified Mist beyond sanity. He slammed Rufus's head into the wall.

Someone was pulling ineffectually at Mist's locked arms. Oliver, and one of the guards; they might have been scrabbling at solid rock for all the effect they had.

In the far distance he heard Stevie say in a soft, cool voice, "Leave him! If he needs to kill Rufus, let him. It's meant to be."

Her words blew through Mist like waterfall vapor. At the point where he could have finished it, the point where Rufus stopped laughing and was plain terrified, turning purple-blue as his life ebbed away—his rage died.

In that moment, someone else appeared. A woman forced herself between Mist and Rufus, emanating a power the others lacked. "Stop!" she said. Not a plea, but a command.

Her hands closed on his wrists. Mist's passion was gone and it didn't take much for her to wrest the poker from him and pull him away. As he gave up the weapon, and dizzily stepped aside, her presence registered.

Shock doused him. Impossible. *Aurata?*

"Stop," she repeated, her voice soft yet firm.

Mist reeled away and collided with Stevie, collapsing into her arms. She caught him as best she could and steered him to a safe distance. Rufus tried to laugh, but the sound was hoarse now, a rasping breath. Turning, Mist saw through a blur of tears that his brother was coughing, rubbing at his bruised and bloody neck and then staring at the blood on his fingertips.

Numb, Mist knew that Rufus, for once in his endless life, had been genuinely, utterly petrified—if only for a few minutes. He thought, *And that might be all the satisfaction I'm ever going to get.*

Perhaps it was enough.

Aurata was fussing over Rufus, leading him to a seat. Her presence commanded the room; her beauty—although more human and less feline than the last time he'd seen her—was unmistakable. Her clothes were plain, outdoorsy khaki. She wore her hair in a glossy bob that tapered to points along her strong jaw, its red-flame shine undimmed. All Mist could do was stare at her while his breathing slowed and all fervor drained out of him.

Aurata. Stevie was speaking but he couldn't hear her. *Aurata!*

"Mist?" Aurata said, approaching as if she didn't know whether to strike him or hug him. "For pity's sake! What is wrong with you?"

"Rufus attacked him," Stevie pointed out. Aurata took no notice.

Mist pushed his hair off his face. "If you don't already know, it's a hellish long list. But you must remember the first and worst thing he did, Aurata. I don't know where you've been, or what you know. Our memories get messed up. But tell me you remember Azantios, at least."

She breathed in and out and spoke softly. "It was such a long time ago."

"No amount of time can make it right."

"I didn't say it was right. But it is ancient history."

Mist laughed: a hollow sound. Aurata came to him and placed her hands on his shoulders. He felt Stevie move away, a draft filling her place. Instead, slanting golden eyes unseen for eons looked into his. Aurata's voice was warm silk, soothing. "Mistangamesh. My beloved brother. This is momentous; the first time we three have met since Azantios fell. I know why you're angry, but please, beautiful Mist, let it go. Let's not fight on this amazing day."

"Aurata." He could barely speak. He bent his head to rest on her hair.

"It's all right," she murmured, embracing him.

"I had no idea you were here."

"No one told you? This is my house, dearest."

Stevie settled next to Mist on the leather seating, close but not quite touching. She felt him trembling like a spent racehorse. She'd no idea what to say, dared not imagine his turmoil. But what if he had succeeded in killing Rufus? That could only have made things worse.

Rufus sat on the far side of the room, his face flushed pink. He started up, as if to approach them, but Mist put out a hand and said, "Keep him away from me."

"Mist?" said Rufus. His voice was hoarse. "Come on, have another go. I knew you'd come back to me one day—if only to take revenge. I deserve it—but have you forgotten that you gave Adam's life to save my unworthy skin, not so long ago?" He laughed roughly. "Of course you're angry. So am I—because how *dare* you wait until I'd finally finished weeping and written you out of my life and 'moved on,' as they say, to make your reappearance? You bastard. Have you any conception of how much I hate you? Yet still I'd rather you strangled me until doomsday than ever left me again."

"It would be my pleasure," said Mist. "And you'd enjoy it; you're that perverse. You haven't changed."

"You know nothing."

Mist looked away. "'How was your rebirth, Mist?'" he said sardonically. "A nightmare, thank you. Yet all you thought about, Rufe, was that you're *so important* that someone else would go to the trouble of impersonating me in order to distress you? That says it all."

"Enough!" said Aurata. "You two will stay on opposite sides of the room until you've both calmed down." Standing in the center of the huge room, she took complete and effortless command. "We should celebrate. We three, together again after all this time—and all you can do is fight? Desist. Let's celebrate peace and new beginnings."

Stevie dared not meet Aurata's eyes, or Rufus's. She was too afraid of being recognized. The idea made her feel like a specimen in a jar. Part of her was still Fela: strong in her own habitat, but vulnerable among the Felynx, like a gazelle among lions. She realized then that she hadn't seen her *fylgia* since they'd escaped from Albin. Her silver pard was gone: she could only think that it had stayed in the Otherworld, and without it she felt bereft.

Staying quiet and calm was the only strength she had now.

Aurata paced around as she spoke. She had an earthy energy that made Stevie think of Frances Manifold in her younger days. Aurata had always been charismatic, Stevie remembered; almost too intense, serene in public but sometimes, in private, disturbingly restless. Always the one in charge of any situation.

"Mist, I know why you're angry. Rufus told me."

"His version," said Mist.

"No," Rufus leaned forward, elbows on his knees. "I told the truth. That I'm an appalling troublemaker and waste of space. I was past caring, so why would I keep anything back? Yet Aurata forgave me."

"Well, I can't," Mist said softly.

"You must, my dear," Aurata said. "I know it will take time, but fate has drawn us together for greater reasons than to squabble like teenagers. We can make a new start."

"Even after Azantios?"

"Even that. When Rufus and I found each other—none of it mattered anymore. Yes, huge mistakes were made, but the past can't be changed. All that matters is love, and I saw that it's time to walk away from the human world, and to begin the future. The fact you're here, Mist, proves it's meant to be."

"But how long have you been here?" Mist asked. He sat back, as if sinking into gradual acceptance.

"Oh, I've owned this place for years. I gathered some Aetherial friends around me, as you see. And I've traveled a lot. I've been learning about the Earth, all the better to understand the Spiral."

Rufus said, "Yes, you should see how busy she's been! She has a doctorate in nearly every science there is. And what have you and I done? Frittered away our time in pleasure."

"Speak for yourself," Mist replied. "I've tried to help humans. Your main occupation was sabotaging my efforts."

Aurata pursed her lips at him. "This isn't a competition to see who's done the most good or harm. Everything I've achieved has been aimed at the renaissance of the Felynx."

She stopped, moistening her lips, as if aware she was close to saying too much in front of Stevie. Without a word, Mist stood up and went to lean against the window, staring out at the ruby landscape beyond. Aurata went to his side. They stood there with their arms about each other's waists. Was Mist weeping? Stevie couldn't tell. A few uncomfortable moments passed in which she, Rufus and Oliver sat without saying a word.

She stiffened inside. Aurata spoke of love, and there was Mist hugging her . . . but wasn't it Oliver who'd taken Daniel, and who'd presumably then sent Slahvin, in his predatory guise, to steal the triptych and the carved disk? None of that was loving.

"Anyway." Aurata turned to face the room again. "When Rufus and I found each other, we knew it was time to come home. We had a long journey, and only arrived a few days ago. So . . . I'm trying to explain that you're safe, Mist. You're among friends."

"Aurata," he said, subdued. "This is a great shock. You're the last person I expected to find."

She gave a wide smile, full of humor. "You thought Rufus had created a villain's lair here, and you'd burst in like James Bond? No, it's simply my home. Yours too, now. So will you make peace with your brother?" When he didn't answer, she added, "Take awhile to gather your thoughts. We've all the time in the world."

No, we haven't, thought Stevie. She bit her lip; she couldn't stop thinking of Albin holding her friends in his subzero coils.

"There's every luxury here. Treat the place as your home. We'll make bedrooms ready for you. And Rufus will be patient until you're ready to see him. Won't you, Rufe?"

Rufus looked up with an expression that put Stevie in mind of Humphrey the spaniel gazing up at Frances: pure, melting adoration. "Only for you, goddess. Since you ask so sweetly, only for you."

Stevie sat forward, addressing Aurata but not meeting her gaze, in case she saw a remnant of Fela in her eyes. She asked simply, "Please may I see Daniel now?"

Aurata came to her, caressed her arms and kissed her cheek. She was so lovely; the Fela-part of Stevie resonated to her irresistible warmth. She couldn't help recalling that they'd shared a bed sometimes . . . so very long ago that the memory seemed unreal, yet was still strong enough to stir a flush of embarrassment.

"Yes, of course you can." Her reply was cheerful. "Oliver? Please take Stephanie to the studio. I'd like to see Mist alone."

"Touch the water," said Aurata. "What do you notice?"

Mist put his hand in the stream and said, "It's warm."

She'd brought him down by a steep precarious path into the bottom of the canyon. All was russet-orange, barren and beautiful, with tall wind-sculpted pinnacles. The layered walls were so steep he couldn't see the house from here.

"You know where we are."

"I don't recognize it, yet it feels familiar."

"We're where Azantios used to be. I know." She smiled at his skeptical expression. "It's changed, of course. Ice ages, floods and winds have been at work. Jigsaw Canyon is the tail end of what we used to call Fire Valley. And don't forget that the Dusklands were very strong here in those days, creating a landscape and climate that was all our own."

"The city's gone, though. What's the point in coming back?"

"Because it was our home. Because it's a boundary place. I need a site that's geologically active. It doesn't need to be as obvious as the San Andreas Fault or Yellowstone. This part of the States is full of hot springs, which means the Earth's crust is thin and full of faults. That's why the water's warm."

"Er . . . yes." Mist was thinking of the red buddhas and Stevie.

"What are you smiling at?"

"Nothing. Well, we saw some unusual thermal springs on our way, with bulbous red geysers like nothing I've ever seen."

"Oh, you stopped at that crummy motel?" Aurata laughed. "Did you know that the red buddhas are only a hundred years old? Someone tried to drill wells to tap the hot water. The result was that all this mineral-rich water exploded to the surface and gradually deposited the minerals into those extraordinary shapes. What's so amazing about the Earth is not just its great age but its *youth*. Did you know there are hills in Iceland only six months old? Volcanic activity is reshaping the world as we speak!"

"So you're a geologist."

"Seismologist and volcanologist too. The disciplines go hand in hand. I actually found Rufus in the middle of an earthquake, which seemed wonderfully appropriate."

"After Azantios," he said quietly, "I tried and tried to find you."

Aurata breathed out. "Ah, my dear, I was dead. Elemental, rather. I was trying to save the Felixatus, but I failed. Veropardus managed to salvage much of it. I came back eventually, but too late to find him or you, so I began a new existence, drifting between Earth and Otherworld, as we do. I found a special house in Venice—ask Rufus—where I worked for years to weave a web that would call any surviving Felynx to me. Mist, I called and called and it's taken you *how* many hundreds of years to hear me?"

He caught his breath, remembering nightmares of Aurata trapped in a strange decaying building, crying out for him to find her. "I had dreams . . ."

"And ignored them?" She groaned in exasperation. "What wretched use was that? Well, only two Felynx responded in any case. Eventually I found Vero—Oliver, rather—and what can I say? He's always worshipped me, bless him. He's my right-hand man and most loyal companion. Later, Slahvin appeared too. He was no more than Vero's servant in the old days, but Azantios changed him into a being of highly unusual powers."

"Slahvin's a monster, Aurata," Mist said darkly.

She shrugged. "A useful one, and loyal to me. We made the Venice house a sanctuary for the few remaining fragments of our civilization, until I found this place."

Mist had a dozen questions, but chose one on which she seemed most focused.

"What is it about boundary places?"

"Ah, continental plates, fault lines in the Earth." She tipped back her head, her eyes liquid gold. "What were we deprived of, in Azantios? Knowledge of the Spiral. Ways into the Spiral. Our birthright was kept secret."

"Only to stop us precipitating a war against Malikala of Naamon, so I understand."

"As if we were children, to need such protection! By the way, I knew long before Rufus found out."

"You did? You kept that quiet. You made a very good job of faking astonishment when he broke the news to you."

She smiled. "Well, I could manage to guard a secret. Some matters need a delicacy of touch that Rufus entirely lacks. But the point is, knowing we were sealed away from the Otherworld, and later discovering there were barriers to keep the realms apart—that's what sparked my passion. Did you realize that the boundary places on Earth are where human civilizations flourished? The huge forces between plates created wonders. Mountain ranges, obviously, but so much more. Molten rock and superheated water created caverns full of gigantic crystals. Seams of copper and precious metals. Underground rivers that could be tapped for agriculture. And I believe these fault lines can be prised apart like clam shells to create new ways into the Otherworld."

Mist laughed in surprise. "Why would you want that?"

"Why wouldn't we want greater access to our home realm? Free and open access, as we will it? Because we were denied it in the past, that's why."

"But we have it now."

"No, we don't. Your journey here wasn't easy, was it? All we have is a system that other Aetherials left us, basically a sort of Berlin Wall with rabbit holes. I want to make changes. Open borders. Isn't it about time?"

She stood with her feet apart, arms folded, gazing up at the deepening blue sky. The canyon filled up with violet shadow.

"To be honest, I don't know," said Mist. "Can you actually, physically do this? Create portals at will?"

"Absolutely. I've worked on the calculations for years, and everything's coming together for the great event. That's why my followers are with me. You asked why we're here, Mist. We intend to reassemble the Felixatus, to mend what was broken, and to create a new home by dissolving the barriers. A new civilization, the Aurym Felynx. We all want the same thing. Even

Rufus. Which is why I dearly hope you can make peace with him, and help me. Your girlfriend too. You must tell me about her another time, but she seems lovely."

Mist was trying to gauge Aurata as reasonable and trustworthy—or not. She sounded matter-of-fact, her words measured. He said, "If you've tamed Rufus, you deserve a medal."

Aurata gave a subtle smile. "That was the easy bit."

"I don't want to state the obvious, but you realize you could be messing with the structure of the Spiral in a way that many Aelyr won't be happy about?"

She snorted in contempt. "Not the bloody Spiral Court. Yes, of course. Why else d'you think I wanted Daniel's paintings hidden? The last thing I want is some hostile force guessing my plans. Do we want Vaidre Daima, or whoever is top dog these days, turning up with his merry band, laying down the law like some overinflated planning enforcement officer? No, we do not."

Mist didn't feel like laughing, but couldn't help it. Her breezy sarcasm had always made him laugh: he'd forgotten. He had to take the plunge, and trust her. "The Court just wants to keep a balance. There are other factions fanatically opposed to any contact between Vaeth and Spiral *at all*. Aurata, we have a really serious situation. On our way here, three friends who were helping us were taken prisoner by a Sibeylan called Albin. He's a separatist, an incredibly powerful one. And we have to rescue our friends, but I don't know how unless someone will help us."

Her eyes flickered with surprise, and perhaps a touch of irritation at Mist's expression of his own agenda. "Lord Albin."

"You've heard of him?"

"Of course. Everyone has. He's nothing, a flea bite."

Mist blinked at her. "I'm glad you think so. More like some mad god of winter when we encountered him. I know you have your own concerns, Aurata, but if you won't help us, who will?"

"Easy answer." She gave a broad, guileless smile. "I will help you, if you will help me."

Oliver led Stevie down a broad flight of stairs, along wide, carpeted corridors. Along the way, other Aetherials passed them, acknowledging Oliver with nods and subtle smiles. Male and female, they resembled smartly dressed humans. Stevie, however, was growing more sensitive to the auras that floated around them, spectral hints of taller shapes in black, red and gold. Felynx auras.

"Who are all these people?" she whispered.

"Friends of Aurata," said Oliver. "The scattered ones, gathered together."

"All the Felynx?"

He put a finger to his lips. "Only a select few survived the fall of Azantios. These Aetherials are more recent recruits who share our ideals. We've had to be very selective, but we're proud of our community. We're Aurata's people, the Aurym Felynx."

Ahead, a heavy paneled door stood ajar. She heard the faint sound of someone humming a song. Aromas of paint and turpentine wove around her.

Oliver left her at the door. Inside, the studio was full of natural light from the huge window. The floor was bare, with a few easels positioned at random and workbenches around the sides. The walls were covered with Daniel's artwork—with the triptych *Aurata's Promise* prominent at eye level as she entered. More paintings were stacked on the floor, sketches scattered on bench surfaces. Amid the creative chaos, she noticed a young man half hidden by the panel on which he was feverishly daubing paint. She saw familiar gawky limbs, unruly brown hair, the glint of spectacles . . .

"Daniel," Stevie cried in relief. She ran and threw her arms around him, nearly knocking him off his stool. He gasped and clung to her with desperate, wiry strength. His body felt too thin, overheated.

"Stevie, Stevie," he croaked in her ear. "You found me. I can't believe it."

"Yes, I'm here. Oh gods, you have no idea . . ."

Alone with Daniel, she stood back to look at him. Relief died. His face was too intense, the pupils overdilated, his skin pasty with exhaustion. The panel on which he was working was a mass of frantic yellow and orange daubs. At the center, a figure was taking shape, like a tarot-card empress resplendent on her throne.

They stared at each other.

"I can't believe you found me," he said, pushing his skewed glasses up the bridge of his nose. His hair had grown out and the beard was a shock. He looked like a bemused younger brother of Jesus.

"I got your message."

"I never thought you would. I was so afraid . . . Fuck, I shouldn't have drawn you into this, but . . . you're part of it. It's scary, but it's amazing. Look." He waved a hand at his work. "I call it *Aurata Enthroned*."

"Yes, I . . . You've done a lot, haven't you?"

"Yeah. Can't stop, that's the trouble. I—I shouldn't have sent the triptych to you. Huge mistake. Oliver needed it, and I didn't mean to put you in danger, because this, this is incredible."

"Well, it wasn't much fun being whacked over the head and robbed, but I survived."

"Jeez, I'm so sorry. Oliver went mad. He sent Slahvin to get it back."

"Mr. Slahvin, the security guy who is so polite?"

"Yes, that's him. I don't know how he can travel so fast, but . . ." His voice fell. "These people are not human. You get that, don't you?"

"I know, Danny. You don't need to convince me." Her skin crawled at the memory of the serpentine shadow attacking her at the museum, haunting Frances Manifold's house and later fighting with Mist in the hotel room. "Mr. Slahvin also stole the carved tablet that your mother found. Fortunately she'd given it to Mist by then, so he was the one who got attacked, not her. You do realize that Frances might have been badly hurt, even killed?"

His face dropped. "My god. I swear, I had no idea this might happen. These people are incredible, but . . . they're ruthless. I've had to accept that. Do as they say, and you'll be fine."

Astonishment at finding him left her wordless. Stevie ran through all she needed to say, trying to streamline.

"I've seen your mother. She's ill with worry."

His face hardened and he looked away. "I never meant to hurt her," he said. "But she hated my art, hated Oliver. I decided it was easier if I disappeared. I can't stop painting these images. No one but Oliver cared."

"How did he find you?"

"He saw my stuff on the Internet." Daniel waved the question away. "He says my work was too important to show the world, because I'm painting the hidden past and possible futures that must be kept secret. So he brought me here to paint just for him and Aurata."

"Right. And you didn't think to ask him any questions?"

"I asked hundreds of questions! He said I should trust him, so I did. He's . . ." Daniel blushed, which made the skin around his eyes look bruised. "He's like no one I've ever met before. Except Aurata herself. I've only met her once so far. It was . . . like being visited by the Queen. She really is a goddess."

"Was your website for her to look at, before she arrived?"

"Yeah, exactly. She was overseas, and Oliver needed her to see what I'd done. Once she'd seen it, he made me delete everything."

Stevie looked narrowly at him, wondering. "And you came here only to paint?"

Daniel turned redder. "Well . . ."

"You were always the worst at keeping secrets," she said. "Are you and Oliver an item?"

He flinched. "No! Well, yes. Sort of. Yes, we are."

Stevie was so startled—despite her suspicions—that she hardly knew how to react. She wandered around, glancing over the display of iconic paintings. Vibrant, fantastical cities, beautiful Felynx, Tashralyr racing in silver-grey blurs that made her heart falter. She recognized some works from the private website she and Rosie had found. There were figures in darkness, gathered around an unseen object that glowed; a blurred battle scene of barbarians invading Azantios; more portrayals of Aurata as a fiery seraph; a row of figures standing in profile like a group of medieval saints: part angel and part animal-god. In shock, she recognized one as Mistangamesh.

What did this mean?

"They're lining up to pay tribute to the fire goddess Aurata," said Daniel as she stood wondering. "That's how I interpret it, anyway."

She turned her thoughts back to him. Yes, Oliver was attractive—but did he actually care about Danny, or was he just using him? She couldn't really remember what he'd been like as Veropardus. To Fela, he'd been a distant palace official, aloof and priest-like. Not so noble, however, that was above having an affair with Aurata. Mist had not liked him at all.

"It makes more sense," she said at last, "that this is about love, as well as art. You know, Dan, you could have told me you were gay at college. I would have accepted it." She smiled. "It might explain why we did so much more talking than lovemaking."

"No—Stevie, it wasn't like that. I didn't *know* at college. I was confused." He grinned, for a moment looking like the Daniel of old. "You were wonderful . . . but I never really knew what I wanted, until I met Oliver. He's different—dazzling, like an archangel. You'd do anything to please him because he's so overwhelming. I loved him from the first moment. I couldn't help it. I didn't mean to . . ." He trailed off apologetically. ". . . disappoint you."

Stevie raised her eyebrows. "Oh, you didn't think I'd come here expecting to resume where we left off, did you? Don't be daft. We ended up as friends, and that was fine."

"Loving friends," he said. "There's no one I love in the world more than you. But with Oliver . . . it's different."

"Frances thought he was a drug dealer."

"Oh, she knew he was more than that. But she couldn't admit it. She was doing my head in, Stevie. I had to make a clean break. I left her a note."

"Which she read to mean that you'd killed yourself."

He dropped his head. "Actually, I nearly did."

"What?"

"Just before I left London. I had a rope in my hands and everything. But Oliver arrived in time."

"Why?" Her voice went hoarse.

"I was tired—exhausted, physically and emotionally." He pinched the skin between his eyebrows, and motioned a hand at the panels. "I've been painting another reality for years now. Sometimes I feel like my brain's on fire. I wanted it to stop. Selfish."

She looked into his bloodshot eyes and her throat tightened. Around one eye was a fading but definite purple-yellow bruise. "Oh, Dan, I'm so sorry."

"What for? I'm fine now."

"Because it started when you met me, didn't it? I feel responsible. And you're obviously *not* fine. Who gave you the black eye?"

"I tripped," he said. "Stevie, you couldn't have stopped this. The visions went on long after we'd parted. With Oliver, it was like floodgates opening. And Aurata said that my images have actually given guidance to *her* about what she needs to do! She's amazing."

Is she? Stevie thought skeptically. "Has Oliver been giving you drugs?"

"God, you sound like my mum. It's worth it. Intensifies the visions, and means I can carry on for hours without needing sleep."

"Maybe your mother had had a point, for once. You'll burn out. You look like you already have."

He blinked. The shadows in his face deepened. "Oliver can be demanding, but so what? If I'm a bit tired or crazy, it's not important. I can't say no to him."

"I think you need to tell him enough's enough."

"You don't understand." Daniel's expression turned dark. "I'm a channel, I can't close myself off. The Felynx need me. They said I'm their *naemur*, a sort of prophet. What I've had to accept since I came here is this: that it's hard, even brutal, but *I've got to do it.* I'm scared, but the end result will be worth it."

"Scared of what?"

He hesitated. "An apocalypse. All I can see is flames. It's as if the world is going to be melted down like molten gold and poured into a new mold to make something absolutely beyond our imaginations. I'm not going to survive, but it will be worth it. A wondrous sacrifice."

Stevie knew for certain then that Daniel was a long way from his right mind. Drugged, abused, burned out, delusional . . . whatever the case, his mental state made him hopelessly vulnerable. It didn't matter that his conversation made sense, or that he wanted to stay in this situation. She *had* to get him away.

"What are you planning to do?" she asked. "Stay here and work until you collapse? I thought sending me the triptych was a cry for help. And your computer message. I came to rescue you, but maybe you don't want to be rescued."

"Stevie, you're my oldest friend. I wouldn't have hurt you for anything. I had some moments of panic, that's all . . . but I'm so, so glad you're here. Honestly, I'll be all right. Everything will be fine because something wonderful is going to happen. You can stay, can't you? Everything feels right, now that you're here." He gave her the sweet, disarming grin that had first snared her heart ten years ago.

She gave a sigh that became a groan. "Danny, your mother's in hospital. She's really ill with pneumonia. It's serious. Honestly, I'm not saying this to make you feel guilty, but you have to come home."

"Don't do this to me!"

But she had to. He went pale as she told him all that had happened.

"I've spent hours with her, I've seen the pain she's in. She's desperately sorry for the arguments you had, for trying to control your life. She understands why you left, but I still think you need to come home. Now. In case she doesn't get better."

His color drained to white. He pulled at his stringy hair. "I can't. I *do* want to see her . . . I would if I could, but I can't leave. None of us can leave now we've seen Aurata's plan."

Stevie was sitting in the middle of a king-size bed when Mist found her.

A friendly but formal Aetherial woman, with hair as red as Aurata's, had shown Stevie to an enormous bedroom where she'd found new clothes laid on the quilt, a selection of luxurious toiletries, and everything else she could possibly need. Except freedom.

On the way she'd bumped into Patrick, who seemed cheerfully oblivious and slightly drunk. "Hey," he said, "I could get used to this place, couldn't you? It's unbelievable."

"They're treating you okay, then?" she asked warily.

"Yes, fantastic. I've been playing pool, and drinking beer in front of the biggest TV I've ever seen. As for the security guys . . . wow. Who owns this place? How come all their employees are so damn good-looking?"

Stevie smiled, couldn't help it. "Sounds like you've forgotten all about your temperamental boyfriend."

"Who?" Patrick said, grinning.

"To answer your question, the owner is Mist's long-lost sister, Aurata. I don't know how long we'll be here. Mist has family business to sort . . . it's complicated. Not long."

"No problem, Stevie. My partner needn't expect me back at work until he's ready to apologize. Let him stew. I'm yours, for as long as you need me. Did you find your friend, by the way?"

"Yes, Danny's here. He's . . . okay."

"Wow, that's a relief. What's the story with him? Sorry, no need to tell me your private business. I'll be in the games room if you need me. Or the hot tub. Or . . . who knows?"

Internally assaulted by images of Sam, Rosie and Lucas, she'd waved Patrick on his way. In her quarters, she showered in a bathroom nearly as big as the bedroom itself, pulled on a soft white robe, and now sat combing her damp hair as the sun set. The view was magnificent, the sky a lake of turquoise, amber and blood-orange, gemmed by a single planet. Venus, she guessed.

Night fell swiftly in the desert. Soon there was not one point of light but millions. The sunset faded to charcoal as Mist walked in.

He stood in the gloom, his head slightly tilted, raven hair brushing his shoulders. He was a serene figure, his long, lean body flattering the cheap jeans and T-shirt into designer garments. His eyes gleamed in the dark.

"Are you just going to stand there?" she asked.

"You look like a mermaid on a rock," said Mist, sitting on the side of the bed. "So lovely."

Stevie moistened her lips. Her breathing quickened with thoughts of the previous night. Even sitting apart, she caught his warmth and the clean scent of his body, as delicious as fresh cotton or warm silk . . . his scent overlaid with heated memories of being held, loved, taken over the edge of bliss.

She grinned. "Thanks. I've been told I scrub up okay. You don't look bad yourself."

Smiling, he placed a hand on her raised knee. "They haven't given me a separate room."

"Funny how that keeps happening, isn't it?"

"I didn't want to make assumptions."

"God, you're so polite, Mist. Not that I'm complaining. Please stay. If I'm in danger, sharing a bed won't make it worse; I think everyone's noticed we're, um . . . whatever we are." She, too, was making no assumptions.

"So how did things go?" he asked gently. "Did you see Daniel?"

"Yes." Briefly, she recapped their meeting. "I was right to be worried about him. He's in a terrible state, manic, exhausted, and scared out of his wits. This Oliver's got him right under his thumb. Brainwashed, and I suspect even abused. He's got a black eye. He said Aurata's people are ruthless. When I told him that Frances is sick, he nearly fell apart and admitted he wants to leave, but can't. No one's allowed to leave, he says, because we've seen Aurata's secrets. Is that true?"

"Possibly," Mist said. "I don't know yet. I'm so sorry. You're right, this is no place for humans. Nor for you."

"Don't say that! We need to get Dan out of here, but we had no hope of freeing him unless we walked into the prison ourselves. I came in here with my eyes open."

He lowered his eyes, lashes falling in long black curves against his cheeks. His grip tightened on her knee. "It's more than that. I wondered if you'd even speak to me after my encounter with Rufus. The last thing I wanted was for you to see me lose control. I've waited so long for this confrontation with

Rufus—and now that it's over, what do I do? I can't kill him—which leaves me where? Nowhere. Stalemate, again."

"No, that's not true. *Something* changed. I saw it."

When he looked up, his eyes shone leaf-green in the gloom. "Did I really hear you telling the others to go ahead and let me kill him if I wanted to?"

"Yes, you did," she said lightly.

"Why?"

"Because I knew you'd do the right thing. And you did. You got him on the ropes, and then you stopped. What you did was exactly right, Mist."

"Such faith in me."

"Have some in yourself. I know why your father wanted you as Sovereign Elect; you always try to do the right thing, no matter what it costs you. That's real strength, not throwing your weight around. I think you're the kindest, most tender person I've ever met."

His hand slid along her inner thigh, pausing half-way. She was naked beneath her robe. He stroked her skin with his thumb, teasing, until she had to stifle a moan.

"No, the kindest person would be you, Stevie."

"How was your audience with Aurata?" Her voice was unsteady.

"Surreal."

"Enlighten me. This place is like a cult, isn't it? Aurata's the queen bee and everyone's here to worship her. She soothes people into thinking all is wonderful."

He gave a wistful smile. "She's always had that effect. You can't help loving her. Veropardus was always in thrall to her, Rufus too, and that hasn't changed. I can't believe she's here. Her presence changes everything. Aurata's the key to this."

Stevie tried to ignore a twinge of jealousy. "In a good or bad way? Fela was in thrall to her as well, but the truth is, I could never make her out. I told you, she had bad dreams sometimes, but everyone does. I wish I had such complete self-belief."

"Ah, she's everything Rufus and I could have been. She's studied science, and brought these Aetherials together: actually done something with her existence. She even claims that Rufus is a reformed character! If anyone *could* reform him, it's her."

Stevie reached out to stroke Mist's side, feeling his ribs through his shirt. "But don't forget that she had Daniel brought here, apparently seduced and brainwashed by Oliver. And that they sent Mr. Slahvin to steal the triptych and the Felixatus base from us."

His hand stopped moving. "It's true, Slahvin is a nasty piece of work and I'm not even sure he's a true Felynx." Mist paused, but didn't elaborate. "Perhaps her staff are overzealous, but she has a good heart."

"Are you sure? My instinct's screaming to free Danny and get back to Melusiel as fast as possible."

"I understand, but there's no use in rushing back into danger without help. There's a bigger picture, and we're all part of it, including Albin. So are Rosie and Sam and Lucas. I'm trying to find a pattern, but I can't see it yet. I don't pretend to know what's right or wrong here. However, Aurata has said she will help us against Albin."

"Would she?" For the first time since they had arrived here, she felt a twinge of hope.

"If we help her."

"There had to be a catch."

Mist's hand slid to her hip. She caught her breath, hoping he intended to do more than talk all night. He went on, "Aurata wants to create some portals into Naamon, our home realm. Without planning permission, so to speak."

"That doesn't sound too terrible . . . does it?"

He undid the cord of her robe so that it fell open, and began to graze gently upward with hands and lips. Stevie caught a handful of his T-shirt and tried to drag it over his head. "If you're going to do that," she said, "take your flaming clothes off!"

He obliged, his hair drifting in a static cloud around his shoulders as he pulled the shirt over his head. Happier now, she ran her hands over his chest. "I'm not sure I can actually get these jeans off," he said ruefully.

"Ah, I see the problem. Let me help you." She smiled, working at the zipper. "I'll be gentle."

And then she didn't care if he was fretting about Aurata or Rufus, or even thinking of long-lost Helena, because he was with *her*.

Perhaps it was wrong and perverse to be doing this while Daniel suffered, while Rosie and the others were stranded in severe danger, Stevie thought . . . yet what else could you do, in the heart of darkness, but feast upon each other as if it was your last night on Earth?

Eventually they lay at peace under the covers, entwined. The curtains were open, starlight silvering the bed.

With a start she realized there was someone else in the room. A shape was slipping towards them, as soft as an assassin. "Mist?"

He noticed at the same moment and they both jerked upright. Stevie hit the bedside light and saw that the approaching figure was Rufus, his long hair wild and his eyes maniacal.

"You've got to help me," he whispered. "Aurata's gone mad."

19

The Book of Azantios

Rufus walked towards them and clambered onto Mist's side of the bed, kneeling on the edge. The two Aetherials stared at each other. "Mad, how?" said Mist. "You expect me to believe anything you say?"

Rufus leaned forward and kissed his brother on the mouth. Mist flinched. Stevie thought for one alarming moment that Rufus was hoping to initiate a threesome. From what she'd heard, nothing was beyond him.

"I don't care if you believe me." Rufus was breathing fast, his eyes glistening. His throat was one huge bruise and his voice still raspy. "I am so glad to see you, Mistangamesh, that you can curse me, strangle me, kick me round the room, anything you like. I'm so happy you're alive that I could cry with joy for a thousand years. I don't even care that you hate me."

"I don't hate you. I have no feelings for you at all."

"You don't mean that."

"Oh, I do." Mist put a firm hand on Rufus's chest to keep him at bay. "Touch Stevie in any way and you will be sorry."

"That's not why I'm here." Rufus turned his gaze to her, smiling. "Not that you don't look supremely touchable, my dear, but I would like my brother to understand that I've learned a very hard lesson."

"And it only took four hundred years," Mist said tartly. "We've been here hardly a day and you're trying to turn me against Aurata? She's not a possession I'm trying to steal from you. There's no need to be jealous."

"Great gods, why did I ever want you back? I'd forgotten what a self-righteous arse you can be. Adam was much nicer." Rufus winked at Stevie. "Did Mist ever tell you that, in his Adam incarnation, he wanted to be a priest? Hilarious. A few sessions with my lustful Aetherial friends soon knocked that out of him. And his agonies of guilt were glorious to behold."

Mist pushed Rufus hard enough to dislodge him from the bed. "Your last warning. Leave Stevie alone."

"Can't you two have a conversation without arguing?" Stevie put in.

"Rufus, I'm not gullible; I don't care what orgies you got Mist or Adam into years ago. Aurata's mad, in what sense?"

Rufus's mocking grin vanished, like a mask falling. "I should speak to my brother alone."

"Fine, I'll leave you to it." She began to get up, keeping the bedcovers over her as she reached for a robe.

Mist pulled her back. "No, stay here, try to sleep." He kissed her forehead. "I'll take Rufus elsewhere."

"As long as you promise not to murder each other," she said. "And I'm serious."

They stood outside on a small balcony that jutted from the huge bedroom. Jigsaw Canyon lay in silver and shadow beneath the frozen snowstorm of the Milky Way. Mist gripped the rail with both hands, barely looking at Rufus. He felt empty. How to treat a brother that you'd tried to kill, only to spare him? A brother who'd responded with a bizarre mix of drama and denial? He had no single emotion that made sense. It was safer to feel nothing at all.

"What's this about?"

Rufus answered very softly, "I love Aurata. I worship her, always have. I know you think I value nothing, but it's not true. I wanted to help her, to support her in every possible way, and I've openly cheered her on and kept my doubts to myself, until now—but I can't any longer."

Mist thought of Aurata in the canyon, enthusing about fault lines and portals. "Doubts? That's not like you."

"What Aurata's planning will rip the Earth apart. Literally, physically tear it to pieces. Perhaps the Spiral, too—it's bound to, in fact, because the two are entwined. We have to stop her."

Mist absorbed this with a mix of skepticism and unease. "Why stop her? I thought destroying the Earth would please you."

"You don't believe me! I knew you wouldn't."

"I'm trying to figure out why the hell you'd say such a thing. Is this some twisted game you're playing? Could it be a misunderstanding between you and her? Or are you actually telling the truth?"

"I know my reputation for honesty isn't great, but this is not a game."

"But you said she saved you."

"She did."

"You were fawning on her, virtually licking her feet when we first arrived. Now you're going behind her back, telling me she's planning to destroy the world?"

"Yes! To save her from herself, because I am at least *trying* to behave half-decently. You've seen Daniel's paintings?"

"Some of them."

"And why do you think Aurata and Veropardus hid them? Because the images reveal what she's planning! She means to rip down all the barriers between this world and the Otherworld. To do that, she intends to crack open every fault line in the Earth's surface and set free rivers of lava. Tell me that won't cause any harm, when a shift of a mere few inches can cause an earthquake big enough to bring down cities."

Rufus's eyes shone so bright that Mist began to suspect his concern was real. He couldn't believe Aurata had the power to cause such a catastrophe. However, it might make sense that her supporters *believed* she could.

"Why would she want to do that?"

"To create the free access between realms that was denied to us in the past. Mist, I adore her, but she's gone crazy. And it's the worst kind of craziness where the person acts sane because they think their ideas are perfectly reasonable. I don't think she *means* to destroy the world, but that would be the result. Yet she can't see it. Or she *can* see it, and doesn't care."

Mist looked at the stars, wishing this would all go away, that there was only him and Stevie. "I thought that destroying Vaeth would delight you."

"Then you don't know me at all! I like the Earth as it is! Yes, I love trouble, I've never denied it. I like tormenting humans, playing with their hearts and minds, upsetting their small lives. I don't want to lose that."

Mist scowled at him. "So you haven't really changed at all. You're still addicted to cruelty. You're worried this might stop your fun."

"The fun stopped long ago, believe me," his brother muttered.

"Vaeth is not a playground designed for your pleasure, Rufus."

"Oh, is that a fact? You're right, of course, you pompous bastard, you're always bloody right—but leaving my selfish urges aside, do you want to see the Earth and the Spiral splitting at the seams, blown apart by a network of gigantic supervolcanoes and boiling away into space?"

"Let me think," Mist said icily. "No. But how can I believe what you're saying?"

"Aurata's possessed. This all goes back to the lies we were told by our elders—when they kept the Spiral secret. It made me angry enough to destroy Azantios. It left Aurata fixated on finding portals. Better still, creating them. Or—how about blasting apart every last barrier between the worlds until Vaeth and the Spiral are one big primal ball of fire? That's not *my* idea of the good old days."

"This can't be true." Uncomfortably, Mist recalled her promise, *I'll help you against Albin—if you'll help me.*

"It goes deeper than you think. She was planning to do something like this with Veropardus in the old days. *That's* why she was so keen to help weave the web that brought down Azantios—they hoped they could unleash the soul-energies from the Felixatus and blast a way into Naamon, but the process failed."

Mist thought of *Aurata's Promise*. The crystal sphere held aloft, and the yellow fissure in the earth—that was her message. *I have tried this before and next time, I will succeed.*

Rufus went on, "Do you know why Aurata's studied geology, seismology, volcanoes and all that stuff? She wants to get it right. She's obsessed. The mere mention of an earthquake practically gives her an orgasm. All those tectonic plates sliding into each other, molten rock bubbling out of the Earth's core, geysers squirting steam . . . ? We're Felynx, Mistangamesh. The fire of Naamon runs in our veins. Aurata is planning to take it to the absolute limit."

Mist leaned back on the rail, looking at Rufus. "How?"

"Come on, she's powerful. These folk around her—they're adepts who can form eightfold, tenfold webs to distort reality."

Mist remembered the horrifying ritual; ten Aetherials, spinning a pattern of energy so powerful that it shook Azantios to rubble. Much of that power had been composed of *his own parents' soul-energies*. He shuddered.

Rufus went on, "I've had a go myself; it's not that hard, and Aurata's a hundred times more dedicated than I ever was. She even claims the ability to weave webs without help."

This woke another echo of Lord Albin in his solitary tower. Mist hadn't told Rufus about Sam, Rosie and Lucas's plight. Rufus would only use the knowledge as a fresh weapon against him. "If this is a game, stop now."

"It isn't. I've changed," Rufus's tone was fervent. "I've seen you horribly killed in front of me—twice, at least. D'you think I could watch that and not be devastated? I confess, I've behaved diabolically in my time. Now I want to do one good thing. I love Aurata, but she needs to be stopped. I love you too. As for the loss of your Helena, and Adam, and our parents—what can I say?"

"Don't say anything!" Mist backed into the corner of the balcony, although this gained him only three feet of distance from his brother. "Don't speak their names. They were nothing to you but collateral damage."

"Not true. I'm . . ." Rufus stopped, visibly struggling. "I'm sorry."

Mist could not speak for a while.

"Gods," he said at last. "I never thought I'd hear those words from your mouth. Still . . ." He felt moisture gathering in his eyes. "All those deaths were my fault as much as yours. More."

"What? The only thing I *didn't* do was to harm Fela. You were the good guy. Why blame yourself?"

"Because I should have taken better care of them."

"Oh, I get it." Rufus slapped his own forehead. "You feel responsible *because* of your noble nature."

"Not noble. As guilty as you."

"Idiot! Don't start being a martyr. You see, this is what's wrong with you! So scared of putting a foot wrong, letting Poectilictis down, of being anything short of perfect. I had to dislodge that broomstick from your backside, don't you see? That's why I couldn't stop baiting you. I wanted you to fall off your pedestal—the harder the better. I wanted you to stop trying to be so fucking *perfect*."

"You should be happy, then," Mist retorted. "No wonder you were laughing while I was trying to squeeze the soul-essence out of you. I was hell bent on killing you, but I couldn't. I expect you're thrilled to find me with Stevie, even though I tried my damnedest not to put her in danger by caring about her."

"Brother dear, you don't have to *care* about her to give her the seeing-to of a lifetime. Which I trust you did, judging by the look of soporific bliss on her face. She's lovely. Where did you find her?"

Mist ignored the question. "I'm not like you. I don't have to seduce everyone I meet, just to prove I can. And I do care about her, which is why I should have been stronger. Rufe, do you think if I was a tenth of the Aetherial I should be, I would have to try so damned hard?"

"You know all this crap is your problem, not mine?" Rufus sniffed, and leaned on the balcony rail with loosely crossed arms. "So, why did you come and find me, really?"

"You know what they say. Keep your friends close and your enemies closer."

"Are we enemies, Mistangamesh?"

"I honestly don't know what we are."

"Yes, I'm evil, and the rest—tell me something I don't know."

"Not evil. You're like a stupid, impulsive child who can't see the consequences of his actions even five seconds into the future."

"You're calling me stupid?"

"I'm not sure there's a scale on which your stupidity is measurable, Rufus. You destroy everything you touch. Even Stevie—you couldn't bear seeing us together for five minutes without trying to drive a small wedge between us, could you?"

"Yeah, that—it was habit, that's all."

"Exactly. Habit, to get Helena and me slaughtered. Habit, to torture poor Adam for decades because you think your own ends justify any means, however depraved."

"You talk about torture? You've no idea how I felt when I thought you were gone for good! Okay, I'm depraved and dumb beyond measure. Yet, guess what? I have feelings. I can still love my own brother and sister beyond all that's rational, can't I?"

"Ah no, you can't use the thin old excuse of love for any of this."

"You despise me. You're furious with me. Fine . . . yet you're *here*. Why?"

"Because I was frightened of you," Mist said simply.

Rufus gasped. "Frightened?"

"I can't forget what Adam went through. And I can't live for hundreds more years, constantly looking over my shoulder, waiting to hear your laughter in the shadows or feel your breath on my neck. I knew you'd find me eventually. So I decided to find you first."

"And kill me. Or not."

Mist looked away. "Well, it was close. As soon as I knew I *could*, the fire went out of me. You laughed. Our reunion went exactly as I could have predicted, yet I walked into it regardless. Which makes me a step down from you on the stupid scale, doesn't it?"

"Look at me," Rufus said. "You are an idiot, Mist, if only for not seeing how drastically you've changed. You've grown. It's the way you carry yourself, as a proud Aetherial again. You have a shine around you that I thought I'd never see. You were so close to extinguishing my wretched life, but you chose to stop. Now I'm the one who's scared of you. Always was, if you want the truth."

Guarded, Mist met his gaze. "Nice words, if it wasn't too late for me to swallow anything you say. Still, let's try to be adult about this, shall we? Now that I've found you, I'm not afraid of you anymore. So, do you really still want me around? Do you want us to be orbiting each other for eternity like two sad, aging planets?"

"Mm. Put like that, it doesn't sound so attractive. But, Mist, it needn't be like that."

"How else could it be?"

"The three of us. If only we can calm Aurata down, we could be a triumvirate to conquer the world."

Mist groaned. "What's the use of conquering the bloody world? You wouldn't know what to do with it once you had it, Caligula."

"Don't knock Caligula. He was a friend of mine."

"Naturally."

"But the three of us: we could be *something* again . . ."

"Wishful thinking. You're not serious. Let it go."

"Fine." Rufus gave a quick, fierce grimace. "At least believe I'm serious about this one thing: the small problem of preventing Aurata from melting the world. What are we going to do?"

Stevie couldn't sleep. She got up, slipped into jeans and sweatshirt, and began to pad through the carpeted passageways beyond her room. There were several doors, all closed. She sensed the house breathing. Not all the Aetherials were asleep . . . murmurs of ecstasy could be heard from behind more than one door. She sensed watchfulness in the air, a rustle of movement and voices barely above the threshold of hearing.

Stars glowed through the skylight above the large central stairwell. She went down one flight to the main living areas, then down a second to the lower floor where she'd met Daniel.

She wanted to see if he was working all night.

The only light in the studio came from the night sky, and from a small door in the far right-hand corner. She heard the whine of a metal drill. Daniel's icons shone with enigmatic scenes from Felynx history, starlight sliding across them as she walked to the half-open door.

The room beyond was a small workshop, with a long bench lit by a single bright desk light. A figure with his back to her was bending over the workbench, which was set up with lathes like a modern, heavy-duty version of her clockmaker's station at the museum.

The figure was Oliver. Light glowed through the tips of his hair, glinting on his panther earring.

"Come in, Miss Silverwood," Oliver said without turning around.

"I was looking for Daniel."

"Contrary to your belief, I do allow him to rest. He's asleep."

"I'll go, then. I didn't mean to interrupt . . ."

"No, come here." He beckoned. "I heard you have an interest in metalwork. No doubt you're familiar with Felynx imagery?"

Not knowing how to answer, she went to Oliver's side. The tang of machine oil and solder were familiar, and made her feel oddly at home. A pang of sadness caught her. And then, to her shock and outrage, she recognized a half-dozen small carving tools as the ones stolen by Slahvin, the night he took the triptych.

"Those are—" She turned hot with the effort of swallowing her anger.

"Yes?"

"I suppose all tools look alike," she said evenly. "You'd think whoever stole mine could have afforded their own."

Oliver gave a minimal smirk in response. Apparently, he couldn't care less. This made her feel even angrier, and more helpless.

On a clear area of the bench, shapes of stone and crystal gleamed. She saw a lens the size of her palm, a spherical crystal shell in two halves intricately carved and fretted with animal forms: lynx and phoenix and salamander shapes. There was a scattering of cogs and metal pieces, bent, broken and corroded.

And another object she knew: Frances Manifold's "unidentified carved stone object," the base of the Felixatus, which had been stolen from Mist.

Fear slithered down her back.

The most intriguing item of all was a simple sphere, the diameter of her two hands cupped together. The material looked like clear quartz but the interior was alive, glowing as if with millions of fireflies.

With a thrill, Stevie recognized everything. This was the Felixatus, disassembled, and the sphere was its heart. It was a vessel, or a prison, filled with countless Felynx soul-sparks.

Were they still alive, after all this time? Sentient? Or mere specks of light?

She also noted a book that looked a thousand years old, hand-lettered in an unknown tongue on rough ivory pages. Open near the middle, the left-hand page was illustrated with a medieval-style representation of the heavens, with moon, planets and stars picked out in gold leaf and lapis. On the right was an ink sketch of the items on the bench, fully assembled; the shell mounted on the base with the crystal globe inside, the lens suspended above it, all held together by a web of curved struts, like an armillary sphere or an orrery.

Stevie couldn't speak.

"The Felixatus," said Oliver over her shoulder. "A sacred object, lost for thousands of years. Now that we have the last piece, we can reconstruct it."

The last piece. He meant the stolen base.

A memory ambushed her: Fela in the chamber, so in awe of this exquisite object that she forgot even Rufus's presence. The details were blurred. She remembered a glow like jeweled cobwebs at dawn, encasing the wild white energy of the heart. A sense of ineffable mystery. No explanation. The Felixatus had simply sat on its column, pointing up at the stars: swollen with pent-up energy.

"Where did the book come from?" she asked.

"It was salvaged from a ruined monastery in the north of England."

"Who wrote it?"

"I did." Oliver stood uncomfortably close to her. "I always retained the instinct to protect sacred knowledge. During the fall of Azantios, I was fortunate to keep hold of the most important parts of the Felixatus; the heart, and the outer casing. It came to pass that I went into elemental form for centuries. Yet when I returned to bodily form and sentience, I remembered who I'd once been. I remembered having the forethought to hide these treasures. I was in a strange world where there was nothing for me to do but enter a monastery and set about writing all I could remember of Azantios and the Felixatus."

"And this was . . . when? The twelfth or thirteenth century? You kept the book with you all this time?"

"Not quite." Oliver's lips thinned. His odd-colored eyes shone. "I was discovered. This very occult and non-Biblical text was frowned upon by the Church authorities. I was arrested, tortured, and burned at the stake for heresy."

"My god. Are you joking?"

She recalled the horrifying sketch Mist had found in Daniel's abandoned studio: a monk twisting in flames, burning, melting in agony. Had Daniel intended to paint the scene?

"Fortunately, I'd hidden the book most carefully before they came for me. And when I returned to a further life—as Aetherials do, when we have unfinished business—I was able to retrieve it from the monastery's ruins and place it in Aurata's safe place in Venice while I sought the lost pieces of the Felixatus."

Stevie was shocked into horrified sympathy. *No wonder he's deranged*, she thought. *And I thought I'd had a difficult time!*

"So you, er . . . heard Aurata's call?"

His face took on a narrow, knowing expression. "Loud and clear. I served her father in the glory days, but I confess a deeper devotion to my lady Aurata. I always saw that *she* was our future. Of course I went to her. Our reunion was inevitable: fate, if you believe in such things. I admit, I was shocked that her own brothers were deaf to her summons. Do we even need them?" He sighed through his nose. "If it's her wish to have them here, so be it."

Stevie didn't respond. It didn't take a psychologist to work out that Oliver would prefer to have Aurata entirely to himself. And would he like to reverse their roles? Did he see himself as the rightful leader, with Aurata as *his* aide? Stevie couldn't see it working the other way around, because Aurata was the natural goddess, and he the instinctive priest. Still . . . the smallest trace of resentment might give Oliver a reason to take his frustrations out on Daniel instead.

Resisting a strong desire to punch him, she said coolly, "So you're trying to reassemble the Felixatus?"

"It's a process that can't be rushed. It must be perfect. I'm afraid the diagrams I made from memory aren't as accurate as they could have been. If I'd made the instrument myself, it would be easier. But it was made by one of the Felynx founders, an Aetherial craftsman long gone. I was a mere custodian."

"He didn't leave a blueprint, then?"

"Sadly not." Oliver gave a slight smile, which helped her see why Daniel had become enraptured by him. "Daniel's images are more artistic than accurate."

"It's a beautiful object. So strange." Quickly she checked herself, thinking, *I'm not meant to know what it is, certainly not meant to have seen it.*

Oliver gave her a deep look; she turned away. Someone was going to see Fela in her, sooner or later, and she didn't trust Oliver one millimeter.

"The Felixatus connected Azantios to the stars. Some say it gave a view of a different sky altogether, the one that graces the Spiral itself."

"And did it? You were its keeper, so I've been told. You should know."

He sidestepped the question. "It is our Grail, in the purest sense. A stone, a dish, a ciborium: a cup filled not with blood but with pulsating Aetheric energy. The symbol of our heart's desire; to become our true selves, the Aurym Felynx."

Oliver fell quiet, fiddling with the lathe. She guessed he would like her to leave, which gave her a perverse urge to stay, if only to show him how to operate the equipment properly.

"Can you remember being Veropardus?"

The question was impertinent, but she took the risk. The unnatural atmosphere of the Dusklands pressed on her. Certainty crept over her that she had no chance of leaving Aurata's house alive. The feeling made her defiant. The more frightened she was, the stronger she would become.

That was what Persephone had taught Fela.

"Not every detail," he answered. "It's dreamlike, in some ways. I remember the important things. Aurata and I are the only ones who held true, all this time, to the essential nature of the Felynx. You? I'd be interested to know how you are so well informed. You are a woman of mystery, Miss Silverwood. Fascinating, the hold you have had on Daniel and Mistangamesh both."

"It's not a hold. We're close friends, that's all. What about Mr. Slahvin?" she asked, eager to change the subject. "Did he find Aurata at the same time?"

Oliver went tight-lipped. Stevie held her breath, aware she was asking too many questions. Perhaps she'd gone too far.

Then he said, "Shortly after me. He was bound to appear. In Azantios, Slahvin was my close assistant. A man of few words but complete obedience."

Stevie frowned. Her Fela-memories did not contain Slahvin . . . except as one of many palace officials, a dark silent figure in the background. She said, "Are you friends with him?"

Oliver looked sideways at her with cold expression. "What odd questions you ask. He's useful, that's all. Why?"

"Because he's dangerous. I did not appreciate being knocked unconscious. How does he do that 'slithering all over the world' trick?"

Oliver shrugged. "All Aetherials have unique talents. He is able to send out his Otherworld form as a kind of astral projection, I believe. Why don't you ask him yourself?"

Her insides tightened. She glanced around and saw Slahvin standing in the doorway.

Over his human shape hung his sinister translucent form; eel-like, black and darkest red, sheened with scales that leaked fire. She caught the dreary, metallic stink of ash . . . felt herself shrink from the memory of his attack in the museum, his circling presence in Frances's house, and Mist's desperate fight with him in the hotel . . .

There was an ambiguous quality to Aurata, Oliver, even Rufus. Any of them might contain a hidden, decent side. Slahvin, though, seemed to be nothing but pure malevolence. So, he'd once served Veropardus, Keeper of the Felixatus, and here he still was. That showed loyalty, but to what? She could hardly bear to stay in his presence.

Was this a trap? Slahvin and Oliver could easily hold her like pincers to interrogate the truth out of her. Unimportant people who knew too much were disposable. Like Fela, like Daniel.

"Everything okay, boss?" Slahvin asked smoothly.

"Excellent," said Oliver. "Miss Silverwood is interested in the workings of the Felixatus, although I'm sure it's as dull as watching someone trying to put an old clock back together. Oh—and she would like to ask you a question."

"Oh, would she?" Slahvin gave her an impassive yet knowing look. Spiders of ice ran over her skin.

"No," she said, with a huge struggle to keep terror out of her voice. "No, not at all, it's nothing. I mustn't take up any more of your time. Excuse me, I should go back to bed."

As if negotiating rattlesnakes, she backed away from Oliver, squeezed past Slahvin and fled. To her complete amazement, they let her go. Behind her, she heard what sounded like faint, mocking laughter.

She was first back to the bedroom and, although she tried to stay awake, fell asleep until long past sunrise. She awoke to find herself alone, but Mist's warmth was on the sheets, and she could hear the shower running.

"Well?" she said, peeling herself off the bed as he reappeared, toweling his hair. Naked, he was like a sculpture, so beautiful that she couldn't keep herself from staring and smiling. "How did things go with your brother?"

"We may have a problem." He sat on the end of the bed. His eyes were softly grey and distant.

"Only one?"

"Yesterday, Aurata offered to help us against Albin, on condition that we help her. I used to think she was the most down-to-earth of us. Passionate and forceful, but sensible."

"If you say so. I was in awe of her, but you know her better than I do."

"Do I, though? According to Rufus, her scheme to create new portals is going to rip the Earth apart."

He recounted his talk with Rufus while she sat hugging her knees, wondering.

"Mist, I don't know what to say. So either we help and risk her destroying the world, or we *don't* help and leave our friends to Albin's mercy? This is . . . god, this is a nightmare."

"I have to talk to her."

"How? Won't it make things more difficult, if she knows Rufus has betrayed her? I know you don't want to think ill of her, but, Mist, there's something really bad here. As I keep pointing out, Oliver effectively abducted Daniel, and sent Slahvin to rob us. Aurata approved all that. This is more than her supporters being overzealous. They're not our friends. They won't *let* us interfere with Aurata's plan. There's a big clue in the fact that her offer to join forces against Albin was conditional. If she cared, she'd have said, 'Yes, of course we'll help you, right now.' No strings attached. Like Rosie, Sam and Luc did. And they didn't even know us. She's your sister."

Mist let go of a heavy breath. "I know. I'm trying to understand her."

"They're not going to let us go."

His gaze came back into focus on her, grave. "How are you so sure?"

She told him about her encounter with Oliver. He gripped her hand.

"Stevie, you shouldn't have risked talking to him. I'm not blind, I know there's danger here. I'll speak to Aurata. In the hierarchy of people she will listen to, surely she wouldn't set a subordinate like Oliver above me?"

"You'd better be right." She let out a soft groan. "I hate to bring this up again, but in my Fela days, she . . . Aurata was a restless sleeper, muttering about being trapped and breaking through barriers. So, perhaps not as cool as she appeared on the surface."

"But she didn't tell you the reason?"

Stevie shook her head. "It wasn't my place to ask. But it all adds weight to the idea that she was making dangerous plans, plotting with Veropardus, even while your parents were still in power. I'm embarrassed talking about this, because of . . . the, er, fact that she and Fela . . . But that was Fela, not me."

"You thought I'd be jealous?"

Stevie frowned. "I should hope so, at least a little bit. Aren't you?"

"That depends. Could she do this?" He slid his arms around her and touched his lips lightly all over her face, working his way to her mouth and kissing her with tender, playful hunger until she dissolved.

"Well, that's not enough to decide," she gasped, when he paused for breath. "Continue. In order to make a full and fair assessment, I need a demonstration of *all* your skills."

Aurata had arranged an intimate breakfast on an outside deck with a spectacular view of the canyon. There was a small table with four chairs; on the table was fresh orange juice, eggs and ham, coffee and croissants.

Looking southwards, Stevie saw a drift of steam that reminded her of the red buddhas, a sight to send echoes of sexual bliss through her. She felt her face flush and hoped no one noticed. Not that it was any secret. Mist's subtly affectionate body language pleased her, but also reminded her that, however hard he tried, he was not very good at acting aloof.

Stevie was surprised to be included at breakfast—she'd assumed the three siblings would want to meet alone—but Mist had refused to leave her out. Aurata was relaxed, leaning back in her chair with her robe falling open to reveal a long, lightly suntanned leg. Rufus looked tired and restless, his eyes very bright.

"So you both managed to make it through the night alive," she remarked to her brothers. "Is this a truce?"

"Apparently," Rufus said with a thin smile.

"I can't forget the past," said Mist. "It's not my place to forgive, because it wasn't just me he hurt. He knows that. But yes, a sort of truce. It's the best we can do."

"*He* would appreciate if you didn't refer to him in the third person," Rufus retorted.

"You must have had quite a talk," said Aurata, pouring coffee into Stevie's cup. "So, Mist, what's Rufus been saying about me?"

Both men went still, caught in a freeze-frame. Stevie held her breath.

"Nothing," said Mist. "Well, apart from gushing admiration for your scientific achievements. And digging people out of earthquakes. All impressive stuff."

"Really?"

"No, he's lying to cover for me." Rufus fixed his restless eyes on his sister. "I said all that, yes, but I also told him that you're intending to blast chasms in the Earth's crust through to the Otherworld, which will turn both realms to a molten blob, and that you don't care and won't listen to me, because you've gone power-crazy. Or just plain crazy."

Aurata put down the piece of croissant she was buttering. "I see."

Mist said calmly, "I didn't believe him. I don't know what to believe."

"It's all right." Aurata sat back in her chair, one bare foot tapping the air. "I'm not surprised. Disappointed, of course, that Rufus keeps arguing with me, but that's my fault for not explaining properly."

"Your explanation was fine," said Rufus. "It's the consequences I'm worried about. But with my age-old record of lying and mischief—who's going to listen to me?"

Aurata shrugged. "It's natural to have doubts, Rufe, but I'd prefer that you don't go spilling them behind my back. Mist, you're the rational one, able to balance different viewpoints. You should be a Spiral Court judge. What do you think?"

"Tell me the options," he said, resting one hand on the back of Stevie's chair. "And the potential consequences."

"The Earth's boundaries are fascinating places," said Aurata, "where continental plates grind against each other, and molten heat leaks out—the elemental heat of Qesoth that first created us. Human settlements formed along those cracks because they gave underground water in the desert, rare minerals, all kinds of riches. But the greatest barriers of all are invisible. The walls that separate Earth and Spiral used to be porous. Aetherials could wander freely in and out . . . but by the time of the Felynx, that had begun to change. We were exiles. The existence of portals was hidden from us, and that was wrong. Rufus, do you disagree with anything I've said?"

"Not so far, but . . ."

"In the earliest days, the separation was no more than rippling air, like the Dusklands. Then like a web, more solid but full of holes. Later—through the activities of Aetherials changing the Spiral, and other forces changing the Earth—the boundaries became denser, riddled with ways through like a rabbit warren. And later still, that barrier was made solid and all portals placed under strict control by the creation of the Great Gates. And that was wrong."

"It was done for protection of both realms," Mist put in.

"Yes, like the Iron Curtain, or those ugly walls that snake through Israel and Northern Ireland," Aurata said sharply. "Hostile, aggressive, the antithesis of freedom. I intend to break the barriers down."

"Like the collapse of the Berlin Wall?" said Stevie.

Rufus muttered, "Only rather more drastic."

"I'm talking about freedom." Aurata's demeanor was calm and open. Convincing. "Aetherials shouldn't be separated into Vaethyr and Aelyr, according to which side we live on. We're all one folk. We should be free to wander wherever we please. Others talk about it, but I'm actually going to do something."

"Are you sure it's possible?" asked Mist.

She pointed at the landscape. "Without detailing the entire geology of the West Coast, thermal areas indicate places where the Earth's crust is thin. Jigsaw Canyon has faults running beneath. It's hardly the San Andreas Fault, but that doesn't matter. Any thin place would do, but I choose this one because Azantios once stood here. We'll weave a tenfold web to strain the fabric of reality to its limit. The energy of the Felixatus will do the rest."

"Simple!" Rufus exclaimed, throwing his hands in the air to describe a fountain. "The Earth explodes like a giant abscess that makes the supervolcano under Yellowstone Park look like a birthday candle. Earth melts, the Spiral vaporizes."

"Rufus has been watching too many disaster movies," Aurata said sweetly.

"What if he's right, though?" Stevie said.

"There might be some damage," she acceded. "For example, if the Yellowstone caldera went up, it would take out most of the States, and the potential domino effect would be quite spectacular." Aurata closed her eyes for a moment, like a cat basking in the sun. "But it won't happen. Any geological disruption would be mere fallout. It will settle."

"Settle?" said Mist. "You mean, on an Aetherial timescale? Over hundreds or thousands of years, during which all life on Earth would be wiped out?"

"Except for the cockroaches," said Rufus. "It'll be just us and the cockroaches. Lovely."

Aurata's eyes narrowed minimally. "Your predictions of catastrophe are a distraction. This change is going to happen, whether you like it or not. I'd truly appreciate your support. I insist on it."

"I'd gladly give it, if this didn't sound so monumentally dangerous. Aurata, are you *sure* you're right?"

"Everything's converged here," she said easily. "The survivors of the ancient Felynx are here, on the site of Azantios. All of you, and the missing parts of the Felixatus. We even have our prophet, Daniel."

Again Stevie and Mist gave each other a sidelong glance. Stevie said, "And what about Lord Albin of Sibeyla?"

Aurata's eyebrows rose into a delicate arch. "What about him?"

"Didn't Mist tell you how powerful he is? The friends of ours he's holding captive—one of them is the Gatekeeper himself, Lucas Fox. You said you'd help us rescue them—and I believe you're the only one who can, if you're as powerful as Rufus says—but how, if melting the barriers is going to cause so much disruption?"

Rufus sat forward, fiercely interested. "Albin, that ice-cold bastard? He had me tried for my so-called crimes without a shred of evidence. He failed. Now he must *really* hate me. Oh, count me in."

"Thank you," Stevie said with a soundless laugh, not knowing how to take an offer of help from Rufus.

Aurata took a minute to reply. Her hesitation stirred Stevie's worst fears; that she didn't care, that her promises were hollow. "Oh, Albin no doubt thinks he's the most dangerous creature ever to walk the Spiral, but he won't be a problem. He knows nothing of my plans. He'll be dust before he even sees me coming."

"Er . . . well, that's reassuring," said Stevie, "I think. But our friends?"

Aurata turned her golden gaze to her. "Stevie, I'll do my best, of course. That's the only promise I can make. I don't know where they are, or what he's done to them. I can't make them my priority."

"Well, try." There was steel in Mist's voice. "One of them is the *Gatekeeper*."

"A bit careless of him to leave his post, wasn't it?"

"Lucas was helping us to get here! And holding him hostage makes it that much easier for Albin to seal all the Gates. He wants separation, as badly as you want freedom."

Aurata gave a quiet sigh. "And as I said, Albin stands no chance against me. He can freeze all the portals shut, but fire melts ice every time."

Mist said, "Aurata, I'd hoped you might see the sense of a middle path. Help us against Albin. Create a new Felynx realm, if that's what you want. But not at such massive cost to Vaeth."

With a soft growl, Aurata left her chair and leaned back against the balustrade. "Mist, don't give me moderation. You don't get it, do you? Must I spell it out?"

She changed form. Where she stood there was now a shape as bright as the sun, as tall as a house, golden wings flaring. "If Vaeth and the Spiral burn, it doesn't matter! We will become fire elementals, our true selves, the chosen of Qesoth!"

Aurata reappeared. A greenish-black afterimage obscured Stevie's vision. Rufus and Mist were both on their feet. Regally, Aurata leaned her head back and added, "Those of us who are strong enough to change will survive. The rest don't matter. For goodness' sake, what are you staring at? Have you never seen an Aelyr transformation before? You can all do the same!"

"You've singed the balcony," said Rufus.

"My point is that I need you to stop flapping about like scared mortals and think on a Felynx scale. You may as well support me, because it's too late for anyone to stop my plan."

Stevie said shakily, "Then why kidnap Daniel?"

"We didn't 'kidnap' him. He was persuaded. My dear, he was leaking our secrets like a sieve. Fortunately we curbed him in time. You know, it's very strange; he's human, yet he claims he's had these visions for years." Aurata came towards Stevie with a warm yet intimidating smile. "Ever since he first met *you*."

"I can't explain that," she said, not quite truthfully.

"He's sensitive, a *naemur*. He seems to absorb a flood of visions from anything Felynx. And it began, interestingly, when he first met you."

"He might have picked up the visions from a lamppost, for all I understood about it." Stevie was trying to stay calm. Mist's hand rested on her back, steadying her. "If you're suggesting I'm some kind of Aetherial spy, that's absolutely not true."

"But you are Aetherial."

"I'm no one. Vaethyr. Practically human."

"Stevie, don't look so worried. I know it's not your fault. It's been fascinating, actually." Aurata sat down and rested her elbows on the table, looking squarely at her. "Enlightening. Daniel's painted events from the past, and things that haven't yet happened—as if he reads my mind. His paintings have given *me* ideas, so the grand plan all feeds around in a circle. And yet it all began with *you*."

She leaned forward and reached out to touch Stevie's cheek with hot fingertips. "I know who you are. And you know me, Fela."

Stevie left the deck, hurried inside, leaving Aurata, Rufus and Mist behind. She wanted to run, but there was nowhere to go. What would happen, now that everyone knew she'd been Fela? If Aurata knew, it followed that Oliver did too, and Slahvin. They must have known from the start, looking down on her with pity and mockery.

Not Felynx, but mere Tashralyr, a creature of the marshes, a curiosity, a decoration.

An Aetherial whose unexplained death had triggered the destruction of Azantios.

She didn't want even Mist near her, because—for all he tried to separate himself—he was still part of the enchanted triumvirate. The more time he spent with Aurata, the more he was drawn under her spell. They might argue among themselves, but the Ephenaestus siblings were still a clique from which she was excluded.

She needed to see Daniel. Patrick, too. There must be someone else who could help her find a way back to Luc, Sam and Rosie, to rescue them or at least assuage her guilt by sharing their fate. She ran down broad flights of stairs to the lower floor.

She heard voices in the studio. Pushing open the door—a big, heavy slab of red wood with carved panels—she saw that Daniel was there. So, to her dismay, was Oliver. He stood in the middle of the room, arms folded over his stocky torso, while Daniel paced about looking thinner than ever, sweat trickling down his pallid face.

They both looked at her, stopping in mid-argument. "Stevie, not now," Daniel said.

"Are you all right?" she asked. She stepped towards him but he backed away.

"I'm on strike," he said, baring his teeth in a feverish smile. "I'm finished. I've got nothing left."

Oliver sighed, rolling his eyes. "All I'm asking of you is one simple thing. An accurate drawing of the Felixatus. Danny, work with me. What's wrong with you?"

Dan pointed at the right-hand panel of the triptych. His hands were paint-blotched claws, trembling. "That's the best I can do. What more do you want?"

"Detail! Not vague decoration, but technical accuracy. Miss Silverwood, can you reason with your friend?"

She turned to Oliver and said, "I think you should leave Danny alone. He looks shattered. If he can't do it, he can't."

Daniel said, "My mother's ill. I have to go home. Look, I'll finish *Aurata Enthroned* and then I'm done. You've squeezed every last image out of me. Please."

Oliver's voice was stone-cold. "Enough melodrama. This is not over until I say it is."

Daniel's response was to run flat-out at the huge window. He hit the glass like an outstretched bird, but the thick, unforgiving pane vibrated and threw him back. Dan crumpled to the floor. Before Stevie was three strides towards him, he was on his feet and fleeing towards the door. "Daniel!"

Only now did she realize that she'd witnessed the end stage of a battle of wills. Oliver must have been wearing him down for hours. Perhaps he'd tried to put Danny in a trance; he'd definitely aided the process with drugs of some kind, judging by Dan's manic, sweaty state. And he'd gone over the edge at last.

"What have you done to him?" she snarled at Oliver, who appeared too startled to move.

Stevie ran to the doorway after Daniel. She was barely two feet away when the door slammed violently in her face. Stunned, she collided with the paneling. There followed the most horrifying noise she'd ever heard; a grunting, strangled screech, like an animal dying in agony.

She grabbed the handle, pulled open the heavy door. In the corridor, by the hinge side of the doorframe, Daniel was on the carpet in a fetal curl, uttering bone-chilling shrieks.

"What have you done?" she cried. She dropped to her knees beside Daniel. His eyes were squeezed shut, his face crimson with pain.

Now Oliver was at her shoulder. He looked genuinely shaken. "It was just an argument," he growled. "Idiot!"

"Oh, gods, I think he slammed the door on his own hand," said Stevie. "Danny? Did you?"

His head bobbed. She burrowed into his curled-up body to find his hands; the left one, undamaged, was cradling the bloody, broken mess of his right. The fingers were crushed at horrible angles, with too many joints. Bones showed through the torn skin.

Stevie put her hand to her mouth, suppressing sickness.

"He needs an ambulance," she said.

"Let me see," said Oliver, moving closer.

"No," Daniel gasped. "It's over."

When Stevie looked up at Oliver, all rational thought fled her mind. He loomed above her, no longer Oliver but a wavering silhouette seen through water . . .

Then she knew for certain.

He was the one who'd drowned Fela. Oliver. Veropardus. But not alone.

Muffled footfalls were thundering down the stairs. The moment stretched; she was aware of others running into the passageway. Aurata and Mist reached them first, then Slahvin with a handful of staff around him, then Rufus, and two seconds later, Patrick.

"What the hell is going on?" demanded Aurata.

"I asked him to draw the Felixatus in detail. He refused." Oliver pushed both hands through his spiky hair. "We argued and the next thing I know, he—first he tries to throw himself through the window, then he slams the door on his working hand!"

Patrick uttered a heartfelt profanity in the background.

Silence. Only Mist moved, kneeling down beside Stevie, slipping his arm around her. Between Daniel's injury and the shadow of Veropardus above her, she couldn't utter a sound.

"What are we going to do with him?" said Oliver. "He's useless to us now."

His indifference made Stevie want to strike him. She could only imagine Daniel's pain; the crushed hand as nothing compared to the blade that Oliver had struck through his heart: *He's useless.*

"Oliver," Aurata said mildly, "why did you want him to draw the Felixatus again?"

"To aid me in putting the damned thing back together." His voice was flat with frustration. "I cannot—it's intricate. I need more detail."

"He's only human." Aurata's voice was gentle. "You pushed him as far as you could. Too far."

"So how about letting him go?" said Stevie. Her voice came out raw. "Can you not see he's had a nervous breakdown? Enough!"

Aurata turned to her with a slow, impassive blink. "We can't let him go. He knows too much. Where would he go, anyway?"

"Hospital. Then home. I'll even pay his bills, if you won't. But you can't keep him here; he needs medical help. Now!"

"We have ways to heal and soothe pain," Aurata said, unmoved.

"It's not just his hand. It's what you've done to his mind! He's broken. He won't tell anyone—and even if he did, who'd listen? You said yourself that no one can stop you anyway."

Aurata came closer to her. "Fair point. But isn't it more about what *you've* done to his mind, Fela?"

Stevie stood up, leaving Daniel in Mist's care. She felt blood rushing in her ears like water. Her legs shook, but held her ground. "This is what we do to humans," Stevie said softly. "We fuck them up. Daniel had the misfortune to be oversensitive—and look how you've used him and burned him to ash. Please let him go. Patrick can take him away—can't you, Patrick?"

"Absolutely." Patrick knelt at Daniel's other side, helping him to sit up.

"I'll get him to the nearest ER, I'll look after him, book his flight home—whatever he needs." He stared up at Stevie as if to ask, *What is this madhouse you've brought me to?* "And you're coming too, right?" he said out loud.

"Not me," she said. "Just you and Daniel."

"Aurata, let them go," said Mist. "This is no place for humans."

"Please," Stevie added.

Hard vertical lines formed between Aurata's eyebrows. "Why should I?"

"Compassion?"

"It will take more than that, Fela. What are you offering in return?"

"Can I speak to you alone for a moment?"

With Aurata at her side, Stevie went back into the studio and pointed to the opposite corner, at the door to the workshop. Painful memories trickled through her like tar but she endured them. "I can give you what Oliver can't," she said. "I'm offering myself."

Darkness.

A concentrated pool of light turned her work area as bright as day. Tiny cogs and pins were taking shape, each one precise in size, shining like gold. Mist appeared at her shoulder. Over the whirr of the lathe, she hadn't heard him approach. She killed the motor, pushed back her protective goggles and looked into his stern eyes.

"Stevie," he said, "What are you doing?"

"Rebuilding the Felixatus. Oliver physically couldn't do it. For all his bravado, he hadn't a clue how it actually fits together. His memory was fuzzy, but Fela's was so pin-sharp that I could do this blindfold."

"So I see," he said very softly. "I meant the question in a wider sense. Aurata says she needs the Felixatus to complete her plan. If you give her this, she'll be unstoppable."

"Perhaps, but mending the Felixatus is the price of Daniel's freedom. I made a promise."

"I know, but Daniel and Patrick are gone. They're safe."

"For as long as I cooperate. She'd send Slahvin after them in a heartbeat if I don't finish this. I presume that's why she trusts me enough to let me work unsupervised."

He touched her shoulder, very lightly. "I wish you hadn't been put in this position."

"Have I played our only card too soon? I've nothing left to bargain with for the lives of Rosie and the others. Aurata has all the power here."

"I hoped my offer of support would be enough, but I don't think she needs it," he sighed. "She knows damned well I won't help with a plan that might wreak devastation. And she's our sister; that's the hold she has over Rufus and me. She's near-impossible to defy, and we can't dream of hurting her."

"I wouldn't expect you to. Look, I've surrendered myself to her. That doesn't mean I agree with her plans, but all I can cling to is the tiniest chance of finding Rosie, Luc and Sam . . . It doesn't matter what happens to me."

"Don't ever say that." Mist pushed his hand under her hair and stroked the nape of her neck. He sounded fierce. "I still don't know if Aurata's ideas are right, wrong, or plain crazy, but I'll never let her harm you. I'll keep talking to her until she calms down and sees the wisdom of a more rational path."

Stevie breathed out, sitting back from the bench. She hadn't yet told him about Veropardus drowning Fela, or other events she'd remembered. It would be an easy way to turn him against Aurata on the spot. However, if he reacted with fury, that would end any chance of him negotiating with her, and might make an impossible situation even worse.

"Jaap de Witt had books like this," Mist said, derailing her thoughts. He was leafing slowly through the volume that Veropardus had written. "Medieval texts, to do with alchemy or completely bizarre theories about the world. Helena and I used to . . ."

He stopped. Stevie picked up a tiny spindle and polished it with a cloth to look busy. "What?" she said. "Laugh at the cartoons?"

"Well, that's not far from the truth. We'd translate, dig out gems of knowledge, marvel at the downright barminess of some of the theories and illustrations."

Stevie tried not to picture their heads bent together, dark and golden, the warmth of their hands gently brushing as they turned over the pages . . . She couldn't allow herself to be jealous of a dead woman.

Once she had full control of herself, Stevie asked, "Mist, do you love me?"

"Yes," he said without hesitation, as if all his breath had rushed out with surprise.

"How? As a friend, or a potential nice memory, or a partner for all time? As much as Helena, as little as Fela, or less or more or differently? Don't answer." She couldn't look at him. Her mouth was dry. "We shouldn't be lovers anymore. We can't."

"Why? Not because of Helena?"

"In a way. I'm not her, I can't replace her, and I won't be second-best."

He stared at her. "Stevie, you are not second-best to *anyone*."

"Thanks, but . . ." She nearly lost her voice. "But that's almost worse, because the main reason is that you mustn't be worrying about my safety every second. You think Helena died because you loved her, and that will taint us forever, if you let it. We have to put our feelings aside. If Aurata unleashes an apocalypse, one or both of us may get killed, and so we both need to be strong enough to carry on without falling down in grief. Make sense?"

The look on his face was one of shock, veiled by resignation. If he argued, she wouldn't be able to bear it. But if he didn't . . . she couldn't bear that, either.

"Stevie, you're my soul," he said, quiet and fervent. "I felt it the first time I saw you. Never second-best. And I never looked down on Fela, either. If anything, I was in awe of her; she was like a distant, silvery moon goddess."

"But you never thought of . . . being with her?"

"No, because she was Aurata's . . ."

"Property?"

"I was trying to think of a better word. No, I wouldn't have tried to 'steal' Fela, because that would have been to behave like Rufus. That doesn't mean I had no feelings for Fela, and just because I lost Helena doesn't mean I can't love again . . . I shouldn't have let this happen, knowing the dangers, but I wasn't strong enough. I'm sorry."

"Why? You are strong. We were both lonely. There was no shame in falling for each other, was there?"

He shook his head, still fingering the leaves of the book. His hand trembled slightly. "If things were different . . ."

"Then we'd never have met. I'd rather have been with you for a few days than not at all. But we can't . . . you know, don't you? I'm being realistic."

His eyes were dusk-grey. His dignity made her heart twist painfully. "Yes, I know what you're saying. Love makes us vulnerable, which we can't afford. We need to focus on the crisis, not on each other. But you know it makes no difference? I'll still protect you with my life."

"No, you won't. You'll do what *needs* to be done. Promise!"

"Neither of us wants to be apart," he said firmly. "We're agreed on that?"

"Yes." The word was nearly a sob. "Agreed, with all my heart, but it's about staying strong."

"You mean this."

"I mean it, absolutely." She hardened her voice.

"Then I promise," he murmured. "But we'll be side by side, like warriors."

His lips briefly pressed her temple. And it was done; the affair ended, a new pact made. And, oddly, it was the first time she'd felt truly in step with him. They were a team, in perfect trust, able to read each other without speaking.

It was the strangest feeling.

Forcing herself to keep breathing, Stevie bent over the workbench, the glow of the soul-orb dazzling her as she tried to remember what she was doing and pretend he was not still there, an arm's length from her. The Felixatus *wanted* to be put back together. Its intangible will pulled like magnetism.

And the pillars portrayed in Daniel's triptych held a code that revealed how the mechanism could be altered to trap souls or release them . . . a code that was carved in her most distant memories.

Mist swore under his breath. She started slightly, unsure how much time had passed. He said, "Gods, why didn't I see this?"

"What is it?"

He pressed his fingers to the book in a pool of light. "It's all here. Aurata and Veropardus. Rufus is right, their plan to destroy the barriers is not new. They were plotting long before Rufus started making trouble. They were trying to use the Felixatus as a kind of weapon. When Rufus told us about the Spiral, and Aurata expressed such shock and outrage—when *Fela* told her— she already knew."

Stevie leaned sideways to look at the text. Since the lettering was hard to read, and her memory of the Felynx tongue rusty, she hadn't tried to read the volume. Now, with careful attention, she deciphered the damning passage.

"When I told her, she did the most incredible job of faking surprise," said Stevie. "Why didn't I notice she was acting?"

"I trusted her. My father trusted both her and Veropardus. Yet all the time, they were planning to overthrow my parents?"

Stevie put her hand over his. The moment to tell him had arrived. "Mist? Look at me. I know who killed Fela. Who killed *me*. It was Veropardus who drowned me in the swamp. And Aurata was there, too; I saw her over his shoulder, a silhouette through the rippling water. And the witness who lied by saying that he'd seen Rufus near the marshes? That was Slahvin. The three of them have been planning this . . . forever."

20

The Felixatus

How to judge right from wrong, Stevie asked herself, *when both sides are equally convinced, and I'm a pawn trapped in the middle, clueless—yet holding the power to change the outcome?*

Maybe.

She leaned over the workbench in a pool of light, the question churning as she worked. Aurata had the iron conviction of a born leader. On the other hand there was Rufus, rebellious and volatile, prophesying disaster. Daniel's icons made terrifying sense at last. "Aurata's Promise" was clear: it was to split open the Earth and make herself the new Queen of Fire.

Mist loved his sister and wanted to believe the best of her. The last thing Stevie had wanted was to tear down his illusions. Yet she'd had no choice. What possible hope was there, now, that he could talk sense into Aurata, or even speak to her at all?

Stevie had discarded all Oliver's attempts at repair. The drawing in his book, which he'd made from memory, was hopelessly inaccurate. His metalwork was inept; the gear wheels were misshapen, their sharp, ragged edges betraying his lack of skill. Starting anew, she buried herself in the process she loved: calculating, measuring, filing and drilling metal, connecting one cog to the next. It was like rebuilding a clock. Simpler, in fact.

As Fela, she'd only had to see the Felixatus once to memorize and understand everything about it. She couldn't explain that flash of intuition. Even now, she heard faint voices trapped within the Elfstone center, crying out for help. *Put it all back together and set us free.*

Yes, she tried to tell them. *I'm doing my best, working as fast as I can.*

The whir of the lathe soothed her. Often she'd find food and drink on the bench without noticing who'd brought it. Pausing to eat, she would read sections of Veropardus's book. The text was more manifesto than history. *In secret we strove to make Azantios equal to Naamon,* read a typical passage. *Our intention was to set ablaze the barriers between worlds, turn them to vapor. Ultimately, we would have overthrown Malikala and raised Aurata in her place. To*

achieve this we must turn the Felixatus into our infallible spear, the pure energy of
dormant Felynx essences into a bolt of lightning that flies truer than any arrow.

Twice a day Aurata would appear beside her, watching silently as if afraid
to interrupt the delicate work. Stevie sensed a glow of approval. She shuddered, thinking, *Déjà vu. There is no way I'll be allowed to live with all this*
knowledge.

Sometimes Oliver would enter and observe for a few minutes. His presence made her skin crawl: his aura was stained by seething resentment. He
must loathe the fact that Stevie could rebuild the Felixatus so easily, when
he'd failed. She'd humiliated him without trying, deprived him of Daniel,
and might yet denounce him as Fela's murderer . . . Oh, there were many
reasons for Oliver to want her dead again. He wanted her gone so desperately
that she sensed his hands sweating.

Stevie slept badly over the next few nights. In bed, she would wake repeatedly and reach out for Mist, but he wasn't there. She held out no hope that
he'd slip into her room, murmuring, "This is ridiculous, we can't be apart."
He was too dignified. They'd made an agreement that couldn't be broken.

If they'd tried to continue, Aurata would eventually have used their love as
a lever against them. The fact was, she demanded everyone's complete devotion. As Stevie had said, she and Mist *had* to focus on the crisis, not on each
other. That was simply practical. And in the end, it might soften the heart-
break of losing each other . . .

Who am I kidding? Stevie asked herself.

Even her *fylgia* had deserted her.

One night she dreamed she was Helena. It was like a flash of memory;
a dark-oak interior in the periphery of her vision as she held up the lens to a
window, only to see all the wrong things: a different sky, unfamiliar stars.
A window onto Hell, Jaap had said, proving that Mist and Rufus were not
scholars, but demons.

She saw the flash of the knife, blood soaking her clothes as she fell, eventually realizing in horror that the blood was not all hers but Mist's too.

"He was no demon. He was the kindest, gentlest of men." They sat in front of a
fire together, Helena bending across to touch Stevie's hand, her hair like
minted gold. *"Whoever loves him, loves him for me. Oh, and don't forget. The po-*
sitioning of the lens is crucial."

Stevie started awake with tears in her eyes. Nice wishful thinking, that a
dead lover would give her blessing to her replacement. A touch condescend-
ing, too. She thought, *No, I don't love him for you, Helena; I love him on my own*
behalf. Yet the dream soothed her in a strange way. She felt sad for Helena,
rather than jealous. *Of course Mist loved others in his time. Who hasn't? It doesn't*
matter now, even if we go on our separate paths, because nothing can change the
fact that the dearest, most beautiful man I ever met has loved me.

"Oh, and the lens!" she said out loud, springing out of bed. "Thank you, Helena."

In the workroom the following day, all the pieces came together under her careful touch.

Struts and brass hoops supported the upper structure on the base. The smaller sphere, the heart, was suspended on a thin rod in the core. Stevie handled the object with awe. Ever-moving light played inside like moonlit water. Warm to her touch, the crystal vibrated, singing to her in gentle, insistent harmonies, like the star song of the Spiral.

The soul-motes sang a message that did not accord with Aurata's plan.

"Who is in there?" she asked, not expecting a reply. It was eerie to think she was holding all the noble families of Azantios between her hands. Even the Sovereigns Elect? Perhaps not. In the violence of the city's destruction, it appeared that while most of the newly dead had been drawn into the Felixatus, some stray essences had escaped. Not least Aurata and Veropardus.

Aurata had meant the sphere to pour out its power, but she hadn't known how to make this happen. Instead it had rolled away like a lost ball, and the souls had stayed trapped.

As the sphere was now, no spirit could pass in or out.

With reverence, Stevie cleaned fingerprints off the surface. Once she fitted the two halves of the outer shell around it, the sphere would be untouchable.

The astrological figures on the carved crystal shell now made sense. They were the symbols of the five inner realms: a sphinx-like creature for Asru, heart of mystery. A hawk for the airy mountains of Sibeyla. For Elysion, a stag, the age-old symbol of the Otherworld. Water snakes represented Melusiel, standing for wisdom and for sinuous passage into the Spiral. And for Naamon, a draconic creature: a winged salamander, not unlike the form that Mist had taken in Virginia's pool.

This was forbidden knowledge in the days of the Felynx, who'd never been told that they were exiles.

She was almost there. On the workbench now stood a globe inside a globe, bounded by hoops within which the structure could rotate to many different angles according to the gearing mechanism she'd constructed. The last item to be attached was the infamous lens through which Jaap de Witt thought he'd seen a demon realm.

This smooth clear piece of Elfstone must be poised above the "north pole" of the sphere. A lens to focus starlight into the heart of the Felixatus . . . or to trap wandering soul-essences? Both, she suspected, although the reason wasn't clear.

Stevie had almost finished when the bitter tang of smoke distracted her. She went into the studio and looked out through the vast window. In the scrubby cactus garden below the house, smoke was curling into the sky, dirty grey against pure deep blue. Oliver was there, on a flat stretch of stone, tending a bonfire.

He was feeding the flames with slats of wood, waiting for each one to catch light before pushing in the next one. Stevie looked around the studio to see that the walls were bare.

Oliver was burning Daniel's paintings.

Her heart nearly stopped. All that work—how could he? Outraged, she banged on the glass, and yelled out loud, "*Stop!*"

He didn't hear. He worked mechanically. There was a glint of moisture on his cheeks—was that from genuine sorrow, or just the sting of heat? If there was any spark of feeling left for Daniel in his flinty heart, she would be astounded.

Stevie watched in dismay as all Daniel's wild, evocative images blackened to ash. Her chest hurt. He'd painted a lost world and a potential, apocalyptic future. Now those visions were lost forever.

"You bastard, you fucking bastard, Oliver," she murmured. "You can't take those images out of my head. Kill Fela, kill me, I'll still keep coming back to haunt you and I'll *never* forget."

Aurata took Mist on a walk to the edge of Jigsaw Canyon and along the precarious spine of the arch that jutted partway into the chasm. At the farthest point, a flat rock formed a high, narrow lookout. The swooping drop of the gorge beneath looked a mile deep. She took him to the very edge and they watched as sunset flushed the folded walls to incandescent scarlet.

"I so wanted you to see this," she said. "While you were searching for Rufus, I bet this was the last thing you expected to find: this place, and me."

"I had no expectations," he replied. "I wanted to kill Rufus, but couldn't. Now we're back on the nightmare merry-go-round. We need to wake up. All of us."

She slid her hand through his arm. Mist suppressed a shudder. How long could he hide what he'd learned? Stevie had made him promise not to confront Aurata about Fela's death. It half-killed him to pretend he didn't know, but he knew if he said a word he might get both Stevie and himself imprisoned, or worse.

The dry, cool wind stirred their hair; carrying a tang of smoke. "It's bound to feel strange, dear, but wonderful, too. Everything is coming full circle."

"What's the plan for the web-weaving and the Felixatus? A ritual of some kind?"

Aurata smiled, patted his arm. "If I told you, I'd have to kill you. It was all in Daniel's images. Oliver is burning the paintings as we speak."

Shocked, Mist looked hard at her. "Destroying the evidence?"

"It's a waste, I know, but we'll soon have the real thing in place of pictures."

"There are still images on the web."

"All thoroughly deleted. Your Stevie's a brave girl; I doubt Daniel would have lived much longer, and she knew it. But I was happy to take her in exchange, because it's her I need now—not Daniel."

"She's not Fela anymore. She doesn't belong to you."

"Nor to you," Aurata said wryly. "Oh, Mist, you're in love with her. Who wouldn't love her? She's gorgeous. I must admit, though, I was surprised."

"Why? Do you still think of her as less than us? That's a delusion. It seems to be a Felynx attribute to imagine we're superior to all others."

Aurata gave a dry smile. "Well, it's surely better than an inferiority complex, isn't it? Of course we're superior. Great Qesoth herself was a creature of fire. Didn't Queen Malikala channel her power for eons to rule the whole Spiral?" Aurata tipped back her head, her hair as scarlet as the canyon. "Qesoth is rising. It's her time again."

Mist was silent for a while, watching his sister as she reached up to the sky, half-dancing in private ecstasy. "Aurata? How long have you known that Stevie was Fela?"

"As soon as I saw her." Aurata turned to face him, the rocks blazing red behind her. "Different form, same aura. You knew, didn't you? I didn't spill some shocking secret?"

"I knew," Mist said, "but her past was locked away. She thought herself to be human until very recently. However, she remembers . . . drowning."

Tension thickened between them. "A tragedy," Aurata said softly. "But it's over, she's back with us. Actually I like her new incarnation: she's smart, with hidden fire."

"More than you know. She'll stop at nothing to help our friends escape from Albin."

"And rebuilding the Felixatus will help. It will be the focus of our newfound power. Energy equals mass times the speed of light squared, and all that."

"Sounds like a formula to turn Vaeth into a fireball. A nuclear reaction?"

"You have to stop listening to Rufus." She placed warm hands on his shoulders, kissed his mouth. "Mist, please believe in me. This is our chance to reforge the world. A new golden age, a new Felynx empire with unfettered access between realms. How can you oppose that? We're fulfilling the legacy of Poectilictis and Theliome. It wasn't Rufus or us who destroyed Azantios, but humans."

"I wonder? Were humans even here when we were?"

"Well, the dates are disputed, but *some* brutish force invaded us—*Homo sapiens*, or another race altogether? We can't know, since they are gone, ground to dust. It's time for the Felynx to rise again."

He stepped away from her, studying the alien gleam of her eyes. "You've changed. I'm not sure it's even Aurata in there. If you ever were who I thought."

"None of us have changed half as much as we need to," she retorted. "Rufus was a maniac, but I understand now that we *had* to break the old Azantios in order to create a new one. New Azantios—how does that strike you as a fine name for the transformed fiery realm of Vaeth and Spiral, united?"

"It strikes me as being a dream, Aurata. Only a dream."

"Do you know how much you wound me by not trusting me?"

"I want to trust you," said Mist. "But the sister I *thought* I knew was loving and sensible and fair. I don't see that person in your eyes anymore."

She grinned. "Perhaps your memory of me is rose-tinted."

"I'm certain of it." He kept his expression neutral, pushing away a vision of dark figures in a swamp, betraying the Tashralyr friend who'd trusted them.

"Oh, I was as headstrong and self-centered as Rufus—just better at hiding it. We couldn't please you, could we? When he and I argued, you disapproved. When we went too far the other way, you disapproved even more. Or were jealous. Or both. Yet you chose to blame Rufus and label me faultless. Is it me that's changed, or your perception?"

"That is a very good question," he said, barely audibly.

"You loved me, and yet I still wasn't good enough to share power with you," she added lightly. She moved to the very edge of the platform, rising on her toes as if to take flight.

He said, "Are you surprised, after your secret plots with Veropardus?"

She laughed. "You still don't understand. We were trying to set the Felynx free! It was *Poectilictis* who wanted them held inside the Felixatus forever! Did you want to end up in that sphere, like a spore trapped in ice? I most certainly did not!"

Her words startled him. He'd never considered before that she might have been afraid of anything. After a moment, he asked carefully, "Aurata, is there anything I can say that will make you pause and think? Put aside your project? Cancel the ritual?"

"What would you have me do instead?"

"Help us rescue our friends. Then return to your scientific work, which might actually do some good."

"But my scientific work was all for this end. Learning about Vaeth's structure, how seismic waves move through the crust and mantle and core, and how to trigger the exact vibrations to make the planet ring and shatter like a wineglass. Did you know that the core is like another planet beneath our feet, a sea of white-hot liquid metal surrounding a solid ball the size of the moon? Scientists think that ball is made of giant metal-crystal forests that create the Earth's magnetic field. Isn't that astounding? The Spiral must whirl around the outside of Vaeth, although Naamon perhaps touches the hostile inner core here and there. The Felixatus is like the world in microcosm. Bursting with resonant energy."

"Have you forgotten that the Felixatus is a sacred object, not a weapon?"

She became suddenly still, as if he'd struck her. She turned to face him. "Don't lecture me about what's sacred. Qesoth is a mighty force. She will channel herself through me. I cannot 'cancel' that as if it were a dinner party."

Mist remembered Aurata's transformation into fire-angel form. He heard Virginia's warning, *Brawth rose, so Qesoth may rise in turn.* "Are you serious?"

"Absolutely," she said softly. "I will become Qesoth."

"A goddess?"

"The primal fire. The heart of the sun." She laughed. "Then the Earth's core would be like an ice cube to pop in my drink."

He stared at her with a feeling of hopeless, unraveling horror. He knew that his sister believed what she said with complete, sane clarity—and had believed it, in secret, possibly for thousands of years. Veropardus had been her priest as well as her lover. Slahvin was—what? Her secret agent, her chief inquisitor-in-waiting? Mist hadn't suspected a thing. He couldn't forgive himself for his own blinkered ignorance.

Still, he persisted. "Do you know you sound mad?"

"Naturally. Do you think I care?"

"Look—these fantasies of power—they're seductive, but they aren't real!"

"Who are you to say what's real? What do you believe?"

"That Azantios is gone, the past is gone! I believe in moderation, justice, all those virtues that you and Rufus seem to find so dreary. So be it—but I'm telling you that we *must* find a way to live in the present. Which includes peaceful coexistence with humans—not deceiving and torturing them as Rufus has. And not this!"

"Well. Some passion at last. Oh, Mist, you're such a gracious, good-hearted soul; that hasn't changed. But moderation doesn't win any prizes. Extreme visions, huge risks and mad ideas—that's our only way forward. Qesoth will rise and act through me. Yes, it sounds insane from a human perspective—but not from an Aetherial one. *We can will our dreams into being.* And I so want your belief and your help. I want you as part of the energy web to make this happen . . . but I feel you holding back."

Mist was quiet, thinking. *As part of the web, I'd have a chance of sabotage.*

"I will help you, if you'll give me the two things that matter. Stevie's safety, and the rescue of our friends from Albin. Their names are Sam and Rosie and Lucas. They're real people, suffering."

She turned an intransigent profile to him. "Dear heart, I've said I'll try. I can't promise."

"That's not good enough."

"It's all I can offer." She exhaled sharply. "Mist, I have a confession to make. I know Albin Wilder of Sibeyla."

"Personally?" He noticed color in her cheeks, her mouth tightening. "This is interesting. He didn't seem a man to have many friends or lovers."

"Albin was once my husband."

Her offhanded tone shocked him as much as her words. Mist turned to her so fast that his right foot slipped off the edge, sending chips of sandstone arcing into the void. He flailed for balance.

"Careful," she said, catching his forearm. "I know, it's a leap of the imagination, isn't it?"

"You could say that. How . . . ?"

She waved her hand, palm down in a gesture of dismissal. "It was a long time ago. I was in the Otherworld, exploring the realms, and we happened to meet at some Aelyr festival on the borders of Sibeyla and Naamon. He knew me as Maia; I never told him my true name and history, and he never asked. He was a very captivating, pale creature, like no one I'd ever met before, and from a chilly high Sibeylan clan. My heat drew him. The disastrous magnetism of opposites. I wouldn't say we were ever truly happy or content. There was passion between us, and a powerful obsession; but he was a twisted soul, resentful because he didn't inherit his mother Liliana's high position as Gatekeeper. The gift leapfrogged from her to our son."

"*You have a son?*" Mist interrupted. "Why didn't you tell me?"

"There was no reason to mention it, until now." Again the throwaway lightness that he couldn't fathom. "Lawrence. A fine Sibeylan boy, but as cold as his father. Liliana wished to take him away into Vaeth to train him, which left Albin more bitter than he'd admit. By then, I knew it was time to leave. An Aetheric pull drew me away, a Spiral call far stronger than my ties to husband and son . . . so I went. I was semi-elemental for a time. I faded into deeper realms where Albin couldn't find me."

"I can understand you leaving Albin, but your son?"

"I couldn't help it." She gave a slight frown. "Lawrence had Liliana. I never felt any great maternal ties. Remember that Aetherials don't cling like humans, but tend to drift apart, as self-sufficient as birds."

"That's true of some," he replied, "but it's a massive generalization."

She shrugged. "You're right. Think me heartless if you will. I can't justify what I did. I'm simply telling you what happened."

Mist didn't feel in a position to judge her. He kept his tone plain. "So you're the mother of Lawrence Wilder? The mother of Albin's son."

"Yes." She looked puzzled. "What of it?"

Mist pushed windblown hair out of his eyes. "Because—didn't you work it out? Of our three friends whom Albin is holding hostage, *two of them are your grandchildren.*"

To his gratification, that threw Aurata. She stiffened, paled slightly. Violet shadow slid like floodwater into the canyon, while the high rocks flared bright amber.

"Samuel Wilder and Lucas Fox are your grandsons," he repeated. "Rosie is Luc's half-sister and Sam's partner. They're three of the best Aetherials, the best *people*, I have ever met. Where do they stand in your schemes? If they turn to ash because they can't transform into fire forms without warning, will that even matter to you? Or is your own flesh and blood as disposable as Daniel's paintings? For pity's sake, Aurata. You and Rufus deserve each other."

She drew back from him, blinking. "I need to think about this, but I can't let it change anything."

He swallowed all the rage that was close to pouring out. "Help them, and I'll help you," he said.

"I'm going back to the house now," she said coolly. "Are you coming with me?"

Twilight filled the workroom. The rank bonfire stink of burned wood had permeated from outside. Stevie put the finishing touches to the Felixatus, testing the small control knobs that adjusted the lens, ensuring the precision-calibrated gears locked or released as they should. She oiled and polished and double-checked. She knew she'd done a good job. The Felixatus, restored, pulsated like some translucent, luminous sea creature. She could almost hear the pleas of the captured souls. *Free us* . . .

Mist loomed over her shoulder, a specter of sooty darkness and shadowed ivory. He gave her a hesitant, somber smile. "Stevie, can I have a word?"

"Of course," she said very softly. "Close the door."

He obeyed. Light from the Felixatus lent his face an eerie magnificence. He studied the object as if it was the most astonishing thing he'd ever seen. "You did this?" he said.

"Well, it's just a repair job, but yes."

"But you've remade all the metal parts from scratch, haven't you? It's exquisite. I had no idea you were so skilled."

Stevie allowed herself a moment of pride. "It's what I trained for at college. Plus I seem to have a photographic memory for things like this. And it's fully adjustable: see the cogwheels, and the degree markings on the meridian ring? I suppose Aurata will need me to show her how to operate it."

"And you wouldn't dream of showing her wrong," he said thoughtfully.

"Er . . ." She had no answer. "I wouldn't dare. Have you seen her again?"

"Yes. She took me to Jigsaw Canyon. Spectacular, for those who are not afraid of heights."

"Count me out," she said with a grimace. "Did you mention . . ."

"You'd have admired my restraint," he sighed. "Yes, I challenged her, but not blatantly enough for a full-out battle. She's planning a ritual, a tenfold web involving the Felixatus. She intends to channel Qesoth."

"Can she actually do that?"

He spoke so softly that she had to lip-read. "I don't know. She believes she can. But she wants me as part of the web, which may be our only chance to stop her. That, and Albin . . ."

"What about Albin?"

He told her.

Stevie was dumbstruck. She made Mist go out into the studio, to make sure there were no Felynx spies lurking. When he returned, she found her voice. "Unbelievable. She and Albin were together? Our friends in peril are her family—and she doesn't care? Fela thought she was a generous soul, in the Azantios days. How did we get her so wrong?"

Mist exhaled. "I wish I knew. We go through so many changes. She saw her city destroyed—which is no excuse, since she was already hatching a deeper plan of her own—but that sent us all half-mad. She turned elemental, wandered in the wilderness, lived other lives including one as someone called Maia who wedded Albin and bore a son, then walked away, slept and woke again . . . So who is the real Aurata? The only one of us who's stayed the same is Rufus. He's always kept to his path of maximum mischief, zero responsibility. I never thought I'd view his stability as vaguely reassuring! Gods, what have we come to?"

"We don't choose our families," she said. "I used to think it would be nice to have a family. Now I'm not sure."

"You don't remember your parents, from when you were Fela?"

She shook her head, uneasy. "No. Only friends, like Karn. I felt I'd always been there. Timeless. More animal or elemental than Aetherial."

"Have you considered that you might be one of the First?"

"How d'you mean?"

"Estalyr, the earliest Aelyr who began as sentient scraps of energy."

She laughed at the notion. "Maybe that's why I love patchwork. I'm made of scraps, like a rag doll."

"A beautiful rag doll," he said tenderly.

"Don't."

"Sorry. Back to business." He put his head in his hands, elbows on the bench. He was not quite touching her, but close enough to wake a hot turmoil of frustration. He said, "I'm serious about the Estalyr issue. 'Scrap' is the wrong word. Energy form, I should say. Our physical shapes, evolution, reproduction, the founding of dynasties—all that came much later. Underneath, we're all primal. Powerful."

"I'm not feeling the power," said Stevie. "I feel mortal. My back aches, I'm tired and frightened. If you're right, why can't I remember?"

"Some Aelyr, like Albin, say we've turned too human. 'Vaethyr' to them means muddy. I think we lock memories away for our own protection."

Like the shell enclosing the core of the Felixatus, she thought. She stroked the crystalline globe. Light glowed red through her fingers. "I still can't believe Poectilictis didn't share the truth about the Felixatus with his son and heir."

He brought his palms to hover over the transparent shell. Motes of lights danced on his skin. "It's still full of Felynx essences. They've even soaked into the base and the lens. That's why we were forbidden to approach it. If I'd been as sacrilegious as Rufus, I would have realized long ago."

She nodded. "Listen. You can hear their song."

His breathing quickened. "Father insisted this was created to save the Felynx."

"Or to imprison them," said Stevie. "Which do you think? Is it fair that they couldn't continue their journeys into the Spiral? Did your parents hope to keep control of everyone, forever?"

"I can't answer that."

"And when your turn came, would you have allowed the process to continue?"

His eyelids fell, lips parting in an expression of dismay. "Yes, of course. I would have done exactly as Poectilictis instructed."

"Wow. At least you're honest." Stevie's words came out louder than she intended.

"Honest, and blind. This is an abomination." His hands trembled, cupping the soul-light. "Thousands of Felynx trapped in here, many of them the folk I knew and loved? It's unthinkable. These souls should be set free."

"That's not what Aurata and Oliver intend, though, is it?"

"They claim they do, but I don't believe them. I suppose you know that Oliver has burned all Daniel's work, to destroy the evidence?"

"I know, I watched him!" she said angrily. "But why do they need to destroy evidence if they're so confident of victory? Oliver acted out of sheer spite, Mist. He's just one mass of rage, jealousy and spite. For Daniel's sake, I'll never forgive him."

"Nor I," Mist murmured.

"I wish I knew what to do," Stevie said, agonized. "Take the Felixatus and run? We wouldn't get past the front door, let alone the razor wire."

"No." His eyes were the color of steel, like shutters falling. "But we can't let this happen. And they needn't think that Fela's death will go unavenged."

"Mist, don't take revenge on my account. I know you still love your sister, or you wouldn't be in such anguish."

"I don't know her anymore! Aren't the most vicious conflicts always between siblings? If I make her choose between me and Qesoth, she's made it plain which way she'll go. She holds all the power."

"I know, and I don't want to die again," Stevie confessed. "Yes, my essence might come back—but with no memory of you or Rosie or anything. I couldn't bear it."

"Nor could I."

He fell quiet, watching as Stevie made last checks to the mechanism and polished the outer shell with a soft cloth. There stood the Felixatus, whole again. A mechanism of precise, gleaming beauty. Carved crystal structures suspended in a cage of hoops, spindles and gears. The repository of a million souls.

And a weapon.

Eventually Mist said, "We both know that we can only change this from the inside."

"The subtlest of changes might do it."

They gazed at each other in perfect wordless understanding.

The door opened and someone flicked on a light. Mist stepped away from Stevie as Aurata strode into the room. Oliver and Slahvin were with her, flanked by some of her followers; five male, five female, neat and menacing in their smart suits. Aurata went straight to the workbench, showing no sign she'd heard Stevie's near-soundless exchange with Mist.

All their attention was on the Felixatus. Stevie slid off her seat and moved aside for them to look. Aurata gave an audible breath of wonder; Oliver was trembling, his expression pinched. Excited, envious? Smudges on his face from the bonfire made him look like a bruised ruffian.

"Finished?" Aurata asked.

Stevie gave a tight nod. "To your satisfaction, I hope."

"Perfect." To Stevie's surprise, Aurata hugged her and shed tears, as if she'd been given a most wondrous gift. "Do you know what it means, to see this whole again? You're a genius."

"Let us hope so," Oliver said aridly.

"Come out into the studio. Stevie, you carry the Felixatus. Oliver, call everyone in."

Sourly he obeyed. Aurata pulled a tall stool into the middle of the space, directing Stevie to place the Felixatus on the seat—hardly a fitting plinth, but it had to do. Within minutes, most of Aurata's disciples were in the room. There were only thirty or so, but their combined Aetheric presence was over-whelming. They exuded a powerful excitement that Stevie, as Fela, hadn't tasted since race days at the height of Azantios. Their lovely faces were bliss-ful. Completely focused on Aurata, they didn't even notice Stevie. She was nothing, invisible.

Aurata waved them into a loose circle surrounding their grail.

"Behold, the Felixatus," she said. "Did we even dare to dream we'd see it whole again?"

The studio felt barren with Daniel's work gone. The globe's light danced on bare wood-paneled walls. The gathered Aetherials emitted sighs of wonder. Some fell to their knees; others showed signs of changing shape, or simply began to weep. "Aurata, Aurata," they murmured, like a chant.

"Where's Rufus?" said Mist. His voice was a stone falling into the fervid atmosphere.

"Oh, you'll see him in a few minutes," Aurata replied.

He moved towards the Felixatus, breaching the sacred circular gap his sister had created. This looked shockingly irreverent.

"Are our parents in here? I don't feel them . . . but how can we know?"

"We can't," said Aurata. "But if Poectilictis and Theliome are there, they'd surely give their strength and blessing to our intention."

Her disciples made murmurs of agreement.

"Mist, step back."

He obeyed, placing himself next to Stevie. She imagined him seizing the Felixatus, making a wild dash and hurling himself through the window; she wouldn't put it past him to do just that. She glanced at Slahvin and his security contingent, who'd arranged themselves around the outside of the group. They positioned their hands strangely; palms down, fingers splayed. Faint lines of light danced between them. Stevie felt pressure in the air, as forceful as magnetism, and she realized. *Of course. They're weaving a web to contain us. We'd never break through it.*

Mist's eyes widened. He knew.

"So, the ritual," said Aurata. "A light supper, a brief rest, then we'll begin. We'll take the Felixatus to the lookout rock tonight. It must be positioned and adjusted to absorb the energy of the stars. When the sun rises and strikes the lens—that will begin the process. The mechanism must be precisely adjusted; can you do that?"

"Of course," said Oliver.

Aurata gave a patient half-smile. "I wasn't talking to you. I was talking to Stevie."

His lips turned bone-white. "But I am the Custodian. It's my duty."

"I'm sorry, Veropardus," she said mildly. "Stevie rebuilt the Felixatus and she's attuned to its energies. I can't trust anyone else to operate it."

"Can you trust her?" he said quietly.

When Stevie looked at him, she saw the face of Veropardus distorted through water as he forced her down into the swamp . . . She had to close her eyes. She felt Mist's hand folding around hers—

The next instant, she and Mist were torn apart.

Aurata had made some sign she hadn't seen. Some of her followers grabbed Stevie, their fingers like claws in her arms. Astonished, she cried out, trying to fight, doubling over with shock and pain. Then she saw why they were holding her.

Slahvin's security guards were seizing Mist. The others were holding Stevie back so she couldn't get involved. Taken by stealth, Mist fought furiously, landing a few good blows before they overpowered him. There were too many of them, bristling with an Otherworldly power that he couldn't match.

"Stevie!" he yelled as he was bundled away, struggling at every step. His anguish echoed in the corridor after he was out of sight.

"What the hell are you doing?" Stevie shouted. "He was going to help you!"

Aurata turned to Stevie with a gelid stare. "Do you take me for an idiot? I know him. He said a lot, but he didn't need to open his mouth for me to know he is not on my side. I wish he'd been different, but I haven't time to waste on sentiment. However, I do need you. So it goes without saying that unless you cooperate, Mist will suffer untold tortures that I'll leave to your imagination. Behave, and all will be well. Do you understand?"

She nodded, faint with pain. "Whatever you want, I'll do it."

"Good girl, sweet Fela." Aurata touched her cheek. "You always were my kitten."

Mist was thrown into a dark, windowless space. There was a shockwave like that of a door slamming as he hit the floor. His eyes adjusted rapidly to wavelengths humans could not perceive and he found himself in a plain grey space, like a giant safe with rounded corners.

In the center sat Rufus, arms wrapped around his drawn-up knees. His hair cloaked his shoulders, pooling on the rubber-textured floor. His chin jerked up as Mist landed full-length beside him.

"Ah, there you are," Rufus said flatly. "You didn't try *reasoning* with her, did you? Fatal mistake."

"What the hell is this?" Mist stared around at the cell, scared and furious.

"I believe it's what they call the panic room. A place for rich folk to hide if intruders raid their mansion."

"How long have you been—?"

"Couple of hours." Rufus sighed. "Should have known this would happen. Aurata doesn't trust us. I never thought she'd go to these lengths to stop us sabotaging her plan. But then, I'm notoriously stupid."

"She's taken Stevie." Mist rose to his knees. "We have to get out of here—surely we can break out?"

"Do we want to? At least no one's assaulting or harassing us in here."

Mist was already on his feet, searching the walls. If there was a door, its edges were seamless. Panic and fury rose as he searched again. "There's no way out," he said.

Rufus looked up, frowning. "There must be."

"Well, there isn't." In frustration Mist hammered on the wall and yelled, "*Aurata!*"

"It won't do any good shouting," said Rufus. "I've tried."

Mist stilled himself, tuning his senses to the atmosphere. At once he felt a familiar pressure, a warping of the air like an unseen semi-elastic cage around them.

"A web," he said. "This isn't a room, it's an eightfold web they've woven to keep us in here. Slahvin and his lackeys."

"Oh, great," Rufus said tightly. "Strictly speaking not lackeys, but Aurata's chosen ones. I used to have followers. I miss those days. You can't get the staff."

"I truly hope you're not going to sit there making facetious remarks," Mist growled, dropping to his knees beside his brother. "Help me, for fuck's sake!"

"Well, this is ironic, isn't it?" Rufus met his glare. "You come here slavering for my blood. Now you're begging for my help! Your worst nightmare in the world was to spend eternity stuck with me—and here we are, trapped in a cell together."

"Yes, the gods must be laughing their fucking heads off."

"Too right, because I'll tell you what's worse—I really liked you as Adam Leith. He was sweet and scared and malleable. Now you've turned back into Mistangamesh, I don't like you one little bit. Damn right, we should have gone our separate ways. Being stuck here with you turns out to be *my* worst nightmare, as well."

"Then help me, you pigheaded fuckwit." Mist grabbed a handful of Rufus's hair and twisted. His brother yelped with pain. "We need to forget that Aurata was ever our sister."

"That's not so easy," Rufus shot back. "She was like an angel, coming to pull me out of the pit. She saved me."

"No. She was just gathering a special recruit. She didn't hesitate to throw you aside the moment you wouldn't cooperate. Maybe it's *me* who's meant to save you, heaven help me."

"Maybe so." Rufus's head was tipped back, his voice tight with pain. "Full circle, she said."

"So work with me for once. We're Aelyr, Felynx, sons of Poectilictis. It's time to reclaim that power and do whatever it takes to stop her."

"Ow." Rufus jerked loose. "Let go! Enough. I'm with you, Mist." He bared his teeth in a smile, half-vicious, half-teasing. "You know I can't resist you when you play rough."

The promontory floated high above the chasm, exposed to the desert's bitter cold. In the dark, overarched by a trillion stars, the height was barely discernible. Stevie could look up, and not think about the canyon far below.

They'd put her into a robe of fine silk, exquisitely patterned like devoré velvet in shades of orange, gold and red, with subtle shapes that echoed the creatures on the Felixatus shell. Aurata and Veropardus—Stevie couldn't think of him as "Oliver" anymore—were dressed in the same ritual garments, as were ten of Aurata's followers. They might have looked slightly ridiculous, if they had not appeared so eldritch, like beautiful demons. The ten wore weightless headdresses like tongues of flame, and masks, too. Their eyes gleamed through holes in elongated, expressionless lynx faces.

The night chill stung as they worked. Aurata had her adherents manhandle a block of stone to the edge of the lookout rock, then directed Stevie to set the Felixatus upon it.

As she did so—as passive as a slave, suppressing all emotion—Veropardus's hands hovered over hers, like those of an adult trying to guide a child. His touch made her cringe. He had no mask, but she would have preferred seeing a mask to his callous, naked face.

"The lens must be angled to follow the constellation of Auriga," he said. "We need to focus the maximum spectrum of starlight into—"

"Veropardus." Aurata's curt tone stopped him. "Stand back. Let Stevie do this."

"It's my duty," he said fiercely.

"Not anymore. We've been through this. She's the one with the delicacy of touch. Would you please set aside your ego for the sake of the greater good?"

"After I've worked so hard in the service of this cause, even *died* for it— you won't let me fulfill my role?"

They paused, glaring at each other in a battle of wills that Aurata was bound to win. She said smoothly, "Veropardus, I won't tolerate an argument on this sacred night. Do you want to help me?"

"Of course."

"Then go back and gather everyone who remains, and have them guard the place where the arch joins the canyon edge. No one must have access to the path. The process begins now and must not be interrupted. That's what I need from you tonight. Strength and protection. Can you do that?"

He surrendered. "Yes, beloved lady of fire," he murmured. He bent to kiss her hand, and, to Stevie's relief, walked away along the spine of the arch.

Aurata continued the explanation. "The Felixatus will concentrate starlight like a battery storing energy. The photons act to agitate the Felynx soul-essences that wait within."

A million of them, yet so tiny, Stevie thought, *each curled up like a glow-worm no bigger than an atom* . . . Just trying to imagine it made her head spin.

"Meanwhile, my companions will be helping me to weave energy webs to weaken the structure of the Earth's crust. And as the Felixatus becomes saturated with pent-up energy, we wait for sunrise."

Stevie caught her breath. "I'm no physicist, still less a magician—but won't the first beam of sunlight cause a massive overload?"

"Exactly!" Aurata squeezed her shoulders. "You get it."

"Do I? Won't it simply explode?"

"Of course it won't. Think, Stevie: after all, you rebuilt it. The Felixatus is constructed so that its force can escape only from a precise point. The sphere will shoot out a beam of fire powerful enough to rip open reality itself. That's the instant at which you swivel the apparatus and direct the beam right into the heart of our energy webs. The Earth itself will crack. Magma will erupt, beginning a self-sustaining process that will vaporize all barriers, melting Vaeth and Spiral one. And we'll achieve our dream: reunification."

"Or the end of everything," said Stevie.

"That's not for you to worry about."

"But all the trapped soul-energies—won't this destroy them? I don't see how they can survive. Are they happy to be sacrificed?"

"In their position, I'd be ecstatic." Aurata's tone held a firm threat. "No more questions, Stevie, for Mist's sake."

She set to work, rotating the Felixatus until it glimmered with evanescent light in response to the stars. Then she made tiny adjustments, a cog tooth at a time, angling the lens until it found the Auriga constellation overhead and focused upon the bright yellow star Capella amid the river of the Milky Way.

At once a distinct thread of white light appeared between the lens and the heavens. The Felixatus began to vibrate, singing in a faint discord that sent shivers through her. Behind her and Aurata, the ten chosen Aetherials formed a circle—more of an oval, as the rock was narrow—and began a slow dance. Energy lines sizzled between them like sparkler trails.

"Good girl," said Aurata. "That's it. Now we follow the star and wait for sunrise. Are you cold?"

"No," she lied. Aurata's concern seemed ridiculous in the context of her general callousness. "I thought Rufus would be here."

"I had to pop him out of the way with Mist. No time for arguments or weakness."

"What will happen to them?"

"Don't worry about that."

"You really don't care about anyone, do you?" Stevie's voice was soft. "You claimed to love Fela, but you killed her without a moment's hesitation."

"Oh, I hesitated, my dear. I'm not your enemy. Real love means putting tender feelings aside for the greater good."

Stevie felt it no longer mattered what she said. "So, how much did it hurt to watch Veropardus drowning Fela?"

"It broke my heart." The response was so quick, it might even be sincere.

"Or to frame Rufus for her death?"

"Likewise. Yet it was destiny—otherwise you wouldn't be here now, holding secrets that even Veropardus has lost. The unseen mechanisms of the universe delivered you to us, like an orrery bringing the planets into alignment. Clockwork."

"If I hadn't met Daniel . . . then Professor Manifold wouldn't have found the Felixatus base . . . Mist wouldn't have found me . . . and we might still be living our small peaceful lives in ignorance. I wish I could've stopped this before it began."

"Don't say that." Aurata's voice was warm. "Stevie, what you're doing is noble. You should be full of joy."

"Well, I'm not. I'm scared. But I've been on this journey before. If I come back as someone else, or dissolve into oblivion—I've no control over that."

"None of us has. That's well said, because I don't know if any of us will survive. The point is, we may not be doing this for ourselves, but for those who come after. Isn't that the greatest sacrifice of all?"

"A sacrifice to Qesoth?" Stevie's voice trembled. She had a vision of the Earth, like molten gold in a crucible, being poured into a new mold.

"And the completion of what we tried to do in Azantios, long ages ago."

Stevie wished she could love and trust Aurata as blindly as her followers did, to share their transcendent ecstasy. It was too late. Dr. Gregory's kind face came into her mind and she longed to ask his opinion: *Is Aurata mad, psychotic, deluded?*

Perhaps her plan was a delusion—but one thing was sure. Fela had died because she'd stumbled onto inappropriate knowledge, and nothing had changed: Stevie still knew too much. At some point, she was certain, Aurata would cast her into the canyon, a sacrifice with no one to save her.

Close to dawn, a wash of luminescence rose from the horizon. "The zodiacal light!" said Aurata. "What a beautiful omen. It's nearly time."

Stars faded as the sky became a vast, paling dome of violet-blue. A line of bright gold formed along the horizon. Aurata rose to her feet, lifting Stevie with her.

Stevie saw the drop yawning below, cold indigo shadow. She felt her legs weaken, her stomach tightening. Unstrung, she needed all her self-control to force the panic down.

She tried to edge back, to gain a few inches of safety, but found she couldn't move. Invisible wires constrained her. The air shuddered with waves of power, woven by the tenfold web of Aurata's new Felynx. Their eyes glowed within their masks and their hair writhed with static charge.

Aurata's palm landed between Stevie's shoulders, caressing her hair like a lover. The long drop below made her so dizzy she couldn't move or think. Then Aurata raised both hands as if casting out a fishing net.

Stevie realized Aurata was using the thickly spun energy of the tenfold web to create a force of her own. Hovering above the canyon, her spell appeared as a vast and quivering transparent disk like a giant lens, deforming the precipice behind it. Sparks raced around its circumference.

"There," said Aurata. "Do you see the vortex I've made? See how it distorts the light? The moment the sun touches the Felixatus, you must rotate the mechanism to send the beam straight into the center of the whorl. Steady hands. Don't rush. Just be accurate. The fire beam will find its true route."

An eerie chanting rose from her acolytes, "*Elysiana, O Melusina, Naamon-a-Asru, O-ah Sibeyla . . .*" They stood with heads tilted back in rapture, weaving a bright complex mesh of power. The changing air pressure hurt her ears and the rock arch swayed alarmingly.

Canyon and sky turned bright red, as if the world were dissolving into blood.

The sun rose, boiling.

The first ray struck the heart of the Felixatus. The globe lit up, dazzling. The earth began to tremble. On the far side of the canyon, rocks cracked and fell.

"Now!" commanded Aurata.

Stevie spun the globe. An answering beam shot out of the lens, yellow-hot and laser-straight, striking the center of Aurata's vortex . . . accurate, except that she'd calibrated the markings on the meridian hoop a hairsbreadth off. Only starfire flew out. Not the souls themselves.

She hoped.

Would this tiny sabotage even make a difference? Her thoughts raced as if each second lasted a minute. *If I do this—my only chance to help Rosie, Sam and Luc—Aurata will destroy Mist. If she doesn't get him, the eruption will. So can I sacrifice him to save them? I have to. Mist, forgive me. You wouldn't forgive me if I didn't. No choice.*

The landscape was quaking, the earth beginning to erupt along the canyon floor. Qesoth's brilliance spilled through. Aurata was transforming into her fire shape, taller than before, pure golden brilliance like the sun's corona.

Her followers were crying out—more in shrieking fear than in wonder. As the rocks trembled, two of them slipped off the rim and went plunging down. Aurata took no notice.

"Great Qesoth, fire of creation, manifest in me . . ." She flung her arms at the sky. "*I am Qesoth.*"

And because she was Aetherial, and believed it, her words became the truth.

Mist wasn't sure how to begin. Albin was right: There came a point when Aetherial powers faded and the flesh took over, leaving Aelyr as limited as humans. He sat cross-legged facing Rufus, recalling how he'd felt in Virginia's waterfall when he and Stevie had transformed. An alchemical mix of terror and exhilaration . . .

He was not comfortable, holding his brother's gaze as he recalled vile memories of Rufus's eyes glinting with cruelty and mischief. Mist forced himself to put all that aside, and stared into his brother's soul without flinching. No anger, no judgment. They joined hands. After a time, discomfort fell away.

They met as equals.

Old skills could be recaptured, however rusty. The air shuddered around them as they wove their own web to push back Slahvin's. Deep inside, Mist felt his lost *fylgia*, his connection to the Otherworld, awakening.

His physical form was expanding, unfolding into something draconic, a great salamander sporting claws and fins. Rufus was changing with him, an expression of glee spreading over his face. Touching, they melded and became a twin creature.

Human doubts fell away. There was only Aetheric force and purpose.

Their prison gave way. Walls melted, swirling into coils, vanishing altogether. Slahvin and his gang of seven were revealed, surrounding them with their eyes closed, all their concentration focused on keeping their prisoners caged.

Eight pairs of eyes snapped open as the web collapsed.

In their dark suits they were like common human guards, no less menacing for that. Handguns swept from holsters. Mist and Rufus were outnumbered. Bullets might not touch their eternal essence, but could still rip apart their flesh, inflict hideous damage to their bodies, even death.

To Mist's surprise, they were in the main living room. Through the panoramic window, he saw a ruby dawn, and strange lights dancing on the canyon's edge.

Mistangamesh gazed at each of their captors in turn, rage smoldering low inside him. Their casual strength, their sense of entitlement infuriated him. Slahvin was the worst, a slithery psychopath too far beyond human to be reached.

"Don't move," Slahvin barked.

He'd been a servant to House Ephenaestus, and still served Veropardus and Aurata to this day. However, his sinister, alien aura suggested he was not Felynx at all but something older and darker. Mist could only guess what he really was, or what resentments had poisoned him over the years. Jealousy of Mist, hatred of Rufus? Like a *dysir*, Slahvin's only purpose now was to protect Aurata.

"A dog can only serve one master," said Mist.

This remark appeared to infuriate Slahvin. In a blink, he changed to a serpentine shape of darkest crimson, nearly black, his eyes burning blood-red.

Mist and Rufus, meanwhile, had slipped back nearly to human shape. Regathering their strength they surged again, extruding claws and barbed fins. Uproar broke out among the guards. They were slow to use their guns, as if wary of harming Aurata's brothers. Instead, heat buffeted the air: the energy of Naamon, rising. But the brothers were also creatures of fire and fed upon it. By reflex they flung up shields to deflect the attack. And the shields became wings, each feather a steel-sharp blade.

Slahvin raised a handgun and fired.

Mist-Rufus dodged the bullet, laughing. They divided in two, Rufus capering to draw their attention as Mist spun around behind Slahvin.

Dragon jerked serpent into the air. Rufus lunged, stabbing Slahvin through the gut with a pinion-feather as sharp as a sword. Mist sliced his throat for good measure. He'd thought it would be harder, but Slahvin went down like a sack of rocks and Mist knew he was dead when he saw Slahvin's soul-essence fleeing—a dark transparent snake flying out of him, vanishing into some deeper dimension.

Dying, or reverting to a more primal form.

With their leader gone, the other guards seemed to be at a loss. The brothers broke through their ranks and left them reeling. As one, Mist and Rufus ran and leapt at the huge plate-glass window, spiking it with sharp beaks that caused the whole pane to implode. Over the balcony rail they leapt, glass showering around them, bullets flying past.

Changing again, they landed as lightly as a pair of panthers and ran on all fours towards the bloody fire of sunrise.

Ruby light flooded the desert. The far walls of the canyon glowed and the strangely contorted promontories resembled weird sculptures, striped red and orange and golden-yellow, as if the whole landscape was on fire, flowing with liquid flame.

Stevie looked down in complete terror. The canyon floor appeared to be miles below. Her heartbeat was a single juddering rush and there was no shred of strength in her body. Where was her Aetherial core, her *fylgia*, her hidden powers? She felt entirely human, helpless, petrified.

She stared at the laser beam from the Felixatus piercing the whorl that Aurata had conjured. It was beginning to burn a portal, she saw, like the sun burning paper through a magnifying glass.

The rock platform shook alarmingly. "Hold steady," came a voice from the goddess beside her, a towering, coruscating figure of fire. Qesoth spoke, from far above, with Aurata's voice. "Let Naamon come to us!"

Yards behind them, where Veropardus stood guarding the path, Stevie heard shouts of anger. Her fleeting impression was that Aurata's web-weavers had fled, but Veropardus wouldn't let them past. The sounds were faint beneath the roar of blood in her ears. She didn't look back.

A strange ecstasy filled her, as if she were about to fly right out of her body. The Earth opened its mouth and grinned.

In the maw, a crescent of white-yellow boiling rock, she saw a black spot. The ground shook and rumbled with the terrible deep tearing noise of lava. The base of the canyon split wide open and the air itself pulled apart, creating a vacuum. Sulfurous fumes rushed up to fill the space as oxygen was sucked out.

"I can't breathe," Stevie said, trying to take an Aetherial form that didn't need breath. Her leaden body was not listening. Flames and magma spread, and at the center of her vision—she couldn't tell if it was down in the lava or floating in midair—the black spot went on spinning and growing . . .

All this happened in a bare three seconds. Stevie knew what to do; it was what she'd always planned, and she was already in motion as the world turned inside out around her. She reached for the Felixatus, wrapped both arms around it and clutched the globe close against her chest.

The beam cut out.

"What are you doing?" roared Qesoth-Aurata.

The only thing I can, aborting the process before it runs beyond control.

She stepped off the edge—only to stick like a fly in treacle. The force of the tenfold web was still holding her, strong enough to resist gravity. She felt Qesoth reaching out to seize her, heat scorching her back.

Then Stevie reached deep into her Aetherial self and pulled out the shreds of her power, just enough to stretch the web. She saw her *fylgia*—real or a vision, it didn't matter—leap out and down towards the spinning black spot—creating a silver wire down which she might slide.

Clasping the Felixatus, she launched herself into nothingness. The bonds of the web fractured. The canyon swung beneath her. Choked by the horrible thrill of falling, she heard a voice yelling her name far above, fading as she arrowed towards a black dot in a lake of fire.

———

As they reached the place where the canyon edge extended an arm towards the lookout point, Mist saw a blur of orange-yellow fire at the far end. The tenfold web distorted reality, so he could see no individuals, only a mad dance of light. A group of eleven Aetherials, led by Veropardus, intercepted him and Rufus. Veropardus squared up to Mist with an expression of pure, gloating hatred.

"Where do you think you are going?"

"To the ritual," Mist said very softly. He wasn't sure how he looked now: part animal, part Aetherial, half in and half out of the Dusklands; a mess.

"You are not invited."

"Nor are you, by the look of things. What went wrong?"

Veropardus's gaunt face turned sour. He went nearly purple with loathing. He raised a hand and commanded his cohorts, "Take them."

At that instant, shots rang out from the house balcony and two of Vero's men fell.

"Oh shit," said Rufus, and laughed.

"Stop firing!" Veropardus shrieked at Slahvin's guards, but the rest of his companions were diving for cover, vanishing behind rocks below the rim of the ravine.

The bullets ceased. Only three Felynx remained in the scarlet-washed landscape. Mist, and Rufus, and Veropardus.

All Mist saw was the creature who had murdered Fela. That could never be forgotten.

He shot a glance at Rufus, who looked back and nodded.

Veropardus came raging at them in a huge tiger-like shape. Fluidly they slid away from his claws. Rufus slashed him across the abdomen. Mist impaled him with a wing barb as long as a spear and katana-sharp, piercing up into his heart. Flinging him down onto the rock, Mist slit his throat. "For Fela," he murmured as he made the cut, severing the head for good measure. It was damage enough to force the soul-essence from him. Finally, Mist hefted the head and body over the canyon edge to bounce down the near-vertical walls . . .

Towards a river of lava.

"Steady on," said Rufus. "Don't you know that Oliver got burned at the stake in one of his previous lives? Hasn't he suffered enough?"

Mist stood panting for breath, sick at heart. "For today, perhaps."

"The brothers Ephenaestus are back," said Rufus, pumping a fist in the air.

Some of Aurata's followers raised their heads from their hiding places, but none tried to stop Mist and Rufus as they set out along the rugged, narrow spine toward the lookout rock. Violent tremors threatened to throw them over the side. In front, a section of the arch collapsed, leaving a great gap between them and the platform where fiery figures were crying out in awe and fear. He saw the tall burning-angel shape of Aurata, Stevie tiny beside her.

Dropping to all fours, Mist ran and leapt the gap. He nearly lost his footing, but clawed his way onto the last stretch of the path and the plate of rock. Rufus was just behind him. Landscape and sky were drenched in red. Below, Jigsaw Canyon seethed with lava.

Too late. Mist felt the tenfold pressure and saw the whorl of distorted reality that his sister had created. He saw the ominous black hole spinning at the center.

He saw Stevie grab the Felixatus and leap—

"*No!*"

He left Rufus standing, rushed past the raging column of fire that was Aurata and threw himself after Stevie. Heat blasted into his face. The rock platform broke under his feet as the canyon itself begin to crumble, shards falling with him into the void.

21

Aurata

Stevie was looking up at green light dappling a ceiling of black rock . . .

No. No. Not again!

The silhouette of Persephone stood over her, unspeaking. With a huge effort Stevie pointed upward, struggling with her whole being to convey her urgent need to stay in the upper world. *There is more at stake than losing my life. Take me afterwards, I don't care—but not now. Still so much to do!*

Persephone raised a hand. She was an immense black archangel, her raised palm a command to go back. Stevie recalled her words, *No one comes here except of their own free will.*

The next moment, Stevie hit a hard surface, rolling. Her body thrummed with the impact. Bruising pain in every bone drove out her breath. Sharp objects stabbed into her ribs. For long seconds, she couldn't move. All around her was pale nothingness: a thick, swirling white fog.

She was lying across the Felixatus, hugging it. The hard edges of the metal framework and the base dug into her, but the important thing was that she'd kept hold and protected it. And the inner sphere was still alive. The unreleased energy of a million Felynx vibrated, sending darts of static into her.

The surface on which she'd landed was cold quartz: sloping, lumpy and rough-textured. She could barely see her own hands in the fog veil.

Terror lay on her like a solid weight. Had she gone nearly blind, or landed in some Aetheric limbo? Trapped in a dimension with no escape? Fine, only if she knew that her sabotage had worked.

The cloud around her was so dense that it hurt her lungs to breathe. Half-stunned, she pushed herself up onto one hand. There was nothing to see in any direction—until she looked upwards and saw a small darkish patch with ragged edges, like an eclipsed sun.

The portal?

A few bright streaks arced down like meteors, gone as soon as she blinked. Falling debris, optical illusion . . . or pursuit?

Her plan—to punch the portal half a degree off so it wouldn't connect with Naamon, then throwing herself through before the hole spread to engulf the world—had been her only chance to thwart Aurata. Whether her actions would help her imprisoned friends or Mist in the slightest, she'd no way of knowing. She might have made things a hundred times worse. *I followed my fylgia, my intuition*, she thought. *They told me that the shadow-self always knows the right path. Oh, my dear friends, you'd better be right.*

With an effort she pulled the Felixatus from under herself and set it upright. Her palms were bruised from holding on so tight. The metalwork bore a few small dents, but no obvious damage to the structure or mechanism. Within the shell of engraved symbolic animals, the central globe shone like a small moon in the gloom.

Whump. A weight hit her from behind, flattening her. Torrid heat overwhelmed her existing pain as multiple hot irons dug into her arms. Her ritual robe caught fire, and pieces floated away like burning paper. A voice grated in her ear, "Fela, what have you done?"

Aurata-Qesoth.

Stevie changed shape without thinking. Deep instinct kicked her into Fela's racing shape, a creature of muscle and sinew, coated in striped silver fur. The fur was her only defense against Aurata's searing heat.

Twisting her neck, Stevie looked into a leonine face inside a caul of flame. Eyes like white-hot suns. A stench of singeing hair, sulfur and burning metal. Her radiance turned the fog to steam, creating turbulence full of ghostly shapes.

The red-hot irons gripping her were Aurata's fingertips. "Let go," Stevie gasped. "Please. I can't run anywhere."

"What did you do?"

"Opened a way to the Spiral, as you wanted."

The voice inside the fire was fierce. "You betrayed me."

"How can that be a surprise?"

"Oh, you still have the spirit for sarcasm, little slave?"

Those two words broke any illusion that Aurata had a shred of compassion for her. In the days of Azantios, their relationship had been about possession. Never love.

The burning grip loosened. Aurata jerked her forcibly into a sitting position, shook her like a doll. Even in Tashralyr shape, Stevie was weak. Every joint shrieked with pain and her muscles felt like wet string. Sizzling heat and raw cold played cruel sensory games.

"Look up," said Aurata, pointing at the greyed-out sun. The disk was drifting away, shrinking, pulling in its tattered edges like tentacles.

"The portal," Stevie whispered. "What's happening up there? Where's Mist?"

"I don't know." *Wrong answer*, thought Stevie; *how can she not know, unless he escaped?* "The real question is, where have you brought us? What is this . . . nothingness?"

Inside Aurata's controlled rage, there was a hint of fear. Stevie replied, "I've no idea. And if you're furious enough to kill me—again—just get on with it."

"Oh, I'm tempted. I can trust no one, *no one*. Those who are loyal are too weak to defend me, while others I thought worthy to be my equals turn against me."

"Because your plan couldn't work!" Stevie ignored the pain, seizing a last chance to defy her. "You can't meld Vaeth and Spiral together and rule both. It's insane. You don't care who gets hurt, even your own family. You were my only hope of helping our friends to escape from Albin, but I knew you wouldn't, because you don't care. Finding out they're your family was an inconvenience, wasn't it?"

"Not true."

"All I hope is that I prevented devastation on Earth. This isn't about a grand plan to rule the universe—which never works for anyone—it's about stopping your megalomania!"

"Have you finished?"

"No. I could have loved you like a sister, Aurata. But you're no better than any dictator on Earth. You don't give a damn who gets hurt while you grab your power, because you're convinced you have a divine right. God's will, Qesoth's will, what's the difference? I'm shouting at a brick wall, aren't I? You *know* you're right."

"And if I were sitting in my dictator's palace listening to this diatribe I would have you dragged out and shot." Aurata's voice was a blade. "One thing I learned from Earth is that if you don't grab power, someone else will. This is not over, Stevie. You've slowed me down, that's all. Your function was only to ignite the process, because true power isn't in the Felixatus. Power is Qesoth herself."

"So where are your followers?"

"Fled, or perished. They tried, but they weren't true Felynx. Too young, too weak. I don't need them."

Stevie drew back. Above, the remaining dot of the portal vanished. "You can't channel Qesoth. The primal powers are long gone. Why should they listen to you anyway?"

"You are so wrong." Aurata stretched out her arms, two long jets of fire. "I told you, Aetherial dreams become reality, if the will is strong enough." She rose to her feet, and kept rising until she was twelve feet tall, a blazing demon. "Qesoth is already here. She manifests through me. Every realm shall bow to her and despair!"

A whip of lightning lashed Stevie's chest and sent her tumbling backwards. Her protective Fela form evaporated. She lay gasping in agony on the rocks, one side of her body freezing, the other scorched.

"Can I trust you with one task, at least?" came a voice out of the flames. "Take care of the Felixatus until I return. I never wished harm to anyone, but you *must* learn to obey me."

Stevie found the strength to sit up. Edging away, she gathered the Felixatus into her arms. "Where are you going?"

"To find the source of this fog and clear it. Then we'll see. We shall literally *see*."

Aurata-Qeosth arrowed upward like a missile; a roaring flame, leaving a jet trail. Steam swirled in the space where she'd been. Stevie was alone once more in limbo, wondering if Mist was even still alive.

Sobbing with pain, she found her feet and began to walk in hope of finding a landmark, some clue as to where she might be. *I'm Aetherial*, she told herself. *We heal quickly. We can change reality, if the will is strong enough . . . Oh, fuck, how did I get into this mess?*

She was climbing a shallow slope. With every step, the clammy haze thickened. Specters moved all around her, forming and dissipating. She caught a brief flicker of her *fylgia* ahead, like a candle flame, transmitting a warning. A ruthless presence was gathering and moving towards her.

It was mere illusion, she told herself. Yet the wraiths continued to shepherd her every step.

Mistangamesh and Rufus each broke the other's fall, tumbling over and over down a slope of loose rock. In Aetherial shape, they were a tangle of spines and feathers, scales and fur and muscular clawed limbs. Rufus rose to all fours, panting like a leopard between curses.

"Where the fuck's Aurata?" he snarled. "Can't see a damned thing. Mist?"

"I'm here." Mist let his damaged Otherworld form shrink to human size, keeping only the blue-black nimbus of his Felynx self around him. "Were you calling to me, or describing this murk?"

"This isn't mist, it's what they used to call a pea-souper. We must be on a mountaintop to be inside cloud like this."

Mist raised his head and shouted, "Stevie!"

His call carried, but received no answer. The pale rock and billowing fog raised a primitive fear, verging on claustrophobia. For a split second he was human Adam again, terrified in the trenches, suffocating on the smoke of battle . . .

"Great," said Rufus. "Now we're wonderfully screwed. Where the hell are we?"

"Still alive, at least. In the Spiral, I think."

"Yeah, but which realm?"

"Sibeyla? I can't tell," said Mist. "This fog . . . It has to be Albin's work."

"Why do you think that?"

Mist raised his head, scenting the air. "I'm getting the same bad feeling as when he held us in his tower. I can't define it. Same cold smell."

"Is it me, or is it full of elementals?"

"Rufus . . . I think that the fog is *made* of elementals."

"Oh, no. That's too creepy even for me. I need to sit down. One of Slahvin's bullets winged me."

Rufus was a dark shape hunched on the rocks, his long hair turning to rat's tails in the damp. "You can't sit down," said Mist. "We have people to find."

"And how is wandering in random circles going to achieve that?" Rufus snapped. "Two minutes. Let's get our bearings."

"All right, but it isn't like you to admit weakness, or to start talking sense."

"Mm." Rufus, now back in his familiar form, glared as Mist knelt beside him. "It's not like you, either, to fight like a berserker and start killing people all over the place."

"Two creatures, who both deserved it," Mist said softly. "They should have gone into the Abyss, from which there's no return."

"I'm not arguing, but I've never in my life seen you kill anyone. I'm impressed."

"Don't be. And shut up. I'm not proud of it."

"Don't feel bad. Sometimes it has to be done." Rufus gave a sigh that turned into a growl. "Look what Aurata's brought us to. All I did was try to talk her out of this lunacy! I'm not her enemy. She knows she's everything to me. I wanted the fun Aurata back, the one who took me to Venice and Las Vegas, made me feel life was worth living after all. That's all I wanted. Not this raving nutcase she's turned into."

Mist put his hand on Rufus's shoulder. "You wanted an illusion. We've all been trying to save her from herself, while she looks down on our feeble attempts from a great height with the disdain we probably deserve." He stood up. "There's someone coming."

"What? Who?"

Figures took shape through the clammy shroud . . . a small Aetherial army. Mist made out a group of at least fifty Aelyr in crouched reptilian forms, clad in dark armor and bristling with spines and claws. He recognized this form as similar to the hunting mode taken by Initiators: those Aelyr who chose to pursue and brand "virgin" Vaethyr entering the Spiral for the first time. These were different—more of an organized unit—but apparently carrying Initiator-style weapons: crossbows armed with glowing, drug-tipped bolts.

A voice shouted, "By the command of Tyrynaia, don't move!"

"Oh, good." Rufus rose and leaned on Mist. "Just when you think things can't get worse, a bunch of prancing ninjas from the Spiral Court turns up."

"Who might help us?" said Mist.

They waited, resigned to capture since fleeing blindly was a worse option.

The unit spread to surround them, fading in and out of view in the greyness. Their commander was a high Aetherial clothed in peacock shades of bronze and green, feathers shivering in his hair.

Mist recognized him. The peacock-man was the spokesman for the Spiral Court, their leader, in effect, at least until another rose to replace him. He'd conducted the failed trial against Rufus. "It's Vaidre Daima."

"So I see." Rufus groaned. "Wonderful! This is all we need. Let's run for it."

Mist caught his arm. "No. He could help. He let you go free, didn't he?"

"Only because there was no evidence against me. The trial was all about Albin grandstanding, and not really about me at all. I'm sure he hates my guts. It's a tradition."

Mist said firmly, "This isn't about you, either. Come on, he's no enemy."

"I wouldn't take bets on that."

Reaching them, Vaidre Daima gave a formal nod, his head feathers rustling. "Rufus Ephenaestus? And . . . Mistangamesh? We had reports of an illicit portal torn from Vaeth. How did you come here?"

"Through that very portal," said Mist. The warriors pressed closer, their eyes gleaming red. He put up his palms to pacify them. "Wait—before you detain us—it wasn't our doing. We were trying to prevent someone . . . we fell through . . . look, it's desperately urgent we find certain Aetherials. We throw ourselves on your mercy."

"Mist speaks for himself," said Rufus. "I'm not throwing myself anywhere."

"Explain. We have a dire situation here. Who or what made the portal?"

Mist hesitated. Even now he was reluctant to name his own sister. "Someone tried to summon Qesoth."

"*Qesoth?*"

"There's no time to explain. If you help us search, I'll explain as we go. Where are we?"

"On a boundary between Sibeyla and Asru, but the structure of the Spiral is dangerously unstable. We're under siege. If we stay in the open much longer, we'll succumb to worse than the cold. The end is closing in . . . so I tell you, if Qesoth were to appear, I'd welcome her."

Mist and Rufus exchanged a glance. Mist said, "Is this fog Albin's doing?"

Vaidre Daima's eyes narrowed. "How did you know?"

"Because we encountered him not long ago," said Mist. "'Fanatical' is an understatement. We sent a messenger to warn the Spiral Court. Iola?"

Vaidre Daima waved a command at his guards to lower their weapons. He began to guide the party downhill. Mist hoped he knew where he was going in the thick grey pall.

"Iola reached us, but there was nothing we could do. Albin wove this fog some five nightfalls ago. It smothers everything."

"I don't understand. When we met him, which was only a few days ago, or so I thought, he had control of just one small island with a tower and few hundred elemental servants."

"Well, now he has control of nearly the whole Spiral. We've no idea how he became so powerful so fast, nor how to stop him. Aelyr refugees have flooded into Asru from the other realms to warn us, too late. It was a stealth attack. This stuff has swamped the whole Spiral. Every realm."

"It's only fog," Rufus said uncertainly. "Isn't it?"

Vaidre Daima's expression was stony. "No. It's a pernicious force that sucks out Aetherial life force and turns us into—I hesitate to use terms like 'ghosts' or 'shells.' Let me say ice elementals, who become Albin's slaves, with no will left of their own."

Memories rose of Sam, Rosie and Lucas, turning to frozen statues. "Every realm?" Mist's voice was raw. "But . . . he captured three friends of ours. One of them is the Gatekeeper himself. The entire Spiral?"

"Only Asru holds out. In fact, only Tyrynaia. That's our last refuge." Vaidre Daima swept his hand through the vapor, stirring it into whorls. "This substance—we've called up all our powers, woven every possible web to push it back, but there's no defense. It creeps everywhere. Even the Spiral can't defend itself."

"You're saying that the Otherworld is effectively . . . dying?"

Vaidre Daima paused, struggling. "Or being held hostage."

"So why the fuck's he done this?" Rufus put in. "Come on, I was accused of all sorts in my time, but I never tried to poison the entire Otherworld, nor to rip the Earth apart. I get blamed for everything, but I'm a rank amateur alongside this! What the hell does Albin think he's doing?"

Vaidre Daima's eyes glazed with rage. "What he's always wanted: to sever the Spiral completely from the Earth. In trying to persuade others to his cause, he lost the argument. So he's taken matters into his own hands. He has overwhelmed us with a force that we never anticipated and cannot seem to fight."

"He's out of his bleeding mind," said Rufus. "I always thought so."

"Rufus is right," Mist said softly. "When we met him, he'd isolated himself. He was full of crazy but calculated plans to change the cosmos." *Like Aurata*, he thought. "Do we all end up mad, if we live too long?"

"I should hope not," Vaidre Daima retorted. "But, as with the human world, it takes only one or two maniacs to cause havoc."

"Oh, this is priceless." Rufus gave a raw laugh. "You always think you can leap into a fast car and escape. You never think you'll be forced into a corner where everything's fucked, no one is going be rescued and we're all actually going to die."

"Rufe, shut up," said Mist. "You're not helping."

"He is being realistic," said the court leader. "And this is my fault. I made a huge miscalculation, the greatest mistake of my service upon the Spiral Court: not in releasing you, Rufus Ephenaestus, but in letting Albin of Sibeyla go free."

"How could you have known?" said Mist.

"I should have paid closer attention. Our best theory is that Albin is more than an individual. He represents the Cold Force that emanates from Brawth. He's become the avatar of a particular ideology that is opposed to the Spiral being connected to Vaeth, and worse: a force opposed to the way Aelyr and Vaethyr live, opposed to humans and even to life itself. And his solution is to flood all but the highest peaks of Sibeyla with this deathly miasma."

His words were drowned by thunder.

High above, the sky exploded. Balls of flame rolled through the clouds, roaring. The storm boiled until the fabric of the Spiral itself began to tilt and shudder.

Vaidre Daima looked flatly terrified. "What is that?"

Rufus grinned, hanging on to Mist's arm for balance. "I think you'll find that is Aurata, trying to clear the fog."

"A cosmic battle," said Mist. "Qesoth against Brawth."

"Come with me!" Vaidre Daima shouted, and they all ran, seeking shelter that did not exist because the storm raged everywhere.

"Mist?" Stevie called as she made her way uphill, blind in the moisture-blanket and deafened by the rumbling chaos far above. "Aurata?"

She wasn't quite alone. The souls trapped inside the Felixatus thrummed frantically against her chest. She felt like a goddess with a whole world in her embrace; and at the same time like a lost child, half-dead with terror. Her *fylgia* drifted in front of her, a tiny dappled leopard.

She was so cold now, she felt she was drowning in liquid nitrogen. Had this happened to the specters around her? There was nothing left of them but amorphous ice entities, presumably extensions of Albin's will. Numb, she could only follow her *fylgia*, the part of her subconscious that was supposed to know best.

She stumbled on jagged rocks and paused, shaken. There was still nothing to see but fleece layers in all directions. She might step over a cliff, for all she knew. The thought made her stomach twist. Once was enough.

Storm flashes from above thinned the murk enough to reveal hints of alabaster landscape. In the cloud ahead, a shape firmed up; a featureless grey spire that remained stable as she edged closer.

Albin's tower.

What a relief to find a landmark, even one so hostile.

She looked up. Flares swept overhead like gigantic fireballs rolling through thunderclouds. The ground lurched. The substance of the Spiral was warping, stretching and snapping back in ear-splitting sonic booms.

The greatest unearthly power of Aetherials was to alter the very fabric of the realms. *That's how we shaped the Spiral in the first place, and why it's always in flux,* Mist said in her memory. *We're spinners and weavers of reality.*

Destroyers, too, she thought. Her dizzy moment alarmed her *fylgia*. Balking, it tried to guide her to the left, but she kept going straight ahead. The tower was her only anchor point in the chaos.

There were no waters of Melusiel anywhere—even without sight, she would have sensed or smelled their distinctive character—only rock. That meant the tower must have moved.

The slope grew steep and treacherous as she neared the tall thin spire. Pausing, she took off what was left of her ritual robe and knotted it to form a sling to hold the Felixatus. With it hung over her shoulder, she now she had both hands free to climb. She still wore smoke-stained jeans, a sweatshirt, and a dewy hint of Fela's fur yet clung to her hands. Changing form was about entering a different realm of reality, so she hadn't burst out of her clothes like a werewolf. However, she was so chilled that she might as well have been naked.

The farther she went, the thicker and heavier the fog grew, slowing her down as if she waded through water. She could barely breathe.

She reached a flat area like a courtyard where she stood shivering and panting for breath. Directly ahead was the tower's entrance, its narrow triangular shape an echo of the spire itself. Pale figures solidified around her. Albin's army, coming to capture her? No. Nothing was moving. She was in a small forest of statues, featureless and translucent like resin: Albin's victims. Were they Aelyr who'd come to challenge him, or supporters he didn't need anymore?

"Can you hear me?" she called out. She caught her breath at the knowledge of who must be among them. "Rosie? Sam?"

No answer.

Warily she wove between the figures. They all looked the same: ice sculptures in human shape. Yet she could still see blurred hints of faces, obscured behinds masks of thick frosted glass.

With growing urgency she worked her way between then, going recklessly close to discern individuality. Yes . . . the harder she looked, the more she saw remnants of personality. Most had Melusiel faces. Outrage brought her to tears. How dare Albin do this?

In front of the tower's entrance, three figures stood in a close, familiar group. She looked into their blurred features, half-closing her eyes for clearer definition. With a silent cry, she recognized them. Rosie, Sam, Lucas.

"I came back for you," she whispered. "Can you speak? Rosie, Luc? Do you know me?"

There was no reaction from any of the three. Tears froze on her cheeks.

"I don't know if you can hear me," she said softly, "but I'm not leaving. I'll be with you, whatever happens."

She set down the Felixatus at her feet. As she straightened up, a hand gripped her wrist.

She jumped with violent shock. It was Lucas who'd moved. His fingers felt brittle, and so cold—dry-ice cold—that his touch made her gasp. She gladly endured the pain, letting him take her warmth. She eased around until she could hold Rosie's hand too, the four of them forming a circle. Then, with all that was left of her Aetherial strength, she willed the heat of her body into theirs.

This is where it ends. If I can't save you, I'll stand and perish with you.

"Albin's fortress," said Vaidre Daima.

He raised both arms to stop his guards in their tracks. Mist saw the familiar sight, like a grey tusk planted in the clouds.

"I thought you were taking us to Tyrynaia," said Rufus. "Are you lost?"

Vaidre Daima made no answer, but his face was grim, one shade off utter panic. "Halt. We're going no closer."

"Why not?" Mist asked quietly.

"No one who went there has returned. We'll retreat."

"And the tower will probably follow us," said Rufus.

At this offhand remark, Vaidre Daima's face blanched. *He's no warrior,* thought Mist. He was an administrator: chairman, judge or mediator, at home amid the coils of the Spiral Court, but a hopeless leader in the field. Few Aelyr were lovers of weapons or combat; why bother, when they had the greater power to alter reality itself? At this moment, the Spiral Court appeared to hold no power at all.

He thought, then, that Vaidre Daima was brave even to have ventured out of the city.

"Stay here," said Mist. He started towards the tower alone.

"Come back, I command you!"

"Mist!" Rufus shouted.

He ignored them. He heard one of the warriors speak, and Vaidre Daima answering, "No! Disarm your weapons. Let him go."

Mist didn't look back. The ground lurched beneath him, and as the rocks swept steeply upward he clung on for his life, grateful not to have the additional menace of crossbow bolts flying at him. He tried to expand his Aetheric body but the press of Albin's power was too much. The air burned his lungs.

Overhead, the battle gave bursts of light, enough for him to see that the tower was still poised on its small island: a plate of quartzite, rough-edged as if had sheared from a slab and been carried here by the massive force of a glacier. Occasionally he glimpsed the equally pale, smooth rock on which the island sat. Then cloud swirled in again to conceal everything. Once or twice he felt the island shift alarmingly, like a curling stone gliding on ice.

He ran the last few steps, weaving between statues. Right by the entrance he found Stevie, too late; she was already joined in a rigid dance with their three friends. They were all as stiff, white and lifeless as mannikins. The amber of her hair was vanishing beneath a thickening layer of frost.

"Stevie," he gasped.

Her gaze rolled towards him. It was clear to him that she couldn't move her head. His heart nearly gave out with despair. He struggled to hear the words from her near-paralyzed lips.

"You . . . oh, thank goodness. Mist, how . . ."

"Come away. You can't help them."

"I have to."

"Please come with me."

"I can't."

He saw then how Lucas's hand was fused to her wrist, and hers to Rosie's. He reached out, intending to free her using his own remaining warmth, but she growled, "Don't!"

"I'm not leaving you like this."

"Mist," she said, her eyes swiveling in the direction of the spire. "Their *fylgias*. You need to release them from Albin. Please!"

In the blurred glassy face of Sam, who stood opposite Stevie between Rosie and Luc, Mist saw the briefest flash of twin aqua sparks.

"Hold on," he said. With no further argument, he ducked through the narrow slit into the dim bluish glow of the tower. He crossed the floor, raced up carved spiral stairs, through the middle chamber where Albin had held them, and up the second flight towards the highest room. The climb was longer and more treacherous than he remembered.

Mist realized then that he trusted Stevie's intuition more deeply than his own. He suspected she was the only one among them who actually understood what needed doing—and had no hesitation in sacrificing herself to attain it.

He was beyond fear. Briefly he wondered what forms Albin and Aurata took as they battled above the ocean of fog, and if they would ever call a truce.

Trapped *fylgias*. How would Albin contain them? In a vessel of some kind?

Mist entered the chamber, recalling details from his trance-dream: a cone-shaped space with a bier of blue lapis stone across its center, with a shelf of arcane instruments beneath a narrow, open embrasure.

All was as he expected, with one difference. It came as a visceral shock to find that the chamber wasn't empty after all. Albin was there.

Lofty and pure white in his feathered cloak, he stood on the bier with his eyes closed and palms raised to the ceiling as if weaving a solitary web. Light fell around him, shining, glittering.

He was in a trance, Mist realized. Fighting Aurata.

The wild atmosphere and warping of reality carried a taste of Albin's thoughts.

She came out of nowhere, falling from a dark sun in the Spiral sky—Qesoth, the primal force, the Fire of Fires. Of course she would come. By his actions, he called her.

The frozen rock of his soul-essence contained no fear, no emotion beyond a calm feeling of triumph. Albin knew himself to be the most powerful being the Spiral had ever seen, Brawth, the end of all things . . .

He rose to join eternal battle: energy forever warring against entropy.

As she vaporized his wintry web, he rewove it with an effortless flow of bitter cold. Yet he was no more able to quench Qesoth's fire than the ocean could extinguish a volcano on the seabed.

Neither could win, Mist knew. They could only rage and fight until their war reduced the fabric of the Spiral to a soup of component atoms.

Feverishly he looked around the chamber for clues. The only objects were those on the shelf; odd instruments, bottles and pieces of crystal. The *anametris* sphere, a small orb that resembled the heart of the Felixatus? No. Albin had said it was a key used to open portals in a different realm, not a device to hold *fylgias*. Mist opened a small brass box, and inside he saw three blue-white shining pebbles. Tiny shapes moved inside, like trapped fireflies. His mouth was bone-dry but he knew without doubt that he'd found what he sought. He took the pebbles and slipped them into a pocket.

"Mistangamesh," said a voice above him.

Albin was awake, glaring at him.

Oh, shit, he thought, as the weight and arctic power of a furious Sibeylan lord descended and flattened him to the floor.

"How dare you invade my domain? Did you summon Qesoth to attack me?"

A snake head poised itself at Mist's throat, the fangs pricking his skin, so cold they burned. The snake was Albin's hand. His own Aetherial powers were drained, numb. He was certain this was his last moment, that he'd soon be another ice carving in Albin's collection.

"No, I did not summon her! I've spent days trying to stop her."

The smooth white forehead wrinkled. "Trying to stop her?"

"She may have transformed into Qesoth, but she is also my sister, Aurata," he rasped, forcing out the last of his breath. "You won't win. You deserve each other."

He thought the blue triad of Albin's eyes would burst from his head. With a swift, powerful move, the Sibeylan shot upright, dragging Mist off his feet as if he weighed nothing. They were floating above the floor. Albin's cloak became wings and he was moving towards the embrasure.

Helpless, Mist found himself pushed out into thin air, with the slender stem of the tower dwindling away below. Still holding him, Albin squeezed through and launched himself off the sill. Wings beating, he powered upwards into the fog.

Mist caught a glimpse of deep blue sky, and the gleaming peaks of Sibeylan mountains like islands in a milky ocean.

"Listen to me," Mist said again. "Neither of you can win."

In response, Albin dropped him.

First he felt rushing air, then, as he hit the ground—excruciating pain.

He managed to force out an aura, producing a framework of fins that was more a broken umbrella than a set of wings, but enough to ease his landing into a long, painful slide. He lay groaning, laughing weakly at the absurdity of his situation: at the simple fact that he was still alive.

All he could see was the side of the spire, a few rocks, the wretched fog mantle, and a lightning storm tearing the cosmos far above. No sign of Stevie. Apparently he'd landed on the far side of the tower and he must crawl around to find her, if only he could move.

He forced himself to all fours and then to his feet, climbing around the tower's base with one hand on the wall for support, until he found her again. Her eyes flashed, as if to ask, *What happened?*

Plainly she could no longer speak. He drew the three pebbles from his pocket and held them out in the palm of his hand. Their light was dim. Nothing changed. Stevie gazed at him, her eyes bright, intense, desperate, and they both knew that nothing would change unless Albin's power broke.

Abruptly the storm settled.

A comet streaked towards the ground. The Spiral ceased trembling, utter silence fell. Only the fog remained.

Stevie saw Aurata land, perhaps thirty paces away down the tumbled rocks. Her aura was a golden oval, hot enough to make the fog hiss into steam.

She staggered, then pulled herself upright, every curve of her leonine form expressing fury. Her brightness thinned the haze around her, revealing a wider radius of flat, pallid stone.

Stevie was facing away from the tower, which meant she could observe, over Sam's shoulder, all that was happening below. Aurata's glow revealed figures Stevie hadn't noticed before: a troop of dark-clad Aetherials, draconic in appearance. She saw a taller man in bronze-green ceremonial robes, and a bedraggled, tawny creature whom she realized was Rufus.

"Vaidre Daima and some warriors from Tyrynaia," Mist murmured. "Floundering."

Aurata turned around slowly, taking in every detail. Her gaze drifted upward to the tip of Albin's stronghold. Her face was a smear at this distance, but her reactions were clear enough: frustrated rage, and swift calculation.

"I should go down to them," said Mist. "I'll come back as soon as I can."

I'm not going anywhere, she told him silently. *Be careful.*

Before he went, he placed the three pebbles on the lens of the silk-wrapped Felixatus. Stevie saw her own *fylgia* curl protectively around them, like a mother cat around kittens. She would have smiled, if she could. Then she watched Mist stumbling away and realized, her breath catching, that he was physically hurt and moving only by willpower.

A fresh arrival startled her. Albin dropped out of the sky near Aurata.

Stevie observed his wings morphing back into a feathered cloak. Undamaged, untouchable, he looked as swan-pale and arrogant as ever.

He and Aurata faced each other as if nothing else existed. Vaidre Daima's party moved forward. Albin only stood taller, like a master sorcerer confronting a band of insolent small children. Mist, reaching the troop, put up his arm to signal, *Wait!*

"That is Aurata?" said Vaidre Daima. "She must also be captured."

Stevie heard every word in the silence. At least her Aetherial hearing was still functioning. She guessed, then, that Sam, Luc and Rosie might be aware and listening.

"Right, and how will that help?" said Rufus. "She's our only defense against Albin, as far as I can see. Got anything better?"

"We need to detain them *both*," Vaidre added in a chilly tone. "This conflict must cease."

"Yeah, good luck with that."

Vaidre Daima called out, "In the name of the Spiral Court, I demand your immediate surrender."

Albin responded with a sneer. Aurata, not even looking round, asked, "Who is that?"

"I'm Vaidre Daima, elected of the Spiral Court." His deep voice cracked and he cleared his throat. "My lord Albin Wilder of the House of Sibeyla,

I demand your surrender. Under the laws of the Spiral Court, you've violated every natural right of Aetherials to live freely in or out of the Spiral."

"I do not recognize your laws." Albin stood cold and defiant, his blue eyes and jewel forming a bright triangle in his skull-white face.

"My lady Aurata Theliet Ephenaestus of the Felynx, I demand your surrender also."

Aurata laughed. "Oh, do try. This battle is between Qesoth and Brawth. You are a mouse trying to place itself between lions."

"You are both now in the Spiral Court's custody." His voice was hoarse. "My authority—"

"Self-appointed, ebbing with every breath. What authority?" said Albin. "Every realm and all Aelyr shall be absorbed by my will. There'll be no one left to 'detain' me." He pointed at Mist and Rufus. "Did you bring these degenerate Vaethyr to help you? A brave try, but pointless."

Stevie felt deceptive warmth creeping into her, a desire to sleep. Hopelessly she thought, *If Mist and I hadn't tried to break Aurata's power, perhaps she would have defeated Albin—or it might have been like throwing a nuclear warhead into the Spiral. How the hell were we supposed to make the right choice?*

"Why?" Vaidre Daima's tone weakened. He sounded . . . heartbroken. Indicating Albin's spectral slaves near the tower, he said, "Why would you do this to your own people, friends, family? Why?"

Albin was unmoved. "You've long known my desire for separation of the Spiral from Vaeth. It can't be a surprise. I tried to persuade, but no one listened. I lost patience. The whole Spiral shall be drowned in elemental fog forever; only the high peaks of Sibeyla will stand clear, where the pure of heart can gather. There are not many of us, I can tell you. The Gates will be frozen, the Spiral sealed."

"This is an affront to Aelyr and Vaethyr in all realms! You cannot do this!"

Albin's pale lips flattened. "What is an affront is that some renegade"—he indicated Aurata—"has tried to burn the Spiral to ruins. *That* is your reward for refusing to acknowledge my warnings. Earth-loving traitors—not content with leaking human pollution into our pristine realms—are trying to split the Otherworld at the seams. If not for me, this avatar of Qesoth would have burned us all."

Aurata listened to all this with mystifying patience.

"Release your white web, Albin," said Vaidre Daima. "You can't maintain it. You cannot keep the Gates shut."

"Oh, can't I? I have the Gatekeeper—the last of his kind, I trust."

Vaidre Daima had no answer. Stevie's breathing quickened: she was horrified to witness his helplessness. Albin went on, "With no one to attend the gates and portals to Vaeth, I can do as I wish. And my first act will be to dissolve the Spiral Court." He pointed at Rufus. "Ah, look! Is anyone surprised to see Rufus Dionys Ephenaestus at the root of this invasion? You let him go free, Vaidre Daima. Now see the result. He brings creatures of fire to attack us."

"Hey, I was trying to *stop* her," Rufus retorted. "Wish I hadn't bothered! Aurata, I'm sorry. What I wouldn't give to see this idiot fried by Qesoth's wrath!"

"Too late now," Aurata said lightly over her shoulder. "This isn't your fault, Rufus. I knew you'd betray me. You do the same to everyone."

"Fair comment, but please. You're never going to be the new Queen Malikala."

"That wasn't my aim."

"But weren't we having fun, sweet sister, before this obsession took over? What's wrong with living for the moment? Why's everyone got to stamp their jackboots into the world?"

"Oh, that's fine coming from you, with your boasting about bringing down governments, winning wars single-handed. Fun, Rufus?"

"Well, I'm over it now," he said in a low tone. "This is how centuries of arrogant self-delusion end. In a bruised heap in the fog. And yet I still love you."

"And yet I still love *you*," she echoed. "I was trying to create a new world. Albin is the one who's intent on destroying it."

Rufus moved to her side, openly sneering at Albin. "And you dared to put *me* on trial? How do you weigh a few mistakes against your own ruthless dogma? You do realize that once you've turned everyone into wraiths, you'll have no one to preach at?"

"And what a relief that will be." Albin stared, and Rufus retreated to Mist's side, his face dark with helpless anger.

Aurata took a step closer to Albin, her presence strangely soft and calm despite her radiant heat. "You had your chance against my brother. Your only concern now is me."

The Aetherial warriors made no move to approach the pair. They were transfixed, as if Albin and Aurata were central characters in a play. Stevie even saw a few of them unfolding from warrior-shape into a gentler Aelyr form as if they'd entirely forgotten their purpose.

"My lady, do I know you?" Albin said softly. "I think that only someone highborn of Naamon would have the impertinence to challenge me as you have. Show yourself. Show your natural form."

Aurata gave a small shrug and let her fire slide away like a falling cloak. She stood there in humanoid shape, smaller yet losing none of her presence.

Albin's face moved. His jaw lengthened. Uncertainty flickered in his eyes. "Maia?"

"Now you see," she said.

22

The Eye of the Cauldron

"*Maia?*" Albin's voice was hoarse with disbelief.

Something was happening to him. Mist saw his power begin palpably to slip. His face turned ashen with plain, numb shock.

"It took you long enough to recognize your onetime wife," she said bitterly.

"How many centuries since I looked upon your face? Yet as soon as your glamour dropped, I knew you."

Rufus whispered in Mist's ear, "What the hell . . . ?" Mist murmured a curt explanation, and Rufus gasped, "*You knew?*"

Albin said, "I've been reviled and condemned by all, even my own family, for my heart of stone. You were the only wisp of heat, my Maia—and when you vanished, the wisp died. I spent eons searching for you, willing you to return."

"I'm not impressed, Albin," she retorted. "Your chilly soul drove me away. I didn't think you would notice I'd gone."

"Hold on," Rufus said loudly. "Aurata? You were wedded to this piece of work?"

"I told you I'd had companions. You didn't ask for details."

Albin ignored her aside to Rufus. "Oh, I noticed your absence, Maia. I minded. And I cursed you for deserting me."

"What curse?"

"That for as long as you were away from me, you would never find peace."

There was a brief, frigid silence. When Aurata spoke, her tone was vitriolic. "Hardly a loving way to tempt me back. A curse? Well, I hope you're gratified, Albin, my sometime husband, because I haven't rested. If you were hurt by my departure, you should look more closely at yourself. I'm fiery Naamon to the bone, and you knew it, yet you tried to change me. It was like being held in a prison of ice. I had to leave. It was nothing personal. Simply time for me to move on, that's all."

"You could treat our union so lightly? We had a son."

"I was a poor mother, I admit. Did Lawrence find you any better a father?"

No answer came from Albin, only the faintest twitch of discomfort in his face. "The call of other realms is stronger than any blood tie. Especially the call of Vaeth."

"And that is why I've sought to seal the Gates!" Albin was suddenly vehement. "Vaeth corrupts us. Vaeth took Lawrence from me, took my own mother, took you. Earth takes every Aelyr who's not strong enough to withstand temptation. No one would make a stand but me. I'm doing this to protect those who cannot protect themselves."

Aurata gave a long-suffering smile. "Ah, Albin, you've changed. You're worse than I remember! It wasn't only your coldness that drove me away, but your arrogance. You treated me as a possession, but I never was. You didn't know me."

His pale lips thinned. "I am wondering who I was searching for. Was 'Maia' an illusion? You never told me your true name . . . and all the time I hunted Rufus, I never dreamed he was your brother. I feel . . . betrayed, a little."

"Brother and lover," Rufus put in, his tone brazen. "It was always me she wanted. Not you, but poor old degenerate *me*."

Albin's gaze touched Rufus, spilling contempt. "Nothing you say holds a grain of credibility."

"Truth hurts," Rufus persisted. "She was with me in the days of Azantios. Now she's with me again. Some Aelyr are bonded forever; nothing can pull us apart, and you lost this one. Tough luck."

Aurata spread her hand at Rufus in a brusque *Shut up!* gesture.

"Ignore him," she said lightly. "If I wounded you, Albin, I'm truly sorry. But we would have destroyed each other. You cursed me never to rest? Well, your curse held indeed. It was partly because I couldn't find peace that I worked so hard to raise Qesoth."

"You should know that curses come back to bite," said Rufus.

"Of course, this is not a matter for hearts," Albin said, pointedly shifting to turn his back on Rufus. Mist edged around so that he could watch both their faces. "It's about balance. Brawth the shadow rose, so Qesoth rose in her turn. I should have known. I didn't expect her to appear in your guise, Maia, but I suppose there is a pleasing symmetry in this."

"And what now?" Aurata said. "You expressed your love for me in a curse! We've fought a battle that neither can win, because Brawth is Qesoth's shadow-self. Without her, he can't exist. So tell me, what now?"

Albin's shoulders rose in a brief, hollow laugh. "It ends here," he said. "Often I told myself that nothing in all the realms could lift winter from me but a glimpse of my Maia's face. A kiss. But Maia was an illusion, and all passion long frozen."

"I was no illusion," she said fiercely. "Everyone thinks that you and I are equally selfish and heartless. But I've always known that my own plan might destroy me, and that I should remember that I'm acting not for myself, but for those who come after." She waved a hand in the direction of Sam and Lucas. "Not least, for our own descendants."

Albin said nothing. Perhaps he'd lost the will to argue.

"Let it end, then," she said softly. "For them."

Aurata moved towards Albin, tilting her face towards his. Their lips met. In the collision of fire and ice, Mist saw all their ambitions evaporate. The power that trailed from their shoulders like cloaks, auroras that filled the universe—all vanished. He saw clearly that their powers had reached a boundary, a membrane like oil and water swirling against each other, unable to mix.

The kiss lasted half a minute, a span of time that seemed endless. At last Aurata stepped back. Her fire had gone. She was fully in her human shape, red hair falling neatly around a strikingly calm face. Albin's expression was bitter, with a distinct trace of sadness.

Mist understood. This was inevitable, yet still a shock. With the kiss, they had each drained the other's strength. Effectively, they had neutralized each other. In doing so, they'd become ordinary, or as ordinary as Aetherials ever could be: a condition that neither of them could tolerate.

Perhaps Albin hadn't realized what he was giving up, but Aurata—always smarter than him—had known. And she'd made a decision to destroy Albin's power by sacrificing her own.

A flash of sanity had prevailed, after all, and allowed her to spare her grandsons.

Mist saw all this in detail, but caught only a glimpse of Rufus snatching a crossbow from the nearest warrior and aiming it at the back of Albin's neck. The bolt shot home. The Sibeylan fell.

Feral, Rufus sprang and landed on Albin's back. He seized the long white hair in his left hand, jerked back the head, and with his right hand—his forefinger a long claw like a scimitar—he slashed deep through Albin's throat.

The color of his blood was a shock. Mist had expected white ichor, not a purplish-red flow, its hue startling against the pale rock as it pooled and spread. Rufus severed the neck almost to the spine, and let the snowy figure collapse in a heap of feathers at Aurata's feet.

The moment Albin fell, the fog dispersed.

The tower remained, its needle-spike pointing at the sky. All around was black-ink darkness—that was a shock, because Mist had seen blue sky above the ocean of vapor. The Otherworld, capricious, could change in seconds.

He made his way upwards to Stevie. Every bone ached as he climbed. Since the Spiral was never completely dark, his eyes adjusted instantly from the cotton-wool fog to clear night. There were strangely few stars, but enough for Aetherial eyes.

On the tower courtyard, the statues were beginning to move. Color was seeping into their empty shells, ice cracking and shattering on the ground. Albin's victims were everywhere. A dusting of bluish light lit scores of figures milling on a plateau that resembled a moonscape, an expanse of jumbled flat plates glistening like feldspar.

On this eerie plateau, Albin's tower and island lay marooned, like a spar on a ship that has run aground.

To one side loomed distant mountains; to the other, a shadowy hint of hills. *This must be the border of Asru*, Mist thought. From that direction, dozens more warriors were arriving to reinforce Vaidre Daima's troops. The Spiral landscape had a tendency to distortion so he couldn't be sure of anything he was seeing. Realms frayed into each other like multiple reflections, even appearing to be in several places at once as if seen through water.

At the foot of Albin's island, Vaidre Daima had regained command and was snapping out orders. His voice carried clearly. "Mistangamesh and all of you near the tower, I ask that you come with me. Rufus and Aurata Ephenaestus, I place you in the custody of the Spiral Court. Surrender yourselves."

Mist ignored him. He felt a duty towards his brother and sister, but his priority was Stevie.

Reaching her, he saw frost evaporating from her hair and skin; saw her eyes come to life. She bent to pick up the three pebbles. They dissolved in her palm and, although he saw nothing, he felt the *fylgias* break free like rushes of spring air. Around her, three glacial specters were returning to life. As each one moved, crusts of ice fell away. Snow sifted from their clothes like powdered sugar. Features emerged from the crystalline coating: Lucas's dark hair and sharp, intelligent features; Sam's bright blue-green eyes, wildly staring around, ready in a heartbeat to fight the nearest enemy; Rosie's face, a creamy oval with wide grey eyes, deep pink lips parted in shock, her hair a red-brown tangle as if she'd fallen through a hedge.

"What the hell?" she gasped. "What the *fuck* just happened?"

Stevie turned, and threw her arms around Rosie.

Mist stood back, not wishing to interrupt the fever of embraces, exclamations and tears among the four of them. While he waited, he let any remnant of Aetherial features drop away, let his form appear human again. He allowed himself a smile.

Then Stevie looked up and saw him.

Gently disentangling herself, she came to him, focusing all the obvious remarks into her eyes so she needn't say them aloud. *We're alive, thank the gods. Is it over?* His arms enfolded her. They embraced in wordless relief that was echoed in the chaos all around them. Bewildered Melusians mingled with Tyrynaians and Sibyelans.

After awhile, Sam said, "Albin?"

"Dead," said Mist. "I'm sorry."

The hawk-like corpse lay in clear sight in a livid lake of blood.

"What the hell are you sorry for?"

"Well . . . he was your grandfather."

Sam and Lucas looked at each other. "No apology needed," Sam said. "I'd have done it myself, if we hadn't been . . . paralyzed, or whatever. Believe me, he's had it coming for a long, long time."

"Can you remember anything?" Stevie asked anxiously.

All three shook their heads. "Fragments," Rosie answered. "Nothingness. As if time had stopped. I knew something was really wrong, but I couldn't work out what. Horrible. But you came back for us! What happened?"

"Have you got all day?" Stevie found a smile.

Lucas said, "Did we dream it, or was Albin doing battle with a red-haired fire goddess? And calling her . . . Maia? Who is she?"

"Oh." Mist paused. "That's my sister, Aurata. Also known as Maia, yes."

"As in Maia, our *grandmother*?" Lucas said quietly. "This is surreal. What should we do?"

Sam said, "This is probably not the best moment to introduce ourselves."

Mist shook his head. "I don't know what will happen, but we may have a chance to see her in Tyrynaia. Vaidre Daima's taking her prisoner. Rufus too."

"They seem to having a difference of opinion about that," said Sam.

Where the island shore met the plateau, Aurata and Rufus were side by side, facing Vaidre Daima across Albin's corpse. There was a negotiation taking place, Vaidre politely but firmly repeating his request for her surrender, Aurata smiling as if humoring a child. Behind him, the Spiral Court troops stayed in their ranks. Mist suspected they were in awe of her, even afraid. Every step the leader took towards her, Aurata took a step back.

"My lady, you must come with us," he repeated.

Aurata said simply, "Not in a million years. You have no power over me."

"You won't be harmed. We need to question everyone."

"Bad luck, because I answer to no one."

Rufus put in, "For pity's sake, Aurata, we may as well go with them or we'll be here for eternity."

Rosie said, "And so will we. Can we sneak away before they notice? I really want to leave, I can't stand being in this place another moment."

Stevie looked at Mist, who nodded. "Yes, she's right. Let's just go. We'll have to find our way around to the far side of the island and hope none of the warriors are there yet. Are you all okay to walk?"

"A bit stiff, and not in a good way," said Sam. "But we'll manage."

Around the base of the spire they went and began to cross the quartz plate of the island's far shore. It was a few hundred yards—farther than Mist had expected—and rising slightly so they couldn't see what lay beyond.

Reaching the rim, they stopped in astonishment.

Nothing. A great midnight curve of space hung above, in front and below. The oval of the plate's rim protruded a good hundred feet over this void.

Sam said, "Holy crap, look where we are. Did Albin know he'd stranded himself halfway over the Abyss?"

"I don't think he did anything by accident," said Lucas.

Stevie gripped Mist's arm. She gasped, tried to speak, gasped again. "To think I was worried about tripping up in the fog!"

Edging as far forward as they dared, they looked down.

The heart of the Spiral was also, somehow, its endless boundary: an ink-black sweep of infinity. Far below was a vast roiling galaxy, a flat spiral trailing long, glittering arms. It was breathtaking with clouds of crimson and violet gas, dense with stars that sparkled blue and white and yellow. At the center was lightless disk, like a bottomless well, a black hole.

The Eye of the Cauldron.

Mist was horribly aware of standing on a thin crust of rock that might break like sugar beneath them. Yet he couldn't tear his gaze from the wondrous galaxy. The black eye was Estel's domain, her cauldron of creation, beginning and end.

To fall into the Abyss is true death, true annihilation, even for Aetherials . . .

"This isn't how I remember it," said Rosie, her voice shaky.

"You've seen this before?" said Stevie.

"It was more a true chasm, like in the Norse myths, with fire rolling down one wall and ice vapor down the other . . . and there was a tree, a gigantic world-tree. You remember, don't you, Luc? We looked down from the branches. I don't remember seeing a huge eye of stars. Why is it different?"

"It's the Abyss," said Sam, "Ergo, it's huge. Of course it won't be the same everywhere."

"And it changes," said Mist.

Lucas nodded, looking pale. "That's the Spiral for you. Different according to who's looking into it, and why." He began to back away. "I can't stay here. The Abyss and me . . . not very comfortable with each other . . . Sorry, I don't feel great and I think we should just go and find a different way back."

Rosie caught his arm, pulling him farther from the precipice. "It's okay, Luc. We all feel like crap. We're not in the best state for admiring the wonders of the Otherworld, so . . ."

"I suggest we work our way back and just go to Tyrynaia with Vaidre Daima," said Sam. "*We've* done nothing wrong—have we?"

"Of course not," said Mist. "I think you're right. You do all look terrible."

"Thanks." Rosie grimaced at him.

"Didn't mean—oh, you know what I meant. So we'll rest until they've finished arguing with Aurata and then go along quietly. Agreed?"

Sam and Rosie began to make their way off the perilous rim, supporting Lucas between them. Mist and Stevie hesitated for a few seconds. It was so hard to stop looking into the awesome majesty of the Cauldron.

There was a shout. Vaidre Daima's voice, again.

"Stop!" Then to his warriors, "What are you waiting for? Capture her! Lady Aurata, give yourself up. You've nowhere to run."

Rufus and Aurata appeared, heading towards the lip of the island. They were barely thirty feet away; Mist ran towards them, calling out a warning. Stevie followed. He told her to go back with Luc and the others, but she retorted crisply, "I'm staying with you."

On the very edge, Rufus and Aurata slid to an abrupt halt. They looked tiny against the vast emptiness beyond.

Vaidre Daima and his guards halted yards away, as if they dared not set foot on the rock plate that hung over the void. Sensible, no doubt, but Aurata had now placed herself in a siege position that might go on indefinitely.

"Aurata, what the hell are you doing?" Mist stopped a few feet from her. She looked unnaturally serene. He had no idea what was going on in her head.

She didn't answer. Rufus shrugged. He looked haggard. "We're not giving ourselves up to the Spiral Court. That's the end of the matter. No surrender."

"Rufe, you're not the one in trouble, for a change."

"Makes no difference," said Rufus. "Where Aurata goes, I go."

"Why?"

"She's the one person who loved me when everyone else hated me."

"She locked you up, not so long ago!"

"It doesn't matter. Perhaps if we hadn't lost Aurata when Azantios fell, the story could have been different. We might have all stayed sane. This is the only true family we have: each other. Maybe you can't stand me, Mist—fair enough, but I still want to be with Aurata."

Mist felt a long, deep pang. *The only true family* . . . "After what she tried to do?"

Rufus shrugged. "She's still my sister, and the love of my life. I've done worse myself; I can overlook a little fire-goddess-channeling lunacy, can't you? So she went mad for a while. Who hasn't?"

"The Abyss," said Aurata, as if she hadn't heard their conversation. She turned to them, her face golden-white like a luminous shell. "Isn't it beautiful?"

"Yes, fantastic," said Rufus. His voice shook. "Now step away from the edge. Come on, Aurata, think about this. They're only going to question us. How bad can it be?"

"I feel safe here. Mist, come closer. See how beautiful it is."

"We've seen," he said. "I know today has been disastrous. Your onetime husband is dead, Veropardus and Slahvin are dead, and your power is gone. But—look, your brothers are still here. We'll help you."

She laughed. "What are you, the men in white coats?"

Stevie said cautiously, "Your two grandsons would quite like to meet you."

"If I was the ordinary Aurata you want me to be, possibly. I wish them well, but I'm a stranger to them. I can't see it would do them any good to meet a madwoman." Her voice turned low and savage. "There are no true Aetherials left."

"Admit your plan could never have worked," said Rufus. "Let's go away somewhere. Like when we were in Venice, remember? Forgive me. It could be you and me again. Mist, too, if he changes his mind. And lovely Fela, if she can forgive you for the swamp business and Daniel and all that. Don't you remember how fond you were of her? What else matters?"

"Nothing," she said dully. Placing her hands on Rufus's shoulders, she kissed him on the mouth. "Nothing else matters. But it can't happen, because the Spiral Court will incarcerate me for eternity. You're right; I was carried away with delusions. Qesoth will not rise, there will be no new golden empire of the Felynx. But what should we have done instead?"

"Anything."

"Not me. I can't live a small life. Even if I was wrong, I hold to my destiny and I do nothing that is not my own choice."

"Don't move!" Vaidre Daima shouted from a distance. A hundred armed crossbows glowed red in the darkness. "Aurata of the Felynx, this is your final warning. Surrender yourself to the Spiral Court!"

"Not a chance," said Aurata. She looked at Rufus, her face aglow. "Are you still with me?"

"Always." He smiled back. They joined hands, both stretching into tawny, lynx-like forms. Laughing.

"No!" Mist yelled. Too late. They bounded and leapt—

Stevie vanished with them.

It was a trick so fast that Mist barely saw it, let alone had a chance to act. In a last stroke of mischief, Rufus had grabbed Stevie's wrist and taken her over the precipice with him.

With a yell of anguish, Mist plunged after her. Missiles whizzed past his ears. He felt the searing pain of a crossbow bolt gouging the skin of his upper arm, but then he was far beyond the range of Vaidre Daima's army. Falling, falling into the Abyss.

How is it possible to fall, Stevie wondered, *when we're out in space with no gravity to seize us? It must be the pull of the Cauldron itself.*

She was too stunned to feel fear. She remembered the sense of calm when she'd drowned. This was the same. She felt wonder and resignation as she stared down into the great spiraling mass of stars, billions of stars that never seemed to grow closer however far they fell. She heard their soft roar, a sound she'd never dreamed could exist, the song of eternity.

Aurata shone like a comet, leading the way. Rufus was still gripping Stevie's wrist, his head thrown back and a cry of exhilaration pouring from his throat. She glanced upward, but could no longer see the edge from which they'd fallen.

All she saw was Mist falling after her. He was reaching out, altering his position like a skydiver to catch her up.

Shock jolted her from calm trance into frantic horror.

"You bastard, Rufus." Mist's voice was thin, carried away by their speed. "You haven't changed, you will never change!"

"But we'll all be together. Don't you want to know the secrets of the Cauldron?"

"Death. True death."

"An awfully big adventure, as some wise man put it. I know now why I could never die. It's because the Spiral itself rejected me! This is how it must end, don't you see? The three of us, together . . ." Rufus's words were becoming drawn out now, slow and breathless. "If one goes, all must go. The four of us. Stevie's part of us now. This way, we will all be together . . . forever."

There was joyous exuberance in Aurata's curving descent. Rufus smiled manically, laughing without sound. Stevie saw the wound in Mist's shoulder, saw his eyes grow heavy as he fought the effects of the drugged crossbow bolt.

Every fiber of her screamed denial.

All the time, Mist was struggling to prize Rufus's hand off Stevie's wrist. He forced himself to stay conscious, would not give up. And she saw Mist's hand suddenly change, sprouting a claw like a butcher's blade.

Stevie saw the claw slice straight through Rufus's wrist. The hand remained clamped around her forearm—but Rufus, cut loose, his mouth wide open in disbelief, floated and rotated away in Aurata's fire trail.

Mist gave a hoarse scream.

She was free, but they were still falling. Beneath them the Cauldron waited, a vast mass of starfire trailing its arms into the void. The great black eye turned, strangely soft and inviting, even merciful—like Persephone's eyes—but inescapable. Stevie knew that they might fall for a thousand years before they reached the center.

Estalyr.

The word dropped into her mind from nowhere, something Rosie had said. She thought, *But we can fly, we can fly, why do we have to fall?*

Stevie pushed deep inside herself, into the most ancient parts of her brain, the long-forgotten core of herself buried like a fossil under layers and layers of time, right back to the beginning. *Wings can't beat if there's no air . . .*

But to the Estalyr, the First, it doesn't matter. Those rules don't touch us. She felt a rush of blue-black energy, strange yet achingly familiar. *How could I forget this?* Heat rushed through her, like a million stars powering her from within. She felt vast wings leaping from her back like sails.

Stevie caught hold of Mist and clung to him as she unleashed her wings in long, powerful beats.

There was no effect at first. Then a slight deceleration, but they were still falling. And then—equilibrium. They hung in the void, but she could not gain height. She realized that Mist, although barely conscious, was also taking winged Estalyr form. His valiant efforts made little difference. Yet, however little, it helped.

Below them, his brother and sister fell, tumbling, swirling downward like sparks of fire. Stevie knew that Mist would swoop down and save them if he could, despite all they'd done. She knew it broke his heart that he couldn't. His body shook with despair against hers. Yet he held on to her with all his strength and worked frantically to help them gain height.

The pull of the Abyss was too strong. Their wings beat like giant sails against nothingness. They were weightless, like astronauts in orbit, losing height again. Even their primal essence was not enough.

"We tried," Mist said into her ear. "Don't be afraid. At least we're together."

"No," said Stevie. "We must try harder. I won't let you fall!"

She saw dark shapes around them like falling leaves. More Estalyr, soaring on great dark wings: indigo-black angels with golden suns for eyes.

Stevie gave her wings an extra, desperate push. Mist reached up with one hand, caught the hand of the Estalyr that was extended to him from above.

The effort was like clinging to twigs in a flood. With infinitely slow progress they all strove against the heavy pull of the Abyss, as if trying to swim up a waterfall. Like salmon leaping upstream, they strove for the impossible . . . and began to win.

A last desperate push, with several pairs of wings sweeping, straining, they reached the lip of the chasm, hung on and climbed, clawed their way, as ungainly as bats, onto flat ground.

Their Estalyr forms dropped away with sheer exhaustion. Stevie and Mist stood clinging hard to each other as they saw who had rescued them: Rosie, Sam and Lucas.

23

Always Summer

"I'm not squeamish," said Stevie, "truly, I'm not, but someone please get this thing off me!"

She stretched out her right arm behind her, turning her head the other way. Rufus's severed hand was locked around her wrist and she feared she might have to wear it like some grisly bracelet for eternity.

There was activity behind her. The pain worsened, making her wince.

"Stevie, it's gone," said Sam.

"I can still feel it!"

She glanced around to see Sam holding the object balanced on his palm, his mouth twisted in a wry expression of distaste. The hand did not look human. It was like a paw sheened with reddish fur, the long, bony digits tapering to neat claws. She hadn't felt it come free, and could still feel claw tips in her skin. She rubbed briskly at her forearm, trying not to gag.

"See?" said Rosie. "It must be like when you pull out a splinter but it still hurts like hell for a while."

"Oh, god," she whispered. "Thanks."

"Right, come on," said Mist, sliding a firm arm around her. His irises reflected the pale rock, matching the ghastly bone-white hue of his face. "Let's get away from here. Nothing Vaidre Daima does can matter to us now."

In a ragged bunch, stumbling from sheer weariness, the five of them made their way towards the warrior horde. The crystalline rock was like ice beneath their feet. They held one another upright.

No one spoke. Stevie kept catching her breath on waves of wonder and horror. Part of her wanted to pour out all the obvious sentiments: *Is everyone all right? How did we all find the strength to become Estalyr? It's supposed to be near-impossible, so how . . . ? Incredible, what sheer desperation will achieve. We've done the impossible, escaped the Abyss . . . I never imagined such terror. We should be dead, annihilated, but we're still alive. We're alive!*

She held all this inside. Words were inadequate. She couldn't believe that Sam, Rosie and Lucas had risked their own lives to save her and Mist, yet they had, and their bravery struck her speechless. Perhaps the same thoughts were in her companions' minds . . . but what could she say to Mist, who'd watched his siblings arcing away like meteors into the void? She couldn't begin to imagine his feelings, still less to comfort him.

He was clearly in such deep shock that she wondered if he'd ever recover. Fear squeezed her heart, worse than anything Aurata, Rufus or Albin had done.

There was a flurry of activity on the rocks where Albin had fallen. A handful of Tyrynaian warriors came to meet Mist and the others, armed but keeping a wary distance.

Vaidre Daima was grim-faced, shaken. Approaching, he began to say something, only for Mist's left hand to shoot out and connect with his chest, stopping him in his tracks. "Do not speak to me. You drove my sister and brother into the Abyss. I assume that's what you intended."

"No! Absolutely not. Only to question them. I made it clear—"

Sam said, "Obviously Aurata didn't care to answer your questions. You might think about putting a safety fence along the edge there."

"As I explained, the Spiral is unstable. The Abyss shifts position. Until the fog cleared, we had no idea it was there. I swear . . . What we've witnessed today is unprecedented, almost beyond our comprehension."

"You should have been there," Sam retorted. "What do you want us to do? We need to rest and then go home. Nothing difficult."

Vaidre Daima's voice was gruff as he retrieved his tattered dignity. "As a courtesy I invite you all to Tyrynaia. Rest, answer our questions, then you can go."

"Yes, we accept," said Lucas. "Would you please tell your guards to lower their weapons? There's no need to treat us like prisoners. We won't resist."

Vaidre Daima made a brusque gesture; all crossbows were lowered and disarmed. Some of the guards moved away and reverted to upright, nonreptilian forms. "I apologize. You are our guests, of course. The guards are here to protect you, an escort of honor."

"Wait," said Lucas, indicating the flutter of white feathers on the rocks. "What about Albin? We can't just leave him there."

Sam led the way, pushing through the Tyrynaians who were grouped loosely around the body. Albin lay where Rufus had felled him, on his side with a purple wound grinning across his throat.

Sam bent down and said, "He's not dead."

Then Stevie saw in shock that Albin's eyes were flickering. His lips moved feebly. It was an awful moment. Everyone gathered around him was paralyzed with pity and horror.

Eventually Mist said, "I can't deal a death blow to him. Not in cold blood."

Sam gave a slight nod, one hand spread in Mist's direction to show he understood. "I wouldn't ask that of anyone." He dropped to his knees beside Albin's shoulder, leaning over him. "He might yet heal, and live." Sam's voice was rough. "The Spiral does that to us."

A faint noise creaked from Albin's lips. "No. Take me into my tower."

Hearing him speak was the worst thing of all. His neck was cut nearly through to the spine and yet he found a voice, like a severed head in a folk-tale.

Mistangamesh looked frigidly at Vaidre Daima. "Will you trust us to do that, at least? Whatever Albin's crimes, he's kin to Lucas and Sam, as Rufus and Aurata were to me. Let them do what they must. Afterwards, we'll come with you."

Vaidre Daima hesitated. Lucas raised his head and glared. "I am your Gatekeeper," he said fiercely. Stevie had never seen him angry before. "Your Court appointed me. If you don't trust me to perform an act of respect for my grandfather and then go willingly to the city with you, I resign."

The Spiral Court leader stepped back, green feathers swaying as he dipped his head, his palms open in apology. "Forgive me. Do what you must. In fact I'll send the guards back and escort you to Tyrynaia alone. That will prove my trust in you, I hope."

"It's a start," said Mist.

Between them, Lucas and Sam, Rosie and Stevie and Mist carried Albin into his spire and up the precarious stairs to the chilly bluish glow of the top chamber. There, as he requested, they laid him on his lapis-blue bier. Sam arranged the swan-feather cloak to cover him from feet to chin.

"You may yet heal, and live," Sam repeated, very quietly. "In which case, someone will have to make sure that you *never* regain your power."

"No," Albin whispered. "Here I will stay. I've no wish for further life, nor power. My time is done."

Sam kneeled down, so his head was on a level with Albin's. Rosie stood with one hand on Sam's shoulder, her head bowed. Lucas, standing on the other side, wept soundlessly. Mist and Stevie stayed at the foot of the bier, watching in silence.

Sam said, "And that's it, is it? No apology? No words for anyone?"

"Maia . . ."

"She went into the Abyss. You probably realized that."

The jewel on his forehead faded to grey. His lips, barely moving, were the same hue. "Tell Lawrence . . . tell my son that his mother and I were too alike. We almost destroyed the world between us. My only purpose in life was to find her, and now that is done . . . I see, in a clear light, that my other ambitions were pointless."

"I wish you'd told Lawrence in person. He never had the chance to speak to Maia."

"You're pure Vaethyr, Samuel. Too human to live in this realm."

"Oh," Sam said softly. "You finally get that, do you? We aren't all the same. Some of us love the human world. You cannot force all Aetherials to be the same."

"Nor can you force me to be otherwise. Heartless and vindictive, you labeled me. Well, vindictive no longer. I am as cold as a dead star, but I am at peace. We are all alone, forever drifting apart like galaxies in the void of space. Our only hope is to accept it. For as long as you deny it, Samuel, and insist on clinging to your human self, your heart will be broken."

"I'd rather that, a million times over, than wall myself up in a tower of ice for fear of getting hurt."

"Fear? I am not afraid." Albin's lips were barely moving now. "I confess to a little sadness. But all is as it should be. Leave me now."

Sam gripped one of Albin's hands, which were stiff and bloodless like wax. "You're not alone, Grandfather. If this is what you choose, we respect it. But you are not alone."

"Lucas," Albin whispered.

"Grandfather?" Lucas took a step nearer.

"Safeguard the Spiral."

The minimal movement of the lips ceased. Albin became a marble effigy. Sam straightened up, and smoothed the feathered cloak. Albin's gaunt white face pointed up at the chamber's apex. The temperature dropped, making their breath form clouds that fell into fine ice needles.

Sam stood away from the bier and grasped Rosie's hand. Mist looked somber, and Stevie felt tears in her own eyes. Lucas was only a shade less pale than Albin himself. *All this sorrow,* she thought, *even though Albin brought nothing but trouble. It's because we aren't heartless. We're capable of grieving for the sheer waste.*

The tower quaked slightly beneath them. Mist said gently, "It's time to go."

"One last thing," said Sam. He took Rufus's claw from a pocket and laid it on the shelf among Albin's artifacts, where it looked ghoulishly appropriate. "Unless you want to give it a decent burial?"

Mist closed his eyes briefly. "No. Leave it there. It seems to belong."

Sam nodded. They made their way in single file down the carved spiral of the stairs—a slow process, as the tower was trembling with alarming violence. Emerging at the base, Stevie snatched up the Felixatus. To her own dismay, she'd almost forgotten it, but here it still was in its silken wrapping. The plateau around them was deserted except for Vaidre Daima, who was beckoning frantically.

The island shuddered beneath them.

They ran. In a few long strides they were leaping off the periphery and onto the moonstone sheen of the underlying ground. Turning, they took a last look at the spire's pointed summit, saw it fading into a shroud of ice vapor: Albin's tomb.

They watched as the island bearing the tower began to slide away towards the edge of the chasm. Silently it went—ice on ice—teetering on the precipice until it tipped beyond the point of no return.

Falling in slow motion, backlit by evanescent glacial light, Albin's tower vanished into the Abyss.

Tyrynaia.

It is a city that reveals itself only to the favored few, Vaidre Daima had told them. *You cannot find Tyrynaia. It will find you.*

He led the way inland from the Abyss, over a high delicate bridge across a ravine and into a landscape that made Stevie think of Chinese porcelain: paths winding around impossibly steep hills cloaked in gnarled foliage. The landscape felt like gossamer floating on nothingness, glowing in semidarkness. Trees stood like exotic bonsai silhouetted against a star-swirled indigo sky. This was Asru, the realm of secrets, a thin crust between the Spiral and the Cauldron.

All the stars missing from the sky above the Abyss seemed to be gathered here instead. The air was warm, almost tropical. The contrast, after she'd been cold for so long, was painful, tingling, delicious.

"Have any of you been to the city before?" Stevie asked.

"No," said Lucas, "but I think it's time."

Stevie carried the Felixatus all the way, refusing Mist's offer to take the burden. There was a task for her to perform. He understood that.

The path wound into a valley: a gentler landscape, full of birch trees and mossy banks dipping into streams. A maze of small bridges and stepping stones guided them across. Fireflies shone from within the trees themselves: not fireflies, Stevie realized, but the eyes of curious elementals, watching them pass by.

She breathed in Asru's wonderful smell, an earthy, humid scent like a hothouse full of orchids. Vaidre Daima stopped at a spring, suggested they rest for a minute and drink from the crystal water. When they looked up again, Stevie saw a vast black silhouette that blotted out half the stars.

"That wasn't there before," she said. "Was it?"

Tyrynaia revealed itself as a dark mountain, a peak as majestic as Mount Everest. As they drew closer, the monumental cutout began to show detail. Colors gleamed like rainbows on oil. Tyrynaia floated in its own realm, veiled from base to summit with a confection of delicate structures—like Azantios in negative, ten times the size.

Mist didn't speak, but his hand was firm around Stevie's arm. She experienced a surge of amazement and recognition. "I have been here before," she murmured. "Or rather, Fela has."

Somewhere deep beneath the floating bulk of the mountain lay Persephone's chamber and the mysterious lake Meluis.

A magnificent double gate stood open in front of them, black filigree patterned with sphinxes and angels. An arch over the top bore the words—in runes she read easily—"Tyrynaia, the Heart of us." A procession of figures was coming down the avenue beyond to greet them.

They were shadows under dusky silk veils, shimmering with elusive light . . . a procession of Aelyr as humans might see them. Stevie felt caught in some wondrous and terrifying dream. Even though she'd plummeted into the Abyss and become Estalyr; even though she'd lived alongside the Felynx, passed through Persephone's chamber and returned to a new life . . . none of it lessened her awe.

"Who comes to Tyrynaia?" a voice asked from behind a veil.

Vaidre Daima pressed his right hand to his chest and gave a formal bow; his left sketched a symbol on the air. "I bring Lucas Fox, Keeper of the Great Gates: Rose Fox and Samuel Wilder, his kin: Mistangamesh Poectis Ephenaestus of Azantios and Stephanie Silverwood of . . . also of Azantios and of Vaeth. Bid them welcome."

The veils were swept back and faces revealed: a dozen different hues and textures of skin and flowing hair, bright intelligent eyes, some faces more animal and others more human—but all stunning and completely unearthly.

Vaidre Daima's voice sounded dry and hoarse; not officious anymore, but the voice of a general who'd been charged with defeating an enemy, and failed. "We have them to thank for saving the Spiral. Those who threatened us are gone."

Tyrynaia was a place to lose yourself. Citadels, spires and arches were interconnected by lanes and stairways snaking upward from one terraced level to the next. Vast statues of black angels stood shining on balconies. Tiny lights gleamed everywhere like rubies and emeralds, sapphires and amethysts thrown onto black velvet.

You could wander for days through the spiderweb labyrinth, Stevie thought. They passed endless dwellings—mansions, villas, palaces—but none seemed private. Pathways cut straight through open-sided halls, or led across balconies like errant rights-of-way. Perhaps the city was a single edifice with thousands of rooms and interlinked courtyards. Perhaps, to live here, all you had to do was find an empty chamber and make yourself at home.

Tyrynaia was built from some species of dark Elfstone, an inky yet translucent crystal that spilled flashes of fire. Fashioned, rather than built, Stevie corrected herself. That was how the Aelyr worked, Mist had told her: spinning reality from intention, rather than from solid stone. Azantios had been the same: Tyrynaia's golden echo.

Vaidre Daima brought them to a high terrace that overlooked the spilling tiers of the city. A gentle breeze blew, carrying incense. From the land far below rose fluting birdcalls, achingly reminiscent of blackbird and thrush and nightingale song. Stevie stood enraptured by the exquisite chorus.

She asked, "Does it ever get light here?"

"The sun appears on rare occasions, according to the unpredictable movement of the Spiral," Vaidre Daima answered. "Yet it's never quite dark, here, either. We have the stars. Otherworld flora and fauna thrive in starlight, or indeed in any conditions, since they seem to have a magical will of their own. It is always summer in Tyrynaia, so our legends say."

"Oh, always midsummer night?" said Rosie, leaning on a balustrade next to Stevie. "So you don't get the blazing heat of noon in the Mediterranean, but always the delicious balmy softness of a summer night? How wonderful."

"It is so," said Vaidre. "Rest here while I send for food and drink."

There were curved marble benches, but the newcomers stayed on their feet, lined up along the terrace wall. The cosmos was breathtaking. Stars whorled in their billions. Planets hung in the sky like fruit, close enough to touch. Stevie saw the mysterious globes of Mars, Venus, Saturn, Neptune, and a half-dozen others she didn't even recognize. She felt drunk on Spiral strangeness, thrilled and overawed to the point of fear.

Mist stood close beside her, not touching. Stevie longed to warm his ashen face with her hands, to drag her fingers through his thick black hair, slide her arms around him and feel his neck and cheeks and lips beneath hers. She resisted. His aura of shock and grief sealed her out, impenetrable. He'd changed. How soul-destroying it would be to lavish comfort on an ex-lover who—through no fault of his own—was unreachable, as unresponsive as a statue.

"Oh, this is weird," said Rosie. "I *have* been here before. Sort of. The first time I changed into Estalyr form—which was *very* trippy—I remember flying over the city, and there was Albin standing on a balcony like this one, pure white against the blackness. He freaked the life out of me but, because I was Estalyr, I wasn't as scared as I maybe should have been. He was full of enigmatic warnings . . . and I wish I'd listened. I never dreamed he'd go to such extremes."

"I still can't believe he's gone," said Lucas.

"Well, I can't believe we were related to him," said Sam. "Yeah, it's easy to get sentimental—ah, he was our grandfather: what might have been if he hadn't acted like a complete Nazi?—but we can't forget how he was. Manipulative. Cruel to Lawrence. Same with Rosie and me, not to mention his smirking indifference when he put Lucas in mortal peril. Cursing his own wife and son! His general hatred of humans and Vaethyr alike. His endless crusade to seal the Spiral off from Earth—and when that failed, he'd rather destroy his own family and the whole Otherworld than admit defeat! No, none of that can be forgotten."

They now sat on the smooth benches as a handful of smiling, dark-skinned Aetherials brought refreshments. They were hosts, not servants: Stevie understood that. They could well be Spiral Court members who would be interrogating them later.

Sweet wine was served, morsels of unfamiliar fruit, olives, cheese, spicy cakes. Stevie had no idea what she was eating and was too hungry to care. The others apparently felt the same, except Mist, who barely touched anything. His face was a bleached shell against the darkness.

"I'll keep reminding myself of that," Mist said. "It's a curse in itself, to love people and hate them at the same time. I'm convinced Aurata believed she was doing good with her mad schemes. I never thought she'd refuse to listen to reason—yet she was pragmatic enough, when she saw she couldn't win, to sacrifice her power, because it was the only way to stop Albin. She didn't hesitate."

"You know why I think she did that?" said Stevie, touching his hand. "Unlike Albin, she wasn't dead inside. Didn't she admit that she might not be reforging the world for herself, but for future generations? There was still some pang of love deep inside her that made her decide to stop. It wasn't only about defeating Albin. She found some compassion for her grandsons after all."

Mist's expression was pensive. "When I mentioned them, I saw her face change. Apart from that, she gave no other clue that she cared. If I was wrong . . . if she still had feelings after all . . ." He sighed. "What a waste that we lost her."

"I think she'd gone too far to be saved," Stevie said gently.

Mist went on, "I truly thought Rufus *had* changed . . . until he pulled that last trick of taking you into the Abyss, Stevie. I knew then that he hadn't changed at all. Maybe he wanted to, but he was too weak. Rufe was the only one who *knew* he was wicked, and reveled in it."

"That's kind of honest, at least," said Sam. "You must realize that when they did their *Thelma and Louise* act into the Abyss, it was only what they deserved."

"Not so much what they deserved, as what they chose. That was my brother and sister all the way through. No one decided their fate for them."

"And how about you?" Rosie asked softly. Mist smiled, but made no reply.

Again Stevie ached to put her arms around him, but couldn't. She felt him drifting away from her and she knew why. It was more than grief. That was why, in Aurata's house, she'd told him they should separate.

Presently Vaidre Daima reappeared with seven Tyrynaians. They glided in robes covered with mantles of jewel colors; purple, green, deep blue. These garments were multilayered and intricately figured with mythic creatures like those engraved on the Felixatus. They wore headdresses of flowers or feathers or leaves that seemed part of their long shining hair. Aetherial fashions? The sight of this delicious dressing-up made Stevie smile, and wish she did not resemble a travel-worn vagrant. She longed for her own dresses and her necklaces of turquoise, amber and carnelian.

"We'll transcribe everything you tell us, in order to keep a permanent record."

"You know something?" Sam said, folding his arms. "We're not obliged to tell you a damned thing. I mean, who are you? Yes, I know you call yourselves a 'court' as if you hold some kind of power over us, but the truth is, you don't. We don't even live here. And even if we did—no one rules the Spiral. Those who try tend to come to a nasty end."

"True." Vaidre Daima cleared his throat. "Still, we function as best we can to protect our realms. Every Aelyr accepts that. And as their elected spokesman, I bear a responsibility to find out the truth. To preserve and learn from it. That's all."

Sam spoke over him: "The problem is, the Spiral Court has no teeth. You lurk in the darkness, being mysterious, trying to control all Aetherials—the phrase 'herding cats' springs to mind—but when a power like Albin or Aurata rises, you're impotent."

Lucas said, "Sam, enough. We can't have this argument now. Let's cooperate, then we can go home."

"I think that's up to Mist and Stevie. They're the ones who had the worst of it."

"It's all right." Mist leaned forward to rest his elbows on his knees. "We'll tell you everything we know."

"Let's keep it brief, then," said Stevie. She cradled the Felixatus on her thighs, feeling shudders and sparks deep within its structure. "We have something important to do."

Later, their stories told, Vaidre Daima led them up to the very summit of Tyrynaia. Such a trek on Earth, Stevie imagined, would have taken a day and been utterly exhausting. In Tyrynaia, though, she felt weightless, tireless. If the air grew thin, she didn't notice. This was another taste of her Aelyr resilience that thrilled and startled her.

At the highest point lay a small round terrace, inlaid with black opal tiles in a spiral pattern. Looking up, Stevie searched the sparkling infinity of stars until she began to pick out constellations, and at last found the topaz-yellow point of Capella in Auriga—or at least its Otherworld twin.

Mist said, "I've been told they call it the Summer Star, or Estel's Jewel."

In the center of the terrace stood a slender chest-high column, carved with designs similar to those on the Felixatus. There were symbols of the five realms, of mysteries into which Stevie had barely dipped her fingertips. On top was a small black angel statue; an Estalyr image, she realized. Vaidre Daima lifted the statue off and said, "Is this place suitable?"

"Perfect," she said. "May I?"

He nodded, and she placed the Felixatus on top of the column. She set to work, rotating the base, adjusting gears until all axes were in perfect alignment. Before, she'd done her best to ensure the souls couldn't escape to be used as Aurata's weapon. Now she reversed those settings. A thin beam of light fell from the Summer Star, directly through the lens into the heart of the crystal sphere.

The Felixatus responded. Specks of light began to dance in their millions, faster and brighter until they became a single mass like a tiny sun. Mist stood with her. She saw dozens of Tyrynaians crowding around the terrace to watch.

The lens shot an answering beam into the heavens.

In an outpouring of light motes, a star-stream, all the soul-essences of the Felynx flew free.

Stevie gasped, laughing. The fierce white rush of fire was beautiful, like the wildest fireworks display ever seen. Night became day. She felt Mist's hand firm on her shoulder. Were those who'd died in the fall of Azantios among them? Even Poectilictis and Theliome themselves?

It was impossible to know. Some questions would never be answered.

Thirty seconds was all it took. The stream faded and the Felixatus went dim.

Then she found herself surrounded by Aelyr from every realm. Their skin glowed in reflected starlight and their eyes were alluring jewels, their hair like streams of silk, all sublime loveliness. After all, why deny themselves beauty when all they had to do was shift form a little to appear exactly as they wished?

Humans would surely kill for such an ability.

There were Melusians, Sibeylans, many others she couldn't identify, even green-skinned beings with iridescent lacy wings, others with draconic or feline features, tall coal-black demigods, smaller nut-brown creatures who could only have formed in wooded glades.

Perhaps some were from different worlds altogether.

They swarmed around her, around Sam and Luc and Rosie too, expressing thanks and praise so effusive that Stevie had to struggle free and fight her way back to Mist.

Now the Felixatus was dim, like an extinguished candle. She saw him breathe out slowly, bowing his head. Color came back into his face, and an expression of peace. A hint of green infused his grey irises.

She brushed the raven-black feathery hair away from his cheek to see him better. "Did we do the right thing?" she whispered.

"Oh, yes. The only possible thing." He clasped her hand. "Thank you, Stevie. Thank you."

"Father?" Sam's voice rang out a few yards away. He was approaching a tall man in the crowd who resembled a fusion of Albin and Lucas; milky skin, ebony hair swept back from stern yet beautifully carved features.

Lawrence Wilder.

He looked, Stevie observed, not unlike Mist. An older, gaunter version.

But he would, she thought. *If Aurata was his mother, that makes Mist . . . his uncle.* She caught her breath on the thought. *And that's why Lucas, too, reminds me of Mist!*

Sam and Lawrence greeted each other in a formal yet affectionate way, clasping hands, exchanging light kisses on the cheek. "Dad," Sam said, and gave him a brief hug. Rosie and Lucas joined him, hanging back slightly.

Stevie recalled what they'd told her. Lawrence had been a formidable figure when he inhabited Stonegate. Much had happened to thaw their relationship with him, but old patterns of behavior lingered. Lawrence Wilder was still a high Sibeylan to be treated with due respect.

"I have been hearing tales," Lawrence said. "Many rumors, chiefly that my father Albin is gone at last. I should mourn him, but I can't. He almost destroyed the Spiral."

"Well," Sam said, taking a breath. "It's worse than that. I met your mother, Maia, and lost her again. If you've heard stories about Aurata of the Felynx . . . that was her. She went into the Abyss." Sam explained quickly, stumbling over the words. "What gets me is that she just went—without wanting to see you, without even thinking about you."

Lawrence's aquiline face barely changed. His eyes were serene.

"Okay, that's fine." Sam took a step back. "I didn't expect a big reaction from you. Definitely no tears. You're a thousand years old, and Maia's long forgotten: why should it mean anything to you? I just thought you should know, that's all."

"Thank you."

"You might want to think about going home to Virginia? She's alone in her cottage. Who knows what effect Albin's games had on Elysion? Do you want to go home to an ice elemental?"

"I am going back to her, Samuel. What, did she tell you I'd left her?"

"No. Only that you wander off sometimes. Fair enough; neither of you was ever a breeze to live with."

Sam stood for a moment, downcast, shoulders slightly hunched. He began to turn away, but Lawrence said, "Sam, wait. Two things. I have seen Maia."

"Oh yeah?" Sam turned back to him. "When?"

"She . . . I received a message many nightfalls ago. That's why I came to Tyrynaia. I didn't know who'd sent it, but when I arrived, she came to me. A stranger, in a crimson cloak and hood. I had no idea who she was."

"You didn't recognize your own mother?"

"It's been such a long time. And we all change. Human, angel, animal—we transform to suit our mood or circumstances. She looked, really, as young as Rosie—although I should have learned by now that age means nothing in the Aelyr realms. The moment she said her name, I knew her."

"What wouldn't I have done to witness that!" Sam exclaimed. "So you knew she was Maia. But did she admit her other identity, Aurata of the Felynx?"

Lawrence smiled; a rare event, Stevie guessed. "No, she omitted that. I only found out today, but it makes sense of her cryptic remarks."

"Come on. Tell all."

Lawrence's eyelids flickered and he looked into the middle distance. "She said she was sorry; that she needed to see me, just once, however reluctant I might be. All Aetherials wander away, she said, but that doesn't mean we love each other less: the sort of stock phrase that would suit a greeting card, I thought. However, I believe she meant it. And she told me that an all-or-nothing change was on its way. Either a new world, or annihilation."

"Did you ask what she meant?"

Lawrence shrugged. "Overexcitable Aelyr of different persuasions are prone to wild pronouncements that rarely have any basis in reality. As a veteran of such events, now content with my peaceful life, I wasn't greatly interested."

"Wow," said Sam. "Father, I'm going to bring you the sleekest pair of designer shades I can lay hands on. You're even more cool than I gave you credit for. What *did* you ask her?"

"Why she wanted to see me."

"And?"

"One simple reason: to see her son, just once, before . . . before what, I didn't know."

"And now you do." Sam exhaled. "Channeling Qesoth, melting the world, skydiving into the Abyss and all that fun stuff . . . I swear by Estel the Eternal, if Rosie and I ever have a child, we'll be the most conventional bloody parents on the planet."

Rosie put in softly, "But Maia came to see you, Lawrence. That's the important thing. At least she came."

Lawrence acknowledged her remark with a nod, a brief gentle glance.

"You said there were two things," said Sam. "What was the other?"

"Oh." Lawrence's grey eyes narrowed. "Second point, a correction. Ancient I may be, but a thousand years old? Not yet."

"Pah, that's nothing." Sam turned, beckoning Mist and Stevie. "Let me introduce you to Maia's brother, Mistangamesh."

Later, they left the Felixatus poised on Tyrynaia's summit and made their way down to the lower levels, moving with the crowd. Mist and Stevie walked side by side, not touching. They stole glances at each other, but there was tension.

She'd made a firm break with him for all the sensible reasons. Certain she wouldn't survive Aurata's ritual, she hadn't wanted him to endanger himself to save her. So much for that. But the problems went deeper. She knew Mist loved her, but would it be enough if he was so numb with trauma that no one could reach him?

She sensed him drifting away, becoming more Aelyr while she wanted to stay human. Tyrynaia might turn him into the remote, ancient Aetherial he was meant to be, someone like Poectilictis or Vaidre Daima. That was fine, if it was what Mist wanted.

And Stevie might even be older than him, one of the earliest energy beings . . . but she couldn't remember that far back. For now, all she wanted was the safe human persona she'd woven. Stevie Silverwood might be far from perfect, but she was *real*.

She had to steel herself for an unknown future: to accept that it was unlikely to be the one she wanted.

Stevie smiled to herself, recalling one of Daniel's paintings: a group of stylized angelic beings dressed in white, blue and black. One had been Mist, taking his place among a high senate that she now guessed must be the Spiral Court. That was Mist's natural, rightful place.

She thought suddenly, *Was I in that picture? Damn, I can't remember. He is a prince of Azantios,* she told herself. *Aetherial royalty.*

I am an unemployed, homeless museum worker from Birmingham.

Yet I'm also Estalyr, one of the primal First . . . and a feted Tashralyr champion who walked among the Felynx and died for the secrets she learned. And Mist— setting aside the burdens of his high status—is simply the most beautiful soul I've ever met.

Isn't it strange, how many different things one person can be?

No kidding, it's a funny old world.

They reached a piazza, tiled with glossy onyx that reflected the stars so it appeared depthless, like a lake at midnight. In the center was a huge obsidian angel with wings folded down its back. From the scores of Aetherials milling about, and the sight of drinks being served from long stone tables, she understood that this was a customary gathering place. Turning, Stevie found Rosie, Sam and Lucas at her elbow. They drew her beneath a quiet colonnade to discuss their next move.

Somehow, in those few moments, she lost Mist in the crowd.

While the other three debated an immediate return to Earth, she looked around anxiously for Mist. No sign of him. A sickening pang plunged through her like a spear, even as she told herself it was best to slip away, with no awkward goodbyes.

She looked at the floor, wondering how far down it was to Persephone's chamber. Perhaps she could slip down there, for old times' sake, and sit in the green glow of Lake Meluis until finding and losing Mist stopped hurting. Then she recalled Persephone's warning, *My realm is timeless. I may not remember you, nor you me.*

She sighed. *Perhaps in another life, dear goddess.*

"The Otherworld and I have a difficult relationship," Rosie confided, startling Stevie out of her thoughts. "It's not all sparkling waterfalls and singing stars. Stuff has happened to us here that's . . ." She opened her palms as if to indicate that the battle of Albin and Aurata was the least of it. "Weird and odd and absolutely terrifying. I'm not ready for it yet. Sam's even more bonded to Earth than I am. We love the place, we have family there, and we are not leaving. And Luc's the Gatekeeper so he has to . . . well, keep the Gates. How about you, Stevie?"

"There's not much there for me but . . ."

"Hey, you've got us. Come back with us. Please?"

"I was going to say that I'm with you. I love Earth too. And I'm not ready for all this strangeness. I've only just got used to being Stevie, so I want to be her for a long time yet, otherwise I'll implode in a big puff of insanity and vanish. So, um, if it's all right, yes, I'd love to. Thank you."

She turned to follow Rosie and the others, then felt a gentle touch on her arm.

"Stevie?" Mist gave a sad, hesitant smile. "Where are you going?"

"Back to Vaeth with Rosie and Sam and Luc."

"Oh." His long eyelashes swept down and up. She couldn't read him. "Won't you stay here awhile?"

"In Tyrynaia?" She tried to keep her manner warm but disengaged. "No. It's been wonderful, but I don't really belong. You . . . ?"

She saw the answer in his darkening expression. "I need to stay in Asru for now. Vaidre Daima wants to talk to me." He rolled his eyes.

"Of course. Heavy Aetherial business. They'll want you for all kinds of important duties and honors. I get that. And you've deserved it."

A slight frown. "But they'll want you too, Stevie. Didn't you realize? You played a bigger part than anyone. You are older than the Felynx, closer to the Spiral than almost anyone here, which makes you ten times more valuable to them than I am. A fount of untapped wisdom."

"Less of the 'old.'" She grinned. "No, they can keep it. It's not for me. I need to go back to Earth."

"Already?"

"Yes. I have unfinished business. I need to see Daniel for one thing, make sure he's okay. And Frances."

"I understand," he said softly. She looked into his eyes and remembered the first time she'd seen him, a hot sensation so intense she'd thought she might faint. The same rush came now, but she pushed it away.

What to say, though? She stumbled into a sentence without knowing where it would go. "Estel watch over you, and maybe . . ."

"Stevie." He took a quick glance over his shoulder. "Here comes Vaidre Daima and crew. If you want to leave, go now. If they catch you, they'll claw you into their web. You won't get away. Believe me. Go!"

She hesitated for half a second, but knew he was right. The peacock-feathered deputation was bearing down on them. This was her only chance to slip under their radar. Mist touched her face, one finger tracing her cheek. "Go safely, be happy."

She went, hurrying after Rosie and the others; glancing back only to see that Mist was already gone, swallowed into the heart of Tyrynaia.

Stevie walked up the drive towards Frances Manifold's front door, gravel crunching under her boots. Pale green leaves were unfurling on the trees and she could taste spring in the air.

Returning from the Spiral, she'd stayed at Stonegate for a couple of days. The first thing she'd done was to phone the Manifold house, hardly daring to expect an answer. To her amazement, Frances herself had picked up the phone and spoken the code phrase that Stevie was supposed to deliver: *"Humphrey has landed."*

Now Stevie rang the doorbell, smiling widely as the door opened and an overexcited golden spaniel scampered out to greet her, tail thumping.

"Stephanie." Frances received her with a heartfelt hug. Her arms were thin but strong. "Come in, my dear."

"You look so much better. I can't believe it. How long have you been out of hospital?"

"Oh, that wretched place. A week or so. At one point I thought I was only going to leave in a box, but somehow they pulled me through. They were all terribly kind, but, you know, I just wanted to come home."

"Is he here?"

"He is. He's been back a few days. I don't know what to say—I haven't got the words to thank you enough . . . but we can go through all that later. Come in, come in."

"How is he?"

"Oh, lord, not in such good shape. But at least he's home! He seems to have acquired a friend, too."

Daniel was sitting half-swallowed by the biggest of the living room sofas. He looked thin and pale, his faded green T-shirt draining what little color he had. His right hand was encased in bandages to the elbow.

Sitting beside him was Patrick. They were drinking beer from cans and watching a tennis match on a small, bulky television set. Dusty sunlight groped in through the glass panes of the conservatory and the French windows.

It was a scene so gloriously normal that tears came to Stevie's eyes.

"So, the world didn't blow up then," she said.

Both young men looked up, then sprang to their feet, beer frothing as they hurried to put down their cans. The next moment she was held in a three-way embrace, voices clamoring in her ears, *Bloody hell, you're back, are you all right, what happened, where's Mist?"*

Humphrey ran in circles on the hearthrug, conveying massive, inexpressible joy as only a spaniel could.

When the hugfest had run its course, Stevie stepped back and was startled to be find her onetime counselor, Dr. Gregory, watching from a doorway. "Stevie!" He came forward, beaming, to give her a warm handshake with both hands. "Wonderful to see you."

"Hi, I, er, I wasn't expecting to find *you* here."

Frances turned bright red and marched away into the kitchen. Dr. Gregory laughed and shrugged. "I was seeing her every day while she was ill. Flowers, grapes, books and all that. Hospital visits turned into quite a friendship. A really wonderful friendship."

"Wow. That's fantastic. Wow."

"By the way, someone was trying to get in touch with you. I'll remind Frances to give you the note before you go." *Fin*, Stevie guessed. "I'll leave you to it," he added, following Frances towards the kitchen.

Stevie turned to Daniel, her thumb pointing over her shoulder, her mouth open in a silent, incredulous question.

"Yes, I know," Dan sighed. "Mum's dating our shrink. Great, isn't it? She's got him on tap to psychoanalyze me twenty-four hours a day." His mouth curved in a crooked smile. "I'm joking. It's great she's happy, and not all alone anymore. He helped her get better, when I wasn't here."

"At least he'll keep her out of your hair," said Stevie. "I always liked him: it was the questions I didn't like. But that's history. So, no supervolcanoes while I was away?"

Patrick said, "There was an earth tremor and some kind of minor volcanic event in the wilds of Nevada. It made a mess of Jigsaw Canyon. You can find pictures on the net, but it barely even made the news."

Stevie took this in with a muted sense of relief. She didn't feel like a hero; the struggle with Aurata seemed very distant now.

"And you, are you okay?" Daniel asked anxiously. "What happened?"

"Everything's fine," she said, losing her battle against tears. "Thanks so much, Patrick, for getting him home. It must have cost you a fortune."

"Oh, never mind that. We got standby flights."

"But the medical bills . . ." She touched Daniel's bandaged hand.

"It's okay," Patrick said patiently. "We can sort out the finances any time. It's not important. Dan had to have surgery on his hand, but the crucial thing is that he should get most of the use back. Hopefully enough to hold a paint-brush."

"I don't know whether I want to," Daniel muttered.

"Mate, there are ways and means!" Patrick spoke fiercely, as if they'd had this talk before. "You've heard of mouth-and-foot painters? Digital art? You can operate a computer just by *blinking* these days, and you're hardly that far gone. A few broken fingers is no excuse!"

"That's not the point."

"Dan, can we have a chat on our own?" Stevie said.

They went into the conservatory. The condensation of winter had cleared, and the garden was greening up beautifully. Water tumbled through the mossy bowls of the water feature.

The first thing he asked was "What happened to Oliver?"

She told him, even the part where he'd spitefully burned all the artwork. Daniel groaned, pain creasing his eyes. A couple of tears fell. He rubbed his eyes dry.

"I'm so sorry, Dan. After the way he abused you, you should be thinking 'good riddance,' but I know things aren't that easy."

"Yeah, because I keep remembering the good parts. When I thought he was an angel who actually loved me . . . I can't just switch that off. The be-trayal makes it so much worse."

"I know. I'm so sorry about the paintings, too. All that hard work, de-stroyed. But they're still in my head, and I'm sure they're in yours, if you ever felt like re-creating them?"

"God, not in a thousand years! No. The funny thing is that I'm almost glad. The whole experience was such a bad trip that I'm glad the evidence is gone." He pointed into the living room. "I put all my sketchbooks on the fire, too."

Stevie was shocked. "Did you? Even the one you left behind at the studio, with the sketch of Veropardus being burned at the stake, and the pictures of the Felixatus base? The first drawing you made of *me*?"

He looked down, his face grey with sadness. "Yes, even that. I'm sorry, but I had to. It was a sort of cleansing ritual."

Uncertain, she touched his hand. "So, how are you, really?"

"I'm fine. Getting there. Patrick's been amazing."

Stevie tried to suppress a smile. "So I gather. And your mother?"

"Oh, she's been great. We haven't had a single argument! She even apologized for all the grief she gave me about my art career and said that whatever I want to do, she'll support me. It's wonderful, it's all I ever wanted. We're bound to start pissing each other off again once she's used to me being home, but for now, it's amazing. I'm so pleased she's got a man friend, I can't tell you. I'll be fine with Dr. Gregory. Tom, rather. He's nearly family. Mother even hinted that, if Patrick and I, er, got together, she would be fine with it. Incredible."

"D'you think you will? Get together with Patrick, I mean? He has a partner in California so I thought he'd be going back.'"

"I know. Patrick said they'd been having problems, and he needs to sort things out." Daniel colored slightly. "So it's too soon to say. But we get on great, like we've always known each other. He's so down-to-earth. I might end up going back to the States with him, who knows?"

"And were you serious, about giving up art?"

His thin face lengthened. "I'm an empty shell. Oliver sucked it all out of me. By the end I was so crazy and exhausted that now, even the sight of a paintbrush makes me feel physically sick. Typical, isn't it? Mother is suddenly fine with my art, and I can't do it anymore."

"I'm so sorry, hon," she whispered.

"I'm struggling, to be honest, Stevie. I keep having flashbacks. I'm on medication, seeing a counselor and all that crap. You know, I'm not being ungrateful, but I think . . . I feel awful saying it . . . but it's probably best I don't see you anymore. You bring it all back, and I need it to stop now."

"Oh." She stepped back, feeling she'd been thumped in the stomach. She understood, but it was still a rejection she hadn't expected. A friendship lost. Unhappy silence stretched between them. She said, "Oh, Dan. If we'd never met, you would have been normal and happy. You'd never have known you were *naemur*, never got drawn into all this. I wouldn't have screwed up your life for anything. Please forgive me."

"Please tell me you are kidding?" A glint in his eyes suggested that he was going to be all right . . . eventually. "Yes, I'm glad it's over, Stevie. But don't get me wrong. It was a hellish ride . . . but even in nightmares, you can learn lessons and see wonders that, only later, you realize you wouldn't have missed for the world."

Stevie stepped off the light railway at Hockley and stood looking up at the station sculpture of giant interlocking cogs. An ache of wistfulness seized her. The curve of the road and the unique mix of old and new architecture was heartrendingly familiar. This still felt like home.

She floated in a mild state of melancholy. The note passed on to her by Frances had been a message from the nursing home where her foster-grandmother lived. They'd been trying to contact her for days, the nurses said. Nanny Peg was fading. So Stevie had gone straight there and sat by her bedside, fingers stroking the wispy white hair. Frail and shrunken, Peg had been deeply unconscious by then, but Stevie had held her hand and spoken softly to her as she drifted away on her last, gurgling breaths.

She saw Nanny Peg's life force leave. It was a tiny bright mote, just like those that had poured out of the Felixatus. No less valuable. The mote had caught on the window pane—a fleck of down from the pillow, the nurse said—but Stevie had opened the window anyway and let the spark fly free.

Afterwards, she'd spent the night in a cheap hotel, barely sleeping. Instead, she kept a kind of vigil, thinking about everything that had happened. Especially Mist.

She hadn't seen her *fylgia* since she'd come back from Asru. Her shadow-self seemed to have stayed in the Spiral, where it belonged. In an odd way, she missed her little ghost cat.

Now she entered the museum, ambushed by a wave of nostalgia and evocative scents: the musty smell of the old buildings, overlaid by the aromas of wood polish and coffee. She looked down the length of the shop and saw Fin behind the till, serving a line of customers.

Fin saw Stevie at once. Her eyes flashed wide with surprise, but she couldn't abandon her task. That put a damper on a dramatic reunion. Stevie waited, feeling awkward. When the last customer had gone, she walked slowly up to the counter and said, "Hi, I'm back."

"Stevie!" Fin rushed out and wrapped both arms around her. "You're all right? Thank goodness!"

"Yep, still in one piece. Most of me, anyway."

"They gave me your job." Fin's voice turned heavy with guilt. "I'm so sorry. I feel terrible."

"Why? Don't be daft."

"Because I know how you loved it. I don't want you to think I was angling for this all along. I wasn't, truly."

"Hey, stop that! I never thought you were—but I'll get suspicious if you keep protesting."

"The truth is, the trustees were *desperate*." Fin grimaced, laughing. "They'd have you back in a heartbeat."

"Oh." Stevie swallowed. "That's—" She swallowed again. "Interesting. Have you heard from Patrick?"

"I have indeed. He's back in the UK, did you know?"

"Yes, I've seen him. As soon as I got back, I phoned Prof. Manifold and she told me that Patrick had already brought Daniel home safely." Stevie felt her face relax into a happier expression. "And Frances is much better. Her house feels like a home, instead of a haunted mansion."

"I'm so glad. Patrick's been worried sick about you. So have I! Such a tale he told me . . ."

"Ah, Fin, you haven't heard the half of it yet. I hope you're still into tales of weird strangeness?"

"Absolutely. Can't wait to hear every detail. So . . . are you coming back?"

Stevie drank in surroundings so treasured that they were part of her psyche: spotlights shining on designer jewelry, the comforting smell of the coffee shop, and the dusty ghosts of the old factory beyond. She remembered her little apartment, how content she'd been there and yet so lonely.

This had been her cocoon. How unspeakably strange it felt, to realize she'd outgrown her old life.

"I honestly don't know. I need to have a think." She exhaled and let herself smile again. "Actually, I came to invite you and your hubby to a party."

Stonegate Manor.

Stevie, Fin and Andy walked towards the double doors, Andy having offered to drive to Cloudcroft and not drink. *Would have been nice . . .* For the twentieth time, Stevie suppressed the wish that Mistangamesh were beside her. It was all right. Her default state was to be alone, and she'd made peace with the knowledge.

The party was for Rosie's birthday, and for the spring equinox, and a general celebration that they'd made it back from the Otherworld alive. The whole village was here, judging by the number of parked cars and the noise from inside.

Rosie greeted them, beautiful with her autumn hair and silver eyes and a long, clingy, burgundy velvet dress with pointed sleeves. She led them into the great hall, which was warm from the press of people and a lively fire in the grate. Dozens of tiny lights were strung around the galleries, and the hall itself was bright with spring flowers. Daffodils and hyacinths released divine scents into the air. Sam and Lucas came to hug her. They both looked drop-dead gorgeous in dark tailored suits.

Stevie marveled at the mingling of Vaethyr and humans. Some wore exotic masks. In one of her patchwork favorites—shades of lavender and aqua with a swirling skirt, and lots of amethyst and fluorite gems to match—Stevie felt underdressed.

She and Fin soon lost each other. Stevie found herself being introduced to dozens of guests, as if she were royalty. There were Rosie's parents, Auberon and Jessica, her older brother, Matthew, with his wife, Faith—who was also Rosie's best friend—and a brood of honey-blond children. There were uncles and aunts, and other Vaethyr clans called Tulliver and Stagg and Lyon . . . *Oh good, I know Catherine Lyon, at least*, she thought. There were far too many names and faces to remember, but all of them looked warmly and shrewdly into Stevie's eyes as if they knew her better than she knew herself.

She was one of the most ancient Aetherials, true Estalyr; one of the very First. With their deep and experienced vision, they recognized this. The knowledge that they *knew* was a shock that made her want to run and hide.

Instead she grabbed a glass of champagne and was soon quite gloriously merry.

Although she felt the ache of Mist's absence, memories of him brought a smile to her lips. She drifted around the manor in a state of pleasure, thinking of neither past nor future.

"Enjoying yourself?" Rosie said in her ear, having tracked her to the upstairs gallery; a nice spot to watch the guests mingling below. "How does it feel to be guest of honor?"

"I don't deserve that."

"Oh, sure. You only saved our lives."

"After we landed you in Albin's clutches in the first place."

"No, you didn't. But you came back for us. You saved the *Gatekeeper*, no less."

"With a lot of help. And don't forget you saved us, too! Let's not talk about it tonight. This is wonderful, Rosie. It feels almost like a family around me . . . something I never had before. It's amazing."

"Stevie, we are your family," said Rosie, looking straight into her eyes. "And this is your home. I mean it."

Sam, bringing fresh glasses of champagne, said over Rosie's shoulder, "As long as you bear in mind the old saying 'Be careful what you wish for.' Stonegate has ghosts, and this family has claws. It's all good fun, though."

Rosie gave him a mild glare. "Honestly, Stevie, we're not that bad."

"So, of all the magical places you could live in the Spiral realms, you chose Vaeth?" she asked thoughtfully.

"Yes, we chose dear old Earth," said Sam.

"Why?"

"Well, it's home. We like it here, don't we? And humans *desperately* need our help." He grinned, exchanging a meaningful glance with Rosie.

"Desperately," Rosie agreed dryly.

"Not the sort of help Rufus liked to dole out, I hope?"

Rosie looked at her in exaggerated shock. "Absolutely not. Not that we're perfect. We're not always . . . good for humans." Her expression went shadowy. "Sometimes we're lethal. I've done things I'm not proud of, but . . . we do our best. According to Luc, we're meant to be contradictory. Sometimes predators, sometimes bringers of blessing. Aetherials are the essence of nature."

"That's our excuse, anyway," Sam put in. "You should know, we need to keep our connection with the Spiral so as not to lose our Aetherial selves and our memories. Hence peculiar rituals and celebrations at various times of year."

"Sounds thrilling."

"Yeah, but I have to be honest." He gave a crooked smile. "Some of the best days of our lives have been spent doing really mundane stuff, like wandering around Birmingham."

"There's nothing wrong with Birmingham," Stevie said indignantly. "I'm a poster girl for the tourist trade. Used to be, rather. Take the Jewellery Quarter: it's a heart of gold, in a literal and intangible sense."

"Any idea what you'd like to do next?" Rosie asked.

"As long as it doesn't involve falling off waterfalls, skydiving, swimming, bungee jumping or leaping off cliffs—anything."

They laughed, but this set Stevie thinking. She'd left the museum, and wasn't sure it was wise to go back, but that didn't mean she had to leave the Jewellery Quarter forever. There were always workshops for rent. She had skills.

She couldn't forget the feeling of the Felixatus taking shape under her hands.

"Come on! Everyone out in the garden, now!" It was Lucas yelling over the noise and music. "It's time for the fireworks!"

"We've got *fireworks*?" said Sam, one eyebrow jerking upward.

"Course," said Rosie, taking Stevie's hand. "Didn't Luc tell you? He's got a specialist firm in to set them up, cost a bloody fortune, so if we're not out there to enjoy the show, there will be *trouble*."

Sam raised his glass and said cheerfully, "Welcome to Stonegate, Stevie Silverwood, and best of British luck."

Mistangamesh slipped through the labyrinth of the Great Gates and emerged onto the flank of a hill. Trees rustled. The wind was light with the scent of spring blossom, new growth, the pungency of peaty earth and uncurling bracken fronds. He began to head downhill, following a path through a copse, following the noise.

The lower windows of Stonegate Manor were open, spilling light and music into the night.

"Everything that Samuel Wilder said is true," Vaidre Daima had told him. "We should have protected the Spiral, but against rogue powers like Albin and Aurata, we were defenseless. We don't fully understand the source of their power. The nature of the Spiral itself is still a mystery to us, even though we're part of it. What if it happens again? In times of crisis, I have proved miserably ineffective. It is time for me to step down. Time for someone stronger to take charge.

"Mistangamesh, the Spiral Court is in agreement. For the good of both Vaeth and the Otherworld, we wish you to become our new spokesperson. Style yourself leader, president, autarch—whatever you will. The Spiral needs strong protection. There will be an election process, of course, but it's a formality, a foregone conclusion. You, the son of Poectilictis, have proved yourself the natural heir."

Vaidre Daima's offer had floored him.

Mist had paced around the city for what seemed days, turning over all the arguments. Strong leadership was needed, for the good of the Spiral. Mist wasn't sure he could fill the role, but then came notions of obligation and responsibility . . .

It's my duty. It's what Poectilictis would want for me. I belong here. Even Daniel saw that. It's time to take my place among the senior ranks. Duty, duty . . .

Finally, Mist had gone back to Vaidre Daima and said, "No."

In that awful gap of indecision, he'd let Stevie slip away. He knew exactly why she'd gone, and yet—in a numb trance of grief—he'd let her go anyway. It had been utter madness. Nothing would bring back Aurata and Rufus; he accepted that. Where was the sense in mourning the past, at the expense of the present? All he knew was that if he lost Stevie, he'd lost everything.

"No?" said Vaidre Daima, his face turning dark with disbelief. "What possible reason could you have to refuse?"

"The very fact that I couldn't make a decision proves I'm not the right person. Or rather, I have made a decision but it's not the one you wanted. I'm sorry." Mist smiled ruefully at him. "You'll find someone else. What about Lawrence Wilder? Or his wife, Virginia? She'd make a far wiser leader than me."

Maybe his choice was irresponsible, but he had human obligations too, not the least of which was the need to find gainful employment and pay back the money he owed to Dame Juliana, with interest. The thought was sheer relief. He'd had enough of high Aetherial matters. He understood at last why Rosie and Sam and so many others relished their life on Earth.

If Stevie could forgive him, or trust him . . . If she could still love him, after all they'd been through . . . If she was even here . . .

It was time to take a risk.

Entering through the open front door, he found the interior deserted. The great hall was dimly lit by fire embers and strings of sparkling lights. Rock music played through the sound system, and a miasma of flowers and perfume and spilled alcohol hung in the air. He followed the murmur of voices through the hall, across the living room and out through the open French doors into the back garden.

Dozens of people thronged the lawn, looking up at the sky for no obvious reason. Through the narrowest of gaps—as if the other guests were all translucent—he saw her instantly.

She was standing with Sam and Rosie near the front of the crowd. Her back was to him, her hair a curtain of amber over the long blue and lilac flare of her dress. He wove between the other guests, approaching so quietly that she didn't look round; didn't even sense his aura.

He had so much to say that he was shaking. In the end he said nothing at all.

Instead he slipped his arms gently around her waist from behind. She started; he felt her stiffen with a wave of astonishment and heat.

And then she went pliant in his arms. She leaned into him, her body softening, her hands folding over his. He rested his chin on her shoulder, and she turned her head until they found each other's lips. With a deep, profound sigh of bliss she gave her answer.

Together they watched fireworks exploding above Stonegate in showers of ecstatic white stars: an echo of the Felynx souls returning to the Spiral. Returning home.

Coda
Gifts and Mysteries

"I wanted to see if this place was real," said Mist.

"The Avenue of Beautiful Secrets," Stevie responded, looking up at the tiled roofs and empty windows. They walked hand in hand along the eerie street. The sounds of lapping water, boats and voices from unseen canals were distant and echoey. The houses had an antiquated grandeur, typical of the surface-world Venetian streets they'd followed to find their way here, but the atmosphere and tints were all of the Dusklands. Greyish violets and dusky blues, touches of luminous gold.

Sometimes an elemental would brush past, making her shiver. Blurred faces appeared in windows and vanished again.

"Do you think we're welcome here?" she said, very softly. "Would this be a peaceful place to while away several hundred years in astral form?"

"Not for me." Mist's hand tightened on hers. "If these Aetherials feel at home here, I'm pleased for them. But I had so many dreams about this place, as if Aurata was trapped here . . . It feels just as nightmarish in reality. I can hardly believe it's real."

"Perhaps we shouldn't have come," she said. "We can turn around now, if you're not comfortable. We could be sitting outside a little café watching the gondolas glide by. I'm dying for some ice cream, and I don't think this is the best place to find any, do you?"

He smiled. "True, but I have to go through with this. I'm all right, Stevie. I'd rather not be here, either, but I *had* to see for myself. I think this is her house . . ."

They looked up at a once-grand mansion with flaking creamy-grey walls and timeworn decoration of lapis and gold around the windows. Mist pushed the tall front door. Unlocked, it swung open to his touch.

They stepped cautiously into a large hall. The great curving staircase and the marble floor put Stevie in mind of a ballroom, neglected for several hundred years. The atmosphere swam with watery aqua gloom and swampy smells, like the decaying beauty of Venice distilled.

"I can feel Aurata here, even though she's gone." Mist's voice was hoarse; he sounded close to tears. In silence, she followed him upstairs, exploring all the haunted yet empty rooms. "I can feel Veropardus and Slahvin, even Rufus, as if they all left their imprints behind."

In the large salon, a flash of gold caught her eye. For a few moments, it seemed the walls were not empty but covered in paintings: all of Felynx history, as portrayed by Daniel's images. She glimpsed statues, and the glowing crystal sphere of the Felixatus itself, and other intricate clockwork models, and even the ghastly severed hand that had belonged to Rufus. But she could pin nothing down. As soon as she tried to look directly, the teasing ephemera vanished.

"Can objects leave ghosts behind, too?" she whispered.

"So it seems." Mist looked calm but rather pale. "I think we should go, before we start meeting projections of my sister or Albin. Let them rest."

When they came back down into the hall again, Stevie stared at the spiral pattern in the floor and felt an irresistible impulse. She stepped onto the first black tile and slowly began to follow the spiral round and inward.

Mist said, "Stevie, I don't think you should . . ."

She hesitated, knowing what he feared. Walking a spiral was to tread a magical path: especially risky, when it was one still soaked in Aurata's rituals.

"Come with me, then," she said, holding out her hand. "If you want to lay all this to rest, don't be scared."

"I am not scared," he retorted. With a wry half-smile he took her hand and they trod the enchanted path together. It was an almost childish pleasure, like following a maze, thrilling yet unnerving.

Not that she expected anything to happen—but as they reached the middle, she received the shock of her life. A tall, translucent man appeared from nowhere, poised like a statue on the round, star-flecked tile at the heart of the spiral. He had black and white robes, sleek black hair, and a dark lynx mask that he now removed to reveal a striking godlike face with golden eyes.

Mist bumped into Stevie as she stopped dead. They clung hard to each other's hands.

"*Father?*" Mist gasped.

"Mist, my dearest son."

Mist bowed to the apparition of Poectilictis, his right hand on his chest. Astonished, Stevie did the same. "What—how can you be here?"

"I cannot explain. An inner call drew me to meet you. Time and place may become a magical intersection that can never be repeated, and we have both waited too long for this."

"What do you want of me?" Mist's question sounded abrupt, but Stevie understood. He went straight to the point, because he knew his time with his father would be precious and limited.

Poectilictis held a small, glowing blue jewel between his fingers and thumb, like a tiny Felixatus.

"I made many grave mistakes," he said. "Not least was trusting Veropardus. And trying to keep our exile from Naamon secret. And another lay in trapping so many soul-essences within the Felixatus."

"But you did all that to protect us, didn't you?"

Poectilictis shook his head. "Did you blame Veropardus for their imprisonment?"

"Yes! I assumed that you acted to keep us safe, while *he* and Aurata wanted to control the Felynx forever. Didn't they?"

"Oh, you think too highly of me," Poectilictis sighed. "None of us behaved well. It's true that he and Aurata plotted against me, and tried to use the Felixatus for their own ends. But *I* was the one who wanted all the Felynx held captive. I wanted our small empire kept together for all time. I believed in unity and control, not freedom. I thought my motives were benign, but in truth, they were not."

Mist took in this confession with a look of near-grief. "This is not allowed. You're my father, you're not allowed to be imperfect! Don't destroy my illusions!"

Poectilictis chuckled. "My dear, best beloved son, I'm telling you for a reason. Don't fall into the trap of thinking that *you're* perfect either. Do you think it's virtuous to relinquish power, to walk away from a position of authority over the Spiral Court? No, you're only putting off the inevitable. One day, *one day*, you will have to go back and take up your responsibilities, because it is your vocation and your duty. Furthermore, I command it. It's your very imperfection that will make you resilient enough to do the job. Do you love your father?"

"Yes! Yes, I love you with all my being."

"Then will you obey me?"

"No, I won't obey," Mist said stiffly. "But I *will* do as you ask, because it's right."

Smiling, Poectilictis stretched out to touch both Mist's hand and Stevie's. "May the blessings of Estel the Eternal fall upon you both. I can go now, find Theliome, and rest at last."

He turned and began to glide away. Mist said, "Father, wait," but Poectilictis didn't react. His tall translucent figure diminished rapidly, as if he'd passed into a remote dimension. The hall was empty again. Stevie looked down to find he'd placed a small blue jewel on a silver chain into her hand. Mist was holding its twin.

Each jewel was set into a delicate pendant shaped like an Aelyr creature. Carved silver snake coils encircled the blue stone, but the creature's head, forming a bail through which the chain was threaded, was that of a lynx.

"Damn," said Mist at last, twisting the gem to catch the light. "There's no escape, is there? One day, I will have to go into the Spiral and take charge, no doubt to defend us against a new threat. Why me? But why not?" He sounded resigned, very nearly cheerful. "Poectilictis laid this obligation on me the day I was born. I give in. There's nothing to do but accept it."

"Not on your own, though. Look, he's placed this bond on both of us." Stevie held up her own jewel with a rueful grin. "What are these? Gifts from the Otherworld?"

"It's never that straightforward. Spiral gifts come with conditions."

"I thought as much. And they're the exact color of the jewel Albin wore on his forehead . . . does that mean something? Deeper sight into other worlds?"

"That would be useful," said Mist. "However, I suspect we'll be sent messages through them, when the time comes. A summoning."

"In that case, mightn't we also be able to contact each other through the gems, if we happened to be apart?" Stevie moved closer to him, turning her head and sweeping her hair from her neck. "Will you put mine on for me, please?"

She felt the cool links on her neck, but he hesitated. "Chains have multiple meanings," he said softly. "These are more than decorative. They're also chains of office, of being bound and constrained by duty."

"Just fasten it, then I'll do yours."

With a sigh, he complied. It felt like an exchange of vows: not exactly a wedding, but something close. Stevie disentangled strands of Mist's hair from the silver clasp, then smoothed the nape of his neck, taking her time. She reflected on the endless journey she'd endured to reach this point, and how far she'd evolved from the terrified, nameless girl who'd crawled out of the silver wood. Not to mention the blessings she'd already received, from Persephone and Virginia, Daniel and Frances, Rosie and so many others. Knowledge, confidence, wisdom . . . and greatest of all, the gift of Mist himself.

The blue gem felt cool yet full of energy on her skin. She said, "Not all chains are bad. Love is a kind of chain that I can live with, can't you?"

"Soft, silvery and unbreakable." He laughed, his expression brightening. "Stevie, I love you for seeing the positive side of this."

"We must, because I think I get it now. Sometime in the future, we'll have no choice but to take the reins of the Spiral, at least for a while, and whatever harrowing experiences we face may still be caused by the fallout from Aurata and Albin's excesses. So I vote we make a pact of sanity and balance. If Sam and Rosie can find equilibrium, I'm sure we can. Peace, love and all that."

"Gods, that is a pact I'm happy to make." He pressed his lips to her temple and wrapped one arm around her, drawing her towards the door. Outside, elemental Aetherials with serene expressions watched them pass along the Viale dei Belli Segreti. "If we have a chance of bringing peace and renewal to the Spiral, I'd seize it in a heartbeat. We don't have to repeat the mistakes that others have made." Mist gave a twisted smile. "Of course, there are no guarantees. We may find a whole lot of *new* mistakes to trip us up."

"True. But we won't be alone. We'll keep each other from screwing up, or going power-mad, right? It might even be fun."

The avenue ended, and they stepped into the real Venice, dazzled by a bright blue sky. Without breaking stride, Mist lifted Stevie, spun her in a circle and set her down again. "It certainly won't be dull. And all we have to do is promise each other not to go crazy. Easy!"

"I give you my word," she said, breathless. "I promise, no drowning of the Otherworld with water elementals, no fire-channeling craziness; none of that, ever—on strict condition that you feed me with delicious Italian ice cream within the next ten minutes."

"I accept the challenge." He grinned. "I'll do my utmost to please you always, Stevie, my brave wild angel, however outrageous your desires may be."

"Careful, Mist," she said, laughing. "Bewitch me with vows like that, and you never know . . . you already know." Her voice turned soft and serious. "Like it or not, I'm yours forever."

Author's Note
Landscapes of the Fantastic

Readers often ask writers where they get their ideas from. Although it may be a cliché, I believe the question is a valid and fascinating one. After all, what *does* go on in our heads?

The basic inspiration behind my Aetherial Tales is simply that I've always been enthralled by the idea of mystical beings who look human but aren't: elves, angels, demons, vampires, faeries, demigods and so on. My Aetherials, or Aelyr, developed as my own version of such a race.

The "others" in the Aetherial Tales are not intended to be traditional elves, faeries, shapeshifters or demons. They are simply themselves. I imagined them as a race that evolved from pure energy, with access to other dimensions and an ability to manipulate reality. Now they have become chameleon creatures, able to blend in with humans when it suits them. Like humans, they are contradictory. Some are good and gentle, and some are most definitely not.

As a writer, I like to get on with a story, rather than creating reams of history and myth for my other-race before I can even start. As a result, my Aetherial "mythos" is developing organically along with the novels. My plan is to catalogue my mythos-so-far and develop it further on my website, www .fredawarrington.com.

Each of the Aetherial Tales series—*Elfland*, *Midsummer Night*, *Grail of the Summer Stars*—tells a self-contained, stand-alone story that you can follow without having to read the others. However, as they're set in the same "universe," there is an overspill of characters and plotlines from one book to the next. *Elfland* tells the story of Rosie, Sam, Lawrence Wilder and others. *Midsummer Night* explores the conflicts of Dame Juliana Flagg, Gill, Peta, Rufus and company. *Grail of the Summer Stars*, rather to my surprise, completes a plot arc over the three books that I hadn't planned or expected until it happened! There are also hints of events and characters from my earlier novels. For example, my Aelyr race—or let's say their distant cousins—first appeared in my epic fantasy *The Amber Citadel*. And when Fin tells Stevie about her friend August, she's referring to events in my alternative history novel about King Richard III, *The Court of the Midnight King*.

It means a lot to me to make these connections, because I'm realizing that, while each of my novels is different, they're all part of a bigger whole. After all, the stories are taking place in the internal landscape of my imagination, my own personal Otherworld, so it's natural to me that characters from different books will sometimes cross paths and say, *"There's something you ought to know . . ."*

Also, it's fun. If readers don't pick up on these moments, nothing is lost, but if you do happen to spot them, I hope you enjoy them too.

About the Author

Freda Warrington grew up Leicestershire, England. She spent her first years out of school as a graphic designer and illustrator and eventually became a full-time writer. She began writing short stories at a very early age, and by nineteen she had her first novel well under way. She has written twenty novels, including the Jewelfire trilogy and the Blood Wine sequence, all of which have been published in the United Kingdom.

Grail of the Summer Stars is the third of her Aetherial Tales novels, and her third book to be published in the United States, after the first two books of the Aetherial Tales, *Elfland* and *Midsummer Night*.

Learn more at www.fredawarrington.com.